P9-DMZ-083

LEAVING CHEYENNE

LARRY McMURTRY

Simon & Schuster Paperbacks

NEW YORK LONDON TORONTO SYDNEY

To Jo, *for her gallantry and her integrity, with my love*

Simon & Schuster Paperbacks
Rockefeller Center
1230 Avenue of the Americas
New York, NY 10020

First Simon & Schuster paperback edition 2004
Published by arrangement with the author

SIMON & SCHUSTER PAPERBACKS and colophon are registered trademarks of Simon & Schuster, Inc.

For information about special discounts for bulk purchases, please contact Simon & Schuster Special Sales: 1-800-456-6798 or business@simonandschuster.com.

Manufactured in the United States of America

10 9

Library of Congress Cataloging-in-Publication data is available.
ISBN-13: 978-0-684-85387-1
ISBN-10:   0-684-85387-6

A portion of *Leaving Cheyenne* appeared as a short story in *Stanford Short Stories 1962*, edited by Wallace Stegner and Richard Scowcroft.

My foot's in the stirrup,
My pony won't stand;
Goodbye, old partner,
I'm leaving Cheyenne.

The Cheyenne of this book is that part of the cowboy's day's circle which is earliest and best: his blood's country and his heart's pastureland.

L. M.

South of my days' circle, part of my blood's country,
rises that tableland . . . clean, lean,
hungry country. . . .

I know it dark against the stars, the high lean country,
full of old stories that still go walking in my sleep.

JUDITH WRIGHT from South of My Days

THE BLOOD'S COUNTRY ☼ 1

When I woke up Dad was standing by the bed shaking my foot. I opened my eyes, but he never stopped shaking it. He shook it like it was a fence post and he was testing it to see if it was in the ground solid enough. All my life that's the way he'd wake me up—I hated it like poison. Once I offered to set a glass of water by the bed, so he could pour that over me in the mornings and wake me up, but Dad wouldn't do it. I set the water out for him six or seven times, and he just let it sit and shook my foot anyway. Sometimes though, if he was thirsty, he'd drink the water first.

"Get up from there," he said. "If you're big enough to vote, you don't need to sleep past daylight. You do the chores today. I'm gonna trot off down in the pasture and look around. One of them scrawny heifers might have calved, for all I know."

And off he went, as usual. The last time Dad done the chores was when I was twelve years old, and the only reason he done them then was because I had let the ax slip and cut my foot nearly off. I never did know what he done down in the pasture every morning; by the time I could get the horses fed and the milking done, he'd be back.

For once though I was kinda glad he woke me up. It was election day, and my sly friend Johnny had worked it around somehow so that he and Molly got to watch the ballot box during the first shift. There was supposed to be at least two people to a shift. What he figured was that nobody would be there to vote till after dinner, so he could do a little courting with Molly on the government's time. Only I didn't intend to let him get away with it. I never liked to see a man cheat on the government.

I done the chores a little too quick. By six-thirty I didn't have a thing left to do, and I knew there wasn't any use getting to the schoolhouse before about eight o'clock. It was just over on Idiot Ridge, about a ten-minute ride. If there's one thing I can't do at all, it's wait. So I got a rag and polished the saddle a little, and that was a mistake. It was a pleasure to polish a saddle like that; the mistake was that Dad walked in and caught me.

"You needn't jump," he said. "And you needn't try to hide it. I found it day before yesterday anyhow. It's a nice saddle. Why ain't you been using it?"

I had put the saddle under a tarp, way back in the dark end of an empty oatbin. But you couldn't hide nothing from Dad.

"Because it ain't mine," I said.

"Hell it ain't," he said, a little surprised. "What'd you do, steal it?"

"You aggravate the piss out of me," I said. "I never stole a penny in my life, and you know it."

"Plenty's waited longer than you to start. Whose is it then?"

"Didn't you see the name plate?" I said. "It's sterling silver, looks like you'd have noticed it. I had this saddle made for Johnny, and I just haven't got around to giving it to him yet."

For once Dad was flabbergasted. I knew he would be, but I didn't see no sense in lying to him.

"Giving it to him?" he said. "You're giving a hundred-and-fifty-dollar saddle to a thirty-dollar-a-month cowboy. That wouldn't make sense to a crazy man. And it sure don't to me."

"Well, I can't help it, Dad," I said. "Johnny did me a big favor, which I ain't at liberty to talk about. Nobody ever did me that much favor before, and I may live to be older than you without nobody doing me that much favor agin. Johnny never owned a quality piece of equipment his whole life. I had the money and I just thought I'd get him something he could use. There's nothing wrong with that."

Dad had real black eyes, and when he wanted to look fierce he didn't look it halfway. He looked fierce then.

"Giving a saddle like that to a McCloud is like pinning a diamond stud pin on a goat's ass," he said. "Favor or no favor. And besides, whatever money you had come from me."

"Johnny ain't sorry," I said. "Being poor don't make him no-count. I worked plenty hard for the money I spent on this saddle, and if you think I'm overpaid, hire you another hand."

"Settle down," he said. "I ain't gonna whip you, you're too old. Let's go outside. You can polish his saddle some other time."

We went out and stood by the water trough and looked at the cattle grazing down in the Field pasture, just this side of the River. I washed the saddlesoap off my hands.

"Ain't this a good ranch?" Dad said. "I put a lot of work and a lot of years into it, but by god I've got it all back in money and satisfaction."

"Go on and bawl me out," I said. "I've got some pretty urgent business to get to this morning."

"You sure have," he said. "You've got to rush over to the schoolhouse and see if you can keep your good friend Johnny from getting in Miss Molly's pants. If you can keep him out, you figure you'll eventually get in. Well, suppose you just sit here and listen about five minutes. You might learn something."

"I don't like the way you talk about my friends," I said.

"Pity," he said. "I'm gonna have to leave this ranch to you some day; now I want you to get to taking that serious. I ain't mad about the saddle. But you took off and left, right in the middle of the calving season. You never gave me no warning or nothing, and you took that McCloud kid with you. And you've never said one word to me about where you've been or why. That don't add up to very sensible behavior, and I ain't too happy about leaving this ranch to somebody who ain't sensible, I don't care what kin he is to me."

"Well, I'm sorry as I can be, and you know it," I said. "But there ain't nothing I can tell you about that. I just had to leave."

He set there and looked off down the pasture. Dad was getting quite a bit of age on him.

"Nobody ever did me favor enough in my entire life for me to waste two hundred dollars on them," he said. "I guess by the time I'm dead ten years you'll have thrown away what I spent fifty years making. Old age is a worthless damn thing."

"Oh, hush," I said. "By the time I've run this ranch for ten years it's liable to be twice the size it is now."

"Yeah and I'm liable to flap my arms and take off from here and fly like a buzzard any minute now," he said. "That sure is a good saddle. I'll tell you one thing, Johnny McCloud ain't no favorite of mine."

"Well, you ain't no favorite of his either, that I know of," I said. I went and put the tarp back over the saddle, and Dad went up to the house to eat.

Of course things never worked like I planned. Dad had found a sick yearling that morning, but he never took time to doctor it himself, so I had to catch a horse and go hunt it up and doctor it before I could go to the voting place. It was after nine o'clock when I got there, and Johnny and Molly had been there since eight. I hated it so bad I could taste it.

They were sitting on the schoolhouse steps when I loped up. She was letting Johnny hold her hand, and they were both grinning. Oh me, Molly looked pretty. She had on a blue and white polka-dot dress, and her long black hair was whipping around in the wind. There wasn't another soul around. Johnny was looking wild and reckless, so no telling what had went on. Molly was just a sucker when it come to Johnny.

"Look who's here," he said. "What happened, you ain't but an hour early? Where's your friend Ikey?"

"I been working," I said. "Hello, Molly." I knew he'd bring Ikey up, but I didn't intend to talk about it. Ikey was a nigger, but he was a nigger that could vote, and he was supposed to be partners with me to watch the voting box. Molly had already promised she would stay awhile with me after Johnny's shift was up, so what I had to do was figure out a way to get rid of Ikey quick. Johnny knew just what I was up to, of course, but it wasn't gonna do him any good.

"Get down," Molly said. She grinned at me, as sweet as ever, but Johnny still had ahold of her hand, and she never made him turn loose.

I couldn't think of too much to say, so I took my horse over and tied him to a mesquite. I went in and was going to vote, but they had been so busy spooning around they hadn't even unpacked the ballots, and I had to do it. I never voted though, I forgot about it. I don't think I voted in that election at all. Molly had finally got her hand loose, and when she stood up we all went over to the cistern and got a drink.

"What's that I smell on you, Gid?" Johnny said. "Smells like screwworm dope. You ought to taken a bath before you come to work for the government."

"You don't smell like no prairie flower yourself," I said. "Been trapping any skunks lately?" When Johnny was just a boy the McClouds had had to sell skunk hides to keep going. They wasn't the only ones, of course, but Johnny hated skunks worse than anything. His folks had finally got better off, but they still just had a little two-section place.

"Not lately," he said, but it kinda irritated him.

Molly, she never taken sides when me and Johnny argued. She would just stand there and grin her pretty, friendly grin, and curl a loop of her hair around one finger. She was pretty as a picture when she done that.

It didn't seem like I'd been there no time when Ikey come. He had an old brown mule that was about half-crippled; he rode the mule bareback wherever he went. We seen Ikey coming and Johnny began to grin. He always had some trick to play on Ikey, and most of them were funny.

"Looky there," he said. "Here he comes, riding that three-legged mule. I tell you what, Gid, some day let's saw that crippled leg off. That way it won't drag and slow Ikey down."

"You hush that," Molly said. "How'd you like to have one of your legs sawed off?"

"I might like it," he said. "You want to saw one off for me?"

"That's no way to talk. Make him hush, Gid." She sidled over toward me just a little bit.

Johnny just looked that much more devilish.

"What he needs is his damn head sawed off," I said. "That's the only kind of sawing that would do him any good."

Ikey arrived about then, and got off his mule. "Good mornin', Mis' Molly," he said. "Mornin', Mistuh Johnny, mornin', Mistuh Gid." The thing that worried me about Ikey was that he was so proud of being good enough to watch a ballot box like the white folks that he probably wasn't going to be in too big a hurry to leave. But I figured I could persuade him.

"Morning, Ikey," Johnny said. "Whyn't you shoot that pore old mule and put him out of his misery?"

I had to grin at that. Ikey was as surprised as if Johnny had asked him to shoot his wife. He thought he had one of the best mules in the country.

"Shoot dis mule?" he said, looking at it real close. "Den how'd I get aroun'?"

"Don't pay any attention to him," Molly said. "He's crazy. Come on in and vote, Ikey."

I was all for that, so I went in and fixed him up a ballot. I thought if we made a big enough thing of him voting Ikey might be satisfied and go on home.

"Boy, this is a big election," I said. "They say every vote is gonna be important. Think it over good, Ikey. Don't be in too big a hurry."

"Naw, don't excite Ikey," Johnny said. "He might stab himself with that pencil. It ain't worth the trouble, Ikey. The man with the most money's gonna get it anyway. It always turns out that way."

"It don't, do it?" Molly said. She never liked to hear anybody run down politics. I guess it was because her old man had been commissioner for our precinct one year; everybody criticized him so she had to take up for him twice as hard as she usually done. He was the most thieving commissioner there ever was, besides the most lazy, and Molly knew it. She just never would admit it, to herself or nobody else. Her daddy didn't get elected because he was the man with the most money; he got elected because he was the man with the most whiskey to give away. There weren't but twelve people in the precinct able to vote, and he gave ever one of them a jug of whiskey and still only won by one vote. The man that was running against him was too decent to vote for himself, and Old Man Taylor wasn't, so he won it. Afterward he got hold of the ballots and found out who voted against him and went around and got his jugs back from those. I know that's true, because one of the ones that voted against him was Dad, and the jug was damn sure all he got back. I guess Molly was the only person in the world who ever liked that old man.

Ikey, though, he never paid any attention to what we were saying to him. He was set up so he could just pay attention to one thing at a time, and right then he was paying attention to voting. He got out his spectacles that he was so proud of and polished them on his pants leg and put them on and adjusted them so he could see over them. It's a damn cinch he couldn't see through them. It would have been like looking through a pair of stovelids. After he got them set so they wouldn't interfere with his vision, he began to read the ballot. That took so long that me and Johnny had to go off behind the schoolhouse to pee before he got through. We left Molly there to help Ikey read.

"You sneaky bastard," I said, when we got out. "How long was you'all over here before I come?"

"Why, I'm ashamed of myself about that," he said. "Don't you think I've got a pretty girl, though?"

"I think Molly's a pretty girl, all right," I said, "but you ain't got her by a long shot. Why don't you take after Mabel Peters, anyway?"

"Why, Mabel's crazy about you," he said. "Watch where you're pissing. You get it on these gabardine pants and your name's mud. I mean it."

Actually I just splattered a little on his boots. "It's about time you were going home, ain't it?"

"Why, yes," he said. "I'll go get Molly."

He went, but he never got her. I went too. She walked out the door with him and he had her hand agin, but she must have told him she had promised to stay awhile with me. He didn't look too cheerful. I went on in to help Ikey.

He was sitting there licking his pencil, and after he'd done that about five minutes, he voted.

"Good lord," I said. "I just remembered something. I was supposed to cut a big patch of cuckleburrs today. Down on the River. Dad's been after me about that for two weeks."

"Well then, why don't you go cut them?" Johnny said. "I'll stay here and do your turn at the voting box. You just go right ahead."

"Oh no," I said. "I wouldn't want nobody to do that. That's my responsibility."

"Don't worry so much," Molly said. I guess she was so sweet it never occurred to her what I was really worrying about. It damn sure occurred to Johnny.

"He better worry," he said. "I wouldn't want Mr. Fry mad at me. I think his best chance is just to forget about this voting and go do his work."

"Well," I said. "Since you're so anxious to help, I wonder if you'd like to lope off down there and cut them for me. It wouldn't take more than four hours."

That got into his quick. "Hell no, I wouldn't like to," he said. "I'm a cowboy, I ain't no damn cuckleburr chopper."

"Well, Ikey, what all do you have to do today?" I said. "Maybe I can hire you to do it. I'll give you two dollars, and you don't need to worry about watching this voting. Miss Molly's gonna stay here a little while and she'll be glad to do your part for you."

Ikey didn't give any argument at all. I wasn't much expecting him to: his normal wage was about a quarter a day.

"I'll cut 'em an' be glad," he said. "I'll jus' be glad." I gave him the two dollars and that settled it. That much money was such a shock to him that he couldn't hardly get it in his pocketbook. Then he folded up his ballot real slow and careful and looked kinda sad about having to drop it in the box. One thing about him, he really liked to vote. Then he got up and put away his spectacles.

"Well, I'll go cut 'em, Mistuh Gid," he said. "I sho enjoyed de elecshun day, Miss Molly. I hope we have anothuh one soon as we can."

Molly kinda laughed. "We will," she said. "We'll have one in November. You be careful, Ikey. Don't chop off your foot, and don't get on no snakes."

Ikey got on his mule and went off. Johnny just grinned and winked at Molly. It was hard to get his goat.

"I wish I was well off enough to hire my dirty work done," he said. "But I ain't that lucky. I always have to do my own."

"I never noticed you doing much," I said. "Besides, I felt sorry for Ikey. I'd like to see him get himself a better mule."

"If that ain't a lie I never heard one," he said. "Ikey's gonna spend that money on whiskey, and you knew it before you gave it to him. And you'll probably talk him out of three-quarters of that. You can't fool me."

"Why, Gid, I heard you quit drinking," Molly said. "I didn't know you started agin."

"I haven't," I said. "Johnny's just spoofing you."

"Well, I got to be going," Johnny said. He'd done all the damage he dared do. "Don't you'all take no bribes under five dollars."

That made Molly mad, so he was smart to leave. She was kinda patriotic, and never liked to hear people hint about crooked government. It was because her old man was so crooked himself.

Anyway, Johnny got on his horse and loped off, and there we were. It was about ten o'clock, and I didn't figure we much needed to worry about anybody coming to vote before dinnertime. Voting is the kind of thing most people like to put off as long as they can.

I looked at Molly, and she was looking at me and grinning. I guess she knew good and well what I was up to, rushing Ikey off.

"Well, Mr. Fry," she said. "You sure was in a big hurry to

chase everybody off. That wasn't very sociable."

"I ain't very sociable with crowds," I said. "Specially not crowds with Johnny in them." I kinda reached for her hand, but I missed. She laughed and stepped out the schoolhouse door. The wind begin whipping her hair up around her face.

"You're grabby," she said. "Grabby Mr. Fry."

"Don't call me that," I said. "And don't put on thataway. Let's go around to the cistern."

"Okay," she said, "let's do. Only you're so unsociable. I might just better go home."

I got her hand after all and squeezed it and she squeezed back.

"I'm a lot more sociable where you're concerned," I said.

I got my big slicker off my saddle and spread it out by the cistern so we could sit down without the grass and the chiggers eating us up. We got on the shady side and leaned up against the rocks and just set there. It was right on the hill, high enough that we could see anybody coming a long time before they would notice us. Molly let me put my arm around her, and she kind of slumped against me, and talked about this and that. I mostly listened. After a while my arm went to sleep, but I didn't dare move. Her hair was in my face. She must have washed it that morning, because it was real clean and I could still barely smell the vinegar she rinsed it in.

"It's a nice day for election," she said. "Look at the way the grass waves. I bet we can see nearly all over the county from here."

I kept wishing she'd turn her face around, but she wouldn't do it.

"Gid-ing-ton," she said, "what are you doing back there where I can't see you?" She called me that sometimes; she thought Gid was too short a name. I was agreeable.

"Don't you wish I'd turn my face around, so you could kiss me?" she said. "Now don't you?"

"I could stand it," I said. "You won't, though."

"You think I should let a boy kiss me on election day?" she said, and then she turned around anyway, and let me. Some of her hair was between me and her mouth; I didn't care. Only after a while she began to giggle and squirm.

"Let me fix it," she said. "Who wants to kiss hair?" She sat up and turned her back, and all I could see was black hair and her polka dot dress. Then she rolled over on the slicker and propped up on her elbows.

"Let's quit," she said. "Let's just talk. What if Johnny was to come back?"

"What if? It ain't none of his business what we do."

"He thinks it is, though." I made her let me kiss her again, but she kept giggling and wouldn't get serious about it. "Johnny thinks it's all his business," she said. "He keeps asking me all about us."

"Well, he can just cut it out," I said. "I'm not going to put up with much more of him. You're my girl now, ain't you?"

"Am I?" she said, looking up at me through her hair, half-grinning and half-serious. "I think I'm too silly for you."

"No you ain't. Why, I'm worse that way than you are."

"No you ain't," she said, and she wasn't kidding. "You're not even as silly as Johnny, and he's not as silly as me. Eddie's the only one who is."

"If you mean he's the only one who's dumb, you're right," I said. I hated that sorry Eddie. "At least I'm a little smart. I'm smart enough to know you're the prettiest girl there is."

I made her let me kiss her agin, and finally it shut her up and she got real quiet and sweet. Once you get Molly quiet she's the warmest, sweetest girl in the world.

"I still think you're my girl," I said.

"Maybe I am," she said. "Lay down here and hush."

She hugged me real tight, and just about that time we heard Ikey's mule. I could tell that mule a quarter of a mile away.

"Damn it all," I said. "Ikey's coming back. I'd like to wring Johnny's neck. I know damn good and well he put him up to it."

"Let's just lay here," she said. "Let's don't get up. Maybe if Ikey sees us he'll go on away. Or we could run hide."

"No," I said. "Damn Johnny anyway. I'll get even with him. I don't want Ikey to see us, and it's silly to hide. I ain't gonna do that."

She got up and I folded the slicker.

"Brush the grass off my dress," she said. "I got off the slicker."

She turned her back and I brushed her off. She didn't really look mad, and she put her arm around me and let me hold her hand even while Ikey was coming up. But she kept looking off across the pasture, off down Idiot Ridge.

"Where did you get that dress?" I said. "It's awful pretty, Molly."

"I made it. Thank you." She looked up then and seen I had grass on my cheek, and she brushed it off with her hand. "You just ain't very silly, are you?" she said.

two

Johnny never would admit he sent Ikey back; he was too stubborn. But I knew he was the one responsible. I finally got Ikey sent off agin, but it was too late. Ikey wasn't hardly out of sight the second time before Dad come, of all people.

Dad made out like he come to vote, but he never: he just come to see what I was doing. He knew I was there with Molly, and he just thought he'd come and spy a little. I hated it like poison when he did something like that. Molly, she never minded. She always took up for Dad, and I guess he liked her for it; he always treated her like she was the prize of the world. Except when I got to talking about marrying her—then he got mad.

"Don't be a damn fool and marry young," he said. "Specially not to no poor woman. Work about thirty more years and make you lots of money. Then go off somewhere and marry a rich widow. Don't never marry somebody who's as broke and ignorant as you are; marry somebody who knows a little about it. Then you might have a chance to enjoy yourself a little."

That was Dad for you. I didn't pay him much mind. He never could understand that he wasn't me.

What I knew was that Johnny McCloud had two things coming: one was a good saddle, and the other was a good whipping. I guess he thought I had a whipping coming too, because he started it all.

About a week after election day, Old Man Ashtoe, the feller Johnny was cowboying for, sent him up to Henrietta with a little bunch of cattle he wanted delivered. Johnny delivered the cattle, all right, but then he bought some whiskey from somebody and got drunk and insulted a deputy sheriff or two and got put in jail. Soon as he got home Old Man Ashtoe fired him, and Johnny was so broke he had to take a job with a harvesting crew. The first day he worked with them was the day they were finishing up harvesting our oats. Dad had me out helping them, of course.

"Ain't this hell?" Johnny said, when we were going out that afternoon for another big load of shocks. "A cowboy oughtn't to do work like this. This here's clodhopper work. It's a kind of disgrace, ain't it to you?"

"Not to me," I said. "I don't have no choice about it. It's a real disgrace where you're concerned, though. If you'd have behaved right, you could be horseback right now."

"I never asked for no sermons," he said, grinning at me. "You've got just as much oatseed in your hair as I have. Where you want to work, on the wagon or on the ground?"

"On the wagon," I said. "You're such a good hand with a pitchfork, I don't want you to get out of practice."

We worked for about an hour, I guess. He threw the shocks up to me with his fork, and I stacked them on the wagon. The wagon was stacked up pretty high.

"I just need eight or ten more," I said. "Let's hurry, then we can take a rest."

He stuck his fork in a big shock, and I noticed him stop to look at it pretty close. I figured there was a rattlesnake under it; we had killed five or six that day. Oatshocks were a great place for rattlesnakes, because so many rats lived under them.

It was awful hot, and I started to take my gloves off to wipe my face. Then Johnny picked up the shock and got ready to heave. I seen it coming and reached out to catch it, but just before I got my hands on it this big snake head came right up between my hands and hissed in my face. It scared the piss out of me and I went to running backward for all I was worth, but the shock kept right on coming till it looked like the snake was going to fall right on my face. I kicked like hell and went off the wagon backward, fighting with my hands to keep the snake out of my lap. I never seen where it went, because I hit the ground like I had fallen off a cloud. I never rolled an inch. In a little while I heard a lot of people laughing and one of them was Johnny. I looked around and Johnny and three or four of the harvesters were about to bust their guts laughing. Then I seen the snake sliding off the wagon wheel: it was an old brown bullsnake was all. It was mad, too, but not no madder than I was. I had to lay back down; I was seeing spots before my eyes.

"We better help him up," one of them said. "He might have busted something."

"Hell no, he'll be up in a minute," Johnny said. "You better get back to work or you'll be the one with something busted."

I propped up on my elbows and looked at him. "You're a damn bastard," I said. "What if that had been a rattlesnake?"

"It couldn't have scared you any worse," he said. "Besides, I seen what it was."

"Well, you better take a good look at the world," I said, getting up on my hands and knees. "You won't be able to see much when I get through with you."

"Goodness me," he said. "Maybe that'll teach you not to fiddle with my girl."

I was beginning to feel the blood coming back from wherever it went to when I seen that snake. Johnny was standing about ten feet away, leaning against the wagon wheel and grinning.

"She's no such a thing your girl," I said.

Then I went for him, and we had it out right there. I nearly got the best of him right off, but then I got to missing ever time I swung at him. I guess the fall had thrown off my aim. Pretty soon I got tired and he did too, but we just kept standing there, pounding the piss out of one another. Finally we both stopped for a minute.

"When you've had enough, say calf rope," I said. "I don't want to put you in no hospital."

"Calf rope, your ass," he said. "You're going to bleed to death if we don't quit."

"Hell," I said. "My nose always bleeds in the summertime."

"Let's quit anyway," he said. "Get a drink of water. You quit first."

"Nope."

"Then we'll just have to stand here till you drop," he said. "I never seen such a stubborn bastard."

We might have stood there till dark, I don't know. Finally the boss harvester noticed us and came over.

"Damn boys," he said, "why don't you fight with the pitch-forks next time? There won't be so much blood that way."

"He started it," I said.

"Load the wagon," he said. "You can fight some more tonight if you want to."

So I wiped off a little blood and Johnny got his pitchfork, and we finished making up the load. He never threw up no more snakes, either. Finally we got all the oats we could haul and went to the barn. Johnny rode on the seat with me.

"Shit-fire," he said. "I'm quitting this job. I ain't no damn clod-hopper, and I ain't gonna let no fat-ass like that give me orders."

"What are you gonna do for money when you quit?" I asked.

"I been thinking about that," he said. "You know what, Gid, I think I'll go to the Panhandle. This here country ain't no place for a cowboy. It's all right if you got your own ranch, like you have, but if you ain't, it's no good. I'd like to go up on the plains, where them big ranches are, and do some real cowboying. I'm tired of sitting around here listening to my old man bitch at me. I think I'll just strike out."

"I wouldn't mind going with you," I said. "Hell, working for Dad's worse than being a hired hand. He thinks he has to tell me ever move to make."

"Then let's go," he said. He was excited about it. But I knew I never would be able to get away from Dad. There was too much that needed doing around the place that he couldn't do. Besides, we had done been gone two months, to that hospital. I pulled the wagon over in the shade of the barn, and we got down.

"Let's go over to the horse trough," I said. "Wash this blood off." I figured if he was going off to punch cattle, I had better give him his saddle. Even if I was still mad at him.

"Well, you coming with me?" he said. Then he bent over and ducked his head plumb under the water and came up shaking it like a wet dog.

"I don't reckon so," I said. "I guess I got too much to do here."

"Too much cowboying or too much courting, which one?"

"You better watch out," I said. "I ain't going to take no more off you today."

He slapped his hat back on without even drying his hair. "Hell, I ain't eager to go off and leave Molly, either," he said. "But a man's got to get out and see a little of the world in his life. I guess they'll be some pretty sweet girls up there."

"Not that sweet," I said. "Let's unload the hay."

"I may not go after all," he said.

But stacking those damn itchy oats in the hot oatbin almost got us down. I guess we was both weak from the fight.

"Oh hell," he said, when we finished. "Piss on this. This here'll kill a good cowboy in a week. It takes weak-minded bastards to stand this kind of work. I'm quitting."

"I don't blame you," I said, and I didn't. It would be the real life, up on the plains, with all those big ranches and cow outfits. I just couldn't manage it, though.

"Come around here," I said. "I got something for you."

We went around in the hallway of the barn, and I drug out the saddle. He never knew what to make of it.

"That's a beauty," he said. "Whose is it?"

"Yours," I said. "I thought you ought to have it for going up to the hospital with me and taking care of me all that time. If you're going off to cowboy, you'll get some use out of this."

"Why, my god," he said. "You don't mean it! Why, ain't it a

beauty. That's as nice a saddle as I ever seen."

"Yeah, it ought to last you a long time."

"Well damn, sure much obliged, Gid," he said, feeling of the leather. "This here's something to be proud of. I never had nothing this well made in my life."

"Let's try it out," I said. "It's too late to haul oats today."

We caught a couple of horses and went for a ride. I never saw Johnny so tickled over anything, or so excited. He rode it awhile and then I rode it awhile, and it rode like a rocking chair. It was a little creaky and new, but he would ride that out of it in a hurry.

We got back to the barn just in time to start the evening chores. Dad was out fiddling around in the lots, watching the milk-pen calves.

"Well, this settles it," Johnny said. "I ain't wasting a saddle like this on this part of the country. I think I'll leave in a day or two. Sure wish you'd go with me."

"Can't make it," I said. "You better wait till them eyes get better. Ain't nobody going to hire a blind man."

"Blind, my ass," he said. "What about your nose?"

"It ain't very bad squashed. It'll straighten out."

Dad finally come poddling over and looked at the saddle some.

"Well, I see you boys been beating on one another," he said. "Too bad neither one of you had any sense to beat into the other one."

"Oh, we wasn't out for blood," Johnny said. Dad got a big laugh when he told him about me reaching out for the snake. Johnny could tell things so they sounded a whole lot funnier than they were.

"What do you think about my new saddle, Mr. Fry?" Johnny asked.

Dad just grunted. "I think it's a better one than I ever had," he

said. "And I'm four times your age and several times your smart."
He walked off toward the house. Johnny winked at me and I
grinned. Dad never got Johnny's goat quite, and it tickled me.

Two days later Johnny rode to Henrietta and pitched his saddle in the caboose and took the train north. That left me and Molly
with the country to ourselves, but I was kinda sorry to see old
Johnny go. He was a good buddy even if he was a smart aleck, and
I felt lonesome whenever he wasn't around.

three

I guess Dad had been hoping I'd change my mind and keep the new
saddle for myself. When Johnny actually took off and left the
country with it, it put Dad in such a bad humor he never got over
it for a month. And when he was in a bad humor he could think
up a million mean jobs for me to do. I spent the last part of July
and the whole damn month of August digging corner postholes and
cleaning out sewer lines and cutting devil's claws and plowing. I
hated the plowing the worst. And all the time I was down in the
field, eating dust and yanking on the damn contrary mules, Johnny
was up on the plains, riding his new saddle and living like a cowboy
should. I got so tired of thinking about it that one day I just come
right out and told Dad I was pretty much in the notion to go up
there too.

"The hell you will," he said. We were riding one of the River
pastures, looking for screwworms, and Dad rode up on a hill and
stopped his horse long enough to tell me off.

"You'll just stay right where you are," he said. "And if I tell
you to plow, by god, you plow."

"But I ain't no damn farmer," I said. "Why don't you hire
your farming done? Why do I have to waste my time doing it?"

"I am hiring it done, and you're the one I'm hiring," he said. "Why pay somebody else to do something we can do ourselves? That ain't no way to get rich."

"I see a few cattle down toward the southwest corner," I said. "What makes you think I want to be rich anyway?"

"Because I bred you," he said. "I know damn well I couldn't breed a boy with so little sense as to want to be poor. You got enough sense to know it's better to be rich than poor, ain't you?"

"That ain't what the Bible says," I said.

He just looked at me. "I ain't responsible for what the Bible says," he said. "If it says that, it's wrong. And I never asked you for no preaching, either. I know there's fools in the world who say poverty is holy, but you let them go without shoes some cold winter, like I did when I was a kid, and then see how holy they think it is. Being poor just makes people little and mean, most of the time. It's a damn degrading thing."

"All right," I said. "Hold your horses. I don't want to be poor. But you can not want to be poor and still not care whether you're rich or not."

"Yes, and them's the kind of people that never accomplish nothing," he said. "They're just damn mediocre. If you're gonna try at all, you ought to try for something big."

"Well, I'll never get nothing big from plowing that worn-out field."

"You might," he said. "You might plow up a diamond, you don't know. I count twenty cattle in that corner."

"I just counted eighteen. Let's go get them."

"I ain't finished telling you what's good for you yet. Now you got the itch to go up on the plains and cowboy, just because Johnny McCloud's up there. Now I'll tell you about Johnny McCloud. He's a good cowhand and he ain't scared of nothing, I'll admit that. But that's the limitation of him, right there. He'll never be nothing but a damn good cowhand. When he dies he'll own just what he's got on and what he's inherited. And that saddle you gave him, if he don't lose it in a poker game first. He'll fiddle around his whole life working for wages, and never accomplish a damn thing."

"That don't make him bad," I said.

"Course not. It don't make him bad at all. I've known a lot of fellers like him, and some of them I liked a lot. The point is, you ain't like that. You've got too much of me in you. Punching somebody else's cows never would satisfy you. But you might waste a lot of time before you figure that out. The man that gets the farthest is the man that wastes the least time and the least energy he possibly can. You ain't old enough to know that yet, but I am. If you can just learn to listen to me, you'll save yourself a lot of misery."

"I guess you know everything in the world, don't you?" I said. "I don't guess you was ever known to be wrong, was you?"

"Oh yes, I've been wrong. I've been wrong more times than most people have been right. But that ain't no significance. I've also done forgot more than most people ever know.

"But anyhow," he said, "it don't take much sense to figure out that you and Johnny are two different kinds of people. Let's go look at them cattle."

We doctored a few worms, and was riding home down the lane, late in the afternoon. It was close to sundown, and Dad had worn down a little around the edges.

"Gid," he said, "now there's no need for you to go around feeling sorry for yourself for two months just because you have to plow an oat field once in a while. Before you're my age you'll have had all the cowboying you need. A man that's training himself to run a ranch has got to be able to do all kinds of things."

"You can say all you want to," I said. "I still wish I'd gone to the Panhandle. I ain't training to be no oat planter. I intend to enjoy my life."

"If that ain't a fine ambition," he said. "Why, any damn fool can enjoy himself. What makes you think life's supposed to be enjoyed anyhow?"

"Well," I said, "if you ain't supposed to enjoy it, what are you supposed to do with it?"

"Fight it. Fight the hell out of it." And then he got to talking about the cattle and the screwworms, and about how dry it was. He said he'd like to build some new tanks if he thought he'd have the pleasure of living long enough to see them full; we didn't argue no more. In a way I wanted to go, and in a way I didn't. Old as Dad was getting, and as much work as there was to do, I wouldn't have been too happy about going off and leaving him. There would be too many times when I'd have to think about him making the rounds by himself, and that would have spoiled the fun. When it come right down to it, Dad and I got along pretty well. All that time I was in the hospital I kept thinking about him home working, and it bothered me worse than the stuff itself. Johnny and me *was* different that way. His dad was just as old and had about as much to do, but it never bothered Johnny to go off and leave him. Course Johnny's mother was still alive, but he just figured his dad could take care of himself.

"If I did stay home it wouldn't make no difference," he said. "Daddy would be out working himself to death anyway, only he'd be working me to death along with him. I can't see no profit in that."

He was right, I guess. It's just all in the way you feel about a thing like that. Me being home never slowed Dad down either, but at least if I was there I didn't have to fight no guilty conscience.

One good thing about having old Johnny out of the country was that I didn't have to watch Molly so close all the time. I knew there wasn't nobody besides me and him she cared much about; not unless you wanted to count Eddie White, and I never. Eddie was a shiftless old boy about my age; he worked around the oil patch whenever he felt like working, and when he didn't he hung around Thalia playing dominos or running his hounds. He was too no-count for a girl like Molly to pay much attention to. I think she just mentioned him once in a while to keep me and Johnny uneasy.

I guess the best time me and her had all the time Johnny was gone was the day I took her fishing. We had shipped a carload of calves to Fort Worth just to try out the market, and Dad had gone with them, to sit around the stockyards a day or two and watch them sell. When Dad took a big vacation like that he always come back wanting to do all the work in sight in the first half-hour, so I thought I better take me a little time off while I had the chance.

It was late September then—a nice warm day, but not too warm. We had had our first little norther about four days before; it cooled things off to where they were just about right. I waited around the house till nine or ten o'clock, then caught my horse and rode across the west pasture and up the hill to the Taylor place.

Old Man Taylor was there of course. He was sitting on the cellar, sharpening his pocketknife and drinking his morning whiskey. He was a terrifying sight. Along his cheeks his beard was white, but all of it that was underneath his mouth was a kind of muddy yellow from all the tobacco juice and whiskey he had dripped on it.

"Clean your feet before you come in this yard," he said. "I don't want none of your damn cowshit in my yard."

That would have been funny if he hadn't said it in such a mean voice. His yard looked like a slaughterhouse anyway. The old man done everything he had to do in the yard, and it showed it: there were bones and chicken heads and empty whiskey jugs and junk iron and baling wire and old shoes and pieces of plank and mule harness and horse turds and slop buckets, and I don't know what all else scattered everywhere. Molly said she tried to clean the yard up once in a while, but the old man wouldn't let her: anything that was there, he said, was there because he might need it. The miracle of it was that such a sweet, nice girl like Molly could have grown up in such a nasty place.

I scraped my feet on the fence wire and the old man never said another word to me.

Molly was in the living room, trying to kill a stinging lizard that had run in one of the woodboxes. She was dressed like a boy, in an old shirt and a pair of pants that had belonged to one of her brothers; they had all left home. But she looked like a girl; I wanted to grab her right there and kiss her, but if the old man had come in there would have been hell to pay.

"Let's go fishing," I said.

"Guess what?" she said, grinning and looking happy. "I got a postcard from Johnny last week. Want to see it?"

"No, I don't want to see it," I said. "I want to go fishing with you. Now do you want to go or don't you?"

"Yes," she said, "let's go right now. I just thought you might like to read Johnny's card. He mentioned you in it too."

I did want to read it, but I wasn't going to admit that to Molly. No telling what an idiot like Johnny would write on a postcard.

"Your dad don't look in too good a humor," I said.

"Get the poles out of the smokehouse and I'll wrap up some bait," she said. "Dad won't bother us. He likes catfish for supper."

I got the poles and propped them against the fence and went down and saddled Molly's horse. The old man was still drinking and sharpening his knife; he never even looked up. In a minute Molly came out with a lunch sack and a bait sack. She went up to the old man and hugged him a little with one arm and whispered to him and kissed him on one cheek and then come on out to me. She really liked that old bugger—it always surprised me to see it. He looked up at the lunch sack, but he didn't say anything.

"Want to go to a tank or to the River?" I said.

"Let's go to the big tank," she said. "South of the hill, in you-'all's place."

It was my favorite tank too, but it was better for courting than for fishing. I never caught nothing there. There was a lot of Bermuda grass around it, though, and shade trees and nice places to sit.

Molly was riding a little gray horse her old man had cheated a feller out of two years before. I was riding old Denver; we named him that because his momma come from Colorado. We loped nearly all the way to our fence before we pulled up. I let Molly go in front of me. Her hair was flying all over the place, and her shirttail come out. She rode good though. There wasn't no cattle around the tank when we got there, and not a ripple on the water, except once in a while when some dragonfly would light on the tank for a minute. We used liver for bait, and I put enough on the hooks to last awhile and stuck the poles in the mud. Molly sat down on the Bermuda grass, in the shade, and I sat down by her and held her hand. We were all set to fish.

It was about a perfect day. The sky was clear, and the sun felt warm like summer while the air felt cool like fall. We lolled around on the Bermuda grass and courted and ate lunch and fished all day. We caught three fish too, two croppies and one nice little cat; I guess we could have caught more if we had tried. We got a lot of nibbles, but Molly was so good to be with that day that I quit paying attention to them. I held her down and told her it was just turtles gnawing at the bait. She knew how inconvenient it was to catch turtles.

Sometime in the early afternoon, when we were over under

the big shade trees and not even pretending to fish, I finally asked Molly to marry me for the first time. There wasn't much grass under the trees, and we were laying on the slicker. We had been kissing a good deal and she seemed to like me so much that I didn't see why not to ask her. I was crazy about her.

"Molly," I said, "say, Molly. We're sweethearts anyway, why don't we go on and get married? Wouldn't that be the best thing to do? I sure would like to marry you."

She kinda grinned to herself and wouldn't look at me.

"Don't you want to at all?" I said. "You're the one for me, I know that for sure."

"You're my favorite," she said, and sat up and kissed me. "Giding-ton. But what in the world would we do married?"

"Why, what everybody else does, I guess. We ain't so different."

"Maybe you ain't," she said, "but I am. I don't want to get into all that stuff yet. It ain't near as much fun as things like we're doing today."

"How do you know?" I said. "You ain't been married. It might be more fun."

She got kinda mad. "Don't tell me that," she said. "I don't want to marry you or nobody else. Girls who get married just to do a lot of things with boys ain't very nice. I don't like it. I'd just as soon do all those things and not be married, and I mean it. I ain't gonna marry till I have to because of having a baby, and I mean that too. And I wish I didn't even have to then."

Well, that shocked me as much as anything I ever heard, Molly saying that. It was just like her though. She never cared what people thought about her. I guess she never thought she was very respectable anyway, growing up with the daddy she had. I knew a lot of people around Thalia who didn't think she was nice, either, but they didn't mean anything to me.

"Honey, don't talk that way," I said. "I'm crazy about you and I just want you for a wife, that's all."

She looked sorry then, but she looked kinda wild, too, and we lay there and hugged one another for a long time before she would talk agin at all.

"I'm crazy about you too, Gid," she said, hugging my neck. "You're the best to me of anybody. But I ain't going to marry, I mean it. I'll do anything you want me to but that. I'll do everything else if you want me to right now," and when I kissed her she was trembling like a leaf. But we never managed it, somehow: it was my fault. I guess I was too surprised at Molly, and I couldn't quit thinking about it. She practically took her shirt off and that was something, but I couldn't quit thinking about it, and I knew it wasn't right, so I made her quit.

"Now we got to quit," I said. "You know it, Molly. Why can't we get married?"

Then she got real cool and mad at me, but I was pretty mad too, and I didn't back down.

"Let's go swimming, Gid," she said. "It's so hot. Then we can talk about it some more." She was cool as ice when she said that.

"You hush," I said. "There ain't no use in you teasing me, and you know it. I ain't no damn kid. We got nothing to go swimming in, so how can we go?"

"We got skin," she said. "I didn't know you was such a scardy-cat. Why do you want to get married if you're scared of girls?"

"Now listen, Molly," I said. "I told you to quit teasing me and you better do it before I shake the hell out of you. I'm sorry. But I ain't scared of you. I just know what's right and what ain't, and you ain't gonna talk me out of it just because you're mad. And if you don't like it, you can just stay mad."

"Don't ask me to marry you any more," she said, only she wasn't mad then, she was kind of quiet. "Get off my shirt, honey. You're too sober, I never could get along with you. You didn't know I was like this, did you?"

I grabbed her and made her let me hold her, even if she didn't want me to.

"I may be too sober," I said. "I guess I am. But I'm not going to get stampeded into doing something crazy even if we do both want to. You got to be a little careful about some things."

"Okay," she said. "You done said that. Shut up about it. Let's fish or ride or do something. I'm tired of sitting here being so careful. I guess you're so careful you won't even want to hold hands with me no more, will you?"

But after a while she got in a good humor again and we walked around the dam and rode horses some and finally went home about five o'clock, just when the shadows were beginning to stretch out. The old man was gone when we got there and I cleaned the fish for her. She cooked them and made biscuits and gravy and we each ate one of the croppie, bones or no bones. We left the catfish for the old man.

After supper we went out on the porch and swung in her porch swing and she was real warm and sweet agin and we kissed all we wanted to. I don't guess things could have been any nicer, except that I had already begin to feel mad at myself for not taking better advantage of the afternoon. But she acted like she'd forgot about it. She teased me a little about Johnny.

"I know why you don't come see me as much any more," she said. "It's because Johnny's gone. You don't really care much about me, do you? You just like to spite Johnny."

She was wrong about that and we both knew it, but it was true that I got a little extra kick out of being with Molly when Johnny was around to notice it. It would have probably been the same with him if he'd been in my place.

I made up with her for the afternoon, only she wouldn't hear a word about marrying. I had to drop that for a while, but I didn't care. She gave me a big kiss just before I got on my horse and held on to my hand until I had to turn loose and ride away. And she stood on the hill and watched me go.

Later I got awful mad at myself for being such a sissy down at the tank. I must have been either scared to death or crazy, I couldn't figure which. At least we could have gone swimming, that wouldn't have been no great crime. The more I thought about it the worse it got, and it was all I could do to keep from riding back over that night. But I figured the old man would be back, so I never.

I guess I always did think things over too much, at least where Molly was concerned. She was a special girl. Johnny, he would have done it and then thought it over later, but I always did the thinking first. The next time I got the chance I decided I would try his way.

But things never worked out too good. Dad rode in the next morning with about a month's work lined up to do, and I had to stay mad at myself all the time I was doing it. By the time things loosened up enough that I could get back over to see Molly, why it was the middle of October and Johnny was home agin, so I had him to worry about. If there was one thing I learned that day, it was not to miss no opportunities. I just wish learning it had done me a little more good.

four

I guess it was being so mad at myself over Molly that caused me to run off one night and court Mabel Peters. I knew at the time I didn't have no business doing it. In the first place it was on a Friday night, and I never got off work till after dark, and I knew I would have to start agin before sunup. And it was nearly six miles over to Mabel's house; I could have gone over and seen Molly with a lot less trouble. But I was still kind of ashamed of the way I acted around Molly; I didn't want to see her that night. Mabel wasn't the kind of a girl I could get excited about in no permanent way, but every once in a while she was the kind I could get real excited about in a temporary way. Her folks were so poor and they lived so far off from everybody that none of the boys courted Mabel much. She was right pretty in a neat, timid kind of way, but she never had no real boy friends, and I knew she was so anxious for a sweetheart she would do most anything. So I wasn't very proud of the reasons I went to see her, but I went, anyway.

Mabel's ma and pa were pretty old and usually went to bed early; except for one or two of the younger kids, Mabel was nearly always up by herself. I rode up to the yard gate in the dark and sat on my horse till the dogs kind of quieted down. One thing I hated about visiting the Peterses was them barking dogs. There must have been six or eight; I never knew Old Man Peters to keep no less. In a minute Mabel came out and stood in the door.

"Who's that out there?" she said.

"It's just me, Mabel," I said. "I'd get down but I'm afraid these dogs would eat me."

"Gid?" she said. "Hush up, Pete, hush that." I guess Pete was the boss dog, because he went running over to her, and in a minute they all quieted down. Then I got off my horse and tied him to their mailbox.

"Have you been to supper?" she said. "Come on in and I'll fix you some."

But I never let her get me in the house. Their little old house always nearly suffocated me. It was an old chickenhouse, was what it was; Old Man Peters had just kinda rebuilt it. It never had but four little tight rooms, and they were so small and squeezed up and had such low ceilings that I couldn't hardly breathe when I was inside. I don't see how they lived through the summertime; it would have been like living in an oven.

Mabel knew I didn't like it, too, and it always embarrassed her. She wanted me to come and see her, but then when I did come she didn't have no nice place where we could go, and that preyed on her mind. Mabel was awful pretty in the face; I was just kinda awkward around her because it took me twenty or thirty minutes each time to get over feeling sorry for her. She'd worked and wanted her whole life, and she always looked like she'd do just anything for somebody who'd give her the chance to have some fun.

"Aren't you going to come in awhile?" she said. "We can't just stand out here on the steps."

"No," I said. "I feel like moving around, how about you? I thought you might like to take a little walk with me. It's such a bright moonlight night we wouldn't need no lantern." That was true. The moon was big and white that night, sailing up over the pastures.

The Peterses' house didn't have a porch, just front steps and back steps, because it was propped up on bricks, but Old Man Peters kept his wagon back behind the barn and I figured that would be our destination. It was a good big Studebaker wagon, and he kept his wagon sheet in it.

Mabel was agreeable enough to the walk.

"That'd be nice, Gid," she said. "Where will we walk?"

"Just here and there." She grabbed my hand herself and held on to me tight. I guess she was afraid of snakes. She walked so close to me I was afraid to move my feet for fear of stepping on her. I went dumb then; I could have kicked myself. I couldn't think of one thing to say. And I was a little snake-shy myself; nobody's very anxious to get rattlesnake-bit. But Mabel didn't mind the quiet; she walked along sort of humming to herself.

"It's sure nice to see somebody," she said. "I swear Ma and Pa have been about to bore me plumb to death."

"Dad bores me a good deal sometimes too," I said. I was beginning to get a little excited from her walking so close to me that way. I never could understand how a little thing like Mabel could get me so excited, but she sure could. She was so thin you wouldn't even notice her if she was standing sideways to you, but once she got near you she sure did make herself felt. We sashayed around by the postpile a time or two and the pigpen once or twice and then I sidled over toward the wagon. I didn't need to sidle. When I asked her if she wanted to sit down awhile she just nodded, and it wasn't two minutes till we were kissing like old sweethearts. Mabel never pulled back a time; it was always me. At first I was kind of wishing it was Molly that was there, but then I quit caring so much, and I guess we'd have done the whole works without no conversation or nothing if I hadn't made the mistake of stopping to ask.

"You can if you want to, Gid," she whispered. "I don't care. And then we can get married and start having babies. That's what I've always wanted to do. You'll be the best husband in the world."

She just barely whispered that in my ear, but it hit me like a bucket of ice water.

"Goodness, we can't do that, Mabel," I said. "Dad would raise too much Cain, and your dad too. Let's go ahead anyway."

She didn't get mad, or say a word back to me, and she kissed me a whole lot more, but it never meant anything then. She had put on all the brakes. I was so mad at her I could have stomped her for a minute, but she kept on acting sweet and happy and never seemed to notice. She did notice, though; she was just too sly to let on.

That was the big difference in her and Molly. Molly was wild, but she was warm, and she wasn't sly. Mabel wasn't really a bit wild, but she was really cold and sly. Mabel's little brain was cold as an icicle.

You couldn't guess that from the way she acted in the wagon. She cuddled up with me on the wagon sheet just as long as I wanted to stay, and I did stay a good while, hoping she would change her mind. But she wouldn't change her mind any more than the moon would change its direction. She sure did want to get married.

Finally I helped her out of the wagon and we walked back to the house. She never talked at all; she knew she couldn't do any good talking. But she kept close to me; I practically had to crawl out from under her to get on my horse.

It was just when I was about to ride away that she began to look real sorry. She had one hand on my ankle, and I was afraid she was fixing to cry.

"Come back to see me," she said. "I get awful bored around here, and I don't like for nobody to come to see me but you." And before I could get away, I was feeling sorry for her agin. I decided on the way home I would have to come back and give her another try. It had been worth it anyway.

Only next morning I wasn't so sure. I hadn't been asleep but two or three hours when Dad came in and started shaking my damn foot to wake me up. That was sure a long day.

five

Johnny got back from the Panhandle on a Sunday night and went to work for us on Monday morning. He rode over about breakfast time, to see how I was doing, I guess. It was branding season and we were getting in some new cattle, so when Dad got back from his morning ride he asked Johnny if he wanted to go to work on a day basis, and Johnny said he did.

"And when I say work, I mean work," Dad said. "I ain't gonna squander no dollar a day for you to sit on your butt."

"I ain't never run from no work yet," Johnny said. "Of course there's some kinds I'd rather do than others. But you're probably that way about it too, aren't you, Mr. Fry?"

Dad grunted. He didn't like much conversation out of Johnny. "The kind I like best is none," he said.

I thought working up on the big ranches might have given Johnny a little responsibility, but it never. He was just as wild and crazy as he'd always been. One thing I noticed, though, he must have done a lot of riding. His new saddle was broken in to where it was comfortable as could be. He let me ride it a time or two, and I liked the way it rode.

He asked me right off if I had been taking good care of his girl.

"Mabel, you mean?" I said. "You bet, ever chance I get."

"Much obliged," he said. "Only she wasn't really the one I meant. I don't guess you know who that would be?"

"I don't guess. Not unless it's Annie Eldenfelder."

We carried on and kidded one another a lot. I was glad to see Johnny get back, really. Things were a good bit snappier with him around.

He hadn't been working for us a week when me and him got into a real scrape with Molly's dad. We never meant to, either, because we both knew how she felt about him, and getting into a scrape with him was the best way in the world to get crosswise with her. But sometimes you don't have much control over what happens to you.

A couple of our yearling steers had crawled through a busted water gap into Old Man Taylor's pasture. Dad seen their tracks going through when he was out on his early morning lookaround, and when he got back to the house he sent me and Johnny over there to get them out. Which wasn't no trouble to do. We found them with the old man's milk cows and drove the whole bunch down to our gate and roped a yearling apiece and drug them through the gate where they belonged. It was still early then, and chilly, with mist hanging over the ground nearly high as a horse's belly. We was glad for a little action to warm us up.

It was when we were going to fix the water gap that we got in trouble. The first thing we done wrong was to ride down toward the creek on the Taylor side of the fence. We knew the old man would raise hell about that if he caught us, but we did it anyway, just to spite him. Then Johnny spotted a coyote. He loped through the fence about a hundred yards ahead of us, and Johnny said he saw him squat down in the grass and stop.

"Hell, let's rope that sonofabitch," he said. "I ain't never roped a coyote, have you?"

"Naw," I said. "Reckon we can catch him?" But I was already making me a loop. I had always wanted to rope one, and I figured this was my chance. Johnny, he couldn't throw his rope in the creek, so I never worried about him catching it. He made a loop big enough for a dinosaur to go through.

"I tell you now," he said. "I can't see him, but he's right over there between them two big bunches of chaparral. Let's sneak up on this side of him, so he can't dodge back through the fence. That way we can chase him clear to the north side if we need to. He ain't gonna sit forever, so when we get past that third post let's charge hell out of him. You ready?"

"He's practically roped," I said. "If you miss your first loop, haze him over my way so I can get a good throw."

We held our ponies down to a slow walk till we got past the post: then we jobbed the spurs to them and away we went, holding up our ropes and yelling like mad. I lost my hat before we even seen the coyote, and Johnny lost his a minute later. In about two seconds we was to the chaparral and up Mr. Coyote come; he jumped plumb over the bushes and it looked for a while like he was running along on top of the mist, two feet off the ground. Me and Johnny was right on his ass, and Johnny was done swinging. I swung to the side to give him room. Johnny had a damn good roping horse, he run right up by the coyote and leaned over, so all Johnny had to do was drop on the loop, but Johnny threw too late and missed about twenty feet, only this throw turned the coyote and it cut right under my horse while I was running full speed. I yanked to the right and went to spurring for all I was worth. Old Denver turned on about fifteen cents and was after the coyote agin before Johnny even got pulled up. By then we hit a strip of mesquite brush and I thought we had lost him, but then I decided to ride like hell and try to chase him through the brush and out into the clearing by the Taylor horse tank, so I could get my throw. Into the brush we went, with me about twenty yards behind the coyote and Johnny somewhere back of me. I ducked and spurred and the mesquite limbs flew. Only if Johnny couldn't rope, boy he could ride. By the time we were past the middle of the brush he went by me on the left just a-flying, waving his rope and his horse jumping trees and bushes and limbs busting like crazy. The coyote was still ahead though, sailing along on top of the mist. I spurred a little harder and we all three hit the clearing about the same time. In a second we were at the tank. I beat the coyote to the water about two steps and turned him over the dam, and Johnny was right there to keep him from ducking back so he went over the dam and down on the other side and I went right over with him and threw while we were still half in the air: caught him clean as a whistle. Old Denver fell then and nobody could blame him; I went rolling off to one side and the coyote to the other. But when we all got up we had a big dog coyote on the end of the rope.

"Good throw, by god," Johnny said. "I thought you was gonna turn a flip off that dam."

"It's a wonder I didn't," I said. I was too out of breath to say much. Johnny got his rope on the coyote too, and we had him where he couldn't do any harm.

"I wish Dad was here," I said. "I bet he never roped one." One thing I could do, and that was rope.

We were about to knock the coyote in the head and get the ears so we could collect our bounty when Old Man Taylor walked up on the tank dam from the other side. He had his .10-gauge shotgun in one hand and a couple of dead squirrels in the other—probably they were going to be Molly's breakfast. When he got up closer I seen his beard was wet, so I guess he had him a whiskey jug hid off in a stump somewhere.

"Goddam you boys," he said, "Goddam trespassers. What are you little sonsofbitches doing on my place?"

We never said a word, but we didn't like it. People can't just come up and cuss you without you getting mad.

"Well, the cat got your tongues?" he said. "Answer me when I ask you something. Didn't your folks teach you no manners?"

"We had to come over and get a couple of our yearlings and fix the water gap on the river," I said. "Then we accidentally run on to this coyote and roped him. That's all, Mr. Taylor."

"Oh you did, did you?" he said. Boy he looked mad. "Young farts ought to have your asses kicked."

We were getting about all we could stand of it, but we didn't know quite what to do. For one thing, we still had the coyote on the ropes, and the old man noticed it.

"Turn that coyote loose," he said. "That there's my own coyote anyway. I don't ever want to catch you roping my coyotes agin. Turn the sonofabitch loose."

That was the silliest thing I ever heard of, claiming that coyote.

"No sir," I said. "We caught him coming out of our pasture, and we'll just have to take him back." I thought I could be just as silly as he was.

"Oh you are, are you?" he said, stuffing his squirrels in his hip pocket. "Now what about you, little McCloud? You get down and turn that coyote loose."

Johnny was half-tickled by it all.

"No sir," he said. "I would, only I'm scared to. I'm kind of a coward when it comes to getting one of my hands bit off."

The old man got madder and madder, but he shut up and just stared at us. That's when I really got uneasy, and I don't know where it would have gone if Dad hadn't rode up about that time. For once in my life I was glad to see Dad. Old Man Taylor was just crazy enough to have shot us.

I guess Dad had missed me and Johnny and come to see what kind of mischief we was in. When Dad was impatient to work it never took him long to miss a person. He rode up like there wasn't nothing unusual about the gathering at all.

"I see you boys been fiddling around," he said. "I thought I told you to come on home when you got them yearlings out. How are you today, Cletus?"

"No damn good," the old man said. "Looky what them boys done. I wisht you'd make them turn that coyote loose. I don't like boys roping coyotes of mine."

Crazy old fart.

"Aw, you didn't look close enough, Cletus," Dad said. "That's my coyote. See that earmark I put on him. Hell, I never even knowed he was out. It's lucky these boys found him. Once your coyotes get off in the brush they're hard to find."

I was flabbergasted and so was Old Man Taylor. Johnny was just tickled. We all looked, and sure enough the coyote did have a piece of his ear missing. And I don't know yet whether Dad was really responsible for it being gone or not. I imagine it was just chewed off in a fight, but you can't tell about Dad. Old Man Taylor like to swallowed his Adam's apple.

"How do you mark your coyotes, Cletus?" Dad asked, solemn as a judge. "I never noticed. If you'll show me, I'll have these boys run what they find of yours back in your pasture."

But Old Man Taylor was a pretty sly old bastard himself—you couldn't hem him up for long. He walked over and grabbed the coyote by the snout and looked at his ear.

"By god, it is yours," he said. "I come off without my spectacles this morning.

"Say," he said. "I like the looks of this coyote, Adam. How much will you take for him?"

That even surprised Dad, only he never much let on. He got out his plug and cut himself off some tobacco; then he offered the plug to Old Man Taylor and he cut off a bigger chew than Dad's. All the time Dad was thinking it over. I bet he thought it was funny as hell.

"Oh, I don't know, Cletus," he said. "I ain't been watching the market too close. I'd have to get about three dollars for him, I guess."

"By god, that's fair," the old man said, and I'll be damned if he didn't take out his pocketbook and pull three one-dollar bills out of it and hand them to Dad. Dad folded them together and stuck them in his shirt pocket. That was a dollar more than the ears would bring in bounty money.

"Good trade," the old man said. "Wonder if them boys would help me a minute, Adam. I might as well earmark him while I got him caught."

"Sure," Dad said. "You boys get down and help Mr. Taylor mark that coyote."

The old man stood back and opened his pocketknife, and there wasn't nothing for it but for us to do the dangerous work. I went up one rope and Johnny up the other, and we managed to get his snout without being bit too bad. I muzzled him with my piggin string and we threw him down and hogtied him with Johnny's. Then the old man cropped his ear and the job was done.

"Much obliged, boys," he said. "Now I'll know the bastard next time I see him.

"Can I borrow your piggin strings and just leave him tied awhile?" he asked, real friendly. "Tame him up a little. After a while I'll send that girl of mine and get her to lead him up to the house. She ain't got a damn thing else to do."

The thought of Molly having to drag that coyote to the house made me fighting mad. But Dad was ready to go.

"Let's get home, boys," he said. "We got all them calves to brand. Much obliged, Cletus. Take care of yourself. Hope he makes you a good coyote."

"Oh yeah," the old man said. "He'll do."

"Well, that was a damn good trade," Dad said. "Three dollars always comes in handy."

"Hell, we caught him," I said. "We ought to get a little of it."

We come to the gate and Dad stopped and waited for one of us to get down and open it. Johnny did.

"Oh you think so, do you?" Dad said. "Well, I don't. He was my coyote to begin with. All you done was rope him. If you was to rope one of my calves, that wouldn't make it yours, would it?"

"What made him yours?" I said. "You wasn't serious about that earmark business, was you?"

He just kept riding and never answered.

"Shit-fire," Johnny said. "I believe I'll quit, Mr. Fry. I better go back and untie that coyote before Molly has to come drag him to the house. I don't want her fiddling with that big bastard. He might bite her hand off."

"I'm with you," I said. "Let's turn him loose. We can get back in plenty of time to do the branding."

"The hell you will," Dad said. "I just got you boys out of one scrape and I ain't got time to get you out of another. Cletus is just waiting for one of you to come back so he can get that extra dollar out of your hide. He'd get it too, don't think he wouldn't."

"Dollar," I said. "You made three."

"Yeah, but Cletus will get two back when he sells them ears to the county. Why, he ain't gonna keep no coyotes. He just spent that money to keep from backing down."

Me and Johnny couldn't hardly believe it.

"You mean a poor man like him would spend three dollars just for that?" I said.

"Who's a poor man?" Dad said. "Cletus Taylor ain't poor. He's just tight. Just because he don't spend money don't mean he ain't got any. I don't spend much myself, and that's one reason I got so much more than most people."

"Well," Johnny said, "if I was a man and I had money, I believe I'd at least buy myself and my daughter some decent clothes to wear. I wouldn't go around dressed disgraceful. I believe I'd spend a little of it enjoying life."

"Most young fools would," Dad said. "That's why most young fools are broke."

Me and Johnny shut up. There was no use arguing with Dad. And he was right about one thing. Just as we crossed the Ridge we heard the .10-gauge go KLABOOM, like a damn cannon.

"One less coyote," Dad said. "And that many more frying chickens I'll get to eat next spring. I'm glad you boys have finally learned to rope."

six

Old Man Taylor got his damn revenge anyhow, only he took it out on Molly instead of us. I could have killed him for it.

Two nights after the coyote roping they were having a big harvest-time square dance over in Thalia. It was about the biggest dance or get-together they had between the Fourth of July and Christmas, and I had an agreement with Molly that me and her would go. I asked her the day we went fishing, while Johnny was still up in the Panhandle. He was mad enough to bite himself when he found out I had done asked her. He ended up having to take Mabel Peters, and it served him right.

Anyway, I got all spruced up and was going to use Dad's buggy. I drove over to Molly's just about dark, and I was sure excited. I didn't care too much about the dance, but the thought of getting to ride all that way with Molly sitting by me was something to be excited about.

But when I got to Molly's the house was completely dark. It surprised the devil out of me. There wasn't no light on of no kind. For a minute I thought Johnny must have pulled some kind of a sneak and taken her off already. I didn't know what to think. It was a still, pretty night, and not a sound to be heard. Finally I hitched the horses and walked across the yard and up on the porch. Still not a sound. I hesitated a minute before I knocked on the door —I decided her old devil of a daddy was hiding in there someplace, waiting to jump out and give me hell about the coyote. I walked around on the porch for a few minutes, hoping somebody inside the house would finally hear me and say something. Molly could have lain down to take a little nap and rest up for the dance.

But nobody said nothing.

"Hell-fire," I said, finally, and went up and knocked on the door good and loud.

"I can't go tonight, Gid," Molly said, and it like to scared me to death. She had been standing just inside the door all the time, but off to one side of the screen, so I couldn't see her.

"You'll have to go on without me," she said. "I ain't feeling good."

"My goodness, Molly, you scared the daylights out of me. Why don't you turn on some kind of light."

"I don't want to," she said, and her voice was trembling. "I just want to be in the dark, Gid." And then it was real quiet, and I knew she was standing there crying, even if I couldn't see her. Molly cried the quietest, she never made a sound at all. Then I heard her move off in the dark and bump into a table or something and run down the hall, and things were quiet agin. The only sound I could hear was the windmill creaking.

I didn't know what to make of it. Something was bothering her pretty bad for her not even to ask me in. One thing I knew, I wasn't going to no dance without her. She could forget about that.

But that didn't solve the problem of what to do. I had to get to talk to her, and the only way to do that was to go in the damn dark house and find her. I wished I had had enough sense to ask her if her dad was there. If she was the only one home, I was all right. But I could just imagine that old man, standing in the living room with a club, waiting for me. The more I thought about it, the mad-der it made me. I remembered how he had cussed me and Johnny when he found us with that coyote. Finally I opened the screen door and doubled up my fists and clobbered on in. About three steps inside I stopped and crouched over, watching for him.

But he didn't come. If somebody had come in with a light, I would have looked silly as hell. Pretty soon I knew damn well he wasn't there. Molly wouldn't have let me walk into no bad situation without warning me. And the old man wouldn't have waited for me to come in: he would have come out. Besides, if he had been there I would have smelled him, he was such a fragrant old bastard.

So I went on down the hall to Molly's room and didn't give the old man another thought. Sure enough she was in on her bed, crying. The moonlight was coming through the window. I went over and sat down on the edge of the old creaky bed and put my hand on her arm.

"Now, honey," I said, "don't lay there taking on. Turn over and tell me where you hurt and I'll see if I can find some medicine." It was strange, because Molly wasn't the kind that went around being sick.

She wouldn't answer me, though, and for a few minutes I just had to sit there, holding her the best she would let me. She moved over under my arm and acted like she was glad to have me there, but she wouldn't look up. She wasn't crying loud, but she sure wasn't happy.

In a little while I fumbled around and found some matches and lit the lamp. The minute I had the light on I seen what it was all about. Her face and throat and the front of her dress was all wet from tears, but the trouble was, she had a black eye. It wasn't a bad one. In fact it kind of made her look prettier or older, in a way, but you could tell she had one. I knew who done it, too.

"Don't you say a word against my daddy," she said. "I know

what you're thinking. He wouldn't have done it if I hadn't been so mean."

That was a lie, but I never said a word.

"I sure am sorry about it," I said in a minute. "But it ain't bad, Molly. It ain't no reason to stay in the dark all the time. By tomorrow you won't even be able to tell it."

I wanted to cuss the worthless old bastard good, but that would have just messed things up.

"I know it, Gid," and the tears were pouring out of her eyes. I sat down and hugged her again. "But the dance is just tonight," she said. "And you're all dressed up and look so nice, you ought to go on. I had my dress all fixed, too. I'd been looking forward to it for I don't know how long. Why does it have to happen at such a bad time?"

I could see how it was a pretty big disappointment. To a girl, especially. Molly never got to go places very often. In fact, it was just very very seldom that she went any place. When you come right down to it, she didn't like much being as cooped up as Mabel Peters, only there was so much more of Molly to coop up.

"Now hush, sugar," I said. "It ain't such a great calamity. This ain't the only dance there'll ever be. We'll get to go to plenty more."

"No we won't," she said. "I don't care." She pulled up the counterpane and wiped her face, but there was still a little puddle of tears in the hollow of her neck. She looked at me kinda mad and I got out my handkerchief and wiped her throat. She was so pretty, black eye or not.

"I wish there never would be another one," she said. "Then I wouldn't have to be so disappointed. I know I won't get to go, even if there's a hundred dances. I guess I'm just too mean."

"Oh hush that up," I said. "You ain't mean, and you ain't hurt, either. We can have just as much fun right here as we could have at the dance."

"But I don't want to stay here. I stay here all the time, Gid. I wanted to go where there were a lot of people having fun."

"Okay," I said, "let's go. It ain't late. That little old shadow on your eye ain't no reason to stay home."

But that just made her cry more. I never knew girls had so much crying in them. Missing that dance didn't amount to a hill-of-beans in the long run, but Molly acted like her heart was broken.

"Now you hush," I said. "This is a silly damn way for you to act. If you want to go, why get up and dry your face and let's go. Hell, by the time we get there everybody will be so drunk they wouldn't notice if you had three black eyes. And if you don't want to go, why hush anyway, and let's go in the living room and pop some popcorn or something. Crying all night won't do any good."

Finally she did hush and just lay back against me. I held her until I was sure she had calmed down.

"That's better," I said. "Have you decided yet?"

"We'll just have to stay here," she said. "I don't want to go to the dance unless I can go looking nice, and I can't do that with this eye. Besides, my dress is all wet. But you ought to go. Just think of all the girls you could dance with."

"I don't know," I said. "Me and you may dance a little ourselves, before the night is over. Johnny can take care of all them other girls."

"He said he wouldn't. When I told him I had already promised you, he said he intended to go to the dance drunk and not dance a single time, just to spite me."

"Sounds like him," I said. "But what he says and what he does are two different things. You know that, don't you?"

"Not when it comes to me, they ain't," she said.

"Where's your dad tonight, anyway?"

"He was out of whiskey and had to go to Henrietta. He may not be back for two or three days."

"Let's go in the living room then," I said.

We did, but we never popped no popcorn. I had had a big supper anyway. We built a big fire in the fireplace; it was the only light we had. Molly started to the kitchen to get something and I caught her in my arms and swung her around a time or two and kissed her.

"Now ain't this dancing?" I said. "Ain't this better'n dancing in a big crowd, anyway? If you ask me, that black eye is the nicest thing about you tonight."

"I wish you'd take off that stratchy necktie," she said. "It's about to rub a raw place on me."

"Boy, I will," I said. "It was choking me anyway." I took it off, and my wool coat too. But I never let Molly get to the kitchen.

"Now let's dance," I said. "Just us two. Let's round dance. You hum the music."

She put her head on my chest and hummed a little bit of some song. I hugged her against me real tight and we moved around the living room floor, in the shadows of the fire. "Let's just imagine the music, Gid," she said. "I can't remember what I'm humming half the time."

"I ain't got that much imagination," I said, but we kept dancing anyway; we danced real slow. Molly's hair had a good smell. I got to wanting to kiss more than I wanted to dance, so I stopped and made her tilt her face up and let me. We stood there so long I expected the sun would be coming up. But it was still dark and shadowy.

"I want to make up to you for the other day," I said. "I sure do love you."

She kept standing there against me with her eyes shut, and didn'- say anything, but when I kissed her agin she seemed real glad.

"It's okay then? If I make it up to you tonight? I've been worrying about it a lot."

"Yes, I want you to," she said, "but let's stand here a little while longer. Let's not think about anything."

So we stood there and kissed some more and got closer and closer together and finally moved on down the hall to Molly's room, where we had been at first. When we got there I remembered something and left her for a minute and went and latched the screen doors. I went back and she was crying.

She grabbed me and I held her tight. "Where did you go?" she said. "You never needed to leave me and go nowhere."

"Just to latch the doors," I said.

She got fighting mad all of a sudden. I had to hold her to keep her from hitting me. "Don't ever leave me like that agin," she said. "I don't care if the doors are latched or not. Next time you leave me, just keep going." And she actually bit me, she was so mad or hurt or something. I almost shoved her down I was so surprised. But I held her in the middle of the floor till she got real quiet and we were close together and kissed a long time agin. I never wanted to leave her, that's for sure. What I couldn't figure was, how I was going to get my boots off without stopping the kissing for a minute.

"Let's sit down, Molly. These new boots are killing me."

"Poor Gid," she said. "Here, sit on the bed. I'll help you take them off."

And in a minute she had, and I was holding her agin. Then I accidentally tore her pretty dress. I thought that would cook my goose, but it never. She put her hand on my neck and kissed me. I started to tell her I was sorry but her mouth kept stopping me. "Don't talk no more," she said, "don't you say another word tonight."

I was the first one awake. I guess I expected Dad to be shaking my foot. But there was just Molly; she was lovely. In a minute she woke up too and yawned and saw me and giggled and snuggled over and kissed me. It was purely delicious. Only I had begun to realize that Dad's buggy and horses were still hitched outside, and that it was past daylight and he was wondering where I was.

"Good god," I said. "Dad'll skin me alive. I ought to woken up and gone home."

"Scardy-cat," she said. "Let's stay here all day. That will show them they ain't the boss of us. I'd like to stay right here, where it's nice and warm and just us, wouldn't you? Can we?"

"Oh lord, I'd like to too," I said. "But Dad is the boss of me, I guess. I better skedaddle."

"Well, I wish we could stay," she said. Then she sat up and grinned, without no covers or nothing. "But I'll cook you some hot biscuits, anyway." And in a minute she had kissed me and crawled over and got out of bed. She was poking around in a drawer looking for some Levis, with just her behind pointed at me.

If it didn't bother her, I didn't see why it ought to bother me. I loved her and I didn't figure I'd have too much trouble persuading her to marry me, after we'd spent the night. Only when I looked down at the bedsheets I couldn't figure it out.

"Hey, sweetie," I said. "Ain't you normal? I thought you was supposed to bleed all over the place."

"Why, didn't you know no better than that?" she said, turning around and grinning at me. She had a pair of Levis in her hand, but she hadn't put them on. "You're the funniest boy, Gid." The morning light was coming in on her through the windows; she pulled on a shirt and never buttoned it, and her hair was down over her shoulders. I thought she was the prettiest thing I had ever seen.

"You didn't have to worry," she said, innocent as daylight. "You only bleed like that the first time."

I was absolutely flabbergasted.

seven

It made me pretty down in the mouth, finding out that I wasn't the first feller ever to spend a night with Molly. I couldn't think straight for a while, I was so upset. But there wasn't much I could say about it, because she got up just happy as a lark, and not the least bit down in the dumps about anything. She fed me some awful good biscuits for breakfast, too. But I never enjoyed my food. All I could think about was wanting to get married to her as soon as I could.

Of course Dad raked me over the coals when I finally got home. He seen me unhitching the buggy, and here he came.

"Well, at least you ain't eloped with her," he said, looking at the buggy to see how stratched up it was. "But I bet it wasn't because you didn't try. Your good buddy Johnny's been down there digging postholes for three hours. Get on down there and help him."

"He ain't my good buddy," I said. "I guess I can change clothes before I go, can't I?"

"I'd just as soon you worked in them you got on," Dad said. "If you dirty them up, you won't be running around so much at night." And I had been out two nights in a month, and one of them he never knew about.

Johnny, he was sweating his whiskey out. But I wasn't in no mood to sympathize with him.

"Where you been?" he said. "Why wasn't you'all at the dance? Hell, I waited for you till one o'clock."

"We got lost and never made it. How'd you and your sweetheart Mabel get along?"

He leaned on his diggers a minute. "Why, she'd be a darling if she wasn't such a bitch," he said. "I had to run backward all night to keep her from proposing to me."

He would have chattered all day if I had let him, but I grabbed my diggers and walked off a hundred yards or so and went to digging. I wasn't in a talking mood.

Well, I thought about it and thought about it, and I couldn't come to no decision. It had to be Johnny that done it, but he never acted the least bit guilty about it, and Molly never either, so I had no way of knowing. The only thing that made me doubt it was Johnny was him not bragging about it. He just naturally bragged a little if he had done anything to brag about. Anyhow, I didn't think it was right for two fellers to have spent the night with a sweet girl like Molly and not either one of them have married her. The more I thought about it, the surer I was about that, and something had to be done about it. If Johnny had been there first, then he ought to have the first chance at marrying her, and if he didn't want to, why I damn sure did. And the way I seen it, Molly could have her choice of me and him, but that was all the choice there was to it. She couldn't go running around single much longer, that was for sure.

All the same, I couldn't help being mad at myself, because I kept wanting to go right back over and spend another night. And I would have, too, if her damned old man had ever left agin; I snuck over several times to check, but he was always there. I hadn't forgot about him giving her that black eye, either.

Finally me and Johnny had it out about her, when we were going to Fort Worth, of all places. About the middle of November, Dad decided to ship the rest of his calves, but he didn't want to go along and fool with them, so he sent me and Johnny.

"I guess I'm a damn fool for sending two idiots when I could just send one," he said. "But maybe if I send two, one will be sober enough to look after the cattle part of the time. I want you boys back here on Sunday, and I don't want you to give them cattle away. If you see any yearling steers worth the money, you might buy me about a hundred of them and bring 'em home with you."

Of course it was the biggest lark in the world to me and Johnny. We struck out early one morning, with a norther blowing cold as hell, and drove the cattle to Henrietta and put them on the railroad cars for Fort Worth about night that same day.

"Them cattle are safe," Johnny said. "Let's go wet our whistles. My damn throat's full of dust."

Mine was too, and we bought some whiskey and went to washing out the dust. About that time we went into a little honkytonk there by the railroad yards and run into the deputy sheriff that had arrested Johnny the last time he was in Henrietta. Only he wasn't a deputy no more and was a good bit drunker than we was, and had two of his drinking buddies with him. Johnny asked me if I'd back him up, and I said sure, so he went over and called the feller a sonofabitch and the other feller called him one back and they went outside and had a fist fight in the street. Me and the other fellers went too, but we didn't fight. The ex-deputy bloodied Johnny's nose, but I think Johnny had a little the best of the fight.

"That'll show you, you bastard," Johnny said. "Next time just try and arrest me."

"Sonofabitch," the man said. "Want me to whip you good?"

That was funny, because they had already fought for fifteen

minutes. Me and Johnny walked over to the pens and climbed around on the cars awhile, and the cattle looked all right to us, so we went to the caboose and went to sleep. Sometime during the night the train come and hooked onto the cars and off we went, I don't know just when. The caboose was awful bouncy, and it woke me up about Decatur. Johnny was sitting up holding his jaw; I guess it had bounced against the floor. There wasn't but one other passenger, a damn greasy oil-field hand, who looked like he'd got on the train about Burkburnett. He was asleep on the bench.

"Hell, let's go outside," Johnny said. "I can't sleep in this rickety bastard. Let's go out and look at the country awhile."

"I'm ready," I said.

We put on our jackets and walked out on the little porch of a thing at the tail-end of the caboose. It was a clear, starry night, but cold as hell. The norther was still blowing, and we was getting it right in our faces. We set down with our backs to the door of the caboose and watched the country go by in the dark.

"I sure like riding trains," Johnny said. "Lots faster than going some place ahorseback."

I watched the rails come out from under the car, and they didn't seem to be coming so fast. But they came awful steady; I kept halfway looking for them to end, and they never did. We went through some little old town, I never have known the name of it, and all it had in it was grain elevators. It was the most grain elevators I knew of this side of Kansas. We could see the shapes of them in the moonlight. It was real exciting to be going someplace.

"This here's where they make all the oatmeal," Johnny said. "Boy, I'm glad I ain't no farmer. There ain't nothing that can compare with a cowboy's life, if you ask me. You don't have to worry about a damn thing."

"It just depends," I said. "What if you own the ranch you're working on? Then you got to worry about making money and taking care of the cattle and all that kind of thing."

"Then you ain't a cowboy, you're a rancher," he said. "I never said I wanted to be a rancher. Damn, I wish I'd brought my sheep-skin coat. I didn't figure it would get this cold in November."

"It's because we're moving so fast." My ears were getting numb, but it was a lot nicer ride out on the end than in that bouncy caboose.

"What you ought to do," he said, "is to forget all that ranch-ing. And forget about marrying, too. Then one of these days we could go up on the plains and really have us a time. When the ranch gets to be yours, you can sell it and not have it worrying you all your life."

"That's just like you," I said. "You ain't got no more respon-sibility than a monkey. That ain't no way to amount to nothing."

"Responsibility ain't no valuable thing to have, necessarily," he said. "Listen at you. It depends on what you want to amount to. I want to amount to a good cowboy."

"Talking about marrying," I said, "that reminds me of some-thing I've been meaning to talk to you about. Something pretty serious. I guess I got to admit you got first claims on Molly, but what I want to know is, do you really intend to marry her or not? One of us has got to, that's for sure, and if you ain't going to, I am."

He looked at me like I was crazy. Finally he laughed, but he was kind of uncertain about it.

"You needn't snicker," I said. "I found out all about it. I know you laid up with her. I done it too, of course, but you was the first, so she's really your responsibility. Now one of us has got to do something."

"I believe you're serious," he said. "And I know you're crazy. What in the world are you talking about?"

"It's simple as mud," I said. "You sweet-talked Molly into let-ting you spend the night with her. Okay. Hell, I don't blame you,

I done it too. Anybody would want to. Only the first one has the most responsibility. It ain't no way to do a good-hearted girl like Molly, and you know it. Now is it?"

"Why, you beat all I ever seen," he said. "After being in that whorehouse and all that mess we went through in Kansas getting you cured, and you still sit there and talk like a damn preacher."

"Now you better watch it, or you'll get a real fight, Johnny," I said. "I ain't talking like no preacher. I'm just talking about doing what's right about Molly."

"I wasn't meaning her," he said. "I was talking about you. She's as nice as they come, I wasn't calling her no whore. But you ain't no more of a lily-white boy than I am."

"I know it," I said. "I just want to get this settled. It's been bothering me for two weeks."

"What I'm trying to get you to understand, there ain't nothing to settle. Molly ain't done nothing to be ashamed of. We've always treated her nice and she likes both of us. You're just ashamed of something that ain't shameful."

"Maybe so," I said, "but I'm pretty crazy about her, and I imagine you are too. But one of us ought to take care of her, and it'll be a shame if one of us don't, that's all I meant to say. You was first, so you get the first chance."

"But that ain't even right, Gid," he said. "I wasn't first, no such thing. I always figured you was first. You was, and you know it. So why try to put the blame on me. I wouldn't do a thing like that to you."

That confused me. "The hell you wasn't first," I said. "Molly told me herself—she wasn't thinking what she was saying, I guess—that I wasn't the first one. Why are you trying to get out of it if you ain't ashamed?"

"Because I wasn't first," he said. "If you wasn't, then somebody else was. Not you nor me. Hell, I never stayed with her a time till last summer. When did you start?"

"The night of that harvest dance," I said. It flabbergasted us both. We never said a word for about fifteen miles, I guess. My ears like to froze off.

"Well, I guess we caught her," he said, finally. "I swear. I always figured it had been you. I wonder who the hell it was."

"It can't be just anybody," I said. "She's too sweet a girl. Who have we overlooked?"

"Aw hell," he said. "We ought to thought of it sooner. It must have been that damn Eddie."

"Not that worthless bastard, I can't believe that." But I remembered one time she said he was the only one silly enough for her. I guess she meant it.

"He's the very one," Johnny said. "He ought to have the shit kicked out of him. What business does he have fiddling around with Molly anyway? That hound-running sonofabitch has probably got fleas plumb up to his middle."

"Yeah, that shit-ass," I said. "Evertime I see him he's greasy to the elbows. What would she want to take up with somebody like that for?"

"Aw, Molly's crazy," he said. He didn't sound too happy, and I wasn't, either. Neither of us could stand that goddamn Eddie. "She don't think like other girls," he said. "Her trouble is, she's too nice. She's lived with that no-count bastard of a daddy so long she can't tell worthless people from them that's got something to them."

"That's about it. That old man's the cause of it all."

"I guess she figures she don't have no chance of being a nice girl anyway, growing up around him. That's probably why she took up with Eddie."

"Maybe there's somebody else," I said. "I'd rather it be nearly anybody than him."

But we couldn't think of another soul.

"Anyhow," Johnny said, "now you see that neither one of us has got to marry her. We don't need to have no guilty conscience. If he done it first, he's the one ought to marry her."

That shocked me worse than anything he'd said the whole night. "My god," I said. "You think I'd sit by and watch Molly marry a worthless sonofabitch like him. Why he ain't got nothing but a few hound dogs and a pair of roughnecking boots. He'd just drag her to one oil patch after another all her life."

"Serve her right, by god," he said. "She oughtn't to taken up with him in the first place."

"I know," I said. "But it don't make no difference. I'll just marry her anyway, even if I am third man. I ain't going to let her marry Eddie."

"Looky there," he said. "Ain't that a sight? I never knowed we was this close."

I looked, and there were the lights of Fort Worth. You never saw so many lights in your life. It was hard to imagine living in a place that big, but it sure was exciting to see all the lights at once. The train blew its whistle.

"That's cowtown," Johnny said.

"It's too early for anybody to be up," I said. "I wonder what they need with so many lights."

"I guess they just leave them lit so jackasses like us can tell when we're coming to a real town."

We stood up and looked, and pretty soon there were houses all around us and we went back in the caboose awhile, to warm up. The oil-fielder was still asleep. We decided he was drunk.

"I tell you what," Johnny said. We took off his shoes real careful and hid them over in a corner and got his shoelaces and tied his ankles together with them. We left a little play in the laces, but we tied about a dozen real hard knots and then spit on them to make them slippery.

"It'll take him a solid hour to get loose," Johnny said.

"It serves him right. It's what he gets for being an oil-fielder." We thought that was a pretty funny trick.

Pretty soon the train slowed down and stopped at the stockyards, and then the fun stopped too, for a while. We didn't know up from down about the stockyards, or what we were supposed to do or nothing, and we got out and stood around in the cold and the dark for about an hour, waiting to unload the cattle. There were a lot of stockyards fellers moving around with lanterns and punchpoles, and a lot of railroad men too, but they never said nothing to us and we didn't bother them.

"Hell, maybe we ought to ask somebody," I said finally. "What if the train goes on and takes our stock with it?"

"I don't know," Johnny said. "My damn hands are froze. I hate to bother any of these men, don't you?"

I hated to too, so we stood awhile longer. Then the train blew its whistle, and that scared us enough that we found a Mexican and asked him. But he only knew Mexican and we only knew white man, so we finally had to ask one of the stockyards men.

"Goddamn, boys, you'all look about frozen," he said. We told him our problem, and, by god, if they hadn't already unloaded our cattle and taken them to a pen way off across the yards. We had been so cold we never noticed and had got by the wrong railroad car, one full of cattle that was going on to the slaughterhouse.

"Well, I guess we can go get a hotel room, can't we?" Johnny said.

"Not till we find them cattle," I said. "What if somebody tried to mix them with another bunch? Dad would have a fit."

So we struck off across the yards looking for them, and just had an awful time. We had to crawl over about a hundred fences, and we couldn't see well enough to tell if any of the bunches of cattle were ours or not. There must have been a thousand bunches of cattle, each one in a different pen. Finally by mistake we got in a pen with a couple of damn boar hogs. We didn't even see them and thought the pen was empty till we got about halfway across it and heard one grunt as he come for us.

"Goddamn," Johnny said. "Run." We took off and hadn't taken two steps till another hog jumped up in front of us. He squealed and come at us too, but we jumped him before he got to his feet good and hit the fence and went up it.

"Shit," Johnny said, "you can look for them cattle if you want to. I'm going to the hotel. I ain't no hog fighter."

The old boars were grunting and squealing around below us like they really wanted blood. I wasn't a hog fighter either.

"Goddammit," I said. "They oughtn't to taken them cattle out of the cars without asking me. I'm the one responsible for them, ain't I? Now I guess they're lost."

"Well, if they are, we just won't go home," Johnny said. "We can work around here for a few days and then catch a train up north. If them cattle are lost, I don't never want to see Archer County agin."

We finally found our way out of the yards and went through the big Exchange building. On the other side of it was the street. We walked down it and came to a lot of honkytonks and hotels; the honkytonks were closed, and the hotels didn't look too lively, but we finally come to one called the Longhorn, and an old feller came out dripping chewing tobacco on the rug and gave us a room for fifty cents apiece. I was worried about the cattle. I figured if I had lost them, I better go farther away than the Panhandle. I better go at least to Canada.

Johnny, though, he wasn't worrying; they wasn't his cattle.

"Me for some shut-eye," he said. "I wonder if that roughneck ever woke up."

It was an awful small, bare room we got, without no bathroom and with one of the littlest beds you ever saw.

"You mean we paid fifty cents apiece just to get a little old bed like that?" I said. "Hell, I slept in a bigger bed than that when I was a baby."

Johnny could sleep anywhere; he pulled off his boots and lay down. "Which you want," he said, "top or bottom? There ain't room enough for sideways."

But I thought I'd look at the street a minute, and when I let the windowshade up I seen it was daylight.

"Why, it's morning," I said. "Get up and let's go look for those cattle."

But he was done asleep and I went on without him. I figured I could do as well by myself anyway.

When I got back to the yards things looked a lot more cheerful; the sun was up and the cattle were bawling and people were charging around everywhere. They had big wide planks nailed on top of the fences, so you could just walk around above the pens and see the cattle without having to get down in the cowshit. I found my cattle in about ten minutes, and was I relieved. There was even a feller with them filling up the hayrack with hay. Them yards was really run right. The hay feller turned out to be a sourpuss.

"Howdy," I said. "I sure am glad to see those cattle."

"You're the Fry boy, ain't you?" he said.

"Gideon Fry. I'm glad to meet you."

"Why'd the hell you sleep so late?" he said. "You done missed two good chances to sell these cattle already. Your dad, now, he was always out at the yards by daybreak."

I never cared much to take a chewing out from an old fat hay hauler in a corduroy cap, so I asked him which way the buyers went. He got up on the fence and pointed one out to me, way across the yards. He bought for Swift & Armour, it turned out. I went over and introduced myself, and I'll be damned if he didn't buy the cattle right there, for a dime a pound. He took me right on in the Exchange building after the cattle were weighed and gave me a check. So that was that. I was so surprised I felt lightheaded; I had expected a hell of a day's work selling them cattle. It was just an hour after sunup and they were already sold.

There was a little lunch counter over in one corner of the big rotunda of the Exchange building, and I went over and bought myself a cup of coffee and set down with it. I just set there, feeling good, drinking the hot coffee; I felt like I could handle anything.

By then it was seven o'clock on a Monday morning, and the floor of the Exchange building was swirling with people. There was a big blackboard over on one wall and two men were at it all the time with chalk and erasers, marking up reports of prices and the number of cattle and whatnot at all the other big markets, Chicago and Kansas City and Omaha and I don't remember where else. The big cattlemen were stomping around the lobby, making deals and ordering people around. You could tell them right off from the just plain cowboys, even if they dressed alike. The cattlemen were the ones giving orders and acting like Dad acts, and the cowboys were taking orders and going off every which way to carry them out. I heard one feller, he was standing about ten feet from me, make a deal for over a hundred thousand dollars' worth of cattle, and he was just standing there drinking coffee, like me. Watching them big operators made an impression on me. They acted like what they were doing was important, and they did things like they meant them. Nobody was ordering them around, like Dad done me and Johnny. They was their own bosses—they weren't nasty about it, you could just tell. I guess it was independence. Anyhow, I went and got another cup of good strong hot coffee and set down to think about it. Dad had probably been right about me. Johnny, he could go off and cowboy if he wanted to; I might enjoy going along for a while, but it just wouldn't suit me for long. I wanted to amount to what all them big boys amounted to.

In a little while I went down the street a few doors and had breakfast at a little café. I started to go get Johnny, but I decided I might as well let him sleep. I felt like I'd wasted too much time in my life, and that cattle money was burning my pocket. There was all them cattle out in the yards, just waiting for somebody to buy them and make money on them. I intended to go make a little.

So I went back and spent the day on the yards. I kept expecting Johnny, but he never come, and I didn't have time to go get him. I had over eight thousand dollars of Dad's money when I started buying and trading and fooling around. Right off I bought a little bunch of steers and sold them not an hour later for a dollar a hundred profit. Boy, I felt like I was on the way. Only then a damn scoundrel from South Texas sold me another bunch too high. I guess I was tired or something and didn't look at them good. It was the ruination of me. I had made six hundred dollars on my first little deal and I figured I'd make that much more on the steers. Then I could buy some real good steers to take home to Dad, and I would still have made money. But, by god, if the last bunch wasn't the worst bunch of cattle I ever bought in my life. When I finally took time to really look them over, I seen how sorry they was, full of pinkeyes and foul foots and crips of one kind and another; looking at them from up above had fooled me. I spent all afternoon trying to sell them: I didn't dare go home with them. Finally I sold them back to the bastard I bought them from, at a four dollar a hundred loss. I lost twelve hundred dollars right there. During the afternoon I did buy some good steers and arranged to ship them to Henrietta, but that didn't make up for the twelve hundred dollars. It was just gone. I seen right then I was going to have to pay better attention if I was ever going to make a cattleman. Only I just gave up for that day. Losing that money kinda made me sick. I wanted to whip that South Texas bastard, but I didn't have a legitimate reason to. He had skinned me fair and square. It just left a bad taste in my mouth.

About an hour before dark I went through the Exchange building and walked on back to the Longhorn Hotel. It was getting cold agin, and I felt sleepy and lonesome and plumb depressed with the world. Who I really wanted to see right then was Molly, in the worst way. Fort Worth didn't look like a very cheerful place any more. In fact, when I looked at it close, it looked like the dustiest, ugliest place I'd ever seen, except that town in Kansas where the hospital was. I would have given another twelve hundred dollars to have been back home, eating supper with Molly and listening to her talk.

But I wasn't there, and I had lost the money, and that was all there was to it. I sure did feel blue. I went up the stairs to our room, intending to get Johnny up so I could lay down and sleep, but when I opened the door I seen he wasn't there. And it was such a cold lonesome ugly little old bare room that I didn't feel like going to sleep in it, even if I was about to drop. The bed never had nothing on it but a little thin green counterpane anyway, and that wouldn't have kept a midget warm.

So I went back down stairs and out on the street. The street lights were done on, and they made the town look yellow and full of shadows. I figured Johnny was at the nearest honkytonk, but he wasn't; I had to go in eight or ten before I found him. Finally I seen him, way back in a bar, sitting at a table with some old feller I didn't know. They couldn't hardly see one another for the beer bottles stacked in front of them. Then I recognized the feller he was with: I had heard Dad tell about him. His name was Sam, and he was kind of a stockyards beggar, I guess; he had one real leg and one pegleg, and he wore a boot on the peg just like he did on the real foot. In his younger days he had been a cowboy on some big ranch and had got his leg pinched off between two boxcars, loading cattle one day. Johnny looked in high spirits.

"Hello, partner," he said. "Where you been all day? I had me a good nap."

"I stayed out on the yards and traded a little," I said. "Wish I hadn't. A sonofabitch got the best of me and I lost a lot of Dad's money. I don't know what I'm going to do now."

"Drink a beer and don't brood," he said. "Hell, don't never brood. Sam can show us where and we'll go lose our virginity; then we can go home plumb busted."

"I can show you, sonny," Sam said. "Call that waitress over here. I'm strangling of thirst."

The waitress was a big fat woman in a red skirt; she was too ugly to look at if you could help it. I drank a couple of bottles right quick, but they didn't improve my spirits none.

"I wished you'd have come out there," I said to Johnny. "I needed you. What kind of a hand are you, anyway?"

"One with sense," he said. "And I ain't drunk, either, so quit frowning at me. I wouldn't get drunk before you did; it wouldn't be polite. Hell, if I had come out the way I was feeling today, we might have lost everything and really been up shit creek."

"I lost enough for both of us," I said. "Goddamn the luck."

"That's what I say, sonny," Sam said. "Goddamn the luck. I been saying that for years. Call that waitress over here, I could stand a little more beer, couldn't you'all?"

We stood a hell of a lot more of it. I don't guess we left the place till ten or eleven o'clock, and by that time the table top was full of beer bottles and we had set so many on the floor we were practically surrounded. We left a little alley for the waitress to come through, between me and where Sam was laying. He had slid off on the floor and went to sleep earlier in the evening and was stretched out nice and comfortable with his pegleg boot propped up on one rung of the chair. They had tried to drag him out, but me and Johnny made them let him alone. He had so much of our beer in him, me and Johnny felt like we ought to protect him. We would have fought like hell if anybody had grabbed him.

About that time, it was funny as hell: we both drank so much beer we got so we couldn't taste it. I don't know whether it was being tired or what, but it got so it didn't taste like beer, it tasted like real good water. And we were both awful thirsty, so we just kept pouring it down and ever now and then peeing some of it out.

"This is the best damn beerwater I ever drank," Johnny said. "How's yours taste?"

"Fine," I said. "Just fine. It goes down like twelve hundred dollars."

"Quit that damn brooding," he said, standing up all of a sudden. "Let's go to the whorehouse so you won't brood. Let old Sam sleep, we can find it. He don't need no pussy anyhow."

"Let him sleep," I said. "He don't need none."

I got up too, but then I fell down. I guess I stepped on a damn beer bottle; anyway, down I went. I fell right in about a hundred bottles, and Johnny he reached down meaning to help me and he fell too and there we were, rolling around in the bottles. At first I wanted to cuss, but then we both got tickled; it was kind of fun to lay there knocking empty bottles over, and we just sort of rolled and laughed and knocked the bottles every which way till I happened to notice we wasn't inside no more. It was colder and there wasn't any bottles and we were laying behind somebody's damn automobile.

"Hell, they threw us out," I said. "Did they throw you out too?"

He was up on his hands and knees laughing like mad. "Hell yes, can't you see me? They threw us both out."

"Want to go attack them?" I said. "Get back in the bottles?"

"Naw. Let's find the whorehouse."

I had forgot about that. Then the next thing this fat streetcar man was shaking me. "You boys need to sleep, go to a damn hotel," he said. "I've carried you far enough."

We were standing on a brick street, not very far from the courthouse, and the norther was blowing right down the street at us. Brother, it was cold.

"There's the courthouse," Johnny said. "Want to go there?"

"No," I said. "There ain't no whores in the courthouse, you damn fool."

"Might be some in jail," he said.

"I guess so," I said.

Then we ran into a damn drunk and he took us right to the whorehouse. He was so drunk he couldn't walk straight; he walked all over the street.

In the house there was a nice-looking redhead and I was going to be friendliest with her, only when we come in she said, "Here come two cowshits," and that made us so mad we didn't go near her. The carpet was so deep it confused me; my boots didn't make no noise; I thought I was barefoot.

Johnny just about fell over the banister going up stairs.

The girl in my room was blond-headed, and I seen her turning back the counterpane on a big white bed. I watched her do that awhile and then I noticed we were laying on the bed and I didn't have my pants with me, just my socks and shirt. But she didn't have nothing on at all and she was getting out of the bed instead of in it; I seen her big floppy fanny going across the room and then she hiked up one leg and washed herself at a little dishpan of a thing.

"That was real nice, sweetheart," she said. "Now be a darling and help me make up this bed."

"We ain't through already, are we?" I said.

"Why sure, sugar," she said. "Can't you tell by your equipment?"

I wished then I hadn't drunk all that beer. Johnny was done downstairs when I got there and we went out.

"How do you feel?" I said.

"Horny," he said.

"Let's catch that streetcar, I'm about to freeze."

Of course we missed the train we was supposed to catch, so the new cattle got to Henrietta about twelve hours earlier than we did. That shrunk them a little. It was dark when we got there; we spent all night and till nine-thirty the next morning driving them home. We kept getting in thickets all night and like to froze to death, too; both of us looked like Ned when we finally got the cattle home and penned. Dad was in the barn loft when we penned them, and he come down and looked them over.

"Well, they ain't the worst cattle I ever seen," he said. "How'd the other cattle sell?"

"Good," I said. "Only I never got home with all the money. I got to cattle-trading and made a little money and let a damn feller skin me and lost all that and twelve hundred dollars besides. Maybe I can work it out in a few years."

I expected him to blow up, but he just kept walking around, inspecting the cattle.

"Got you in a little trading practice, did you?" he said. "Good. You may learn yet."

And he put us right to work, branding the new stock. I was so surprised at Dad that I never even minded the work. Dad was one man I never learned to predict.

eight

It took us till past the middle of November to recuperate from the trip to Fort Worth. Johnny, he swore off beer drinking forever, but his forevers usually just lasted about a week, and this one wasn't no exception. I couldn't enjoy myself much for worrying about when Dad was going to come down on me about the twelve hundred dollars. He just seemed to forget it, and Dad wasn't the kind to forget that much money.

One pretty warm fall day we worked like hell dipping cattle and hadn't much more than got to bed when somebody come riding up to the back gate just a-screaming. I jumped up and grabbed my pants and run out; Dad was done there. It was one of Mabel Peters' little brothers.

"Daddy says come tell you our house is on fire," he said. "Grandma burned it up."

We took his word for it. Dad yanked the kid off the horse and told me to take it and get on over there, he would follow and bring the kid in the wagon. So I grabbed a Levi jacket off the back porch and went.

When I got there it was just a nice campfire left; an old chickenhouse don't take long to burn. The Peterses were all out in the yard, squatting around patting the dogs and crying: it was the only time in my life I ever saw that family all in one place, and I was surprised at how many of them there was. Six kids younger than Mabel, her momma and dad, and her grandma.

"Well, she's gone, Momma," the old man said. "Now we'll just have to trust in the Lord."

The grandma was taking on the worst; she had started the fire. She was about ninety-five. One of the boys said she had sloshed some kerosene out of a lamp onto the tablecloth. Mabel's mother was hysterical because she missed the boy they had sent to our place and thought he was burned up in the fire. There wasn't any fire fighting to do at all, and it was pretty miserable standing there watching the Peterses try to figure out what they had to go on living with. The old man had run out on the back porch and took out the milk strainer; it probably wouldn't have burned anyway. One of the boys had grabbed a Montgomery Ward catalogue and let the Bible burn, and Mabel had brought out a dish of pecans that was sitting on the new chair. The chair was the only new thing in the house, but nobody ever thought of grabbing it, and the two littlest boys had already eaten about half the pecans.

"Well, son," the old man said, coming over to me, "we're burned out."

"Dad's coming," I said. Then I went over and got Mabel and made her squat down close enough to the fire that she could at least keep warm. She was barefoot and never had on very warm clothes.

Pretty soon people that had seen the fire began to come. Dad was the last one there, but he had filled the wagon up with quilts, coffeepots and stuff to eat, so he done the most good once he come. We raked off a little of the fire and made some coffee, and gave each of the Peterses a quilt.

"Ain't it a mess, Gid?" Mabel said. Her teeth were chattering. "Now's when I wish I was married," she said, looking at me; the fire lit up her thin little face. She was pretty as could be in the face.

"If I was married," she said, "it wouldn't be so bad. We could all go over to my husband's house and live."

That about made my teeth chatter. I felt sorry for the Peterses, but nobody would have wanted all them kids and old folks swarming into their house.

"I wisht I'd got the chair," she said, starting to cry agin. "Why didn't I get the chair? Instead of the pecans."

Dad told Mr. Peters that if his family would all get in the wagon and wrap up real good in the quilts, I would drive them to Thalia. Mrs. Peters had a sister there, and they could stay with her a day or two, whether they liked it or not.

Everybody went home and Dad caught one of the Peterses' mules and went home himself, and I started down the road to Thalia with the biggest wagonload of sad people you ever saw. A norther had come up; I didn't have on a shirt under my jacket, and like to froze. All the Peterses went to sleep, but about halfway into town Mabel woke up and came up on the seat by me. She let me have a little of her quilt.

"We're much obliged to you, Gid," she said. "You're the nicest one that came tonight.

"Some of these days I'll marry you and make it all up to you," she said. "You see if I don't."

I started to tell her that I didn't want her to get her hopes up, but she squirmed over and kissed me and was like that all the rest of the way to Thalia. I could barely drive. It livened up the ride a whole lot.

"You remember what I said," she said, when we were coming into town. Her face was all white and excited, and neither one of us was particularly cold any more.

I got the job of going in and waking up Mrs. Peters' sister. Everybody else was afraid of the dog, but I beat him off with the wagon whip. When the lights came on all the Peterses climbed out and clobbered into the living room, looking like some Indian nation in all their quilts. The lady took them in, and I got ahold of two quilts and started back. Before I could get off, Mabel ran out and wrapped around me for about ten minutes. "Come and see me," she said. "I'll get awful lonesome in here."

After that, the Peterses had a real hard time of it. The sister kept them a week, and then they moved into the firehouse, and finally ended up back at the place living in their barn. People scraped up for them and gave them preserves and bacon and old clothes and a little money to get started on. But the old man never had the energy to start, and the boy had the energy but not enough sense. They were the poorest folks in the country, and Mabel felt disgraced. Finally they all left but her and went to some little town in Arkansas, where they had kinfolks. Mabel got a job in a grocery store and a room in a widow's house and stayed and tried to make herself well thought of. But she was still the poorest of the poor, and it was a long time before she got over it enough to have any prosperous boy friends.

nine

As much as I worked around Dad, it looked like I would have been able to figure him out. A man as set in his ways as he was ought to have been more predictable. But he could always keep about a jump ahead of me.

We had three fair rains in October and a damn good slow three-inch rain the second week in November, and all our country looked good. We had more grass than we had cattle for, and it didn't look like it would be too hard a winter. I figured Dad would stock some more calves; that would have been the logical thing for a cattleman to do. One morning he sent Johnny off to check the water gaps, and told me to hitch up the wagon, we were going to Thalia. That was okay with me.

"Well," he said, once we were started, "I think I'll let you plant a little wheat this year. See what kind of a wheat farmer you are. Thought we'd buy some seed today.

"And don't go getting red in the face," he said. I was. "You ain't got no say-so about it, so just keep your mouth shut. I got the damn toothache this morning anyway."

"A toothache ain't got a damn thing to do with it," I said. "If you ask me."

"I never asked you. What I mean is, I can't stand no long conversation with my tooth hurting this way."

I got all nervous. It's terrible to be in a wagon when you get mad; you can't make it go no faster or anything. You just have to poke along when you feel like whipping and spurring.

"Well, I don't intend to do no farming," I said. "Your tooth can stand that much. You're crazy anyway. We ought to be buying cattle."

"Knock hell out of that mule," he said. "Keep him out of the ditch. He don't need to graze all the time.

"I figure it's gonna get dry," he said. "We've got some dry years coming. We might need this grass next summer more than we need it now, so I ain't gonna stock very heavy. It won't hurt you to try a little farming."

I began to get the Panhandle on my mind when he said that. It would take something drastic to bring Dad to his senses about me. Maybe if I run off for a little while it would do it.

We got to Thalia and got the wheat seed, and while I was loading it and fooling around the feed store trying to bargain with the feller for half a load of cottonseed hulls, Dad went up and got the doctor to pull his tooth for him. It must have had roots plumb down to the collarbone, because Dad spit blood all the way home.

"That was three dollars throwed away," he said. "Next time one wears out you can pull it."

"Okay," I said. "I'll do it for two and a half and save you the trip besides."

"I wish it would quit coming these damn cold northers," he said. "My blood's getting thin."

We didn't say much going home till we got to the place where the road went over Idiot Ridge. When we got there we could see the Taylor place across the long flat on the other hill, and off to the west of us we could see the Peterses' barn.

"Which one of them damn girls do you reckon you'll marry?" Dad said. "We may as well thrash that out while we're thrashing."

He beat all. "Why, I may not marry at all," I said. "I can't see that it's too much of your business, anyway."

"Oh, I guess it is. I was just curious as to which kind of trouble you mean to get yourself into."

"Well, if I marry either one it will damn sure be Molly," I said. "You couldn't get me to marry Mabel with a thirty-thirty."

"That so," he said, spitting. "He said not to, but I think I'll chew a little tobacco. I'm bleeding to death through the head."

So the rest of the way he split blood and tobacco juice, instead of just blood.

"Okay," he said. "Mabel ain't the kind of girl you want; she's just the kind of girl that wants you. Molly, she don't want you."

"She damn sure does," I said. It made me mad. "What makes you think you know so much about her? Me and her get along real well."

"Oh, of course," he said. "I never meant to say you didn't. But you ain't gonna catch her, and your buddy Johnny ain't either, that's plain as day. And it's a damn good thing. She'd run you ragged if you did."

"How'd we get to talking about this, anyway?" I said. "I may not even marry. But if I do, it'll be Molly."

"Don't make no bets," he said. "And don't be sorry if you don't. If you stay loose from her, she'll make you the best kind of friend you can have. If you do marry her, you'll have ninety-nine kinds of misery. And you remember I told you that. A woman is a wonderful thing, goddamn them, but a man oughtn't to marry one unless he just absolutely has to have some kids. There's no other excuse."

"Well, you married, didn't you? You survived it, didn't you?"

"Yes," he said, "but your mother didn't. And I'm surprised I did. It like to done for us both."

"Anyhow, you're wrong about Molly," I said. "I can tell you that."

He kinda grinned at me. "You might tell me the time of day," he said, "if you had a better watch than mine. That's about all you can tell me. Of course if you marry the Peters girl, that'll be hell too, but at least you won't lose no friend."

"I swear I can't talk to you," I said. "You don't no more know me than the man in the moon. You think you know everything about me and you don't really know a damn thing."

"You're probably right," he said. "Maybe I'll improve." He got tickled at something and set there popping the reins on the mules and laughing to himself for the next mile or two.

"Did you mean you think I ought to marry Mabel instead of Molly?" I said. "I'm just curious."

"Oh no," he said. "I told you already I didn't want you to marry till you were forty or fifty years old. By then you might have enough judgment to marry right. Only I can see already you ain't gonna have enough judgment to last that long. I just mentioned it to see how much you knew about yourself."

"I'm sure you know more about me than I do," I said.

Dad sighed. "People are the hardest animals in the world to raise," he said. "And it's because nobody ever got them to breeding right in the first place."

"You don't breed people," I said.

"No, and it's a damn pity," he said. "I can take me a bull and get him with just the right cows at just the right time, and I won't have to worry much about the calf crop. But the chances of anybody getting the right man anywhere near the right woman are as slim as chances get. That's why I don't mind so bad being old. If I was young agin, I'd probably mess up even worse than I did."

Dad said that in a pretty sad way. It bothered me to hear him.

"That's a pessimistic damn thing to say," I said. "Why, I think life's a damn sight more fun than that."

"You ain't lived one," he said. Then he told me how much work we were going to get done that winter.

ten

Dad kept me so busy with one thing and another that it was after the first of December before I got over to Molly's to ask her to go to the Christmas dance with me. One afternoon I got off early, though. Dad decided it was going to come a storm, and he wanted to leave the cattle alone till it was over. Johnny never come to work that day anyway; his old man had kept him home to help him kill their hogs. Dad said he didn't need me, so I saddled up and got my sheepskin coat and rode over to the Taylors'. It was cloudy and cold and looked sleety back in the northwest. I seen a big flock of geese going over. I hated the wintertime; it sure made the cow-work mean.

Molly was hanging out clothes when I rode up. She had on an old red flannel shirt and a pair of overalls and was actually barefooted out in that cold. I guess it was a habit. The Taylor kids hardly ever put on shoes before Christmas, and they had them off agin by Washington's birthday. She looked as pretty as ever. When I walked up she put her hand on the back of my neck, and it was cold from the wet clothes.

"Don't you hope it snows?" she said.

I kissed her right quick and made her let me help her hang up clothes. It was so cold they practically froze while we were getting them over the clothesline. There were scraps of burned tow sack floating around the yard, so I figured the old man had let the windmill freeze and Molly had had to thaw out the pipes.

Molly's cheeks were red and her hair all blowy, but she didn't seem to mind the weather. "Dad said he might kill a goose," she said. "If he does, maybe you can come over and eat some of it."

"Maybe I'll kill one myself," I said. "Let's go inside for a while."

I got the bushel basket the clothes had been in, and she caught me by the hand and led me in the house. The kitchen was nice. It was so warm the windows were fogged over. Molly had made some cookies that morning, and we sat down at the kitchen table and ate them.

"It's about time you came," she said. "I been missing you so much." She reached her foot under the table and kicked me with her toes.

"Dad's been working the daylights out of me. By the time I get loose from him I ain't fit company for a pretty young lady."

"I guess I could stand you," she said. "Ain't these good

cookies? I feel so good today now that you showed up."

I pulled my chair around by hers, so we could sit close together. I decided I would start taking more afternoons off.

"Johnny comes by a lot," she said. "He said you'all had a pretty big time in Fort Worth. I wouldn't mind seeing Fort Worth sometimes."

"Maybe we'll go there on our honeymoon," I said.

She looked at me, half-grinning and half-serious; part of what was in her eyes was mischief and part of it wasn't. She had my hand in both of hers.

"I told you about that once," she said. "I don't intend to get married till I'm going to have a baby."

"Oh, now hush," I said. "That's silly. We'll get married by next summer, I don't care what you say."

She shook her head and thought about it to herself for a while, and wouldn't look at me.

"Anyway, don't go getting no black eyes week after next," I said. "We don't want to miss another big dance."

"I'm sorry about that, Gid," she said. "I knew that was why you come over. I already told somebody else I'd go with him."

That knocked a hole in my spirits. But when I thought about it a minute, it didn't surprise me. Johnny rode within two miles of her place every day; it was no wonder he'd asked her.

"Well, I guess he deserves to take you to one dance," I said. "Anyway I'll get to dance with you a lot. Johnny won't care about that."

"Oh, it wasn't Johnny," she said. "He asked me a long time ago. I promised Eddie I wouldn't go to dances with anybody but him any more."

I didn't have no idea what to say to that. I couldn't believe it.

"Are you plumb crazy?" I said. I started to bawl her out, but I seen she was sitting there about ready to cry. I held up.

"Well, has he asked you to this dance?" I said. "I haven't seen him lately. He may not be in this part of the country."

"No." She didn't let herself cry, but her eyes spilled over once. "I guess he's in Oklahoma," she said. "He ain't been here in a month. But I promised him anyway."

"But, sweetheart," I said. "He may not even be back in time for the dance. You don't want to miss it, do you?"

"No," she said. "You know I don't. But he told me not to go unless he was here to take me. So I better not."

"That beats anything in the damn world," I said. "I ought to spank you right here. What kind of a feller is he? That ain't no way to treat a girl." But I hugged her anyway, and her face was all wet against my neck.

"He's not any count," I said. "You know that, Molly."

"Sometimes I wish I hadn't promised him," she said. "But I did. You're my favorite."

We set in the kitchen for a long time, kissing and not talking much. She wouldn't say another word about Eddie or the dance. I didn't care. It was a comfortable time, and I didn't think much about the dance.

"Stay for supper with me," she said. "We butchered the milk-pen calf, so we can have beef. Dad may not be coming home to-day, I don't know."

So I decided to stay, and I meant to make it all night if she'd let me. I milked and done her chores for her and chopped enough wood to last her through the cold spell. I even put my horse in the barn. Then we ate and got real cheerful. We found some pop-corn and went in the living room to pop it in the fireplace. The living room was neat, so I knew the old man hadn't been there for a while. When he was around it was always full of junk and whiskey jugs.

"Wouldn't you like to get away from here?" I said. We were

sitting on the floor close to the fire. Molly had unbuttoned her shirt a little and I was watching the firelight on her throat and chest.

"Why no," she said. "I couldn't leave here. This is where I intend to live. Anyhow, who'd look after Dad?"

We salted the popcorn and buttered it and ate it, and when Molly kissed me after that she tasted like warm butter and salt; I'll always remember that.

"I sure do like you," she said. "You can come stay with me anytime you want to, you know that, don't you? It doesn't make any difference about the dances."

She lay down with her head in my lap, and I looked down at her.

"I sure do like you too. But it makes a difference to me. You're the one I want and I don't want no other fellers around you."

She grinned and sat up and gave me one of those butter-and-salt kisses. The firelight lit up our faces. And just that minute we heard the back door kick in and the old man stomped into the kitchen. We heard him stamping around trying to get his over-shoes off.

It made us both so sad at first we didn't even move. Then we sat up, and by the time he came into the room we were eating popcorn, just as innocent as you please.

"We're in here," she said. "It's Gid and me."

"Oh it is is it?" he said. He turned and went back to the kitchen and we heard him getting a glass out of the cabinet. When he came back he had a glass of whiskey in one hand and his bottle in the other. It was the first time I ever saw him drink out of a glass. He still had on his big sheepskin coat and his old dirty plaid cap, with the earflaps still pulled down over his ears and tied under his chin. He didn't look in too good a mood; it kinda scared me, actually. I kept on eating popcorn.

"Go get some firewood," he said. "It's a goddamn cold night."

I didn't know whether he was talking to me or Molly, but I got up and went to the woodpile and got an armful of wood.

"Put it over here," he said. So I dumped it right by his chair and he took his gloves off and picked out a chunk and leaned over and pitched it in the fire. Sparks and ashes flew everywhere, and Molly had to jump to keep them from getting on her. It made me mad.

"Good way to catch the house on fire," I said. "Let me do it for you, Mr. Taylor."

"Hell no," he said. He sat the glass down on one side of the chair and drank out of the bottle. I never did see him drink out of the glass agin.

"All right," I said. I didn't want no argument with him. "It's dangerous though."

"Danger-rus, my ass," he said, grinning at Molly like he was fixing to tell her some big joke. "This here's my house anyway, if I want to burn it down then by god I'll burn it down. Never asked you nohow. Get on out of here and go home. Who asked you over here in the first place?"

"He's just visiting a little," Molly said. "He ain't doing any harm, Daddy." She said it kinda timidly.

He gave her a hard look. "I never asked you to take up for him," he said. "A little licking wouldn't hurt you, sister. You ain't fixed my supper, so what are you sitting here for?"

She looked hurt and sad: I think she was really scared to death of him and didn't know it herself. She picked up the popcorn bowl and went to the kitchen without saying another thing.

I stood up and put on my coat and went over to the fire to warm my hands a minute.

"Get away from there," he said. "Don't stand between me and the fire, don't you know better than that? A little licking wouldn't hurt you none either, you damn coyote roper."

I didn't see why I needed to take any more off an old surly bastard like him.

"You ain't gonna lick me," I said. "You're too drunk."

He grinned, but it was a pretty mean grin.

"And quit trying to court my girl," he said. "I'd chop her in two with an ax before I'd let a feller like you have her."

"You're so damn tough my teeth chatter," I said. "I'm a good notion to stuff you up this fireplace right now."

That was the first time in my life I ever said anything bad to a person older than I was. It scared me a little, but the old man just took another drink.

"You're a little piss-ant," he said. After that he just stared at the fire, and I left him to his bottle.

Molly was in the kitchen crying and stirring stuff on the stove.

"Don't argue with Daddy agin," she said. "Please don't, Gid. I won't like you any more if you do."

I went up behind her and hugged her. "Yes you will," I said. "I sure hate to go off and leave you tonight, you know that, don't you?"

She turned loose of the frying pan a minute and turned around and kissed me, but we were both uneasy because the old man was so close by.

"You're my girl," I said. "You're the only one I'm ever going to have." I let her go then and started to leave, but she shoved the frying pan off the fire right quick and went out the back door with me, into the cold. And she still didn't have no more clothes on than she had that morning.

"I'll go help you get your horse," she said. "Dad's done forgot about supper, and he won't think of it till I remind him."

I hugged her up against me as close as I could. "What made him so mad?" I said. "I wasn't doing anything wrong."

"Hush," she said. "Don't talk about Dad. I don't want you putting the blame on him."

I shut up, but it still seemed an awful way for a girl's daddy to act.

"I don't think he'll lick me tonight," she said. "He was just talking." Molly was funny. She didn't seem to realize there was much wrong with him licking her.

The wind was singing down off the plains cold as ice, and by the time we got to the barn, Molly was about froze. I made her take my sheepskin while I caught the horse and saddled him. We lit the barn lantern and she held it so I could see what I was doing; even so the barn was mostly shadows and the horse didn't like it. When I got through I set the lantern down and rubbed her hands to get them warm.

"You'll probably take pneumonia," I said. "You ain't got many brains to be so sweet."

She put her cold hands on my neck. "I just came out so you could kiss me goodnight," she said. "It ain't much fun in the kitchen when somebody else is around."

I did, and it was funny: she was so cold on the outside and so warm underneath it all. Molly was always the warmest girl I knew. I blew out the lantern and led her and the horse out into the cold. I put her in the saddle in front of me, where I could hold her. The moon was up, and the little thin cold clouds were whipping across it, going south.

"I'd hate to be the moon," she said.

At the yard gate I got down and helped her off. But I held her up against the horse for a minute, so he could warm her on one side and me on the other.

"Come on to the dance with me," I said. "If Eddie bothers you about it, I'll stop him."

She kissed me for a long time then, and kept changing from one foot to the other. I guess they were about to freeze. Then she pulled back and looked at me.

"You ain't the only kind of good person," she said. "How do you know you're any better than him?"

"The same way you know it," I said. "Only you won't admit it. Come on and go with me."

"I can't, honey," she said. "I done promised. But I'm so glad you come over. Come back and see me a lot, Gid."

"You'll see a world of me before it's over," I said. "That's a promise I can make."

She held my hand even after I was on the horse; then we remembered she had on my jacket and she took it off and gave it to me.

"Now get on in before you freeze," I said. "I'll see you pretty soon."

"I wish you could stay," she said. "I hate to see you go off. You're liable to freeze."

But she's the one who would have frozen, if I hadn't turned and ridden off. I don't think she wanted to go back in very bad. I know I sure did hate to leave. I rode off about twenty steps and stopped to button my coat. "Don't get lost," Molly said.

"Go in, honey," I said. "It's awful cold." I guess she just grinned, I don't know. The last time I looked she was still standing there by the fence, with the wind blowing around her.

eleven

Johnny and me talked it over and decided we would go to the dance anyway, and not take no girls. Neither one of us wanted to take anybody but Molly.

"Course I might take Mabel home," Johnny said. "If she comes. But I ain't going to take her both ways."

"She won't go home with you," I said. "Mabel's got more pride than that."

Neither of us could understand why Molly would make a promise like that to a no-count like Eddie. But we knew it had to be stopped.

"I think we better whip him," Johnny said. "You and me can fight over her in our own good time."

"Naw, we better not fight him," I said. "That would just make her feel sorry for him. I guess that's why she goes with him anyway. I'll just tell him to stay away from her."

"He won't pay a damn bit of attention to you," he said. "Hell, I don't pay much attention to you myself."

At least it was a pretty night for a Christmas dance, and not too cold. When we crossed Onion Creek we both got the real dancing spirit, and we loped the rest of the way into town. But we sure weren't the first ones there. Half the horses and buggies in the country were hitched outside the dancehall, and there were even quite a few automobiles.

I wanted an automobile myself, but Dad was too tight to buy one. Johnny said he wouldn't have one of the things.

We came in right in the middle of a square dance and didn't

have any way to get in on it, so we stood around patting our feet. The hall was nearly full, and the people were stomping and drinking a lot of eggnog and having a real good time.

"There they are," I said.

Molly was dancing in a set just across the floor from us. Her black hair was flying around her shoulders, and she looked her rosiest. Eddie had on his roughnecking boots, so you could hear him all over the hall when his feet hit the floor. He wasn't dressed up or nothing, and he looked like he was already drunk. It made me so damn jealous I could hardly stand still. Once when him and Molly met to do-ce-do he swung down and kissed her big before he went to the next girl; she never seemed to mind. I guess she was having such a big time being away from home that she forgot herself.

"Why do you reckon all these old folks want to get out there and dance?" Johnny said. "It's just making a spectacle of themselves, if you ask me."

I thought so too. The whole town was there. All the little kids were running around screaming and chasing one another and talking about what they were going to get for Christmas; their mommas and poppas weren't paying any attention to them at all. Everybody that could move danced. Fat ones and skinny ones and ugly ones and pretty ones. Of course there were a few bachelors off in the refreshment room, emptying the eggnog bowl and talking about the war, but there wasn't over a dozen of them. I even seen a preacher dance one set, and that was a pretty rare sight.

"I think I'll partake of a little eggnog," Johnny said. "Then we'll see what we can do about Molly."

I let him go. I didn't intend to drink much myself till after the dancing was over. I had a hard enough time dancing as it was.

When the set was over I started across to Molly, but it was

crowded on the floor, and of course about fifty people stopped me to shake hands and ask how I was and wish me Merry Christmas and ask how Dad was and how the cattle were and all that, so that they started a round dance before I could get over to her, and Eddie hugged her up and was dancing with her. It made me so mad I could have bitten myself. I didn't see how she could breathe he was holding her so tight.

I was right on the spot when that dance was over, though. Johnny was across the hall, talking to Mabel and some feller she was with. Eddie was grinning and red in the face and his cowlick was falling down in his eyes. He was in an awful good humor.

"Howdy, cowpuncher," he said, "dance with my girl awhile. I got to have me a drink. This dancehall is hot." He handed me Molly's hand and went outside; I guess he had him a bottle somewhere.

"Merry Christmas, Gid," Molly said. "I'm glad you'all finally got here. Guess what? Eddie's bought him a car."

I never asked her the story on it; it made me blue enough just to hear it. It was just the kind of thing that crazy bastard would do. He never owned a shirt in his life that didn't have fifteen patches on it, neither. We found out later he got the car secondhand for forty-five dollars. I guess he made the money roughnecking.

The next one was a round dance too, and we danced real slow. Molly had on a dark blue dress, and she had little tiny shadows under her eyes, like she hadn't been getting enough sleep. Her neck smelled like lavender. But her breath smelled a little like whiskey; I guess Eddie got her to take a drink. I wanted to say a lot of things to her, but she laid her head on my shoulder, and we didn't talk. Then I let Johnny dance one with her; I told him it was his Christmas present. I danced one with Mabel; she talked a blue streak.

After that I got to dance a good square dance with Molly, and that was fun. Eddie come in in the middle of it, but he had to sit down and wait. I figured I would give up on it for the night and get drunk myself. As I was leading Molly off the floor I told her I had her a Christmas present.

"Let me come over and get it," she said. "Dad hasn't been in too good a mood lately."

Eddie grabbed her and hugged her; he was about five degrees drunker than he had been. Johnny was getting drunk too; he spent most of his time with Mabel.

"Old Josh is going to take her home," he said. "I asked. But she said I could come by later and she'd make me some hot choclate. You know how I am about hot choclate."

I went in and took after the eggnog pretty heavy. I liked to sit and listen to fiddle music, so I sat down by the refreshment table and listened to "Sally Goodin," and "Four Little Ladies," and "The Texas Star" and all the others.

Then all of a sudden Molly run in and squatted down by me and whispered in my ear. I seen she was crying.

"Go stop them, Gid," she said. "It's such a nice dance; I don't want them to fight. Eddie gets so mean. Tell Johnny I won't never like him agin if he fights."

"What happened?" I said. "I been drinking too much. Where'd they go?"

"Outside," she said. "Go stop them, Gid."

Most of the people still seemed to be dancing and having a good time. Usually when there was a fight a lot of the men would go out and watch.

"They went off behind the cars," she said.

When I stood up I didn't feel so drunk. "I doubt if I can stop them," I said. "But I'll try."

The cold air felt real good after the dancehall, and my head felt clearer. Sure enough, they were over behind the cars. I guess they had already fought a little, because Johnny had a nosebleed. It didn't mean much; I think his nose bleeds just from excitement. Six or eight of the bachelors were standing around watching; they had turned some car lights on, so everybody could see better.

Eddie had one fist doubled up and his arm drawn back, and Johnny was just standing there watching him; he had his thumbs hooked in his pockets. Johnny was drunk as a bat; they both were.

"You're a damn oil-field hound-running coward," Johnny said. Johnny looked happy about it all; he never minded fighting. But Eddie was serious about it; he kept his fist doubled up. Eddie was a coward, that's why I wouldn't have wanted to fight him; somebody that's scared of you can really be dangerous. Johnny never noticed things like that.

I started to say something to Johnny, but decided not to. They were going to fight anyway. Eddie kept standing there, holding back his fist and sneering that mean sneer of his, and all of a sudden Johnny made a run at him and they went to the ground. Johnny was a quick bastard when he started. They went to rolling and bumping on the ground, each one trying to get a choke hold and neither one doing the other much damage.

"Hell, them boys ain't fighting," a man said. "They're just wallowing on the ground. Get up from there and fight, boys, if you're gonna fight."

They did, and that was Johnny's mistake. Eddie got him off balance and knocked him down and went to pounding on him. Then Johnny nearly got up agin and Eddie jumped on him and began to pound him against an automobile.

"Now that's fighting," the feller said.

I was getting nervous. It looked like we were going to be disgraced. Johnny couldn't get his balance, and Eddie kept pouring it on. Finally he got Johnny down agin, only he didn't go down with him. He stood back with his fist doubled up. I guess he thought he had won, because he kinda laughed.

"You goddamn cowpunchers, you can't fight," he said. "Hell, it takes a roughneck to fight."

And that was Eddie's mistake, thinking Johnny McCloud would quit fighting just because he was beat on a little. I knew damn well Johnny wasn't done with the fight because his eyes were open; Johnny never quit nothing while he still had his eyes open. I guess he was resting. Eddie sneered and Johnny come up and stayed up. Eddie tried to kick him back down, but Johnny got the leg and set Eddie down himself. And while he had his leg he managed to yank off one of the roughnecking boots and he threw it out in the darkness as far as he could throw. Then he run Eddie against an automobile. They were out of the light then; I don't know exactly what happened. Somehow Johnny got Eddie up on the hood of a car and shoved him clear off on the other side. He ran around the car right quick and we did too, but the show was over. Eddie was holding his neck and spitting and wouldn't get up or say anything; I think he had bitten his tongue when he hit. Besides the sheriff came out about that time.

"These boys ain't hurting one another, are they?" he said.

"Naw, they're just fighting, Gus," a feller said. "I guess they're about done."

Eddie stood up, but him and Johnny were both too tired to say much. I motioned at Johnny to keep quiet but he didn't see me. The sheriff didn't mind fighting, but he couldn't stand nasty talking.

"So you leave her alone," Johnny said. "You horse's butt you."

Eddie walked off to look for his shoe, and the sheriff turned around and took hold of Johnny's arm.

"I don't like that filthy language," the sheriff said. "Who started this fight anyway?"

"I did, by god," Johnny said. "And by god I finished it, too. And I'd whip you too if you didn't have that damn badge on."

That was just the kind of crazy thing Johnny would say. The sheriff started off with him. "Taking the Lord's name in vain is one thing I won't stand for," he said. "Not even at Christmastime. What if a lady had heard you say that?" And off they went.

"Don't think that Gus won't arrest them," the feller said. "He won't stand for no goddamn cussing, and I don't blame him."

"No, but you know something," another feller said, "he'll never get elected in this damn county agin. That's just how goddamn sorry people are getting."

I danced a round dance with Molly and told her it was okay.

"They wasn't neither one hurt," I said. "Eddie will be back when he finds his shoe. I guess I better take Johnny's horse up to the jail and see if I can talk the sheriff into letting him out."

Molly felt a little better when she was satisfied there was nobody killed.

"I wish I could take you home," I said. "Even if he has got an automobile."

"It makes me mad the way you talk about Eddie," she said. "Working in the oil field ain't no crime, is it?"

"No, and you're too sweet to argue with." We walked off the floor and I got my coat.

"I hope they let Johnny go," she said. "Tell him to come and see me when he can. I'm sorry he got in trouble on my account."

She wouldn't go outside with me, even for a minute—afraid she would bump into Eddie, I guess—but I made her promise to come over and help us with the hog-killing, the next week. I figured I could give her her Christmas present then. I sure did hate to leave her at the dance.

The sheriff of course wouldn't let Johnny go. I guess Johnny cussed him all the way to the jail. He was a funny sheriff. He never got mad and he never got tickled, either.

"That boy talks too nasty," he said. "I ain't gonna have that nasty talk around where there's ladies. Why, that would be a disgrace to the county."

"I know it," I said. I thought I better agree with him. "If you'll let me have him, I'll take him out of town quick, so there won't be no danger."

"No, I'll keep him tonight," he said. "Just put his horse in the barn. Be a good lesson to a boy like that. Besides, I want to give him a good talking to before I let him go, and he's done asleep."

So I went on home, eighteen miles by myself.

twelve

The Wednesday before Christmas, Dad decided it would be a good time to kill the hogs. We had four big shoats to butcher; more hog meat than me and Dad could have eaten in two years. Dad had done made arrangements to sell three of the carcasses, though; the fellers he sold them to came over to help us. Dad had gone over special and asked Molly to come cook for the crew, and Johnny was there, of course, mostly just getting in the way. When you took Johnny off of his horse he was the worst hand in the world.

Me and him did the actual killing, shooting, and sticking, while Dad and the other men built the fires and got the water ready. Dad, he wouldn't have wallowed around in the hogpen mud for half the pork in Texas. Johnny worked the gun and I worked the butcher knife, and we laid them low. Then we got our horses and drug the carcasses up to the fire one at a time.

Johnny bitched around so much while we were scraping the carcasses that Dad finally sent him off down in the River pasture to drive in a yearling he thought was getting sick. Actually Dad must have liked Johnny; he let him get away with a damn sight more than I ever got away with.

About nine-thirty Molly come riding up; she had on her red mackinaw. Just seeing her made me feel so good I could have jumped six feet. I never realized how lonesome I stayed till I got close to Molly. Not even then. When I realized it was when I had been close to her and one of us was leaving. Then for a day or two the world would look twice as bad as it really was.

I took her down to the barn and put her horse where ours wouldn't kick hell out of him. I got her back in the hallway, out of sight, and gave her a kiss.

"Silly," she said. "Who ever heard of kissing in the morning?"

She wouldn't let me hold her hand when we got outside because she was afraid everybody would tease us. She was right; they would have.

It was a good day. We got the hogs butchered without no trouble, and Molly cooked a big dinner and everybody enjoyed it and complimented her on it, and that made her feel good. Johnny even made it back in time to eat; for once he showed pretty good manners. In the afternoon we made soap and cracklins and the other fellers loaded their pork and went home. It was nearly suppertime before we got all the kettles cleaned, so Molly decided to stay and fix supper, too. Johnny went on home. Dad gave him a quarter of pork for a Christmas bonus and he told us all Merry Christmas and went off with it tied to his saddle. Watching him leave made me blue for a minute; it was strange. I knew right then he'd never get Molly to marry him, only for a minute I wished he could have. It would have been nice for him if he could have.

"Well, we done a good day's work," Dad said. "Let's go inside where it's warm. I could stand some supper."

We went in and the kitchen was nice and warm. The lamps

were lit. Me and Dad sat at the table and watched Molly working around the sink and around the stove, not paying us much mind; it was a treat for us just to watch. Me and Dad had batched for nine years, and we thought we got along pretty well, but having Molly in the kitchen eating supper made the way we usually done it seem pretty flat and dull. The house was just so much fuller with her in it. I guess Dad felt it too.

"Sure do appreciate your coming over to cook," he said. "This here'll beat Christmas."

Molly turned and looked at him a minute; she had a pan of biscuits in one hand and a gravy bowl in the other, and I don't think she even heard him. She just smiled and went on cooking, and Dad never repeated it. He was looking too tired, Dad was. He hadn't been feeling too good, I didn't think. Course he never said a word about it.

Molly fed us beef and beans and biscuits and gravy and pie, and we ate plenty of it. I couldn't take my eyes off her, and I couldn't keep from wishing I could get her to marry me. Then we could have her around all the time. She sat down at the other end of the table and drank her coffee, not saying anything but perfectly content. We were all quiet, but it was a real easy quiet.

Finally Dad got up and said he had to go to bed. He offered to pay Molly something, but of course she wouldn't take nothing. So he gave her a quarter of pork and some cracklins and told me to ride home with her to see that she got there all right.

Then it was just me and her in the kitchen.

"Let's go over to my house, Gid," she said. "Dad's gone to Wichita. You and him won't bother one another tonight."

"Okay," I said.

When we got there we built up the fire in the fireplace and sat in front of it a long time. I gave Molly her Christmas present, but I wouldn't let her open it, and we sat there not talking much or kissing much or anything, just resting together. Then she leaned forward and took some pins loose and shook down her long hair and lay back against me so the firelight shone on her face and eyes and mouth. I was half-sick, I loved her so much and was so excited by her. In a minute I was all wrapped around her. She wanted to go in the bedroom, and pulled her shirttail out as we went down the hall. It was cold as ice until we had been under the covers for a while, and then it got toasty warm and only Molly's fingers were cold. And there wasn't no old man to worry about, so we could go ahead. Only I was so excited about her I didn't do no good; I don't guess I knew enough about what I was doing.

"Oh hell," I said. "Dammit. I wouldn't blame you for marrying somebody else."

"Be still and hush," she said, and kissed me.

"I don't see why you put up with me," I said.

"You're my favorite," she said. "You ain't done nothing wrong. You just enjoy me a whole lot, I can tell that. And that's what I want you to do. Go to sleep, sugar."

And I did: it was the best sleeping in the world. When I woke up I could hardly believe I'd slept so good. Molly was still asleep and I was holding her. It was pure enjoyment. Finally I woke her up because having her asleep made me feel lonesome. We hugged and talked awhile. But she wouldn't say she'd marry me.

"That would be wrong," she said. "I don't love you that way." And then she leaned over and looked me right in the face, with her hair touching my chest. "But you love me that way, don't you?" she said, as if she had never thought of it before. "You do love me that way, Gid," she said. "That's going to be so sad. I don't love anybody that way." And she lay with her face tucked into my neck a long time, so I could feel her breath on my Adam's apple.

About daybreak we got up and had a real good breakfast and were cheerful as we'd ever been. I went home and worked and was all right that day. But the next day when I woke up I was so lonesome for her I was sick. All I could see that day was her face leaning over me, and her hair.

thirteen

It didn't seem like I was going to be able to stand not having Molly around more of the time. Every time I thought about her I got bluer and bluer. And if that wasn't trouble enough, Dad had me farming. It was a warm January and looked like it was going to be warm all winter. Johnny was doing most of the cow-work, and Dad was just mostly piddling around; he still wasn't feeling good. So for four days in a row I had to go down and follow them worthless mules around that worthless field, thinking about Molly all the time and wondering when I'd get to see her.

Then one Monday about the middle of the morning Johnny come through the field on his way to the League pasture. He was jogging along looking pretty discouraged, and I waved at him to come over. I was tired of kicking clods around anyway, and he got off his horse and we set by the plow awhile.

"Don't you get tired of this?" he said.

"Naw, I love it," I said. "I'd like to do this for the rest of my life. What are you so down in the dumps about?"

"Oh, Molly, I guess. I wish I wasn't so damn sweet on her. Hell, I oughtn't to be. She don't care nothing about me. At least not like I want her to. She just ain't got no sense."

"She's got the wrong kind of sense," I said. "Anyhow, what's she done now?"

"Nothing she hasn't done before," he said, looking real sour. "I rode all the way over there to visit her last night and the first thing I saw was Eddie's damn automobile. I never even went in."

"See 'em?"

"I looked through the kitchen window. He was sitting there eating vinegar cobbler and she was waiting on him just like he owned the place."

That made me plain sick. We sat there for about ten minutes, neither one of us saying a word. I couldn't think of one hopeful thing.

"Shit on the world," I said. "Let's go someplace. I'll be damned if I'll plow my legs off while she cooks cobbler for somebody like Eddie. Let's just go to the Panhandle and show them all."

"All right," he said. "You going to leave the plow here?"

I did. I rode in on one mule and unharnessed. Dad was up at the house, sitting by the fireplace trying to shave a corn off his toe. He looked pretty tired, but I wasn't in no mood to sympathize.

"Dad," I said, "things are just going wrong. I've had enough of this country. Me and Johnny are going up on the plains for a little while. I hope you can hire you a little help."

"Going, are you?" he said. "That oil-fielder running you off?"

"Not by a damn sight," I said. "I'm sorry to leave you."

"Oh, I guess I can do the work," he said. "I always have."

I seen he wasn't gonna act nice, so I didn't say any more to him.

"Let me hear from you now and then," was the last thing he said.

So we rode to Henrietta that night and arranged with an old boy to take the horses back to Archer County for us. We got good and drunk, and along about midnight we caught the train north. Our spirits weren't too good, but we were the only passengers, and we each got a bench and went to sleep. I dreamed that Dad was out terracing in the moonlight. When I woke up Johnny was still asleep and I had a headache, so I went out on the porch of the caboose. I guess we were about to Childress then; anyhow we were on the plains. The cold air kind of cleared my head. It was exciting to see all that country stretched out around me, but I felt pretty sad, too. I was split: I was glad to be where I was, and yet I wanted to be where I had just left. Looking down the rails, I couldn't help but think of the people at home, Dad and Molly mostly.

Thinking about them, I got lonesome, and went in and woke Johnny up. We stayed awake the rest of the night, talking about all the different big outfits we could work for. It would be the JAs most likely, or maybe the Matadors, depending on where we decided to go from Amarillo. We had about fifteen dollars apiece, cash money, and our saddles and saddle blankets, so we felt pretty well off.

We got off the train at the big brick station in Amarillo, and it was like getting off at the North Pole. The wind whistled down those big streets like the town belonged to it, and the people were just renters it was letting stay.

"Goddamn," Johnny said. "I never realized it was this cold up north in the wintertime."

We got a hotel room and decided to take the day to look around. Only the hotel room was so toasty and warm we stretched out and slept till almost six o'clock. When we went outside the lights were on and the streets were plumb empty, like the wind had blown everybody away. We found some saloons, though, and the people were in them.

"Let's celebrate before we go to work," I said.

He was agreeable, and boy did we celebrate. I wished we'd eaten supper first. I guess around home we never drank enough to keep in shape. We found some girls, too, even if they wasn't no raving beauties. We would have kept them for the night but they said our hotel was too respectable for them. They wouldn't take us to their places, so we went back to the saloons and drank some more and did without.

When we finally got back to the room we agreed we'd have to get up at four o'clock and look for a job. Boy, it was a bad night. If the hotel hadn't had a bathtub, we would have ruined the place. I brought up a good gallon, myself, before morning, and I wasn't nothing to Johnny. He made twice as many trips as I did. About the time it got light I seen him on his way to the bathroom agin, only he was crawling.

"What are you doing crawling?" I said. "Can't you even walk?"

"I might could," he said, and crawled on in anyway. I thought that was pretty funny.

"Hell, I can at least walk," I said. He was in asleep on the bathroom floor.

We never made it up at four, but we did get downstairs by about six-thirty. I had got emptied out and was feeling okay, but Johnny wasn't. I made him eat some breakfast, though, and he kept it down.

"That'll make you good as new," I said.

"I'll never be that good agin," he said.

By the time we got our hotel bills paid it was after sunup. The wind was still cold as ice.

"How much money you got?" I said.

"Oh, few dollars," he said. "Enough to last."

But, by god, when we counted, we had three dollars between us. Where the rest of it went I'll never know.

"We better go to Clarendon," he said. "That's the place to get jobs. Hell, we'll be broke by supper."

So we got railroad tickets to Clarendon; they cost a dollar apiece. Johnny went to sleep right off, but I sat up and looked out the window. That old plains country sure did look cold and gray to me, and I wasn't so sure I liked it. We ought to have waited till springtime to leave home. But still, it was a good feeling to be loose like we were; it was a kind of adventure, in a way, and it didn't too much matter about the cold. It mattered more about Molly and Dad. I was just glad Johnny was along. It wouldn't have been much fun by myself. I couldn't figure out what had happened to all our money.

They put us off in Clarendon about one o'clock. Johnny was all refreshed, and we turned up our collars and went walking down the street to see the town. It would have been a nice walk if it hadn't been for carrying the saddles.

I guess we were lucky; the first thing we struck was a horse auction. They were auctioning off a couple of hundred broncs some fellers had driven in from New Mexico. A lot of cattlemen were there. After we watched the bidding awhile we saw a funny-looking old man who didn't look like he could be very important, so we asked him if he knew where two cowpunchers could get a job. He was pretty friendly.

"You boys cowpunchers?" he said. "What else can you do? Can either one of you ride broncs?" He was a grizzly old feller and didn't have but half an ear on one side of his head.

"Both of us can," Johnny said. Which was a damn lie; he couldn't ride a bronc if all four of its feet were hobbled. He was an awful good hand on a horse, but he wasn't no hand to make a horse, so I contradicted him.

"I can ride broncs and he can do everything else," I said.

"My name's Grinsom," he said. "I could use a couple of hands myself. I'm gonna have a bunch of horses to drive home when this is over, and then somebody's gonna have to break them, I damn sure ain't. You boys come along and I'll try you for a week. I'll give you a dollar apiece to give these broncs a good ride, and if we get along with one another it'll be fifteen a month and bunk and board. That suit you?"

It didn't seem no great amount of money to me, and I couldn't figure a little dried-up feller like Mr. Grinsom owning much of a ranch, but Johnny thought it was fine, so we hired on. It turned out Mr. Grinsom owned thirty-eight thousand acres. He bought nineteen broncs and offered me and Johnny our pick of them to ride to the ranch.

Since Johnny had spoke up about being a bronc rider, that was pretty funny. He got throwed four times on the way to the ranch. I only got thrown once, and that was an accident. I was looking around and not paying enough attention to what I was doing.

"You ain't gonna break no broncs that way," Mr. Grinsom said to him, after the fourth buck-off.

Johnny was about half-crippled by then, and too mad to lie. "Hell no, I ain't no damn bronc rider," he said. "Gid can break these horses; he likes that kind of stuff. I'm a cowboy. I like to ride a horse that already knows something, so I can get work done. You keep me a week, and if I don't turn out to be the best hand you got by then, why by god just fire me."

Mr. Grinsom got tickled. He had pretty much of a sense of humor, at least about some things.

"My boys may give you a little competition," he said.

It turned out he really meant *his* boys, too. He had a big fat good-natured wife and seven grown sons. He had two hired hands, too, but he never worked them half as hard as he worked his own boys. All the boys' names started with J: Jimmy, Johnny, Jerry, Joe, Jakey, Jay, and Jordman. I never could tell them apart, but they were nice enough old boys. They had a great big bunkhouse, and me and Johnny and the two hired hands and the seven boys all slept in it. We ate supper at the big house, and Mrs. Grinsom explained to us that after they'd had the fourth boy it had got too noisy in the house and they'd put them out in the bunkhouse with the cowboys when they got big enough to get around. I don't know where all the noise went; the only words I ever heard them say were: "Thank you for the supper, Momma, it sure was good." Each one of them said that to Mrs. Grinsom after their meals.

Me and Johnny thought it was a pretty strange family. But the other two cowboys, one's name was Ed and the other's name was Malonus, they *really* thought so. They were so glad to have new hands around that wasn't in the family that they just about hugged us.

The next morning the old man asked me if I really wanted to break the horses. I said for a dollar apiece, like he offered, I'd give them a good first ride.

"How many do you want to ride a day?" he said.

"Oh, I ought to be done with them by three o'clock," I said. "There ain't but eighteen left. I rode one yesterday."

He acted like he didn't believe me. He sent Johnny off with the boys and the other hands and stayed around the lots all day, doing little chores and watching me out of the corner of his eye.

I didn't care. I felt real good that morning. The cold didn't even bother me. I made a good strong hackamore and went after them broncs. By dinnertime I only liked six being done with them, and I got the six in another three hours. I even saddled up a few of the worst ones and rode them agin, just so the old man would really get his money's worth. By that time he was sitting on the fence. I bet he chewed a whole plug of tobacco that afternoon. When I got done and turned them out in the horse pasture, he walked off to the house without saying a word. But I didn't care about that, either. I had been throwed seven times and was stiff and sore as hell, but I felt like a million dollars. I felt like I could have ridden fifty horses if I'd just had somebody to do the saddling for me.

That night the old man did a strange thing. He paid me at the supper table.

"By god," he said, after supper. "Now, Mother, make these boys be quiet." None of the boys had made a sound anyway. "I want you all to notice," he said. "This here's one feller that can do the job. He rode eighteen wild horses today, I seen him myself. And one yesterday." I was real embarrassed. The old man got up and stomped off to the bedroom and came back jingling a sack full of money. "I'll pay you right here," he said. "It might put some ambition into these boys of mine." And he counted me out nineteen dollars, mostly in silver money. There wasn't a sound in the room but the money clinking. Even after I gathered it up and put it in my pockets, there still wasn't a sound. Later that night Ed told me the old man never paid the boys atall, just give them a dollar apiece at Christmastime. That didn't surprise me much. Mr. Grinsom wasn't the first tight feller I'd ever seen.

We worked pretty good for about a week. Me and Johnny never had no trouble matching the other hands; by the time the week was over Johnny wasn't in no danger of getting fired. The old man was funny. He treated us like friends and his own boys like hound dogs.

But there were two things I couldn't get over: one was making nineteen dollars in one day, and the other was being homesick. If I could make nineteen dollars in one day, I was stupid to work a whole month for fifteen. And besides, I remembered the time in Fort Worth when I'd made four hundred in about two hours. Cowboying was fun, but it wasn't near enough fun to make fifteen dollars a month worth while. I knew I could beat that.

The homesickness was the worst part of it, though. I didn't mind the work, and I didn't mind the company; I didn't mind the country, or even the cold weather. I just minded feeling like I wasn't where I belonged. Home was where I belonged, but tell that to Johnny and he would have laughed like hell. He didn't feel like he belonged to any certain place, and I did. He was born not five miles from where I was, too. When you came right down to it, Dad was right: me and him was a lot different. I couldn't get over thinking about Dad and Molly and the country and the ranch, the things I knew. The things that were mine. It wasn't that I liked being in Archer County so much—sometimes I hated it. But I was just tied up with it; whatever happened there was happening to me, even if I wasn't there to see it. The country might not be very nice and the people might be onery; but it was my country and my people, and no other country was; no other people, either. You do better staying with what's your own, even if it's hard. Johnny carried his with him; I didn't. If you don't stick with a place, you don't have it very long.

Me and Johnny argued for ten days. I just plain wanted to go back, and he just plain didn't. I got so I couldn't sleep; I would wake up and lie awake for hours. Then one Saturday, Johnny was in Clarendon and run into a man who had a ranch out near the New Mexico line; he wanted a cowboy or two to look after it through the winter; it was so dull he couldn't stand the winter there himself. He offered double what we were getting, and said besides he had a pretty little Indian woman who would stay out and do the cooking. So Johnny hired on for both of us, but he told the man we had two more weeks to go for Grinsom. I told him right off I wasn't going any farther west or north, but he thought I'd change my mind. Then on a Tuesday, Mr. Grinsom sent us out in one of his big pastures to look for sicklings—that was all he had for us to do—and I just decided I was through. I pulled up and stopped.

"Hell with it," I said. "I'm going to Archer County. There ain't no use in me loafing around here any longer."

We turned our backs to the wind and watched it whipping across the high open flats. He tried to talk me out of it. "Don't do nothing rash," he said. "Wait till we get on the new job. Think of that Indian woman."

"You go on out there," I said. "I don't want to spend no winter in New Mexico. What would I want with an Indian woman when Molly's just three miles from home?"

"Yes, but Molly's crazy," he said.

"I never stopped to argue," I said. "You coming or staying?"

He hunched his neck down into his collar and frowned. "I hate to see you miss a good winter," he said. "What'll I do for company if that woman don't talk English?"

But he was staying. "There ain't as much at home for me as there is for you," he said. "This here's more the life for me."

And I was crazy enough to want to stay with him, even when I knew I was going home. We were pretty good buddies.

"Well, I hate to run off and leave you," I said. "But I got to go. You'll be coming home next summer, won't you?"

"Oh sure," he said. "I just don't feel like going that direction right now, Gid. I hate to be stuck off out here with no company, though."

"Well, write me once in a while," I said. "I believe I'll lope on back. I might could get to Amarillo tonight."

"Say hello to the country for me," he said. "Give old Molly a big kiss and tell her she's still my girl."

"I'll sure do it," I said. "Don't let no crazy horse fall on you."

"Oh hell," he said. "Won't nothing hurt me unless I freeze to death. You watch out yourself."

I guess we should have shook hands, but we never. He kinda nodded, and turned and tucked his head down and trotted off into the wind, headed north. I set there a minute, watching him cross the windy pasture. Then I loped back to the ranch, gave notice, and talked the old man into loaning me a horse to ride to Clarendon.

"Why you running off?" he said. "Too dull? I may buy some more broncs in a week or two."

"Oh no," I said. "I just guess I'll go run my own ranch."

It was a pretty lonesome trip home. I had to wait till way after dark for a train out of Clarendon, and was the only one on it, then, so I didn't have a soul to talk to. I never slept a wink all night, I was too excited about going home. Only I wisht old Johnny had come; train riding was dull without him. I got off in Wichita Falls about ten the next morning and found a man with a wagon going to Thalia. We drove in about an hour before dark, and the first person I saw was Mabel Peters, coming out of the dry goods store where she worked.

"Why, if it ain't Gid," she said. She had put on a little flesh and was dressed nice and looked real cheerful. In spite of all I could do, she made me go home and have supper with her at the boardinghouse. All the boarders were there, so she didn't dare ask me up to her room, but she followed me out on the porch after supper and hung on to me for an hour, she was so glad to see me. She asked me four or five times if I would come back and see her.

It was so late when I left Mabel that I had trouble finding anybody to borrow a horse from, but I finally got one and rode home. I was practically sick at my stomach I was so glad to be going home. It was good to ride over some familiar country. I even went by Molly's, but there wasn't no light; I sat on my horse by the back fence a minute, thinking about her.

Our place was dark too. When I got in the first thing I did was tiptoe down the hall to Dad's door, to listen a minute. He was snoring like he always did. Once I heard him cough and hawrk. I was glad he was asleep. I guess I was afraid I would find him out in the moonlight, plowing that old oat field.

fourteen

The morning after I got home I remember Dad came in my room real early, but he never woke me up. I was about half-awake and I seen him standing inside the door. But I guess he figured I needed the rest, because he went on out and I stayed in bed till nine o'clock.

When I finally got dressed and outside he was down at the lots filling up the hayracks. It was a cold morning, with a big frost on the ground.

"Well, how's the Panhandle?" he said. "I guess you got rich quicker than I thought you would, or else you went broke quicker. Which was it?"

"Aw, I just got homesick," I said. "How's ever thing here?"

"Run down and wore out," he said. "Specially me. Why don't you get the horses up? A couple of them need their shoes pulled off, and I ain't had the energy."

Dad sure looked bad. He hadn't hired no help at all; I knew he wouldn't. But he wasn't lying when he said he was worn out. He didn't have much flesh on him any more, and he had been a big fleshy man. When I first got home I thought it was from working too hard, but it wasn't. He was just sick; he didn't have no wind any more, nor much grip in his hands. But he wouldn't go to a doctor for love nor money.

I felt real bad about having gone off and left him so long. I know it wouldn't have made any difference to his health if I had stayed, but it would have made some difference to me.

"Hell, you ought to go see a doctor, Dad," I told him. "You probably just need some kind of pep-up medicine. Why do you want to be so contrary?"

"I ain't contrary," he said. "I just don't want to pay no doctor to tell me what I already know. There ain't no medicine for old age."

"You're just tight," I said. "You oughtn't to let a few dollars stand between you and your health."

"I am tight," he said. "I'm rich, too."

"You don't live like it," I said.

"No, because I want to stay rich. The best way in the world to get poor is to start living rich."

I couldn't do a damn thing with him. He kept on working, day in and day out, warm or cold. And the thing was he wasn't much help any more, only he didn't seem to notice it. I was doing nine-tenths of the work, and it kept me busy and worn out and tired. It was just miserable old hard cold work, no fun to it, like loading cake and hay and feeding cattle and building fence and all kinds of winter work like that. I'd been home three weeks before I ever seen Molly.

But then she come over to see me one day and cooked us supper, and I guess she seen right off how Dad was. I think it worried her, but she was real cheerful that day and never mentioned it to me. But she started coming over two or three times a week and cooking for us. Sometimes she even got there in time to ride a pasture with me, or help me with the chores. It was real good of her to come; I was crazier about her than I had ever been. I was pretty lonesome anyway, and worn out and worried about Dad, and it was awful nice to have somebody warm like Molly to be with once in a while. But no matter what I said or how I said it, she wouldn't marry me.

"I know you want me to, Gid," she said. "But it might be bad if I did. You might be sorry you ever asked me," she said.

"That ain't true," I said. "I wouldn't be."

She thought a minute, and grinned, but a sad grin. "Then I might be," she said. "That would be just as bad."

One night after Dad had gone upstairs to bed we sat by the fireplace awhile, and we got to talking about him. Molly was the best person there ever was for sitting by the fire with. Every time she came over we got off by ourselves a little while, and those were about the only times I got unwound.

"You better make him go to the doctor," she said. "If you don't, I think he's going to get real sick."

"He's too damn contrary," I said. "He just won't go."

"Don't talk bad about him," she said. "He's a real good man. He treats me better than anybody I know, you included." I don't know what that had to do with it, but it was true. Dad always let Molly know he thought she was about tops.

"I don't reckon he'll die," I said. "You don't, do you?"

She hugged me then. "He might, Gid," she said. "He's just getting sicker and sicker."

I thought that over for a while and it really scared me. I couldn't imagine Dad not being around to give the orders. Even sick he was just as active as he could be, and never missed a thing.

It was hard to think of Dad being any other way than alive.

"Dad couldn't keep still long enough to die," I said. Neither one of us thought it was funny, though.

"I sure am glad my dad's healthy," she said. "I guess he'll live to be a hundred. If he was to die, I think I'd just plain go crazy."

"I don't guess anybody lasts forever," I said. "Funny thing, I've always been sure Dad would outlive me. I just never thought of it any other way."

We sat for a long time, thinking about it. But I couldn't believe it would happen. I guess I knew it had to sometime, but I just couldn't believe it. Not even in my brain.

"Well, if he'd just quit working and set around and rest up a little," I said. "I think he'd get all right. He stays on the go too much."

She shook her head. "That ain't his trouble. I think that's good for him. If your dad had to die, I'd want him to do it working, wouldn't you? Just to go on working till it happens. That's all he loves to do. If he was to sit around in a rocking chair, he'd get to feeling useless, and that'd be worse than being tired."

I kissed her and we sat on the couch for another hour or so. I meant to ride her home, but I was too tired, and she wouldn't let me.

"Much obliged," I said. "Come back whenever you can. We sure are glad to see you."

"Why, I enjoy it, Gid," she said. "Next time Dad goes off I'll come over." When she rode off into the wind it reminded me of Johnny, up there on the plains. I missed having him around.

Life is just a hard, mean business, sometimes. Here we were worrying about my dad, and three days after we had that conversation Molly's own dad staggered into his smokehouse drunk, looking for some whiskey, and picked up a jug of lye by mistake and drank a big swallow of it and it killed him. He never even got out of the smokehouse. Eddie and one of his cronies was over there at the time; he had been drinking with the old man, and he went out and found him. It was a windy, dusty evening. And the first thing Molly said to me when I got there was, "Well, Gid, my poor old daddy never lived to be a hundred after all." And she just about did go crazy that night.

It was the end of any respect I ever had for Eddie White. I guess he was just scared of dead people. Anyhow he sent his damn oil-field crony over in the car to tell us. Dad had gone to bed, and I didn't wake him. I left a note on the kitchen table, where he'd see it in the morning. And then I saddled up and got over there on the run, and when I got there Eddie and his buddie were just driving away. I don't know where they were going in such a hurry, but they left Molly by herself with her dad, and there wasn't no excuse for that, drunk or not. I rushed in and she was in the kitchen, bawling her head off—she didn't even know Eddie was gone; the old man was dumped on a bed in his bedroom, with just a quilt thrown over him. I never mentioned Eddie and she never either; maybe she was so torn up she forgot he had been there.

She wanted me to do something for her daddy, clean him up a little; but she didn't want to go in the room with me and I didn't want to leave her by herself for fear she'd get to taking on agin. I made her drink some coffee, and I got a towel and wiped her face and kinda dried her eyes, and then we washed the dishes. There was a lot to wash; I guess she had cooked supper for Eddie and his friend. Washing them calmed her down some. When we had the kitchen good and clean I made her hold the lamp while I went in and straightened the old man out the best I could. He looked terrible, and I didn't know a thing about what I was doing, but I got his boots off anyway, and got him wiped up some and laid out and covered up neater than he had been. It was a mistake for Molly to come; it made her sick at her stomach. She vomited in the bedroom first, and then I carried her to the bathroom and held her head while she finished emptying her stomach. She was awfully white and shaky. I walked her down to the bedroom and made her take her clothes off and put her nightgown on and get in bed, and she laid there and cried while I went back and cleaned up in the bathroom and the other bedroom. Then I left the lamp on the kitchen table and got in bed with her. She thought some people might come; she thought Eddie must have gone to tell some, when she remembered him. But I didn't expect him to tell a soul that night, and he didn't.

"But what will I do, Gid?" she said. "You know I can't do without Dad."

"Hush, sugar," I said. "Let me just hug you tight. Let's don't talk for a while."

And I did hold her. For maybe half an hour her eyes were wide open and she was stiff in the bed, but then she got warm and relaxed and her eyes shut and she was asleep. I stayed awake just about all night, holding her, and she never moved or turned over till morning. She was lucky to be able to sleep, I thought. She was so helpless, in a way. And when it got light and she woke up I was watching her and still holding her. I saw just as plain as day when she remembered what had happened, and I thought she would get bad again, but she never. She looked real serious and then she pulled my head down and kissed me and got up and put up her hair standing by the bed, and she never cried at all until later that morning, when Dad and the other people begin to come.

fifteen

Dad finally did go to a doctor, in fact he went to five of them, but he had been right all along. They never done him no good. One of them kept him in the hospital for two weeks, though, and that threw ever bit of the ranch work on me. It was around the first of April before I got Johnny off a letter, and then I never said much.

DEAR JONATHAN:

I know you love that name so much I thought I would just use it on you.

Well, how was the winter up there? I guess you have got a family of half-breed kids by now, or did that deal ever turn out? Let me know, I am sure curious.

I guess the big news down here is about Molly's old man. He drunk lye last month and died, it was awful hard on Molly but I think she is over the worst of it now. She is getting sweeter all the time, and I mean it, I think I am going to get her in the notion of marrying me one of these days, then when you come back you will really know what you've missed. But I guess you will bring your Indian sweetheart home, so you won't mind too much.

Eddie is acting sorrier than ever, I may have to fight him yet.

Well, I wish you would come home, we could sure put you to work, we might even give you a raise. Our steers wintered good but the calf crop is pretty puny. If we don't get some rain the grass will all play out by June.

I guess that's all the news I know of. If you see Old Man Grinsom, say hello for me and ask him if he thinks I can ride or not. I have got a new sorrel horse by the way, he can foxtrot like nobody's business but he ain't no cowhorse yet. He's just a four-year-old though. I give thirty-five dollars for him.

Write me sometime and send me the news from New Mexico.

Your friend,

GID

I guess old Johnny must have been sitting at the table with his pencil licked when he got my letter, because I got one from him in less than a week's time.

DEAR GID:

I would use the rest of your name too, but I ain't the kind that has to get even with ever mean trick that's played on me.

Well, this is the life for me, and I don't mean maybe. This place I'm at is the rancho grandy for sure, there ain't no damn mesquite to get in your way, but I do kinda wish it had a few more windbreaks in it. It like to blown us all away in Feb. and March, them was just fall breezes you got when you was up here. Jelly, she made a big wool bandanna to keep my neck warm.

Jelly ain't her real name, but that's what the boss called her so I use it too. He wasn't kidding when he said she was pretty. Boy I never would have made it through the winter without her.

Well, tell Molly I'm awful sorry about her trouble. I'm just sorry for her, I ain't gonna miss the old bastard personally, are you? I wish I had been there though.

If you do fight Eddie, don't let him get the first lick. Get the first one yourself, with a two-by-four if one's handy.

I ain't losing no sleep over you and her getting married, I know she ain't that far gone.

We had quite a bit of snow in early March, never had much before that. It's all the moisture we've had. This here ain't a very big ranch, really, and it's a good thing because there's just me to take care of it.

The coyotes have got six calves so far, I even seen one Lobo but didn't get a shot at him. There ain't a decent horse on the place.

Well, write me agin. I like to hear the news. I may come home one of these days if I don't get lost in the sandstorms. Tell Molly I'll be seeing her.

Your friend,
JOHNNY

sixteen

We had a good rain in early February, and it looked like that would be the last we'd ever have. We never had a sprinkle in March, and by the middle of April the pastures were looking like they usually looked in July. It never helped Dad's disposition, or mine either. We had to feed the cattle, and it was such hard, hot work Dad just couldn't do it. Between the dry weather and Dad being sick, I wasn't in a very good humor.

One morning I run into Eddie. I was down in the River pasture, feeding. The cattle could hear me well enough, but it was hot and they didn't want to come to the wagon. I hollered around for an hour and only got sixty-five or seventy. I was just about to go ahead and feed them when three damn floppy-eared turd hounds come loping up through the brush, barking like hell. The cattle took off in about ten different directions. I got down and chunked the dogs and went on and got most of the cattle back together agin, and I'll be damned if the dogs didn't come up and run them off agin. My horse was tied to the back of the wagon, so I got on him and took my rope down and went after some dogs. I didn't rope them, but I whipped the shit out of two of them. The other one was too much of a dodger. When I was trotting back to the wagon, coiling my rope, I seen Eddie slouching across the flat. I might have known they was his dogs; nobody but him had time to run hounds that time of year. He had on an old khaki jumper and some patched pants and some roughnecking boots and looked like he hadn't seen a razor in about ten days. Both of us were mad.

But I didn't start off unfriendly. "Howdy, Ed," I said.

"Goddammit, Fry, that ain't no way to treat dogs," he said. "No telling where they are now. I been looking for them all morning, and now I got it to do over agin."

"I'd been after these cattle they run off a good while, myself," I said. "I guess the dogs will come home when they get hungry, won't they?"

"But maybe I don't want them home," he said. "I might want to hunt some more."

"Listen here," I said. "I don't give a plugged nickel what you want, if you're asking me. But what I want is for you and them dogs to get out of this pasture. And the next time they scare off cattle of mine they ain't gonna get off so easy. Next time they're gonna get the shit drug out of them."

"I'm a notion to whip your butt, right now," he said.

I got off my horse.

"Have at it," I said. "I hope you brought your lunch. You may need it before you're through."

"Aw, hell no," he said. "Then I'd have to carry you to the hospital. But let me tell you, you got one coming. Write it down in your little book."

"Don't wait till I get too old," I said.

"Another thing," he said. "Stay the hell away from my wife. I don't even want to see you on her place."

"Stay away from your what?" I said.

"My wife!" he said. "Just leave her the hell alone."

It was like lightning had hit me, only not fast lightning but a real slow bolt that slid all the way down me. By the time it got to my feet I was plumb numb. I couldn't have said boo.

"Why, you look surprised," he said. "I guess that shows you, now don't it. You and your long-legged buddy, too. Hell, we been married three weeks, and she's a real dilly. Me and her we really take after one another. I never had a woman so crazy about me.

"Well, ain't you gonna congratulate me?" He winked and grinned.

I got back on my horse and went on back to the wagon, and he went off after his dogs. A good many of the cattle had come back, and I fed them.

That afternoon I went out with the posthole diggers and the wire stretchers, but I didn't do no fencing. I went down to the far tank and sat under a big shade tree, watching the mockingbirds and the kildeers fly around. There were a lot of bubbles on top of the water; I should have fished. I just couldn't understand Molly doing it. I wouldn't have cared if lightning *had* struck me. There didn't seem no reason left to work or nothing. I got to wondering if I would ever see her agin, and I couldn't think what I'd say if I did. There wasn't no clouds to look at, just water and sky, so I watched the water awhile and then I watched the sky. I didn't do much thinking; I just sat there feeling tight and sick. About sundown I rode home. Dad noticed there wasn't no dirt on my diggers, but he was tired too, and he never said nothing about it. We had cold steak and cold potatoes for supper, and I made the coffee too weak. It wasn't such a good supper.

seventeen

It looked like the world was going completely to pot. Dad was getting worse instead of better, and three or four days after I found out about Molly I got another letter from Johnny.

DEAR GID:

Well, I've got so much time to kill now, I thought I would write you agin. I have been in a real scrape, it's what I get for riding sorry horses, I ought to know better. I was off riding line and my horse buggered at a damn skunk and off I went, only I got caught in my rope and he drug me about half a mile. I guess I am the most skinned-up person you ever saw. Besides, my hip was broke, and I was about ten miles from home; it was a pretty hard crawl, I tell you for sure, I was out lost all one night. If it had been cold the coyotes would have ate me by now.

Jelly she got me into town and now they got me cemented up so I can't turn over. It's pretty tiresome, so don't ever break no hips if you can help it.

The horse come in, so I ain't lost the saddle.

These doctors are no-count, they give me a lot of trouble. I guess it will be June before I'm worth anything agin.

Wish you was up here, we could play some cards and talk over old times. Write me when you get time and let me know all about Molly and your dad and what's happening down that way. I ain't had much news lately.

Your friend,
JOHNNY

So he wasn't having no luck, either. I didn't know what to write him, all the news was so bad. I wished I could have gone up and stayed with him like he done with me, but it just couldn't be managed. Finally I wrote him a note.

DEAR JOHNNY:
We are all sorry to hear about your trouble, that's a cowboy's life. I would come and stay, only Dad's pretty sick now and there ain't nobody but me to run the ranch.

Molly has married Eddie, I guess that's the end of that. I haven't seen her. He is too sorry to talk about.

We haven't had no rain, either.

I wish you would come on home when you get well, we could sure use a good hand.

Your friend,

GID

Dad was looking low. I would have given anything to talk to Molly about it, but the times when I could talk to her were over and gone. I did go in and see Mabel Peters a time or two. She was a nice old girl, but she wasn't much help. She was after me to marry her, and I was half a mind to. I didn't see how I could be no worse off than I was. At least we'd have somebody to do the cooking and the housework. I wanted to hire somebody, but Dad wouldn't let me.

"Hell no," he said. "A hired woman would get the best of me in no time. We'll just get along by ourselves."

One day me and him drove a little bunch of cattle down to the League pasture. On the way back we stopped on the Ridge and talked and rested awhile. It was a pretty day. The mesquite was leafed out, and everything smelled like spring. Dad had got down to pull up a devil's claw, and said he didn't feel like getting back up right then; we sat under a post oak and talked. I had got where I liked to talk to Dad; it taken me a long time. From where we were sitting we could look off west and see halfway across the county, to the little ridges above Onion Creek, where Dad's land ended.

"I got a good ranch," he said. "That's one thing that cheers me up. The best land in the county."

He was right, I guess. To me it didn't seem like much consolation.

"The nice thing is that I'm a damn sight nearer worn out than this country. I'd hate to get old in a worn-out country."

"You ain't worn out," I said. "You're just damn pessimistic. If you'd stay in the hospital awhile, you'd get well."

He didn't say nothing for a minute.

"Well, it's too bad she married him," he said, looking across the country. "She'll make a good one. But just let me tell you something, son, a woman's love is like the morning dew, it's just as apt to settle on a horse turd as it is on a rose. So you better just get over it."

"Aw, I ain't hurt much," I said. "Why in the world did she want to marry a bastard like that? It just don't figure."

"Well, she's got a lot of sense when it comes to taking care of herself," he said. "A lot more than you have. She'll make it."

"Why, she ain't got no sense, when it comes to taking care of herself," I said.

Sitting on the ground, you could smell the spring coming right up through the grass and into the breeze. It was sad Dad felt so awful at such a pretty time of year.

"It's my fault you don't have more," he said. "You've always had me to give you orders. I never put you on your own enough. She's been on her own since she could walk.

"But there's no use in you sitting on your butt sulking," he said. "Sulking never made a dime nor kept a friend."

"We better get on home," I said.

By the time we got to the barn it was late evening, and the last of the sun was shining on the weathervanes above the barn. Dad was tired. He drank some buttermilk and went to bed. He had seemed a little bit worried about me.

"Anyhow you're stubborn," he said. "Stubbornness will get a feller through a lot of mean places."

The next morning he never woke me up, and there was a note lying on the table when I come down.

DEAR GID:

Miserable night. There's no profit in putting up with this.

I think I'll go out on the hill and turn my horses free, or did you ever know that song? It's an old one.

Take good care of the ranch, it's a dilly, and don't trust ever damn fool that comes up the road. Always work outside when you can, it's the healthiest thing.

Tell Miss Molly I appreciated her coming and helping us, just tell her much obliged until she is better paid.

Well, this is the longest letter I've written in ten years, it is too long. Be sure and get that windmill fixed, I guess you had better put in some new sucker rod.

YOUR DAD

The rifle wasn't in the closet, so I knew that was that, and I sat down and held my head. I wisht old Johnny had been there, or Molly, but they wasn't. Directly I went outside and turned off the windmill and went on down to the barn and hitched the wagon and put the wagon sheet in it and headed off across the hill. He was right on the west side; he had on a clean khaki shirt and Levis and had taken his hat off and was laying on his back on the grass.

Once I seen him I wasn't so scared, for some reason. He just looked natural, like Dad, and comfortable. I put him in the wagon and took him up to the house and laid him on the couch in the living room and got a counterpane to cover him with. It was worse in that cool darkish dusty old living room than it had been out in the sunshine. I hated to be the one to start treating Dad like a dead person. It was a long time before he seemed dead to me. For three months after that I would wonder in the morning why he hadn't come to wake me up.

I guess Dad had been better known than I thought; there was a big funeral and a lot of talk about what a pioneer he had been. It never done him much good, or me either. The worst of it all was seeing Molly. After I went into town to the undertaker a lot of people came out to visit me and bring stuff to eat. Molly, she came too, and brought a cake, and it was so awkward I got a headache from it. I knew she was remembering when her dad died and wishing she could really help me, but she couldn't. All those people were there trying to cheer me up, and it just made me bluer. Every once in a while I would see Molly looking at me from across the room, and she would be crying and looking so sad I wished I could have gone over and hugged her and told her it was okay. Finally I did talk to her just a minute.

"Molly," I said. "One of the last things Dad did was tell me to thank you for helping us last winter. He sure appreciated it."

"I hope you'll come and see me sometime, Gid," she said. "When all of this is over." Right after that she left. I seen her at the funeral, but just at a distance. Eddie was even there. I guess old Johnny was the only one that wasn't. I wrote him a card and told him a little about it, but he never answered. In September, after he was back, we had a kind of little funeral ourselves: we took Dad's old white saddlehorse that he called Snowman out on the hill and let him loose in the pasture; nobody ever rode him agin. We left Dad's saddle hanging in the harness shed. Sometimes when I'm doing the chores early in the mornings, I wonder if Dad and that old pony aren't still out there, maybe, slipping around through the misty pastures and checking up on the new calves.

eighteen

One afternoon about ten days after Dad died I decided I ought to look over the ranch. Of course I had been over every inch of it a hundred times, but it had been Dad's ranch then, and not mine. It was a nice sunny day, with a few white clouds in the sky, and not too hot; the week Dad killed himself we had a two-inch rain—it was just his luck to miss it—and the country looked wonderful. We had lots of grass, and the weeds weren't too bad yet. Dad had about ten thousand acres; he had had the whole county to pick from, and he picked careful. There was a creek to the southeast and a creek to the northwest, and the River down the middle, so if there was water anywhere in the country, we had it. And of course he had built good tanks. I saddled old Denver and started off east, through the Dale pasture and rode down our east fence plumb to the southeast corner; then I cut back across Westfork and rode west between it and the River, winding through the brush till I got nearly to the west side and then turned north and rode up on the hill in the south pasture and rested awhile. The whole south end of our land was brushy, mesquite and post oak mixed; the farther north you went, the more mesquite and the less post oak. Dad said when he first saw the country there wasn't a mesquite tree anywhere, or a prickly pear. Then I crossed the River and rode northwest till I hit Onion Creek, and turned and came back southeast agin along the top of Idiot Ridge. There wasn't no mesquite on the Ridge; it hadn't got that far north. The north end of our land was still prairie, but you could look south off the Ridge and see the brush coming. Our headquarters sits southeast of the Ridge, on a long hill. Finally I rode back through the League pasture to the barn and turned old Denver loose. I sat on the lot fence awhile, resting and thinking. It was about an hour before sundown, and I didn't much want to go up to the house, since there wasn't nobody there. At least the milkpen calves were a little company.

For a day or two after Dad died I had actually been in the mood to sell the place, just dump it, and go where I wouldn't have to be reminded of Dad all the time, or of Molly. But I got over wanting to do that. For one thing, I got so I liked being reminded of Dad. Of course I didn't like to think of Molly and Eddie, but it would have been pretty yellow-bellied to let them run me out of the country. Most of the time I hadn't paid much attention to the country; Dad had done that. But what I saw that afternoon looked pretty good to me.

I didn't think no more about moving; but even staying took a lot of thinking about. One thing for sure, I wasn't no solitary owl. I couldn't stay on the place by myself; in about a month I would have been dead of lonesomeness. So I figured the best thing to do was marry Mabel. She was the best girl left in the county, and I figured I could get along with her okay. She would be so grateful to me just for marrying her that she shouldn't fuss none for about fifteen years.

Then if Johnny ever come back, I could hire him to help me run the place. I wanted to buy some new land if I could; I didn't intend to stop with what I'd inherited; that would have been pure laziness. Of course Mabel and Johnny wasn't too fond of one another, but I figured that would iron out once me and her was married and he quit trying to get in her pants.

I sat on the fence and never even noticed sundown. I happened to notice the moon's reflection in the milklot water trough. The house looked so lonesome I just didn't go in, I caught old Denver and rode to Thalia without even eating supper.

When I stepped up on the boardinghouse porch I could see Mabel hadn't gone to bed. She was sitting in her chair, patching a quilt. I felt sorry for her. When I knocked she had to put on a bathrobe before she let me in.

"Why, come in, Gid," she said. "I was just thinking about you.

"You look kinda blue," she said. "Want some hot chocolate?"

I said no. Her bedroom was neat as a pin.

"I guess I am a little down in the dumps," I said. "You want to sit out on the porch awhile? It's a real warm night."

"Okay," she said.

We got in the glider and rocked, and she snuggled up against me, warm as a hot-water bottle. We seen the moon, way up there, and I wondered if its reflection was still down at the ranch, in the water trough.

"Honey, let's get married," I said. "I'm sick of this living alone."

"Why, I am too," she said, and she squeezed my hand right hard.

I hugged her and kissed her and stood up, thinking she'd go in and get her clothes on, so we could wake up the J.P. and get it done and go on home, but boy she fooled me. I never seen her run backward so quick.

"Why, I couldn't hold my head up if I got married that way," she said. "What are you thinking about?"

She talked like it would take us two weeks, just to get married.

I never knew she was that silly about things before. She wouldn't even let me spend the night with her. I ended up having to pay fifty cents to spend the night in the damn hotel.

But I didn't back out. There wasn't nothing to be gained from that; not that I knew of. Only I told her the next morning that I wasn't going to wait around no two weeks, I had too many other things to do. She said I'd have to at least ride back to the ranch and get my good clothes; I had just come in like I was. So I done it. While I was gone she quit her job and packed her suitcases. And when I got back to town I hunted up a feller I knew and just bought me an automobile. I figured if Eddie White could afford one, I could too. He showed me how to drive it and I got it to the rooming house and put Mabel's stuff in it. Then we walked over to the Methodist preacher's house. It was a pretty day and Mabel was dolled up like a hundred dollars; I had on a wool suit and was about to cook. Anyway, the preacher called his wife in to witness, and he married us. I gave him three dollars. Mabel hung on my arm all the way back to the rooming house, and I guess everybody in town knew what we'd done. I sure was hot and embarrassed, but Mabel didn't even want me to take my coat off till we got out of town. It took a lot of wrassling to get that damn car home, no better roads than there were; I wisht a hundred times I'd never bought it. But we finally made it, and I yanked the car stopped by the back gate.

"Well, here we are," I said. "Man and wife." And I started to get her stuff out of the rumbleseat.

"Gid, you ought to be ashamed, ain't you going to help me down?" she said. "I see I'll have to do a little work on you." And she never wasted no time starting.

nineteen

The first month we were married, I don't think we saw a living soul but one another. I guess I must have run into a few other people, here and there, but I sure didn't say much to them, and I didn't give them the chance to say much to me. If there was one thing I didn't feel like putting up with, it was jokes about newlyweds. Just being one was joke enough.

Of course, it really wasn't that Mabel was so bad herself. She was a good person, a real good person, I guess, and she damn sure wasn't lazy or anything like that. She did her work, and she looked after me a damn sight better than I had been looking after myself. And there was a many a time when I was awful glad to have her around.

Still, it never changed the facts, and the facts was that I had done an awful ignorant thing. When I first realized just *how* ignorant, I was flat embarrassed for myself. A ten-year-old kid could have showed as much judgment as I showed. I guess Dad had been right when he said I didn't know anything about taking care of myself.

Mabel was a big surprise to me, of course. I thought I knew her to a T before I ever went in to marry her. I hadn't been married to her two weeks before I knew that a blind idiot could have found out more about her than I managed to. For one thing, she was a lot prouder of herself than I thought she was, and for another, a lot less proud of me. I soon found out that she didn't consider me no particular prize, but I had better be sure and let her know that I considered her one. She seen herself as the belle of the county; nobody was going to talk her out of that view. I soon gave up trying; she could see herself any way she wanted to.

It come down to two things: the first was that Mabel just wasn't a very generous person. I guess she never had anything to learn to be generous with. For every nickel's worth of her she put out, she wanted a dollar's worth of me. And got it, too.

The second thing was that I was still crazy about Molly. What few little times I'd been with her meant more to me than a lifetime with Mabel could have. I had feeling for Molly, and didn't for Mabel. And Mabel had none for me.

It wasn't very long before I was hanging around the lots till dark for a plumb different reason. It used to be I didn't want to go to the house because nobody was there; pretty soon I was working late because I didn't know what to do at the house when I got there. I seen the moon in the water trough many a time, and I seen it in the sky, and if one thing was for sure, it was that the moon didn't care. What I did didn't make no difference to it, or to nothing, or to nobody, I felt like. I did get a card from Johnny, but I didn't have the guts to answer it.

I never was bluer than I was that first month. If a feller has to be lonesome, he's better off being lonesome alone. But I'd kicked that advantage away forever, and there was no use sulking about it. It was done and that was final; I would just have to make the best of it. Only it didn't look like a very good best.

It reminded me of something Old Man Grinsom had said one time; it was the day we first run into him in Clarendon. Just to make conversation I asked him how long he had been in the Panhandle.

"Since '93," he said. "I come here with nothing but a fiddle and a hard on. I've still got the fiddle." And when we seen them seven boys we knew where the other went. My case was a little different. I got married with a ranch and the other, and I still had them both. And to be right honest, I guess it served me right.

twenty

It was late April when we married, and May was the month we stayed by ourselves. By June I knew I had to do a little better than that for myself, someway. I was getting where I didn't even enjoy my work. One morning I had to fix a little fence on the northwest side, and when I got that done I decided it was time I went and checked up on my neighbors. The closest one was Molly.

When I rode past her barn I didn't see no automobile, and that was a great relief. It took so much nerve to get me there I would have hated to have to ride away agin. But Molly, she was there, out in the back yard hanging the washing on the line. There was a good breeze, and the sheets were flapping, so she didn't notice me riding up. She looked like the same old Molly, only more so, wearing Levis and an old cotton shirt with the shirttail out; she had a clothespin in her mouth and three or four more in the shirt pocket. Her shirttail was damp in front, where the sheets had flopped against her. And her hair was loose, hanging down her back and getting in her face now and then; I seen her brush it out of the way with one hand. I thought she just looked lovely.

I got off and tied old Willy to a mesquite tree; then I walked into the yard and stopped behind her, at the windmill. I didn't know if I could talk.

"Hello, neighbor," I said. "How are you getting along?"

She turned around with a tablecloth in her hands; I thought she was going to cry. She had those little dark places under her eyes. She dropped the wet tablecloth in the grass, and I went over to pick it up.

"My, Gid," she said. "You scared me."

For some reason I was real embarrassed; I squatted down and picked up the wet tablecloth and was going to try and wipe the grass off it. But Molly squatted down too and put one of her wet hands on my neck, and then there was her face and she kissed me. I shivered clear through. But her face against mine was as warm as sunshine, and I had to sit down in the grass and hug her.

"Now ain't this some way for old married folks to be acting?" I said.

She grinned, but it was just half a grin, really, and her mouth quivered.

"It's nice, though," she said. "I'm so glad to see you. Let's go in the house."

I helped her up and put my arm around her; we let the table-cloth and the clothespins lie where they fell. I asked her if she wanted to finish hanging out the washing, and she shook her head.

"No, but let's sit on the cellar awhile," she said. "It's too pretty to go in; I just don't like to sit on the dewy grass."

The cellar was stone, and the sun had warmed it up. She held one of my hands.

"Where's Eddie?" I said.

"Just relax," she said. She knew what I was thinking. "He's gone to Oklahoma, working in the oil fields."

"Good lord," I said. "He's a strange feller. I don't see how he can stand to go off and leave somebody like you."

She snickered. "That's because you ain't Eddie. He ain't the married kind. He'd go crazy if he couldn't get off and run around."

I wanted to ask her why in the hell she married him, then, but I bit my tongue and didn't.

Molly was in the sweetest, happiest mood. She kept glancing at me and smiling and she rubbed my hand between hers.

"Well, I'm just so glad to see you," she said, and in a minute turned around and kissed me. I held onto her for a long time, and then I figured I better tell her something for her own good. Only she knew what was on my mind agin.

"Don't be so scared," she said. "That's no way to make me happy. It's just us here, you know."

"I know," I said. "And you're the sweetest woman I ever had hold of, I don't mind saying that. But now listen. We got to get something straight. I'm married and you're married, and I ain't the shy old kid I used to be."

"Good," she said, grinning. "What's shy got to do with it?" She reached up and pulled a thread off my shirt collar and rubbed my neck with her hand.

"It's got a lot," I said. "This kissing and hugging is just inviting it. The state I'm in, it's whole hog or nothing."

"That's so nice," she said. "One thing I've always hoped is that you'd come over here some day ready to be whole hog in love with me. I hoped sooner or later you would."

That just flabbergasted me.

"Honey, good lord," I said. "I been whole hog in love with you for the last ten years. Maybe more. Surely you know that."

She looked me in the eye for a long time, a little sad, with one corner of her mouth turned up just a little. "I know you think so," she said. "But you haven't, Gid. You ain't even this morning, yet."

"Well, what do you mean, whole hog?" I said. It seemed to me, looking at her with her face so close to mine, that it was impossible to love a person more than I loved her, and the way she sent that cool look up at me made me mad. I could have hated her. It was a bad feeling; I felt myself getting mad, and I didn't want to.

"I mean just you loving me," she said. "And nothin' else. Just pure me and pure you. But you're always thinking about Johnny or Eddie or your ranch or your dad or what people will think, or what's right and what's wrong, something like that. Or else you're thinking about yourself, and how much you like me. Or else you just want to get me in bed. Or else you just like to think about having me for a girl. That ain't loving nobody much. I can tell that."

"Why, goddamn you," I said. "That's some way for you to talk." I was thinking about her marrying Eddie.

"That's the way I've always talked to you, darling," she said. "You ain't thinking about me, you're thinking about Eddie." She reached up her hand to my cheek and smiled, but I was too mad then to care; it was like my blood vessels had busted. I yanked her back across the cellar, I seen later where it skinned her leg, and held her down and kissed her. It's a wonder she didn't get fever blisters. And for a long time we stayed that way, and she kissed back, only I knew it wasn't working somehow, it wasn't convincing her of anything. I let up and looked at her: she felt warm but she still looked cool, and there was a terrible strain inside me; I didn't know what to do or how.

"Molly, what do I have to do?" I said. "You drive me half-crazy, don't you know that?"

"I wish I could drive you all the way," she said, holding my hand against her chest. I could feel her breathing.

"I didn't know you were like that," I said. "Why do you want to hurt me that way?"

"Oh, Gid," she said, and tears come in her eyes, "I don't want to hurt you. I just want you to turn loose of yourself for a minute, so you can hold *me*. That's the only thing I want."

She got upset then and cried and I was ashamed of myself for getting mad. At the same time I was still mad. I didn't see how she could go marry Eddie and then expect much of me. But I didn't want her sad.

"I just don't guess I know how to do that," I said. "If I did I would."

She sat up and wiped away the tears and smiled at me, her

cheeks still wet. "I know you don't," she said. "But maybe I can show you."

She took me in the house then, and it was nice and cool and shady, after the sunshine. I made her let me put some iodine on the big skinned place on her leg; it burned like the devil. I felt silly, to have done a rough thing like that. But Molly never mentioned it. I was all nervous and tense and jumpy and nearly sick, and she kind of loved it all out of me, like a fever. I was so upset that for a long time after we had done it I couldn't go to sleep or be still in the bed, but she stayed with me, I remember her face, and I finally did sleep and slept good. When I woke up the afternoon sun was pouring in the windows and the room was hot. Molly was still with me and was holding my hand against her chest. She had thrown all the covers back.

"You're a good sleeper once you get to sleep," she said. "You slept four hours without even turning over."

I pulled her down so my face was right against hers. "I'm not going to let you go," I said. "I'm going to give you everything I've got to give; you're the only person that's worth it. I don't know why you wanted to take up with somebody worthless like me agin, but it's too late for you now."

She swung her head back to get her hair out of her eyes, and it fell all over my face. I lay for a hour, I guess, smelling her and listening to her breath; I could tell she was pleased about something. She was a mystery to me, but I was glad I had finally pleased her someway. After a while the sun moved and the sunlight came right on the bed, so we were laying in a shaft of it, with a million little dustmotes in the air above us. Things looked lovely and funny for a change.

"I swear you smell like a gourd, Molly," I said. "I never noticed that before."

"Maybe I never smelled that way before," she said. "I'm starving, you stay here and let me get us something to eat."

I was pretty hungry too. Only not hungry enough to get up; I never felt so good and lazy in my life. Maybe I would just stay there in Molly's bed for a month or two. That would have set people on their ears. Molly crawled out and wound up her hair, standing by the bed with the sunlight across her stomach.

"You're a shapely hussy," I said.

She snickered and pulled on her Levis. I must have dozed off agin for a little while. When I opened my eyes she was sitting on the bed cross-legged, with just her Levis on, eating a piece of cornbread and drinking buttermilk. There was some for me, with a couple of pieces of cold chicken, sitting on a chair by the bed. It wasn't there long. When we finished there were cornbread crumbs all over the bed and Molly had buttermilk on her upper lip. I wiped it off with a corner of the sheet. I wanted her to lay down agin, but there were so many cornbread crumbs in the bed that it wouldn't do, so we both got up and I put on my pants and we went in the living room and sat on the couch and hugged and talked awhile.

"When I come over here today I was going to ask you a lot of questions," I said. "Like why you married him, and all that. But I've just about forgot the questions, and I don't guess I really care about the ones I remember. What do you reckon caused that?"

"Me, I guess," she said. She was eating a piece of stick candy she had found somewhere, and was slouched back against my arm without nothing on but her pants, just as relaxed as she could be, and in a perfect humor. She wouldn't let me have any of the candy, but when I kissed her now and then I got her taste and the candy's too.

"One thing I do want to settle, Molly. What do you want to do about these people we're married to? Do you want us to go off somewhere or anything like that?"

"Do you want to go?" she said.

"No," I said. "That's kind of against my style."

"I'm glad," she said. "Because I wouldn't go. Right here in this house is where I always want to live."

We got a quilt and stretched out together on the living room floor and stayed there till plumb dark. I just couldn't quite get my mind made up to go home, and she didn't hurry me.

"Gid, I'm ready to have a baby now," she said. "I'm convinced you'll make a good daddy."

"Good lord," I said, sitting up. It was all shadowy in the room; she rested her head against my chest. We sure didn't get very far from one another that day. I guess she had been as lonesome as me.

"You're a strange woman," I said. "How come you don't want your husband for its daddy?"

"Oh, Gid," she said, "he wouldn't make no good daddy. Not as good a one as you.

"You don't really care, do you?" she said, looking up at me. I could barely see her eyes, but her voice was real serious. "I mean if me and you have a baby. Of course I'll let on it's Eddie's, just you and me and the baby will know."

I thought about it a long time. Here I was married to Mabel and her to Eddie. It was strange to think of a baby coming out of Molly, but I knew one thing, if one did I wanted it to be mine.

"No, I don't care, sweetheart. I'd like for you to if you want to."

She curled around me. "I knew you'd come to me sometime," she said. And that was all we said that day. After a while I got up and dressed to go, and she walked out to my horse with me. We stood there awhile, looking at the Milky Way and the Big Dipper and all the rest of the summer stars. Finally I got on.

"I'll just get over when I can," I said. "Okay? I probably can't stay this long ever time. I sure will miss you."

"Okay," she said. "Me too."

I rode on home by moonlight; it was bright enough I seen a big old coyote loping into the brush ahead of me. I should have been thinking about a story for Mabel, I guess, but I was thinking about Molly instead, and what a tender sort of person she was. And yet she had something fierce in her, like Dad had in him. I saw her agin, all the ways she'd looked that day, hanging up clothes in the morning, with her shirttail out, and sitting on the couch that evening, without no shirttail atall. She had the most changing kind of face, for it always to be the same one. Riding across the League I run into Dad's old horse, and he nickered. I sure did miss Dad.

twenty-one

It was just amazing how seeing Molly ever once in awhile improved things for me. I begin to kinda take an interest in life agin. And I never seen a whole lot of her, either—I hardly ever got over more than once a week. Lots of time I was too busy, and other times, when I did ride over, I'd see Eddie's car and have to go back. There wasn't no sense aggravating him. But it didn't bother me too much if I missed seeing her one occasion or another. I knew that if I was a little patient, there would be a time when we could get together. Those times were worth the wait. Molly was awful good to me.

And good for me, too. In the meantime, between visits to her, I had the ranch to run, and Mabel to live with, and I began to see that I had better get busy and try to do a little better job of both than I had been doing. It wasn't fair to Dad and Mabel not to.

At first I was pretty worried that Mabel would find out I was courting somebody else, but that was just because I still didn't know Mabel too well. In those days she was so proud of herself I couldn't have convinced her I was in love with somebody else if I'd come right out and told her. Which I didn't. I was fond of Mabel, and a little sad for her, but not as torn up about marrying her as I had been. And I made her a pretty decent husband too. I got to understanding her a lot better as time went on. We never was much of a delight to one another, I had to admit that, but I know I treated her better after I took up with Molly. Mabel was just a combination of proud and scared; she never had anything, and she always thought she was entitled to everything. It made me blue that I couldn't be more wholehearted with her, but I just couldn't. She wasn't the one. But anyway, she kept such a close eye on herself all the time that she hardly noticed me. She didn't have much notion of what was going on with me, and a good thing she didn't. After I got over my first blueness and began to treat her about half-nice, she thought I was plumb crazy about her.

"Well, I see you're beginning to learn how to treat a lady," she said one night. It was after supper, and we were sitting on the porch. I had complimented her on her cobbler, or something like that.

"I guess I ain't had much practice," I said.

"Well, you can get a lot on me," she said. "And don't think I won't tell you when you make a mistake. I ain't bashful about that." She scooted a little closer to me on the step.

I put my arm around her and hugged her and never said a word. It was dark, and we could hear an old hoot owl hooting somewhere in the pastures to the east. There wasn't no moon that night, but there was a good breeze from the southeast, and the country smelled good. We done had lilac in the yard. Life always seemed so complicated in the evenings. Mabel seemed perfectly happy, and I was sitting with my arm around her, about two-thirds melancholy. "Let's go in, honey," I said, "before the mosquitoes get to biting." "Well, you've got to kiss me first," she said. I did, and then we went inside and lit the lamps.

twenty-two

Early in June I spent a hell of a day. Mabel woke up in a bossy mood and practically chased me out of the house, so I done the chores and doctored a few sicklings and then decided I'd go to Antelope. That was where we got our mail, then, and I thought while I was there I'd hire somebody to come up and thrash my wheat. We had a pretty fair wheat crop and I was ready to get it thrashed; it was the last farm produce I ever intended to raise.

I rode old Dirtdobber that day, and I guess that was a mistake. He was the oldest horse on the place, and I never rode him nowhere except to get the mail. I think he was twenty-three years old. When I got to Antelope I tied him up and gave him a good rest, while I talked with the boys a little. I found an old boy with a thresher, said he'd be up after my wheat the next day. While I was fiddling around it come up a real mean-looking cloud in the northwest, and I figured then I'd do good to get home without getting wet. Besides which, the Montgomery Ward catalogue had come that day, and it was so much extra weight I didn't know if old Dirt would be able to carry it. He was particular about weight.

But I stuck the catalogue in my saddle pouch, and we headed out. If it rained like it looked like it aimed to, that old boy wouldn't have to bother about my wheat. But I was wrong about the rain, it never rained five drops. What it did was hail.

And I mean hailed. It started out the size of plums and moved up to pullet eggs, and before it was done there was hailstones on the ground bigger than anything our old turkeys ever hatched. Course me and Dirt were right out in the open when it started, and getting him to run was out of the question. I tried holding the catalogue over my head, and dropped it in about two minutes. Finally we got to a little old half-grown post oak, and I figured that was the best protection we would find. I unsaddled right quick and crawled under Dirt and then under the saddle too, and scrunched down tight. The first thing Dirt did was try to piss on me, but I wasn't worried about that, I was worried about my skull. I jobbed him a time or two to cut him off and damned if the old sonofabitch didn't jerk loose and step right on my hip and run off. So far as I was concerned it could hail him to death; I wasn't going after him. I got on the downwind side of the tree and hid as much of me as I could under the saddle, and stayed put. At least none of the big ones hit my head. My saddle got dents in it that never did come out. It hailed for a solid hour. Finally I didn't have to worry so much, I reached out and raked me up a kind of igloo and was pretty cozy. I had one less worry anyway, and that was the damn wheat crop.

When it quit the country looked like it was under a snowstorm. The sun came out in a little while and started melting it off, but some of the big piles didn't melt for two or three days. I was in a hell of a shape; Dirt had about halfway squashed my hip. I could hobble along, but carrying the saddle and blanket I couldn't make no time, particularly over that slippery hail. I guess Dirt had weathered it all right; I seen him about half a mile away, poking along toward home. "You old bastard," I said, "wait till I catch you." But all I could do was hobble on over to the Eldenfelders', they was a Dutch family that lived about half a mile away. I hated to run the risk of getting dog-bit—they had about fifty damn mean turd hounds—but it was the only place in hobbling distance. However, it turned out all right. They fed me a little rotten cowmeat and sent their big old dumb girl Annie to haul me home. A lot of the boys thought it was smart to get in Annie's pants, because she was willing and about a half-idiot, but I never fooled with her. She seemed kind of pathetic to me. The creek was up, so that was as far as she got me, but I gave her a dollar. "Bye-bye," she said. It's a wonder she could drive the wagon. I waded the creek and went on home. My hip was beginning to unsquash a little by then.

Old Dirt was in the barn when I got there, trying to kick in the door to the oatbin. The old fart had so many knots on him I didn't have the heart not to feed him.

But when I got to the house I wished I was back outside in the hailstorm. The ten or fifteen broken windowlights hadn't improved Mabel's humor. I was thinking I might get a good hiprub, but I could have staggered in on two wooden legs and she wouldn't have cared. I didn't see no signs of supper, and I guess I said the wrong thing.

"Hello," I said. "What's for supper, hail soup?"

"I'll hail soup you," she said, "going off and leaving me in a storm like that. Where you been all afternoon?"

"Well, I been coming home," I said. "It wasn't a very quick trip, I'll admit."

"I bet you was," she said. "I bet you was sitting down in the Antelope domino hall, losing some of your inherited money."

I let that pass.

"Where's the mail?" she said.

"Wasn't none but the catalogue, and I lost that in the hail. I guess we'll have to get them to send us another one."

She got so mad it tickled me.

"What kind of a husband are you?" she said. "We'll do no

such thing. You just saddle up and trot back and find it; I want to do some ordering out of that catalogue before it gets too old."

"Why, you're crazy," I said. "Hell, it's beat to pieces by now, anyway. I imagine we can borrow one."

"We ain't going to borrow nothing," she said. "You go get it. You lost it."

I tried to grab her and hug her, hoping it would get her in a better humor, but she just stomped out to the bedroom, and I let her go. I got the milk bucket and milked, and when I got back, no sign of her. I cooked myself some bacon and eggs and ate supper. Then I washed the dishes, and still no Mabel. I went in the living room and did some figuring in my little daybook; I was thinking of buying three sections of land that joined us on the northwest.

About nine o'clock I heard her, and she came in in her bathrobe and nightgown, looking like she'd had a good nap. She was a shapely woman, too, when you caught her looking just right.

"Hi," I said, and she set down on my lap and kissed me and seemed fairly friendly.

"Where's the catalogue?" she said.

"Good lord," I said. "Ain't you forgot that yet? It's right where I dropped it, and that's where it's going to stay, as far as I'm concerned."

"Well, I knew you was ignorant but I never thought you was lazy," she said, and she jumped off my lap and went out the back door just boohooing. I would have swore she was crazy.

But I went out to get her; I didn't want her to run around barefooted and get on a snake. That would really aggravate her. When I came out on the backsteps she ran down in the storm cellar. It was pitch dark down there, and I went over and stood on the steps.

"Now, Mabel, come on out of there," I said. "There's no use in you taking on so over a damn catalogue. You'll get on a stinging lizard down there if you ain't careful."

"I hope I do," she said. "I hope they sting me to death, so I won't have to live with you."

I started down, and damned if she didn't grab a jar of peach pickles off the shelf and threw it; I heard it hit the steps below me and break. Then she threw two more, just whatever she happened to grab.

I thought what the hell, there wasn't no use in provoking her to ruin all the preserves.

"Okay," I said, "sleep down there if that's how silly you are." She didn't say nothing, so I went in and went to bed. There was a cot in the cellar, and it was a warm night; I didn't figure it would do her any harm.

Only I couldn't sleep worth a flip. I went back out twice more to try and persuade her, and all it did was cost me preserves. The last time I went was about three-thirty, and I just sat down in the kitchen and read the almanac till it got light. Then I went down in the cellar, and she was curled up on the cot asleep, peaceable as a baby. But the cellar steps looked like a cyclone had hit a jelly factory. I went in to cook breakfast, and I heard her hollering at me. So I went out.

"No, I ain't gone after the catalogue yet," I said.

"Could you carry me up these steps?" she said. "I'm barefooted and I'm afraid I'll cut my foot off on all this broken glass."

"No, I'm afraid to carry you, I might drop you and break your precious butt." I went and got a basket and a broom and the ashes shovel and cleaned up the mess, while she sat on the cot and watched. Then she came in and made coffee and never said another word about it. And for a day or two, she was sweet as pie.

twenty-three

One morning early in July a damn horse kicked a hole in the water trough, and while I was down patching it, getting wet up to my ears, I looked up and seen a horseback rider loping across the Ridge toward the barn. By god, if it wasn't Johnny, he'd come home, and he was riding the prettiest little sorrel gelding you ever saw. He called him Jack-a-Diamonds.

"Well, by god," I said, standing up to shake his hand. "Where'd you get that horse?"

"Bought him off a feller," he said. "How you been?"

"Oh, fair," I said. "How long you been home?"

"Since last night."

"You're walking just like a normal feller. You don't look crippled."

"I finally growed back together," he said. "This country sure looks good to me."

"Well, we had four inches of rain in May. Course we had that hail."

"Heard about that. See it smashed hell out of your wheat."

"What I get for raising it," I said. "Tie up your horse and stay awhile, I got to patch this water trough."

"I'll help you," he said, and he did. If he hadn't I wouldn't have got the damn thing patched by dinnertime. While we worked he told me a million funny stories; he was the same old Johnny. I was sure glad to see him back.

That night, of all things, me and him and Molly went coon hunting, and had a hi-larious time. Johnny's dad had a new coon dog he was proud of and Johnny wanted some excitement, so he asked me if I wanted to go with him to try the dog out. I said sure, and after supper I told Mabel where I was going and met Johnny on the Ridge. We decided to go over and see if Eddie was home, and if he wasn't to take Molly. She was there by herself, peeling potatoes in the kitchen, and she put on an old pair of boots and was ready in a minute. Johnny had brought the dog with him across his saddle, and we all struck off toward the creek, walking. It was a hot night with plenty of moon, but we took a lantern anyway.

"I hope we don't get snake-bit," Molly said. She had been bit once and was afraid of snakes. Sure enough we killed three rattlers that night, but we didn't have any close calls.

We hadn't been out thirty minutes when the dog treed a big old fat coon in a live-oak tree. I didn't much want to kill him, because we'd have to lug him around all night, but we went ahead and done it. After that we got pretty excited, and the dog soon struck another trail. Johnny had the lantern and the gun, and I had the coon in one hand and Molly's hand in the other, so I could help her through the brush.

"I like this," she said. "I'm glad you'all came by."

Then the dog treed in the shaft of an old hollow oak, and from the squealing we heard it was a momma coon and two or three little ones. We never brought an ax, but the old tree was just barely standing, and me and Johnny pushed it over. Only no coons come running out.

"Now what?" Molly said.

"I'll stomp it open, I guess," Johnny said. About the time he said it the momma coon went scooting out the open end of the tree, right between Molly's legs. She jumped about three feet. I had the gun and couldn't shoot for Molly, so it was up to the dog, and he let the old momma get plumb away. He was a good dog for treeing, but he wasn't worth a shit for fighting. She got in the creek and he didn't have the backbone to go in after her.

"Don't you all kill the little ones," Molly said. "I want one for a pet."

"Sure," Johnny said.

We blocked up the open end and then Johnny stomped a hole in the old rotten wood. One little coon jumped right out into the dog's mouth, and that was all for him. I got down on my hands and knees and managed to grab another one by the neck and drag him out. He was nearly half-grown though, and I sure needed something to tie him with. Baling wire was what I needed, but that's the way, when you need baling wire you can't find it and when you don't need it you're tangled up in it.

"Do you think you can gentle him?" I said, holding him out so Molly could see.

"Probably not," Molly said.

Then Johnny yelled. He had kept his foot in the stomp hole, so the other little coon couldn't run out, only he discovered that his foot was stuck. I wasn't very worried.

"Pull your boot off," I said. "Or sit down or something."

"Hell no," he said. "If I was to sit down wrong, I'd break this hip agin and be laid up in the hospital another three months. My heel's stuck. See if you can stomp more hole."

Molly and me thought it was funny; we stood there and laughed. Only I didn't laugh long. The little coon that was in the log decided it was time to come out, and he did, right up Johnny's leg. Johnny yanked backward and fell a-spraddling. The coon went right over him and off, and the dog never seen it. I got so tickled I forgot I was holding anything, and the little coon I had whipped around and bit clear through the palm of my hand. When he turned me loose I was glad to do the same for him. I howled like a banshee.

So Molly didn't get no pet, and we went home with just one and a half coons and a cowardly dog, but we had fun anyhow. When we got to Molly's she bandaged my hand and we sat up in the kitchen, eating all the stray food and talking over old times. We were all in high spirits and Johnny told us a lot of stories about life on the plains. Finally me and him slept awhile on her living room floor, and about sunup she came in in her nightgown and bathrobe and woke us up and cooked the best breakfast I ever ate. We did her chores for her and about six o'clock rode off toward home, with Molly standing by the yard gate with a milk bucket in one hand, watching us go.

There was a big dew that morning, and the country looked as green and sparkly as it ever had in July. We stopped our horses on the Ridge and talked about the grass and the cattle for a while.

"Well, are you home to stay?" I said. "Did you quit your job?"

"Yep, I'm here for good," he said. "You need a hand?"

"Boy, you bet," I said. "If you want a job you can start today. And live in our bunkhouse and we'll board you if you want to."

"Fine with me if it's okay with Mabel," he said.

I said it was. We hadn't said two words about her.

"Course you might be ready to go in business for yourself," I said. "I wouldn't want to stand in your way if you do."

"I am in business," he said. "The cowboying business. You can have the ranching business; I don't want no part of it."

"Okay," I said.

"I'll go home and tell my old man and get my stuff," he said. "See you after while."

And him and old Jack-a-Diamonds went off along the Ridge west in a long easy lope, neither one of them carrying a care in the world. I just about envied Johnny, but I didn't quite. He was the most carefree, but I thought I had a few more good things than he had. I meant to swap him out of his horse, though. The sun was drying up the dew, so I got rid of Molly's bandage and went on home and ate another breakfast.

twenty-four

Johnny sure made a good hand. Me and him got things done in a day that I would have fiddled around with a week if I had been by myself. Besides, he was enjoyable to work with. At least most times. Sometimes he was the most aggravating feller I knew. Ever once in a while he acted like he still intended to try and court Molly some, but I didn't figure he'd get very far with that.

Having him to do the cow-work left me more time to get ambitious, and the land bug began to bite me pretty bad. I had already decided that land was something I'd never have enough of. So one day I buckled on my spurs and rode to Wichita to the bank and borrowed enough money to buy them three sections that joined me on the northwest. They were a good place to start extending. I had a deed drawn up and took it with me for the other feller to sign, and started home.

I rode hard that afternoon; the automobile was broke down or I would have gone in it. The weather was terrible—it was late August—and I didn't need no thermometer to tell me it was over a hundred degrees. When I crossed the Taylor place I decided to take the deed up and show it to Molly. I was proud of that deed, and I already knew Eddie wasn't there; I had looked that morning.

Molly was, though, ever inch of her, and she couldn't have

looked better to me if she'd been Lily Langtry. I knocked at the back door and went on in, and she was just turning away from the stove. She had been putting up the last of her garden stuff.

"You're about as hot as I am," I said.

"I'm glad you come," she said. "Let's sit down and cool off."

I drank a couple of dippers of water out of the water bucket. She sat down at the table and I offered her a dipper full.

"I believe I will," she said, and she took the dipper and tilted her head back and drank. She had really been working: the arms of her shirt were sweated halfway down her side, and the tip ends of hair around her neck were wet. Her old shirt was plastered to her stomach. But she looked like the real thing to me; when she took the dipper down I leaned over and kissed her and she reached up to put her hands behind my head, so the dipper dripped water on my shoulder.

"You know why I'm glad you come?" she said. "I've been saving something to show you."

I grinned; I sure felt good. "What have you got I ain't already seen?" I said.

"This, Gid," she said, standing up. She grinned to herself and pulled the ends of her shirttail up and stuck her stomach out at me. It didn't look much bigger than it ever had, but it looked a little, and I got the message. Besides she grabbed me and hugged me.

"Don't that make you glad?" she said. "We've got one started. That makes me so proud. It's just what I've been wanting."

I didn't know what to say. It was okay with me, but I wasn't wildly happy about it, like she was. I was more excited about the deed.

"Why sure, Molly," I said, "if it's what you been wanting. And it's ours for sure?"

"It's ours for sure."

There was nothing else *to* say. She was happy enough to faint; she just sort of slid on me.

"Well, sugar," I said, after it was too late for it to have done any good, "I don't know about all this. You're so excited about it, we want to be careful and not jar it loose."

"This bed's just a puddle of sweat," she said, crawling over me. "I'll get some water and sprinkle us, so we'll be cooler." She brought in the dipper and sprinkled the sheets with me in them, and then sat down by me and caught my hand.

"It won't jar loose," she said. "I'm so glad the first one is yours. I wouldn't have wanted anybody else's to be the first."

"Honey, you're an awful strange woman," I said. "There ain't another like you in the world."

"That's okay," she said.

"See how this stretches the elastic," she said, sticking out her stomach agin when she started dressing. She had just got into her underpants.

"I thought it was supposed to make women less exciting," I said. "It sure hasn't you."

She flopped back on the bed and laughed a big one. I liked the way Molly laughed. "These sheets are still nice and cool," she said. I was done half-dressed but I lay back down a minute and grinned and kissed her.

"And you're my honey," she said. In a minute we got up and dressed. I showed her the deed, but it didn't impress her a snap's worth. But I must have impressed her a little; she wouldn't hardly turn loose of me that day.

"Gid, have you got time to see what's wrong with my windmill?" she said. "It just barely has been drawing lately "

"Sure, come on out with me," I said.

"I'll be out in a minute," she said. "I want to pin up this old hot hair." She raised her arms to pin it.

I got a pair of pliers and a couple of wrenches out of her tool box and climbed to the top of the pipe. It was just the sucker rod loose, and I tightened it in two minutes. But I didn't climb down, I rested a minute on the crossbars while I waited for Molly to come out. Dad was the only thing missing in life; I hated it that he had missed such a good year for cattle; it was just the kind of year he had always waited for. From where I sat I could see my new land.

I had my hand on the top of the pipe, and the damn rod went down and mashed my finger before I noticed. I damn near fell off, but caught myself. I had a blood blister to suck, and a big one. Some grayish clouds were building up in the northwest, so we might get rain.

Molly stepped out on the back porch, buttoning her shirt, with her hair pinned up high in a knot and her neck looking cool.

"Come on down," she said. "I'll get a crick in my neck looking up there."

"I'm surveying my new land," I said. "Except for your place I own everything west of here that I can see."

"You and your land," she said, "you ain't getting mine. Come on down here to me." She was shading her eyes and looking up.

So I climbed down. "I like to pinched my finger off," I said. "I better get on home before I get in more trouble."

She took my mashed finger and put it in her mouth and wet it; the finger still stung but I didn't much want to go home.

"You're supposed to kiss it," I said, "not slobber on it."

"I can't feel him yet," she said. "I ought to pretty soon."

"One of these days I'll repipe your windmill," I said, and then I remembered Eddie. Molly looked a lot thinner with her hair up on her head; it made her look cool and tender.

"I see you ain't interested in babies," she said. "Come with me to milk. It's cool enough now."

I got the bucket. The old brindle cow was already in the lot, waiting.

"Want me to milk?"

"No, she don't like strangers. You'd have to hobble her." So I put the feed in the stall and old Brindle went in. Molly got out her milking stool from under the trough and set down on it and went to milking. The old cow was an easy milker, but she kept switching her tail at flies and hitting Molly in the face. I got tickled.

"Here," I said. "I'll hold her tail." The old cow never noticed.

"If she ever steps on your foot you'll learn to wear shoes," I said. I squatted down by her and put my free hand on the back of her neck, where her skin was cool. I slipped my hand on under her shirt and rubbed her back and belly a little; a trickle of sweat slid along her ribs from her armpit.

"I wish I understood you," I said. "I never know just what you want from me. You'll make a good milker yourself." I felt in front and she grinned.

"I just want your loving and a little less conversation," she said.

We left old Brindle in the lot, eating prairie hay. I carried the milk bucket and she put her arm around my middle; we walked up to where my horse was tied. I set the milk bucket over in the yard and came back and kissed her bye. She poked her belly against me, but I got on my horse anyway, and she stood there grinning, fiddling with her shirttails.

"Aw, I'm glad, Molly," I said. "I just got this new land on my mind. I better go, I'm getting lonesome for you and I ain't even left yet."

"I guess I know what's good," she said. "Say hello to Mabel."

"I will, you say hello to Eddie." It was a kind of joke. If either of us actually did it, it was her; she was just that crazy.

"If I come by agin in a day or two, will you chase me off?" I said.

"That's one thing I've never been guilty of," she said. The little barn swallows come out and begin to flitter around, and she looked up at them. "I love the cool of the evening," she said.

I loped across the hill and left her standing by the fence, fiddling with her shirttails. It was strange riding off from Molly; I never done it in my life that I didn't want to turn and go back a dozen times before I got out of sight. She always stood right where you left her, as long as she could see you. I remembered her in the kitchen that afternoon, all sweaty and loving, drinking the dipper of water and her throat wet. I felt like Molly was just as permanent as my land. Old Denver wanted to tear out for the barn, but I held him to a lope and we got to the lots just as the sun was going down behind the Ridge.

Ruin hath taught me thus to ruminate,
That Time will come and take my love away.

SHAKESPEARE, *Sonnet 64*

RUIN HATH TAUGHT ME ☼ II

Johnny came in one afternoon and caught me crying. I had been listening to Kate Smith.

"My god, cheer up, Molly," he said. "You're going to ruin the oilcloth."

"Sit down," I said. "I know it's silly." I got up and poured him a cup of coffee, and he blew on it awhile and didn't say anything, and finally he reached over and squeezed one of my hands.

"Now look, quit this stuff," he said. "It's a beautiful day. You ought to be out making a garden instead of sitting in here like this. What brought it on?"

"Oh, the radio," I said. "Listening to Kate Smith. Ever time I do that I get blue." And not because of her, because of the songs. "God bless A-mer-ica, land that I love . . ."—she always sang that. I just wanted the war over and my boys home. My boy home.

"Aw, quit listening to all this patriotic stuff," he said. "It's just depressing. And it don't do no good."

"You make me mad," I said. "It wouldn't hurt you to be a little more patriotic. You ain't gonna cheer me up talking that way. I just wish we knew something definite about Joe."

He rubbed my hand and drank his coffee.

"Well, I do too, honey," he said. "He was my boy too. But imagine he's dead; be better for us to face it. Missing over a year. We can't just sit here and quit."

He made me get up and go outside with him, and he was right, it was a real pretty day. Being outside cheered me up. We sat on the cellar awhile and he took his hat off and put his arm around me.

"I knew you'd smile sooner or later," he said.

"Look how tall my corn's getting," I said. "Three more weeks and I can cook you some roasting ears. Where's your boss today?"

"He's off trying to buy him another ranch for me to take care of," he said. "Gid's plain land-crazy."

"Well, you just let him go ahead." Johnny was always trying to slow Gid down. "Everybody's some kind of crazy." It was so clear we could see half the county. May was usually my favorite month.

"What kind of crazy are you?" Johnny said.

"Just plain crazy," I said. "I haven't got enough brains to be any other kind." Then he leaned over and kissed me; I figured he was getting about ready to. He'd had it in his mind ever since he came in.

"Well, Molly, I'm woman-crazy," he said, holding my shoulders and grinning his old reckless grin. He tickled me. I couldn't help loving Johnny, even when I wasn't much in the mood for him. Even when he was acting the soberest there was something about him that was like a boy; he never lost it, and it was one of the nicest things about him; when he was around I could have a boy and a man in the same person. Not like Gid at all—Gid never had been a boy; I guess his dad never gave him the chance. And that was why Jimmy was so much harder for me to raise than Joe. I never had any trouble handling Johnny and Joe.

"You want to help me tie up my tomato plants?" I said. "I might as well do that today."

"Well, now, you might as well not, either," he said. "I'd like to be treated like company for once, not like a damn hired hand. If I'm going to have to work, it had just as well be for Gid. He pays me."

"Pardon me," I said. "You was the one that mentioned gardening."

"Yeah, but you had the war blues then. Actually, why I'm here, I came a-courting." He kissed me agin; he was so funny.

"Why yes, honey, I'll marry you," I said when he quit. "Just let me go get my pocketbook so we can pay the preacher."

That always embarrassed him, even if he knew I was kidding. If there was ever a bachelor, it was Johnny McCloud.

"Aw hush," he said. "I'd just as soon marry an alligator."

It really got off with Johnny when I mentioned marrying; I should have quit doing it. I guess Gid kidded him about it all the time, and he was probably ashamed of himself for not wanting to marry me. If he had ever really asked me, I could have really turned him down, and he wouldn't have felt that way any more. I wouldn't have married agin anyhow; Eddie was enough husband for me. At least not Johnny. Gid I might have. But that was a different story.

"Well, I guess the tomatoes won't get tied up," I said, and took his arm. I wasn't too eager to go in the house with him then—for one thing, it was so pretty outside—but he was eager to go with me, so it was okay. I was the only woman Johnny had ever been able to count on, and I usually tried to give him what he needed—it wouldn't have been very loving of me not to.

He had a big ugly-looking blue spot on his hip where he said a horse had pitched him off against a tree stump, and I went in the pantry and got the liniment and made him lay back down while I rubbed some on it.

"You're sure nice to me," he said. "I'd have probably been a cripple years ago if it hadn't been for you."

"It don't take much to rub on liniment," I said. "You could have done that much already if you weren't so careless of yourself."

"It's so much more pleasant when you do it," he said. "You can rub my back a little if you just insist."

That was another difference in Johnny and Gid. Once Johnny got in a bed, no matter for what reason, he'd think of excuses to stay there for hours on end. Gid was just the opposite. You practically had to tie him down to keep him in bed ten minutes. I had been trying to break him of it for nearly twenty years; I hadn't made no progress, and in fact I'd lost ground. When we were both younger I could entice him to relax once in a while, but the older we got the less luck I had. Mostly, I guess, it was because Gid had so much energy he couldn't hardly stay still; but partly it was because he was ashamed of himself for being there in the first place, especially if it was in the daytime. At night he wasn't as bad, but then I never got to see much of him at night.

Not Johnny. He could lay around and enjoy himself for hours.

"Say, Molly," he said. He was lying there watching me; he was such a watcher it tickled me sometimes. "What'll you take to patch my britches pocket before I get them back on? I'm afraid I'll lose my billfold and all them valuables in it."

"I may not have any blue thread," I said.

"That's all right, I ain't particular."

I put my brassière on and patched them for him, while he dozed. His clothes were always just on the verge of being worn out; I think he just wore that kind when he visited me so there would be something for me to patch. I watched him sleep. Joe had his features to a T, and his eyes, and his recklessness; if he hadn't had the recklessness he wouldn't have got in no bomber crew to begin with. But that pleased Johnny. One day after Joe had already been reported missing, Johnny told me he'd rather have a dead hero for a son than a live coward.

"I'd rather have Joe than either one," I said, and I don't think he knew what I meant. Men don't think like women, or maybe it's that they don't feel the same kind of feelings. Gid had said practically the same thing to me when Jimmy got sent to the Pacific. And the boys were the same way, I guess. Joe actually enjoyed living over in England and flying in the bomber. I guess he had a million girl friends over there; I was always afraid he'd marry one of those English girls and bring her home to Texas and not know what to do with her. In his letters he never mentioned things like that. "How's the place, Momma?" or "What's Gid and Johnny doing?" or "Momma, I sure do miss your cooking, these army chefs sure can't cook like you. Why don't you send me some cookies?" Letters like that. Joe was the liveliest kid in the world, and the best natured. I waited till he was sixteen to tell him Johnny was his dad—it had bothered Jim so much when he found out Gid was his. But it tickled Joe flat to death. I imagine he pretty well suspected it anyway, but when he grinned at the news I cried for half an hour I was so relieved. I doubt Johnny and him ever talked about it. They usually just talked about horses and ballplaying and rodeos, things they were interested in. They probably never even mentioned it. Things like that just didn't worry Joe like they did Jimmy.

Johnny was sound asleep. He was woman-crazy all right, at least where I was concerned, and he tickled me the way he let me know it. But he wasn't as crazy as he had been. One time years before he had come charging into the kitchen in such a hurry that he hadn't even seen me and knocked me flat on my back—it scared Jimmy to death. I guess the time was coming when Johnny wouldn't barge in on me in the afternoons, and I would miss that, mood or no mood. I put the needle in the pincushion and got back in bed and made him turn over so I could lay against him, under one of his arms. I never did doze off, I just lay and looked out the window and counted Johnny's pulse once in a while, for the fun of it. It looked like a cloud was building up in the south. Ever once in a while Johnny would grunt like a hog, just one grunt, and then be quiet agin. One time straightening out his leg he stratched me, so I jumped; he was the worst in the world about toenails. Once I gave him a pair of clippers and he kept them about two days and broke them trying to cut a piece of baling wire. The arm I was holding had his watch on it, and when it got to be six o'clock I got up right quiet and put on my dress and cooked supper. Steak and gravy and black-eyed peas was about all we had, but I had a few fresh onions from the garden, and Johnny loved fresh onions.

When I went back to the bedroom the room was full of shadows, except for the one west window where the last of the sunlight was coming in. I sat down on the bed and gave Johnny a shake.

"Get up if you want any supper," I said.

He opened his eyes and stretched. "Aw hell, you're done dressed," he said, and grinned.

"You heard me," I said.

"We ain't wrestled in a long time," he said. "You want to?"

"Not specially," I said. "I've lost my girlish strength."

"You never had none, you was just awful wiggly," he said.

I went on and set the table and he stomped around dressing and washing up for ten minutes before he ever showed himself in the kitchen.

"Boy, where'd you get them onions?" he said. "Have you milked?"

"No," I said. "You can milk while I wash the dishes."

"These dishes won't need washing," he said, and they didn't much.

He went to the barn with me but I did the milking. He let the cow in and made conversation, but milking was a little beneath his dignity. Gid would grab ahold and do anything, but Johnny was finicky about the things he worked at. A lot of that rubbed off on Joe, only I never let Joe get away with it. One time I sent him out to hoe goatheads, and when I went out to see about him he was playing with a stick horse and hadn't hoed a lick.

"What are you doing?" I said. "I thought I sent you out here with a hoe."

He had really worked his nerve up by that time. "Momma, go to hell," he said. "I'm riding. Cowboys don't hoe."

"I'll cowboy you, sonny," I said, and I did. Johnny, he laughed about the whole thing and just made Joe worse, so the next time he came loving up to me I told him a thing or two. "Go court your horse," I said, "cowboys don't fool around with girls."

"Aw, honey, now you ain't mad at me," he said, but he didn't get nowhere that day.

When I finished the milking Johnny opened the gate so old Muley could go out, and I started to the house with the milk bucket. He came up and put his arm around me and made me slosh some milk out on my foot, so I gave him the bucket to carry.

"I never was no hand at milking," he said. "Think of the time it's saved me."

The only time I ever got Johnny to do chores was the winter after Eddie got killed, when I come down with the flu so bad. Gid and him took turns with my chores until I got over it. Both the boys had it too.

It was a warm, pretty evening. I strained the milk and Johnny poured himself some coffee. I got a jar of plum preserves and opened it for him; he loved to drink coffee and eat plum preserves. After he had spit about a hundred seeds into his coffee saucer I took the jar away from him and put it back in the icebox.

"It's a wonder you haven't took sugar diabetes, as much sweet stuff as you eat," I said.

"It's a wonder I haven't tooken something worse than that from associating with old widow women like you," he said.

I walked over behind him and squeezed his neck a little. "I always get old after supper," I said. "In the afternoon I'm still young and pretty."

"I've noticed that," he said. "I wonder why it is."

We sat around awhile and then he put his hat on and we walked out to the back gate. There were plenty of stars showing, but there was a good bit of lightning back in the west.

"Well, I guess Gid's bought him another five sections by now," he said. "It's all I can do to keep him from working me to death. You'd think a man forty-seven years old would begin to slow down."

"Gid got a late start," I said. "He didn't really catch hold till after his dad died."

"He's making up for it."

"Tell him to come and see me," I said. "I don't get to see too much of him since they moved to town." And when he did come by he was in such a hurry I didn't get to talk to him long.

"He comes by often enough without me telling him to," Johnny said. "I'd just as soon not encourage the competition."

"How are him and Mabel making it?" I said.

"Oh, they're having trouble, Molly. But when ain't they? At least now they got a house big enough that they can kinda keep out of one another's way."

"I'm sorry," I said. "Gid deserves better."

"I think so too," he said.

"We never heard the news tonight. I forgot about it."

"We didn't miss nothing," he said. "You keep up with this war stuff too close."

"Well, you're an American," I said. "Don't you want to know what's happening?"

"Not particularly," he said. "When the Japs or the Germans cross the county line, then I'll be interested."

I didn't say no more; it was a sore spot with us. There was no changing Johnny. But I think he was sorry he said it, because he knew it made me blue.

"I 'pologize, honey," he said, patting my arm. "I didn't mean to hurt your feelings. Sure enjoyed the meal."

"I'm glad," I said. I kissed him on the cheek and he got in the pickup and started off. Then he stopped and leaned out the window.

"Much obliged for patching them pants," he said.

"You're welcome." He bounced on across the hill, hitting all the bumps. I could see the taillights bouncing. Johnny was a sorry driver and so was Gid. Joe and Jimmy could drive circles around either one of their dads. I stood by the fence until the taillights went out of sight. It seemed like I'd spent a lot of my life watching Gid or Johnny or one of the boys drive off across the hill. That was all right. I enjoyed being there where they could find me if they took a notion to come back—and they always had. After I watched the clouds awhile I decided it wasn't stormy looking enough to worry, so I went in and went to bed.

two

It wasn't but a few nights after that that it come a real bad cloud. Just before I went to bed I stepped outside to look around, and it was as pretty a night as anybody could want—I could see ever star in the Milky Way. I went back in and read a piece or two in the *Reader's Digest* and went to sleep. When I woke up the wind was blowing a gale and the limbs of the old sycamore tree were thrashing against the roof. I got out of bed and made sure the windows were all down, and then went out on the back porch to see if I could tell anything about the cloud. The wind was out of the southwest and just about took my nightgown off. That was too much wind to sleep under, so I went back to the bedroom and got my bathrobe and a pillow. There was a cot with several quilts on it already made up in the storm cellar; I had learned long ago to have things like that ready.

I sat down at the radio a minute and tried to get a weather report, but all I got was static. Anyway, the way the sycamore thrashed was weather report enough. I put an apple in my pocket, in case I got hungry, and shut the back door good when I went out. Just as I stepped off the porch the big raindrops began to splatter me; there was an awful wind, and a big old tumbleweed came swooshing across the yard from the south and bounced right into me. In the dark I never seen it coming, and it scared me, and stung a little, but I got loose from it and went on to the cellar and shut the door after me. The sandstone steps felt cool on my feet; it was pitch dark. I had a kerosene lantern sitting on a table, but before I could work my way over to it I stumped my toe on an old pressure cooker that was sitting on the floor. I never could remember to throw it away, and I stumped my toe on it practically ever time I went to the cellar. From down there I could still hear the wind singing, but it didn't sound dangerous; nothing sounded dangerous from down in the cellar. I lit the lantern and looked through the quilts to be sure there wasn't no stinging lizard in them. The cellar was clean, and there never had been many stinging lizards down there, but it never hurt to look; not near as much as it hurt to get stung. Then I blew out the lantern and snuggled down in the quilts and ate my apple. It was a nice sweet one and smelled fresh, like it had just come off the tree that day.

When I got done I dropped the core under the cot. I had such a good taste in my mouth; it was one thing I liked about apples. Lately I had got so I always belched peaches, so I didn't eat them much, except in homemade ice cream. I felt nice and cozy and relaxed snuggled in the quilts, and I wasn't too worried about the storm. Where cyclones were concerned I was awful lucky. One time one went right between the house and the barn, and all it done was turn Dad's old wagon over; it never even hurt the chickenhouse.

I thought I would doze right off to sleep, but I didn't. I lay there wide awake. It began to rain real hard; I heard it beating against the tin door of the cellar. After I lay there thirty minutes or an hour I knew I was going to get real blue before the night was over, and in a little while I began to cry. I didn't even try to stop myself. At first I was just barely sniffing, but then all my feelings rushed up to my chest and my head and I heard myself crying over the rain on the door. I was crying so hard I thought I had fallen off the cot; when I was coughing and trying to get my breath I pulled back one of the quilts and felt the canvas with my hand, so I hadn't fallen. My breasts just felt like empty sacks. I turned the pillow over on the dry side and cried some more hard crying, and finally I quit and pushed the pillow off the cot and lay on my stomach with my head on my arms. I was all upset and knew I wouldn't go to sleep, but I didn't feel any more like I was going to die.

There was no cure for being upset that way; I just had to grit my teeth and wait for the feelings to die down. Being lonesome itself was just part of it—mostly I couldn't stand not having anybody to do for. I never was happy when I just had myself to do for, or even when I had somebody else wanting to do for me. That was nice, but that wasn't the main point about loving, at least not with me. The main point was having somebody I could let my feelings out on. And I couldn't do that very well at a distance, I needed to have somebody right around close, so I could touch them and cook for them and do little things like that. It was always men or boys, with me. I never knew a woman I cared for—not even Ma. Men need a lot of things they don't even know about themselves, and most of them they can't get nowhere but from women. It was easy to do for them, most of the time, and it made me feel so comfortable. A lot of times it wasn't easy, of course, but it still felt better to try. With Johnny and Joe it was easy; they were just alike and

needed exactly the same kind of handling. With Gid it was sometimes awful hard because Gid was too honest; he never would fool
himself or let nobody else fool him, even if it was for his own good.
I tried it enough times to know it couldn't be done, especially if he
was having hard times with Mabel. It had nearly always been hard
with Dad, and with Eddie, and it was hardest of all with Jimmy,
who was just Gid times two. At least Dad and Eddie liked themselves, even if they didn't like me, and I could figure out what to
do from that. But Jimmy, he never liked himself or me, and that
made life hell for him. And he hadn't changed. Wherever he was,
over there in the Pacific, he was wishing he was somebody else's
son besides mine. I never even put my hand on Jimmy, not even on
his arm, after he found out that Gid was his daddy, and that I was
still letting Gid and Johnny get in bed with me. Only I wasn't letting them come, I was wanting them to: Jimmy didn't know that, or
didn't understand it, but if he had he would have just hated me
more. I blame some of Jimmy's troubles on religion, but I can't
blame them all on it; I have to blame most of them on myself. If I
had married Gid instead of Eddie, Jim might have been a happy
boy. But if that had happened, Eddie would have killed Gid, or Gid
and Johnny would have fell apart, and there might not have even
been a Joe. I don't know that I done very wrong. But I know that
Jimmy's miserable; some of the time I am too. Four men and two
boys were what I'd had for a life, and laying there on the cot I
could picture every one of them, plain as day. But there wasn't a one
of them I could get my arms around, and right then, that was what
I wanted; I would rather have been blind and had the touch than
like I was, with just the picture.

Everybody gets hard nights, though, I guess. It wasn't the first
time I'd ever felt sick with my feelings, and I wasn't girl enough
to think it would be the last. When you lay around feeling cut off

from folks, crazy things go through your mind. I would see men's hands and faces and other parts of them, sometimes even their stomachs, Eddie's or Johnny's or Gid's. Probably if I had gone on and married Johnny, it would have been good for both of us, but he wouldn't have done it, even if I had really wanted to. He was too responsibility-shy. Besides it would have made Gid feel terrible; he had wanted to marry me all his life.

Once I almost decided to marry Gid—I guess I was just jealous of Mabel. We were in my bedroom.

"If you've got the guts to quit her, I'll marry you," I said. "If you don't, I wish you'd quit wishing out loud."

That was when Gid was having terrible times at home, and when I said that he looked like he was about to split in two.

"Honey, you know it ain't a matter of guts," he said. "If I didn't have that much guts, I wouldn't be here now. But I don't believe in divorcement—it ain't right. If Mabel wants to do it, she can. I ain't going to."

"If it was conscience, you wouldn't be here," I said. "So I still think it's guts." I talked awful to Gid sometimes; I don't know why he didn't choke me. I would nearly drive him crazy.

"Well, let's just be quiet for a little while," he said. "Honey, I got to go in fifteen or twenty minutes."

That made me feel terrible, and I pulled him over to me. We had some rough times, me and Gid, a lot rougher than any I ever had with Johnny. Or with Eddie either. Nothing was rough with Johnny, and when things were bad with me and Eddie it was just because he plain enjoyed being rough and mean to women; I was hardly ever hard on him like I was on Gid. Sometimes I hated Gid, and I never felt that strong about Eddie one way or the other.

After I had cried enough, and thought about things enough, I finally did go to sleep. It wasn't good sleeping—I felt like I had fever, but I guess I would have slept all morning if Gid hadn't been good enough to come by and see about me. First thing I knew someone was banging on the cellar door. Down where I was it was still pitch dark.

"I'm down here," I said. "You can open the door."

Bright sunlight fell on the steps and across the foot of the cot, and I seen Gid's old boots on the top step and knew it was him.

"Well, thank goodness," he said. "Can I come on down? I was scared you'd blown plumb away." He took another step, so I could see about to his knees.

I sat up and pushed the hair back out of my face. "My lord," I said, "I've overslept. What time is it, Gid? I bet the milk cow thinks she's forgot."

"Oh, it's not too late," he said. "About seven. I can get them chores for you. Can I come down?"

"Please come on down here," I said, pulling the quilts up around my middle. "Did the house blow away?" He came on down the steps, I seen his legs and his belly—he was getting a little bulge—and then all of him, standing there kinda grinning at me but looking like he had been worried. Gid was always my favorite; sometimes when I seen him the delight would shoot right through me, as sharp sometimes as a sting.

"Well, Molly, I sure was worried about you," he said. "I heard on the five o'clock weather report there was two tornadoes sighted out this way."

"Oh, sit down here," I said. "I'm all right." And when he sat down on the cot I couldn't keep from hugging him. He hadn't shaved that morning, and I felt the bristles on his face against my neck and his arms squeezing my sides; it made me feel good clear to the bottom. He was tense and tight as a drum. Gid always came to me tense. I held him and rubbed my hand on his neck and down his back, and in about two minutes he kind of sighed and let things loosen inside him.

"I don't know what I'd do if you was to blow away," he said.

"Hush," I said. "I won't." I made enough room on the cot that he could lay down by me; it wasn't comfortable, but for a few minutes it was okay; I felt like myself agin. Then Gid got embarrassed that I would think he came for bedroom stuff—as many times as he had come for that he still got embarrassed if he thought I knew it—and he sat up.

"Well, I never meant to come out here and go back to bed," he said, picking his hat up off the floor.

"I guess you're the silliest man alive," I said. "Maybe that's why I love you so much. When you were young I didn't think you were silly at all."

I got up too and slipped my bathrobe on and we went up the steps and outside. The yard grass was wet and cool against my bare feet, but it was a clear day, and the sun was drying things up fast. I guess it was the latest I'd slept in two or three years. There were a lot of broken limbs and leaves and tumbleweeds in the yard, and it had blown a few shingles off the roof, but I didn't see any serious damage. Gid went around the house, inspecting everything, but I felt too good to worry about wind damage; I stood by the cellar, yawning and stretching the kinks out of myself, soaking up the sun. Gid went in the house and got the milk bucket and came and stood by me a minute. He had a look on his face that meant he really wanted to spend the day with me but wanted to do fifty other things too.

"'I'll go milk," he said. "I never ate breakfast in town, I could eat with you. I got a million things to do today."

I rubbed my head against his neck; it embarrassed him a little.

"Go on and milk," I said. "I'll get breakfast. But you needn't be planning on rushing off."

"I got to, Molly," he said. "I just wish I didn't."

I went in and cooked a big breakfast, eggs and bacon and biscuits and gravy, and pretty soon he came in with the milk. We sat down and ate.

"What do you hear from Jimmy?" he said, while we were drinking coffee.

"Nothing." And that was all he said during breakfast. I knew he was getting up his nerve to leave.

"Well, that was a good breakfast," he said, pushing back his chair. "I hate to eat and run, but I guess I better. I got many a mile to make today."

"Don't leave this morning, Gid," I said. "Just stay around here."

When I came right out and asked him, flat like that, he had to at least look at me. He was too honest just to dodge behind his hat.

"You need me to help you do something?" he said.

I could have slapped him for saying that. I needed him to help me live. "No," I said. "I just like to be around you."

It was like I had run a needle into his quick. He shoved his hands in his pocket and shook his head. He didn't say anything, and I sipped my coffee.

"I'm glad you do," he said, finally. "I'd like to stay a month. But you know what I'm up against. I've got a few more obligations than you have."

I felt miserable for being so hard on him, but I got harder in spite of it.

"Okay," I said. "Come back next time there's a storm."

"Aw, now be fair," he said, and I could tell he was trembling. "I got things I *have* to do; I'm a husband. Can't you understand that?"

"I understand you ain't going to stay," I said. "It's pretty plain what you don't want to do." Before I could finish saying it he had stepped over and yanked me out of the chair so quick I didn't even see his hand, grabbed my hair and yanked my head back so tears sprang out of my eyes, and my face was about two inches from his. But after he held me that way a minute his hands began to tremble.

"I'm sorry, Gid," I said, and we walked outside together and stood in the yard.

"I'm the most worthless white man alive," he said. "I'll stay a week."

"No, honey, go on and work," I said.

"You got some gloves? We might as well patch up them old corrals of yours."

We went down to the barn and he got out the tools, and we spent the whole morning patching on the lots, putting a new board in here and there and resting with one another and doing odds and ends and talking. We just piddled, and enjoyed it. Then I fixed him a big dinner and about two o'clock hugged him and sent him on. He was thinking about taking me in the bedroom but I didn't encourage him; if he had that day, he would have been down on himself for a month and wouldn't have come to see me all that time. If we held off, he'd be back in a day or two, when he felt easier, and and it would be better for him. Gid was a complicated person, but I had been studying him a long time, and I knew his twists. We had given one another a lot of good times, of one kind or another, since that summer I got pregnant with Jimmy. That seemed an awful long time ago. I guess the times we spent together, the good ones, not the bad ones—there were enough of them, too—were the best times either one of us ever had.

Three days later, about the middle of the afternoon, Gid came back over. I had been working in the henhouse all day and was sweated down, but I was still glad to see him. I wiped off my face and took him right in the house.

three

One day about the middle of June a man from up around Vernon came by and wanted to sell me some alfalfa hay. I hadn't bought any alfalfa in three years and it sounded cheap enough, so I told him to go ahead and bring me ten ton; he said he'd be there with it the next day.

That afternoon about three o'clock I put on my overalls and got the hull fork and climbed up to see what I could do about cleaning out the loft. I didn't want the men to have to do it when they got there with the hay. It was a pretty hot day for that time of the year. I turned on the faucet at the water trough and washed my face and got a big drink before I climbed up. Working in the loft was like working in an oven.

I opened the loft doors at both ends, so there would be a little ventilation. There was plenty to do, I seen that. The loft probably hadn't been cleaned out since Dad built the barn. The wastage and chaff from all the hay we'd put up was about shin deep, all over the loft, and it was full of all kinds of mess that Dad had left around and I never had bothered: baling wire and hay hooks and buckets and whatnot. I got to poking around, and there was every kind of nest you could imagine in the old loose, dry hay. Rats' nests and mice nests and cats' nests and barn owls' nests and possum nests and probably even a skunk nest or two, if skunks can climb. Many a time, in the winter, I would go up in the loft and find a big old momma possum curled up in the hay, snoozing where it was warm.

There were fifteen or twenty rotten bales of leftover hay that wasn't good enough to feed, so the first thing I did was get a hay hook and drag those over and shove them out the north loft door; that way the milk cows could find them and eat what they wanted of them. I left one bale, to sit on.

Moving the bales was work itself, and when I got done I could feel the sweat dripping down my legs and down my sides. I drug my sitting bale over by the south door where I could get some breeze, and rested awhile. From the loft I could see way off south, to where Gid's fence line ran across Idiot Ridge. I wisht I could see more of Gid. I missed him when I didn't get to see him regular; but I guess he came over ever time his conscience would let him. I never had been able to talk Gid out of his conscience, or love him out of it, either; I had tried both ways. Me and Gid were in a situation where neither one of us could completely win, and I used to wonder why we let ourselves get that way. Maybe we didn't—I don't know that there are situations where you can completely win. Not where you can completely win something important.

A lot of medium-sized thunderheads were blowing around in the sky, so that patches of shadow would come over the pastures and sometimes right up to the barn. Then the clouds would go on north, and it would be bright and sunny till another bunch came along. When I had rested enough I got up and took the hull fork and went to raking the wastage out the loft door. The old stuff was so matted down that it made hard raking. I was always scaring out rats; most of them run along the rafters till they found a hole and went down into the saddlehouse or the oatbin. When Jimmy and Joe were little boys they used to take their rat terrier up in the loft and let him kill rats; it was how we lost that dog, actually. One day he ran a big rat out the loft door and went right out after it. The dog broke his neck and the rat got away. Joe come running up to the house, screaming; he was just heartbroken. It was the first time anything he loved had died. I picked Joe up and ran down to the barn and Jimmy had already carried the dog over by the post pile and was digging a hole to bury him. He was crying, but he wasn't hysterical. He had had one dog die of a rattlesnake bite. Joe couldn't understand why he was putting Scooter in the ground.

"We don't want the buzzards to eat him," Jimmy said, but Joe didn't know what a buzzard was. He had crying fits for three weeks after that.

I had raked out the east side pretty thorough and was trying to make a start in the northwest corner when my fork struck something that made a glassy sound, and, of all things, I fished up one of Dad's old whiskey jugs. It surprised the daylights out of me. No telling how long it had been back in that corner. It was still corked, and had whiskey sloshing around in it. Nobody had touched it since the day Dad set it in the corner.

I laid my hull fork down and picked up the jug and went back to my sitting bale. I felt real strange. Picking up the jug brought Dad back to me, and it gave me the weak trembles. Dad's beard and his hat pulled down over his eyes. When I pulled out the stopper and put my nose to the mouth of the jug, the strong whiskey fumes went right up my nostrils and made my eyes water. His eyes and his eyebrows and skinned-up hands and yellow fingernails and two broken-off teeth and the gray hair under his hat, around his ears. The whiskey smell was Dad's smell: I never got close to him in my life that I didn't smell it. The night Eddie and Wart brought him in out of the smokehouse they didn't even pull off his boots; Gid had to do it after he came.

For a while I sat by the bale, just holding the jug. It was brown, that thick glass kind. The outside was dusty, but the dust hadn't got through the stopper; it hadn't even rotted much. If I had drunk the whiskey, it would have made my tongue numb in a second. Twice in my life Dad had made me drink whiskey, and it scalded my throat both times. The first time I was just a little girl, three or four years old, and Johnny and his dad came over. The men were drinking. I don't know why they did it, but they caught us kids and made us each take a swallow of whiskey out of a tin cup. We cried and then ran off down to the pigpen together, me and Johnny; that was the day we got to be friends. That night Dad got me on his lap and teased me. "How'd you like that likker?" he said. "You want a little more? You can have some if you want it." Momma had done gone to bed. I hugged his neck big so he wouldn't make me drink any more.

The other time was years later, three or four years before he died. I had slipped off somewhere with Eddie while Dad was gone to Henrietta. Dad got back first, and when Eddie and me seen the wagon we knew he'd be mad. Eddie wouldn't come in with me; he let me off at the barn.

"Hell, he's your dad," he said. "You can handle him better than I can."

But I couldn't, really. When I went in the kitchen and told Dad where I'd been, he grabbed me and like to whipped the pants off me with his razor strap.

"When I leave you at home," he said, "I want to find you here when I come back."

My feelings were hurt and I hurt from the whipping too and wanted to go to bed, but Dad felt lonesome and sorry for himself and he made me sit up till midnight, keeping him company. We sat at the kitchen table and he poured me a big glass of straight whiskey and told me not to drink it too fast and not to leave till I drank every drop of it. I vomited half the night.

There was only one time in my life when I ever drank whiskey of my own accord, and that was the afternoon Eddie told me he wanted me to miscarry Jimmy. He didn't know I was pregnant by Gid, either; he thought it was by him. I cried and argued and argued with him about it.

"Shut up arguing," he said. "I told you before we started all this I never intended to have no kids. All the time I was growing up I had them little brothers and sisters of mine under my feet constantly, and I don't intend to fiddle with no more kids. They're just trouble. You should never have let it happen. If you don't get rid of it yourself, I'll take you to a man who'll get rid of it for you."

"What kind of a man is that?" I said. "And how do you know about him?"

"I done rung the bell a time or two before, in my life," he said. "It cost me fifty dollars, both times, but that's a damn sight cheaper than raising a goddamn kid. If you're smart though, you can save us that fifty dollars. Go horseback riding a lot."

"No, I want to have him, Eddie," I said. "I won't have any more, but I want to have this one." I was crazy about Gid in those days; he was all I could think about.

"I told you what you better do," he said, finishing his beans. "And you better do it, if you don't want no operation. Because I'll take you if I have to drag you, you can believe that, can't you?"

I could believe it. Eddie was just like Dad when it came to doing what he made his mind up to do. The only way to stop either one of them was to be stronger than they were, and I never was that strong, at least not physically. Once in a while I could stop them another way.

That afternoon I cried and cried. I could already feel Jimmy kick against my belly. Then I got one of Eddie's whiskey bottles and kept mixing it with water and drinking it till I guess I got drunk. My head felt like it had smoke in it, and everything in the house looked funny. I decided I would try to get Gid to run away with me, and if he wouldn't, I'd run away myself. I had fourteen dollars of Dad's money that Eddie had never found. I figured I would catch a train to Amarillo; that was where Gid and Johnny went when they ran away. I guess I was crazy. I changed clothes three or four times that afternoon, trying to decide what to wear to go see Gid. And I never had that many clothes; I changed into some twice. When Eddie came in I just had on an old cotton slip and was down on my hands and knees fishing under the sink trying to find a tow sack or something to use for a suitcase. I must have been drunk; I never knew Eddie was in the house till I felt his hips jammed against my behind and his hand around my middle. But I knew it was his hand; nobody's hand behaved like Eddie's.

"I'm glad I got me a wife that goes around half-naked," he said. "That's the most exciting kind."

I was crazy, I didn't even know what he was saying. "Eddie, have you seen a sack?" I said. "I need a good big sack." For a while he wouldn't even let me back out from under the sink; I couldn't even raise my head.

"Sack, my eye," he said. "You don't need no sack, sugar-doll," and his hand gave me fits and he got to wanting to kiss me; then he let me out. I couldn't get it out of my head that I was leaving; I wouldn't even know he was kissing me till he would quit for a minute. I had to vomit a lot that day too. When Eddie woke up he told me I could have the baby.

"I learned something today," he said. "It's more fun wallowing around with you when you're pregnant. I never knew that before. I wonder why it is?"

I was feeling so bad the news didn't penetrate to me till later.

"I guess it must be the tilt," he said. "The tilt's a lot better this way. I hope it keeps on improving, I like to have something to look forward to."

I guess it did, because it was him wallowing that made me start with Jimmy, when the time came. I never even tried to get him to quit; that wouldn't have worked with Eddie. The day the baby was born he left and didn't come home for three months, and that meant that Gid could come every day or two. I was happy. And Eddie liking the tilt so good made things a lot easier when Johnny got me pregnant agin, three years later. Otherwise Eddie would have either beat me to death or left me, then and there. Or both. If there was one thing Eddie never had much of, it was patience with me.

And Dad never either. Smelling the whiskey made me think of things about Dad that I hadn't thought of in years. He always felt the worst when he was the nearest sober; I guess it just took whiskey to make life look good to him.

One of the worst times I ever had with Dad in my life was the afternoon he told me and Richard about the facts of life. It was four or five years after Momma died; I was about seventeen. Except for one trip to town when I was a little girl, I had never been farther away from home than the schoolhouse. Eddie wasn't even in the country then, and since we were all too big for school, I didn't see Gid or Johnny more than a few times a year. Once in a while they would stop at the windmill for a drink of water. I had never even thought of having a boy friend—my brothers were the only boys I really knew.

And it was the same way with the boys—none of them ever had a girl friend till after they run away from home. Richard never, I'm sure; he only went to the schoolhouse two years. Me and Mary Margaret were the only girls he ever saw, and him and Mary Margaret fought like cats and dogs.

One evening I was rolling the flour to cook the supper biscuits, and Dad came in and sat down at the table. It was March or April, and the sand had been blowing; Dad's hair was full of grit, and he sat at the table and stratched his head. He never said a word to me. I started to ask him if he wanted me to give him a haircut; I gave all the haircuts my family had, as long as I had a family. Except for one burr haircut Joe got while he was in high school; it made me mad because he sneaked around so about it.

But Dad didn't want one. He was in a strange kind of mood, and I didn't bother him. I was getting ready to grease the biscuit pan when Dad went to the back door and yelled at Richard. In a minute Richard slouched in.

"Just leave them biscuits awhile," Dad said. "Come back here with Richard and me." They went off down the hall, and I wiped some grease off my thumb and followed them. They had gone into Daddy's bedroom and it was the biggest mess in the world. Dad never even let me make the bed.

"Shut the door," Dad said. He sat down on his bed and pushed back his hat. He sat there about ten minutes, just thinking, and I wanted to get back to my biscuits.

"What did you want, Daddy?" I said. Me and Richard were just standing there. Except Richard wasn't impatient. He never was.

"I guess Richard's old enough for me to show him a few things," he said. Neither one of us had any idea what he was talking about. Finally he grinned at Richard.

"Take your pants off," Dad said. It didn't surprise Richard; I guess he thought he was going to get a whipping, was all; he took off his overalls. It had been cold and he still had on his long johns.

"My god them's dirty underwear," Dad said. "Take them off too."

"Aw, it's cold," Richard said, but he started unbuttoning, anyway. In those days me and Richard and Mary Margaret all slept in the same bed—just Shep got to sleep by himself—and I had seen

Richard pee a million times, so he never thought of being embarrassed just because of me. I was just a little bit embarrassed—not so much that as worried, because Dad was acting so strange. Richard was cold-natured and got goose bumps all over his legs.

"Now, Molly, get your clothes off a minute," Dad said.

I had been about to giggle at Richard's goose bumps, but that surprised me. "Why do I have to?" I said. I knew better than that. Dad looked at me for the first time since he'd come in.

"The next time you ask me why when I tell you to do something, you'll get a real tanning," he said. But he wasn't mad, he was just warning.

"What all did you say take off?" I said.

He was cutting himself some tobacco then. "Ever stitch," he said. "I need to show Richard about women, and you're the only one around. Hurry up."

That was the first time I ever felt funny being around a boy. I took my pants and shirt off, but I sure did want to keep my underwear.

"I'm cold too," I said. "Ain't this enough, Daddy?"

"I'm gonna warm you in a minute," he said. "I told you what to take off."

I still had on long johns too, only the legs were cut out of mine. I went ahead and took them off and stood there naked, holding my underwear in front of me. Dad never looked at me, but I felt awfully embarrassed; it was a strange feeling. Then Dad noticed I was holding my underwear and he snatched it out of my hands and threw it down on the floor. That made it worse.

"All right, now, Richard, looky there," Dad said, nodding at me. "That's how they look." Then he looked me up and down himself, a real long look. "Molly's a real pretty gal," he said. "You're lucky to get to see such a pretty one. She's a damn sight prettier than her momma ever was."

"What am I supposed to look at?" Richard said. "All I see is Molly, and I know her anyway." If it had been anybody but Richard, I would have been even worse embarrassed. There wasn't no harm to Richard.

Dad laughed. "You ain't looking good," he said. "Come up here by her and squat down where you can see. See where that hair's growing on her?"

I didn't know what to do with my hands. I knew Dad didn't want me to cover myself up with them. Finally I held them behind me. Richard had squatted down by me and was really looking.

"Oh yeah, that's where she pees," he said. "I see that. Why's all that hair grow there? It's on me, too, but not as much."

"That's to make it hard to get into," Dad said. "The thing to remember about it is that's where you make babies, right up in that crack."

"It don't look like a big enough place," Richard said. "I'm still cold without my pants."

"Stand up here," Dad said. "You can just stay cold. You ain't much of a boy, anyhow. Make him stiffen up, Molly, so I can tell him how it works."

I knew what he meant, or thought I did, and I didn't move. I didn't want to touch Richard.

"Take ahold of him," Dad said. "He don't know the first thing."

"No, I don't want to," I said. "Richard don't want me to, either. He understands it, he's seen the bulls."

"You're the contrariest damn girl I ever saw," Dad said. "Do like I told you."

Richard's was hanging there, about arm's length away, but I knew I wasn't going to touch it, not even because Dad said to. In a minute I started to cry, and tears were running down my chest and stomach.

"I'll give you something to cry about," Dad said, and stomped out. I knew he was going after the razor strap, and I couldn't think of anything to do, I just stood there crying. But the minute Dad left Richard's got stiff. When Dad got back it still was. Richard and me were both surprised.

"Well, did she help you?" Dad said, when he seen it.

"Naw, it just done it by itself," Richard said. "I'm sorry. I never meant for it to." He was as embarrassed as me.

"Why, hell," Dad said, "that's what I've been trying to get you to do. Now you see, when it's like that it fits the crack in Molly. And most of the time it makes a baby, so you got to be careful where you shove it."

"You mean if you don't put it in you don't have no babies? Then why do people have babies anyway?" Richard said. Richard had a hard time understanding it. But I did too. I just stood there wishing it was over.

"Because it feels so good when it's up in there," Dad said. "You'll feel it some day."

Richard perked up at that; he loved to feel good. "Oh," he said. "Then can I try it with Molly right now? I'd like to know just how it does feel."

Dad hit him across the behind with the razor strap.

"No, and get your pants on and get out of here," he said. "I've shown you all you need to see. You don't never do it with your sister; not never. And you better remember that."

I reached to pick up my underwear, but Dad shoved me back away from it.

"I'm going to have a little talk with you," he said, and Richard left.

"Why didn't you do what I told you to?" he said.

I tried to think of a good answer, but I couldn't. I didn't know why, actually.

"I don't know, Daddy," I said.

"Do you want me to whip you with this razor strap?" he said, standing up.

I shook my head. But I knew he was going to.

"If I brought that boy back and told you to do it agin, would you mind me this time?" he asked.

I thought about that a long time. From the way Dad looked I knew about all I could do was take up for myself. Besides, I didn't want to touch Richard.

"No, I wouldn't," I said, "I sure wouldn't."

"I'll make you think wouldn't," he said, and I got the worst whipping he ever gave me. But I never did say I would, and he finally quit. He would always quit if I took up for myself long enough. Sometimes it was real hard to do, and it was hard then.

Of course Richard was a pest after that. Dad had got his curiosity aroused, and he soon forgot the part about not doing it with his sister. He pestered me for two solid years. But he wasn't no danger; he was just a nuisance. I could always fight Richard off.

Dad always expected his kids to mind him without asking no questions, and whenever I got in trouble it was always for not minding, or for asking questions first. But I still thought he was an awful good daddy, and that's what Johnny and Gid could never understand. They never liked Dad; neither did Eddie. But all they seen was his rough side. Dad never went around making over me, but I could tell he liked the way I fixed things and took care of him. It used to make me blue that I was the only one he had to love him. Momma and him wasn't suited for one another; Dad was rougher on her than he was on any of us. The boys all hated him because he worked them so hard, and Mary Margaret couldn't stand him.

Him and Eddie did manage to tolerate one another, I guess because they both liked to drink whiskey. Likker was the only thing Dad ever gave away; mostly because he liked company when he drank. And Eddie liked free likker. He took advantage of Dad that way.

Once Dad even told me that if I got married, to marry Eddie.

"He ain't much count," he said. "But at least, by god, he'll treat you like a wife ought to be treated. He won't pussyfoot around with you, I'll tell you that."

That may have been part of the reason I married Eddie. We hadn't never been considered respectable, and he hadn't either. Eddie and Dad were a lot alike; they never tried to get ahead like most men do. They spent their time trying to enjoy themselves, and a lot of the time they were miserable anyway. All Eddie's folks were living in Arkansas, and he never had a soul to look after him or take up for him.

I had liked Johnny ever since I knew him, but I never took marrying him serious. He wasn't the marrying kind, and we both knew it. So it was between Gid and Eddie. I liked Gid better, and there were times when I stayed upset for days, trying to make up my mind to marry him. Sometimes I wanted to so bad I could taste it. But I thought Eddie needed a wife the worst—I was dead wrong about that. And then I thought I was too wild and bad ever to suit Gid; I was afraid if I married Gid everything I did would disgust him—and I was dead wrong about that. I married Eddie, and everything I did disgusted *him*, and nothing I did ever made Gid stop caring for me. I'm more like Gid, in the long run, than I am like Dad or Eddie, but I was years and years finding that out.

I wasn't just sorry for Eddie, either; I was crazy about him sometimes. I was just crazy about him, about the way his hair was always shaggy and curly on the back of his neck. That may have been what I liked best about Eddie; it may have been why I married him, silly as that is. He never got a haircut and I was always dying to put my hand on the back of his neck.

But thinking about old times never got no loft cleaned out. I finally stoppered the bottle and got up, and then I pushed the sitting bale out the loft door, so I wouldn't be tempted to sit down and daydream no more. It was four-thirty or so, and cooling off, and by the time I got the west side of the loft raked it was six or after, and milking time. I stood in the loft door and wiped the sweat off my neck and face with my shirttail and watched the milk cow come up. When I got down I hung the jug on a nail in the saddle shed, with the whiskey still in it. It was good and aged, there wasn't no use pouring it out. While I was milking Johnny drove up in his pickup and I talked him into staying for supper with me. He wasn't very hard to persuade.

four

I hadn't got a car till 1941. Besides being expensive and dangerous, I thought they was just plain ugly. I couldn't understand why so many people took such an interest in them. Both the boys were big car-lovers, of course: the first hundred dollars Jimmy ever made he spent on an old rattletrap Hupmobile. He run it for three years and sold it to Joe for fifty. From that time on they were both on the road constantly, going somewhere. I just let them go. Them driving didn't worry me like me driving. They grew up in a time when cars were the thing, and they knew enough about them to handle them okay.

After I had driven two years I got so I could wrestle the car to town and back without any serious danger, unless the road was slick or I met somebody in a narrow place. Gid and Johnny had taken me to Wichita and advised me when I bought the car. It was a Ford, a black one. We looked at about fifty, and it was the one Gid said I ought to get. I was enjoying the company, and I didn't care. Johnny was in a hi-larious mood that day.

"I wisht you'd get that red convertible," he said. "A widow like you needs a car like that to haul her boy friends in."

"I wouldn't mind it," I said. "I think I'd like one open, so I could climb out if I needed to."

"You'd need to if I was with you," he said. We had stopped to drink coffee and Johnny had drunk beer instead. It was old watery café coffee, so I wisht I'd drunk beer too. I was feeling good that day. We all were.

Gid was solemn as a judge though until we got the car bought. Spending that much money, even if it wasn't his, always made Gid sober. Just to tease him I made them take me around to the Cadillac place, and I even got out and went in. They had the nicest salesman we met, too; I would have just as soon bought one of his cars. But Gid rushed me off.

"Whew, I'm glad to get out of there," he said. "He'd have sold you a limousine in another ten minutes."

"Well, I guess if I had wanted it I'd have bought it," I said. "It's my money, you know."

"I know," he said. "But it won't be long."

After we bought the Ford he loosened up a lot and we went to a big cafeteria and ate lunch. Johnny cut up with all the waitresses; it's a wonder they let us stay. Gid was just cutting up with me.

"Well, we got that done, we can enjoy ourselves," he said.

After dinner they flipped a coin to see who would drive me home in the new car, and Gid won. Johnny didn't care. He took off in Gid's car, and I bet he went right to some beer joint and tanked up.

Gid had on new boots and a new gray shirt that day, and he looked fine and handsome. He was just getting rich then; anyway he had a lot of confidence in himself. It was before Mabel made him move to town.

"Well, since we're here," he said, "let's just make a holiday of it. You want to go to a picture show?"

"I guess so," I said, "I'm just with you."

So we went and he bought some popcorn and we sat right in the middle of the theater, and Gid put his arm on the seat behind me, so that when I leaned back I could feel it against my shoulders and neck. It was such a comfortable feeling, and once in a while he would put his hand against my neck or my hair. Nobody else made me feel comfortable that way. I don't remember what the picture was, or what it was about. I never can remember picture shows; most of them are so silly, anyway. When we came out of the dark show the sun was so bright I could hardly see, and he had to practically lead me down the street to the car. It was a shiny, new-smelling car then; after I'd hauled chicken feed in it for a month or two it smelled different.

Gid drove, and we rode out of Wichita toward Scotland, into the open country. I took off my neck scarf and unpinned my hair; the bobby pins were hurting my head. It was nice to get out in the country agin; so far as I was concerned, Wichita Falls was the ugliest place on the earth.

"Drives like a good car," Gid said. "Just stiff. You bounce it over them old dirt roads awhile and it'll get broke in."

189 • RUIN HATH TAUGHT ME

"It better be good," I said. "I intend for it to last me the rest of my life."

My hair itched from being pinned up all morning, and I combed it out while Gid drove home. It was early fall. The boys had both volunteered in August, and they were still in boot camp. After that Jimmy got sent to New Jersey and Joe to California. All the way across the country from one another.

"Well, I guess the boys are doing okay," I said. "The worst thing they've complained about is the cooking."

"Oh, have you heard from both of them?" Gid said.

"No, just from Joe." We were past Scotland, over in the dairy-farming country; I began to notice milk cows grazing in the pastures. "But he said Jimmy didn't like the cooking either."

Gid was looking blue.

"Don't get depressed, honey," I said. "We've had such a good day. There's nothing we can do about him now."

"Well, I wish we could think of something," he said. "I wish we could make it up to Jimmy someway, whatever we done wrong."

Gid's little girl Sarah was six years old then, and Jimmy had been on his mind a lot longer than she had. She was a cute little girl, but you could sure see her mother in her.

"You know we can't," I said. "We'd have to do over our whole lives. We just have to hope he'll outgrow hating us for it."

"Oh, he don't hate us, I don't guess, does he?" Gid said. He couldn't stand to think that. I had lived with Jimmy, and got so I could stand it long ago.

"Oh yes," I said. "He does. I'm just surprised he hasn't killed us."

"The army might change him," he said. "He might be a little more tolerant when he comes back."

I was looking at my comb. There were some hairs stuck in it, and the sun through the windshield was turning them golden. I was wondering how I would have been if I had been a blond; even worse, I guess.

"It won't change Jimmy," I said. "Any more than it would have changed you. We could have changed him if anybody could, and we didn't."

I had begun to cry. He wanted me to scoot over by the wheel, but I wouldn't do it. I sat by the door till after we turned off on the dirt road, and all Gid could do was pat me on the knee with his hand and try to watch the road.

When we got about a mile off the highway, out with the pastures on both sides of us and no cars anywhere, he stopped and pulled on the emergency brake—it squeaked, and it still squeaks—and took out his handkerchief and moved over by me and wiped my face. I took his hat off and laid it in the back seat; he done had some gray in his temples.

"You oughtn't to cry," he said. His handkerchief was plumb damp; I took it and put it in my purse, so I could wash and iron it for him. I looked out the window when he hugged me. I had my knees up in the seat, and he pulled back my skirt a little and rubbed his hand down the calf of my leg.

"If it was Mabel, she'd have on stockings," was all he said.

In a little while he drove on and I scooted over by him and finished combing out my hair. It was such a pretty afternoon, so cool and sharp and clear.

When we got home I let Gid know I wanted him to come in with me, but he was ashamed from thinking about Jimmy, and wouldn't do it. Gid's car was there and Johnny's pickup was gone, so he had beat us home.

"You don't have to go," I said. "Nobody will come."

But he stood on the back porch and kissed me and wouldn't

come in the house. It was me he was ashamed of, someway. He wasn't very often, but when he was it hurt me like a nail.

"You can stay," I said.

"I know I can," he said. "But, Molly, I better not."

I turned and walked off from him, into the cold house; one of the few times in my life I walked away from Gid like that. I guess he left; when I came out to milk he was gone. It made me feel terrible, because I knew he was mad at himself and in the awfulest misery, but there was nothing I could do about it but wait till he came to see me again. It was two months, two of the worst ones I ever spent. But he came back, and I made it up to him. Then for maybe six months he came every day or two.

The night we got the car, though, Johnny came, and for once in his life wished he'd stayed away. I was sick of myself and sick of ever body that night, and it was a lot more than Johnny could handle. I would wake him up and say terrible things to him. Finally he got his clothes and left. In three or four days I went over and found him and apologized, and it was all right.

Who needed to have been there that night was Eddie. He would have really thought I was nasty if he could have spent that one with me. I would have run him off too, or else he would have laid me out with a poker. Maybe that was what I tried to provoke Johnny into doing. Eddie might have done it; he wasn't scared of being mean.

Of all the boys and men I loved, Jimmy was the one I completely lost. His eyes and the way he went about things was Gid to a T; everybody knew it, and that made it worse. Eddie was dead before Jimmy got big enough for it to show, so it never bothered him. Actually it didn't bother Gid too much; he was proud of

Jimmy, and couldn't help showing it. Mabel thought I was so trashy anyway, she was probably glad to have Jimmy and Joe for proof.

But it broke Jimmy. He was too smart to try and fool. Maybe the boys made fun of him—he and Joe both had lots of fights. Joe never minded them. Jimmy did. Jimmy was crazy about me till he was eight years old. Then he wasn't sure about me from then till he was thirteen. When he was thirteen I told him Gid was his daddy; then he was sure about me, and he hated me. He had been the most loving little boy; for eight years I couldn't turn around without him being around my neck, and when the coin turned he was just that hard a hater.

When he was ten or eleven his teachers at school started him going to church. There was a man teacher that liked Jimmy a lot—his name was Mr. Bracey—and for a long time he drove out ever Sunday and got Jimmy and took him to church and Sunday school, and then brought him home. He never even asked to take Joe—it was always Jimmy—but Joe didn't care. He probably wasn't in a church five times his entire life. And in the long run, Mr. Bracey done Jimmy more good than harm. I never was mad at him, even after Jimmy told me what he done. I never told Gid about it.

But it was the church people that really turned Jimmy into a hater; the more he took to religion, the more he turned against me.

When I told him Gid was his daddy, he didn't bat an eye. We were sitting at the table.

"I'm never going to call him Daddy, though," he said.

"I didn't mean for you to. I just wanted to tell you."

"I'm not ever going to call him anything," he said, and he didn't. Gid tried his best to get Jimmy friendly with him; he offered to take him cowboying and fishing and lots of places, but Jimmy wouldn't go. When he was real little he idolized Gid, but after he found out, Mr. Bracey was the only daddy he had.

Jimmy was the only person I ever saw I couldn't have a little effect on. Even Dad I could help a little, and even Eddie. But I might have been a stone so far as Jimmy was concerned.

He had friends, though. Him and Joe were always close brothers, in spite of being so different, and Jimmy had plenty of other friends, too. He went out for all the teams, mostly just to keep from coming home and doing chores, but he made them all. They tell me he was an awful good player; the whole town bragged on him. He was twice as good as Joe; he went out too, but he never took it seriously, and was just medium. I never went to any of the games Jimmy was in, because I knew he didn't want me too. I did see Joe play a few times.

Jimmy and me only talked about things once. He had been off to a religious camp one summer and they convinced him he was going to be a preacher. I didn't have much to say about it—I kept thinking about how much his grandaddy would have said. Gid didn't like it, but he never said a word about it. Johnny kidded Jim a little, but it was all right. Jimmy liked Johnny in spite of himself, and Johnny's kidding never made him mad.

But one Sunday night Jim come in from church. I guess he was eighteen or nineteen then, and I was sitting in the kitchen shelling peas. It was summertime, and I got up and fixed him a glass of iced tea. He tolerated me enough to drink it. I guess his resistance was down that night; he started asking me questions.

"Have you ever been to church in your life?" he said. "I just want to know."

"Oh yes," I said. "I used to go to camp meetings."

"Don't you like it in the Lord's house?" he said, looking at me through Gid's very eyes.

I didn't know what to say, except no, because I didn't, really.

He kinda looked down his nose.

"The minister says I ought to bring you to church so he could try and save you," he said. "But I don't think I will. You wouldn't go anyway."

I tried to grin, but it was hard. "No, I wouldn't go," I said.

"Molly, you don't believe in salvation, do you?" he said. Once in a while he called me just by my name, I guess to hurt me. He didn't like to call me Mother. But I couldn't stand him calling me Molly, as if he were just my friend.

"Jimmy, if you can't call me Mother don't call me anything," I said. "I mean that. Honor your father and mother, ain't that in the Bible?"

He didn't say a word; looked at the sugar in the bottom of his tea glass. His forelock fell down in his eyes and I kept wanting to reach out with my hand and brush it back out of his face.

"I don't guess I do believe in church salvation," I said.

I went on snapping the little peas and shelling the big ones, and he sat across from me a long time without saying a word. When I looked up from my fingers he looked me in the eye. He was like Gid; he always looked you in the eye when he hurt you.

"You committed adultery and fornication," he said. "That's about as bad as a woman can get." When he said it, though, he sucked at the corner of his mouth, and looked like a little boy trying not to cry.

"You don't know how ashamed I am of you, Momma," he said. "I'm so ashamed of you I can't tell you."

I let the peas alone. "You're telling me, Jim," I said. I would have given the best touches of my life to have been able to hold Jimmy then. I probably would have died right there if it would have taken what was bothering him away, but I knew nothing that easy would happen. He couldn't say any more, and I was choked up so I couldn't talk. We just sat.

"Fornication and adultery is what you did, Momma," he said.

I guess what he wanted was for me to deny it, to tell him I hadn't really done neither one, and that everything the preacher said about me was wrong. I sat the peas on the table.

"Jimmy, those are just two words to me," I said. "Even if they do come out of the Bible."

"But you did them," he said. "In this house we're living in, too."

"I wasn't saying I didn't," I said. "And I wasn't saying I'm good. I guess I'm terrible. But words is one thing and loving a man is another thing; that's all I can say about it." And that was true. The words didn't describe what I had lived with Gid, or with Johnny, at all; they didn't describe what we had felt. But Jimmy hadn't felt it, so I couldn't tell him that and make him understand.

"There's such a thing as right and wrong," he said. Like his daddy used to say.

"I guess so," I said. He wanted me to argue, and I just couldn't. I felt too bad and worn out. I wanted to cry and never shed a tear.

He finally got up and went to the door. "Yes, but there is," he said. "And if you live unrighteous, you'll end up turning on a spit in hell." He sounded like a little hurt boy trying to convince himself. It was silly to think of turning on a spit the way I felt; I couldn't be seared no worse than I was. In a little while I went on and shelled the peas.

Him and Joe left for boot camp about two weeks apart. Johnny and me took Joe to the train in Wichita, and I would have taken Jimmy, but he wouldn't let me. He hitchhiked, and he walked the three miles over to the highway, too; he wouldn't even let us take him that far. When he was out on the front porch ready to go I gave him twenty dollars but I didn't try to kiss him. He said good-by and walked out of the yard and off across the pasture without ever looking back. Just before he went over the Ridge he shifted his suitcase to the other hand.

I sent him a lot of cakes and cookies. He probably wouldn't like them, but maybe his buddies would.

five

When I started thinking about Jimmy I always ended up thinking about Eddie. One morning out gathering the eggs I got him on my mind. It was funny, and Jimmy never would have understood it, but if I really done them two things he accused me of, I done them with Eddie, and he was the one I was married to.

I guess it really was the way the hair on the back of his neck was so shaggy that I liked best about him. A lot of times I felt completely crazy when I was around him, and I didn't care what I did. That's why he never liked me very well and was mean to me. He wanted somebody that acted real respectable to play like they was his wife while he went on and did what he pleased.

But I guess it was a good thing I married him. I read in the paper about these sex fiends who are always killing people because they can't get enough woman, and it wouldn't have taken very much of a push to make Eddie one of those. In fact, when he would be after me three or four times a day I thought he was one, and I told him so. It made him so mad he would almost choke me, because he thought I was to blame. He thought I was always stirring him up on purpose. And I did once in a while; but not no four times a day. He didn't really like me very much.

"You're a nasty bitch," he used to say. He said it so many times it finally quit bothering me. And the less I let things like that bother me, the meaner he got. Lots of times when one of his hounds was in heat he'd grab me and drag me out in the back yard and make me watch while all the dogs fooled around with her. I soon quit fighting that too; it didn't bother me that much to have to watch. I don't guess it really bothered me at all.

"Looky there, sweetie," he said. "Why, she's just like you, ain't she? Just the same. What do you think about that sight?"

I wouldn't answer, or wouldn't say much. "It's just dogs breeding; it ain't too unusual," I said. Once in a while he would be fiddling around with me and make me mad.

"Well, honey," I said one time, "I didn't know you like to watch so much. I feel sorry for you. Let's go in and move the mirror over by the bed, so you can watch us." I knew how to take up for myself where Eddie was concerned.

What I said surprised him, but he couldn't back out. "All right, by god, let's do," he said. We went in and moved the mirror. I liked to drove him crazy that day. Eddie had to feel that he was the most exciting man that ever went in me, and when I didn't let him feel that way, he squirmed. That day we moved the mirror I lay there and laughed and giggled at him for fifteen minutes, and I could have been a feather pillow for all the good he was doing. He knew it, too. Every time he looked in the mirror I was grinning at him. I guess that was one of the times I hated him because I had married him instead of Gid. That was the time he squeezed my hand so hard he broke my next to littlest finger.

"I'm tired of your goddamn laughing, let's see you cry a little," he said, and squeezed it. But I wouldn't cry, either, I just looked at him, and he got up and dressed and went to Oklahoma and was gone six weeks. About the time he came back I got pregnant with Jimmy.

Our times weren't always bad though, mine and Eddie's. I was only mean to him four or five times, when I couldn't help it. He would come in sometimes when I was washing dishes and grin at me and untie my apron and stand there behind me, fiddling with my hair or rubbing my neck or back or sides or front till I would finally turn around and kiss him, and leave soap on his shirt.

I never seen but one of his girl friends; she was a redhead. She was at his funeral, and she came in with Eddie's sister Lorine. Lorine didn't mind letting me know that the redhead was the girl Eddie ought to have married. They never brought Eddie home after he was killed; he was buried in Chickisha, Oklahoma, where Lorine lived. I went up there on a train; it was the longest trip I ever made in my life; it was right in February, cold and rainy. Eddie looked nice. I didn't think the redheaded girl was too pretty, and she didn't act very kind. I rode all night on the train, back to Henrietta; it was a pretty sad trip for me. I kept seeing my face in the train windows; I couldn't see out at all. It was hard for me to believe Eddie was dead; I kept thinking I would feel his hands on me agin. When I got off the train in Henrietta it was after sunup, and Johnny and the boys were there waiting; I had left them with him, and they stayed in a little hotel; it was the first time the boys had ever been away from home. Johnny looked tired—I guess they had run him ragged—but I was so glad to see him. When they saw me the boys were too timid to say anything, but Johnny came up and put his hand on my forehead; his hand was so cool.

"Molly, you've got fever, honey," he said. "You've worried yourself sick."

"I sure don't like to travel," I said. I squatted down so the boys would see I wasn't mad at them, and they came and hugged my neck. Johnny bought them some doughnuts for breakfast; they hadn't ever had any before. Neither had I, I don't guess. While we ate he fixed the tarp over the wagon; it was drizzling rain. We had plenty of quilts and he fixed us a good pallet and me and the boys curled up and slept nearly all the way home. The boys were just worn out from missing me. They didn't let me out of their sight for days. Just before we got home I woke up and got on the seat with Johnny. He tried to make me wrap up, but the misty rain felt good. When we seen the house up on the hill, I cried till we got to it. That night I woke up in the bed and Johnny was asleep and snoring, with his arm around me. I kept imagining Eddie, but it would never be Eddie agin. I cried till the hairs on Johnny's arm were all wet, but he never did wake up.

I had the eggs gathered and was changing the chickens' water when Gid and Johnny drove up in Gid's car. They never got out, but sat by the back gate with the motor running, watching me. I knew they wouldn't be staying no time, or they would already be out of the car and in the kitchen, so I went on and fixed the water. Gid was in a hurry somewhere and Johnny had just managed to stall him a little while by coming by to say hello to me.

"Boy, I'm sure having a scrumptious dinner today," I said, when I did get over to the car. Gid still had his gloves on and his hand on the steering wheel.

"Well, I hope you've got a big appetite, so you can eat it all," he said. "We've got two days' work to do before dinnertime. How are you?"

"Except for being short of company, I'm fine," I said. "You look awful prosperous today."

"Hell, he is," Johnny said. "Who wouldn't be, hiring cheap help like me?"

I walked around to his side.

"That was dangerous," he said. "Didn't you know Gid had his foot on the footfeed? He might have run right over you."

"I ain't that bad," Gid said.

"I should have gone around behind," I said.

"No, you should have climbed over. He's just as apt to back up as he is to go forward."

They kidded with me a minute and said they would see me in a day or two; then they left. I got a little blue, because I knew some day I would have to show Gid the letter from Jimmy. It would nearly kill him. But the war would be over some day, and there wasn't much hope of getting out of it.

Gid never understood much about sex stuff, or at least I didn't think he did. Maybe I didn't understand it, or was wrong about it. I guess we were just raised different. Except for that one time with Richard, Dad never mentioned it—and then he hadn't been talking to me, anyway. Momma died when I was still pretty young, but she wouldn't have said anything about sex if I had got up one morning with triplets. It just wasn't nothing Momma would have talked about. Whatever ideas us kids had about it, we come up with on our own. I guess I just didn't have the background for thinking it was especially wrong; by the time I was eighteen or nineteen I would just as soon have had a baby as not.

Gid and Johnny were the boys I started out liking, and they weren't really go-getters in that respect. I guess their folks had thrown a scare into them. Then Eddie came along, and he knew just exactly what he was after and how to go about getting it. I didn't have no idea atall how to stop him, or even that I was supposed to stop him. Besides, Eddie was exciting. But I hadn't seen him five times when he got me down where I couldn't get up, and then it wasn't exciting, it was just plain hurting. I yelled to beat the band. It didn't matter to Eddie. And he hurt me ever time, for six months or a year; I couldn't see why a woman would ever want anybody to do her that way. But then I kinda begin to see one reason why: it was because a man needed it, and had it all tangled up with his pride, so that it was a sure way of helping him or hurting him, whichever you wanted to do. I hadn't been doing nothing atall for Eddie; just letting him have a good time. He was really nasty about it and I thought I'd quit him. Only before I did I started getting where I enjoyed it as much as he did; then I got so I enjoyed it more than he did. And that's when he quit caring anything about me: because he didn't want me to like it—not for my sake—he just wanted me not to be able to help liking it if it was him doing it. But of course I could help it, and by that time anyway Gid and Johnny had got a whole lot bolder, and I seen where it could really do wonderful things for a man if a woman cared to take a few pains with him.

I guess for a while I must have been pretty exciting to Eddie. It was after Joe was born that he completely quit caring about me. He still fooled around with me a lot, but he quit paying any attention to whether I liked it or not. He done what he pleased, and when he got done he stopped. One day I was just laying there watching him, and he said so.

"Well, there ain't but so much peaches and cream in any one bowl," he said.

"That's right," I said. "And when they're all eaten up you don't have nothing left but a dirty dish."

I think Eddie just married me to show up Johnny and Gid.

Gid was just the opposite of Eddie. He thought I was nice and pure and he was nasty and bad—it shocked him to death to find out he wasn't my first boy. He just couldn't believe sex was right. I don't guess he left my bedroom five times in his life that he wasn't ashamed of himself—in spite of all I done. I had to be careful where I touched him or he would jump like he was electrocuted. But he was the thoughtfulest man I knew, and took the most interest in me. He just wasn't able to understand that I loved him and wanted him to enjoy himself—he got it in his head, but he never got it in his bones.

Old Johnny did though. He had more pure talent for enjoying himself than Gid and Eddie put together. He could enjoy himself and pat me on the shoulder and sleep for a week, and I loved that about him. The right or wrong of it seldom entered Johnny's mind.

I always wished I had known Gid's daddy better. I think he could have straightened me out on a lot of things that it took me years to learn by myself. He had the highest standards of any man I ever knew—to this day Gid worries because he can't live up to those standards of his dad's.

One evening three or four months before he died me and him had a little talk. We were sitting at his kitchen table; Gid was out doing chores. I went over there a few times and cooked supper; they had had to batch for so long I felt sorry for them. Mr. Fry was in pain a lot of the time. I think he liked me, but I was always a little scared of him.

"Well," he said. "Some have to take and some have to give, and a very few can do both. I was always just a taker, but I was damn particular about what I took, and that's important."

"Why, Mr. Fry," I said. "Look at all you've give Gid."

"Oh yeah," he said. "A good ranch he ain't old enough to want and a lot of advice he ain't constructed to use.

"Them biscuits smell good," he said. "Let's get a head start on old Gid."

He buttered himself four biscuits. But I still had my mind on what he said.

"I don't guess I've ever done much of either one," I said.

"Aw hell," he said. "You could take a million dollars' worth, if you would. But instead you'll give out twice that much to sorry bastards that don't deserve it. And they won't put much back. I'm glad you and Gid won't marry. You'd smother him in sweetweed and he'd loaf the rest of his life. Misery makes a man work."

I was embarrassed, and he went on and ate his biscuits.

"Anyway, it ain't hurt your cooking," he said, and he looked up and gave me one of the longest looks I ever had in my life. I remembered that look a hundred times, whenever Gid or Jimmy looked at me across a table; they both had Mr. Fry's eyes.

"Molly, if I was just ten years younger I'd take your whole two million myself," he said. "The rest of the pack could go hungry. Gid would probably be the first one starved."

I couldn't say a word. My legs trembled, and I was glad they were under the table. I was looking at his hands. Finally he took a match out of his pocket and whittled it into a toothpick. I thought when I seen him in his coffin that if he had been ten years younger he would probably have done just what he said.

six

On the last day of July I went into town to get some groceries and my mail, and to buy a war bond. Old Washington at the feed store had some new kind of chicken feed he wanted to sell me, and I stood around there talking to him about one thing and another till the middle of the morning. I never did buy the feed; I had more eggs than I knew what to do with anyway. I bought the war bond though—it was about the only patriotic thing I knew to do. When the war started they made me a plane spotter and gave me a lot of materials on what to look for, but no airplanes ever came over except the oil company's Piper cub, flying the pipelines. Once in a while a big one would go over at night, but I couldn't tell anything about it.

I stopped in the drugstore a minute and drank a four hundred, and then went to the post office. My *Good Housekeeping* had come, and a new *Reader's Digest*, and the rest of the box was full of sale circulars of one kind and another. When I pulled all them out, the letter dropped on the floor. I threw all the circulars in a wastebasket before I picked it up. Then I went over to the counter and opened it and read it, and my mouth felt dry, it felt like my lips were chapped. People kept going by me to get their mail; I don't know who; they were just like shadows. Finally Old Man Berdeau, the postmaster, came out and tacked some kind of notice on the bulletin board, and then he came over to me and offered me his handkerchief. I didn't think I was crying, but I was.

"I'm mighty sorry, Mrs. White," he said. "I guess they're going to get all the boys before it's over."

It was a month before I remembered to give him back his handkerchief. I walked out and started to look for Gid. I knew he had built a new house on the west side of town. On what they called Silk Stocking Avenue; he said they ought to call it Mortgage Row. People in cars kept stopping and offering me rides. I don't know what I said to them. I knew the house by Gid's car setting in front of it; then I seen him way at the back, digging postholes; he was putting up some kind of pen. He looked so surprised when I came running up to him; I put my face against his chest, so I couldn't see anything. I could smell the starch on his shirt and the sweat under his arms when he put them around me.

"They killed my last old boy," I said.

"Molly, would you like to go in?" I looked at his house a minute, it was a big ugly brick house.

"Let's go home," I said.

He took me to his car and put me in the front seat. "I've got to go in a minute," he said. I was hoping he wouldn't bring Mabel out, and he didn't. We went off.

"Stop at the post office a minute," I said. "I left my magazines."
He went in and got them; Mr. Berdeau had put them up.

When we crossed Onion Creek I scooted over by him. "What's
life going to leave me?" I said. And when we stopped at the back
gate I noticed the car wasn't there. It was still parked at the post
office, with the groceries in it.

I didn't really see Gid till we were sitting at the kitchen table.
I had drunk my coffee but his was getting cold in the cup, and I
reached out and put my hand on his wrist. When I saw the look in
his eye I was ashamed of myself for being so selfish.

"Drink your coffee," I said.

And I quit grieving for Jimmy; it was strange to feel myself
quitting, but I couldn't have cried any more right then if I had
wanted to. I didn't really think about him agin that day, and when
I did the next day it was not me losing Jimmy I thought about, it
was Jimmy losing his life and never getting to have it.

Gid was there with me, at the table; I had never in my life
been able to think of two men at a time. One would always crowd
the other out.

"Stay here tonight," I said.

That afternoon we sat on the porch, in the glider, and Gid
talked more than he ever had in his life. He told me about his business, and his trouble with Mabel, and a lot of other things. It was
a hot day, and we could see the heat waves rising off the pastures.
I had a hold of one of Gid's arms.

"We're the ones should have got married," he said, during the
afternoon. I didn't say anything. I never did like to think about how
much better things might have turned out if we hadn't acted like
we did. We *did* act like we did, and some bad things happened, but
others would have happened if we had acted some other way.

We did the chores and I cooked us a little supper and we turned on the lights and sat in the living room, and there wasn't much to do.

"Let's play dominos," I said. So we got out the card table and the dominos and played for three or four hours; neither one of us was sleepy. I got a lot of good hands and won more games than Gid.

"Domino," he said, and I laid down my hand and shuffled for long time. Gid had asked to see the one letter Jimmy wrote, and I had lied about it and said it was lost. Actually I had hidden it in a shoebox. I felt dry inside and out when I lied to Gid—he was so trusting and it was so easy to do. And part of me wanted to show him the letter; if I had he never could have left me again. But thank God I didn't.

"Well," he said. "Maybe you'll locate it one of these days. We can't do nothing staying up."

It was hot that night; no breeze at all. I told Gid he ought to take his undershirt off, but he didn't. He went right off to sleep. I got up three or four times during the night to sprinkle the sheets with water. I couldn't get cool; I was dripping sweat. Once Gid woke up and raised up on his elbows a minute and seen I was awake.

"We've covered a lot of miles together, haven't we?" he said, and then went back to sleep. He always slept on his stomach. We had covered a lot of miles together—and we had covered a lot when we weren't together, too, I thought. Tomorrow night I would just have the moon and an empty bed. I put my hand on his neck and there was sweat in the little wrinkles of his skin.

I guess I slept a little; Gid was pulling on his Levis when I woke up.

"I'll go get the chores," he said. "You stay here and rest."

"I can stay in bed the rest of my life, if I want to," I said. And I got up and cooked while he tended the animals. We didn't have much to say that morning. I went in to town with him so I could get my car. When we got to the post office I leaned over and kissed his cheek.

"Many thanks for staying," I said.

"Why, Molly?" he said. "He was the only son we'll ever have."

As soon as I got home I went to the hall closet and got the letter out of the shoebox and took it to the trash barrel and read it agin.

DEAR MOLLY:

This is just a note to tell you I won't be home after the war, so don't you'all look for me. If I never see Texas agin it will be too soon, as there are lots of other parts of the world I like better.

Joe wrote me that you was afraid I would marry some Filipino girl and bring her home without telling you. Don't worry, I am not going to marry no girl, Filipino or otherwise. I'm not very religious no more, this war has caused that, and I don't take after girls any more, I take after men. I have a friend who is rich, and I mean rich, he says if I will stay with him I will never have to work a day, so I am going to. I guess we will live in Los Angeles if we don't get killed.

JIMMY

I hope his rich friend loved him. He was a cruel boy, but I guess I had it all coming. After I burned the letter I went and got the basket and gathered yesterday's eggs.

seven

I guess Gid told Johnny, because he came over right after dinner, that day that I burned the letter. I was glad to see him; he was just the one I was in a mood for. We sat on the glider awhile too.

"Did you see Gid?" I said. "How did you think he looked?"

He kinda grinned. "He's taking it hard," he said, "because he decided not to work this afternoon. That's unusual. The last time Gid took an afternoon off was the day Sarah was born."

"It could have been worse," I said. And in two minutes I had told him about the letter. Telling him didn't make me feel any better—it just made me feel disloyal to Jimmy. But I had to tell it.

"That's terrible," Johnny said. But the surprising thing was, Johnny was in a good mood. He tried to act solemn and sad, but he just wasn't—Jimmy had never been close to him. Once in a while he would grin to himself about something.

And I guess I was a bad mother to the end, because I began to feel good too. It was such a relief, somehow, that Johnny wasn't really sad. Johnny could still sit there and enjoy life—I guess I had thought everybody would stop enjoying it forever because my sons were dead.

"You know what I'd like to do this afternoon?" he said. "I'd like to gather up a pretty woman like you and go fish that big tank in the southwest corner. We ain't fished that tank in nearly a year."

"That's right," I said. "It was last September, wasn't it, that we went down there?"

"Well, you're the pretty woman I had in mind," he said. "Do you want to go?"

"Did you know I'm forty-three years old?" I said. "That's about too old to be thinking about pretty."

"Why, I'm older than that, and I think about it all the time," he said. "Besides, I know a lot of young pullets that ain't thirty yet who'd trade looks with you this afternoon."

"It's because I've had you to keep me fresh," I said, and I smiled too. It felt good to really smile.

"I'll get us some worms," he said. "You get your fishing clothes on."

I packed the old picnic box with some bacon and eggs and potatoes and the coffeepot and part of a mincemeat pie I had left over in the icebox. I thought we might just stay out and have supper by the tank if we felt like it.

"Well, I didn't know we was going camping," he said, when he saw me putting the box in his pickup.

"I just put in a skillet and some stuff to eat in case we don't catch nothing," I said. "I thought we might have a fish fry and do a little night fishin'."

"I got enough worms to catch half the fish in the ocean," he said. "Look at them big fat grubs." We put the poles in, and a few quilts to sit on, and left.

The tank was still as a mirror, and the fish weren't biting much. "I guess they don't want to risk getting yanked up in this heat," Johnny said. We spread the quilts at the south corner of the tank dam, under three cottonwood trees. The trees made pretty good shade.

And Johnny couldn't resist shade. Before we'd been there an hour he was sound asleep on the quilts, and I was left to do the fishing. I didn't mind. We just had three poles, and they weren't much trouble to watch. In the summertime I usually did my sewing while we fished. Johnny's shirt had a rip in the shoulder, and I sewed it up and patched one of his socks while he slept. The tank and the country around it were just as still: there wasn't even enough breeze to stir the cottonwoods. I watched the water and sewed and fished a little, and couldn't keep much on my mind. Since Jimmy was dead, I could imagine that we had been closer than we were, and I let myself make up a lot of little scenes that never happened, where we were having fun together. Later I got to believing a few of them. I made up that Gid and I had married, and one fall he and Jimmy and me went to Dallas to the Fair. I never had been to the Fair, but Jimmy and Joe both went once, and Joe tried to bring me home some cotton candy; he didn't have much luck. Johnny slept two hours and I only caught four fish worth keeping: three nice little cat and one good-sized perch. I quit on worms and tried a little bacon for bait, but had no luck. I was feeling too lazy to go catch grasshoppers. When fish don't bite you might as well leave them alone.

About five I woke Johnny up, because I knew when he slept too long he always felt sour and sluggish.

"Supper ready?" he said.

"I just do the catching," I said. "You get to do the cleaning."

"I believe I'll swim a little, first," he said. "You want to come in?"

I didn't think it would fit too well with the day, for me to go in, so I said I would just dunk my feet. Johnny and I swum together a lot in the summertime, usually. I sat on the dam and cooled my feet down by the four fish, and he swum the tank a time or two and came out spluttering. He looked so cool I wished I had swum after all.

"Let's have a little target practice," he said, and he got his twenty-two out of the pickup and threw three cowchips out in the water and we shot at them till we had used up a box of shells. I had shot that gun so much I could shoot it nearly as well as he could.

Then we dug out a little place not too far from the water, and I laid the fire and got out the supper stuff while he cleaned the fish. The sun was easing on down and it turned the water gold when you looked across it. Five of my old cows came to drink on the other side of the tank and stood and looked across at us and bawled. I guess they were hoping I had a little cowfeed for them, but they never came on around. I greased the skillet and cooked the fish and some of the bacon and made the coffee, and we put the potatoes where they would bake. I had forgot to bring any pepper, but it was a pretty good supper, anyway. The sun went into the mesquites, over west of us, and just a few streaks of light got through and struck the water. Then it was gone and there was just the afterglow, and the killdees and bullbats were swooping down over the water.

"You ever eat a killdee?" Johnny said. "They don't make two mouthfuls." We seen some crows going to roost. The dam's shadow began to stretch across the water.

"My potato didn't get quite done," I said.

"Now if you ask me," he said, "this is the good life." He was leaning back on one elbow drinking his second cup of coffee.

"It is good," I said. "I wish the boys could have lived some of it."

"They did, some of it," he said. "At least Joe did. I reckon old Jim was the one missed out."

"Reckon they'll ever find Jody?" I said.

"No, I don't imagine."

Mine would just be scattered, I guess. Dad was buried in Decatur, where his ma had lived, and Eddie was in Chickisha. I forget the name of the place where they buried Jim, and Joe was nobody knew where. I felt calm and rested, but pretty sad.

Johnny moved over by me. "What would you think if I was to steal a kiss from a pretty forty-three-year-old woman who's lost her boys?" he said. "She can cook the best fish I ever ate."

That was a funny speech, coming from Johnny. His voice kinda trembled. I smiled and leaned back against him.

"I guess you would just be kissing her because you feel sorry for her," I said.

"I guess that wouldn't have nothing at all to do with it," he said.

We kissed once and sat by the tank listening to the bullfrogs. There wasn't much moon that night, just a little sliver. We heard a snake get a frog, and the frog squeaked a long time. That sound always made me wince. Johnny turned on the pickup lights so we could gather up the stuff.

When we got to the house he helped me get the stuff in, and I figured he would stay all night. But he kissed me agin at the back gate, and went on.

"Aw, I'm too rambunctious," he said, when I asked him why. "You got too much on your mind to have me around. I'll be over in a night or two."

"Well, I hope so," I said. I hadn't had a bath in three days, so I went in and took one. The bed was empty and there wasn't no moon either, but I went right to sleep. I guess Johnny knew I was completely worn out.

eight

One day the last of August I cleaned out the cellar. I had preserves and canned goods in there going back ten years or more. Some of it I had put up when the boys were little and we were real poor; I thought we had better keep as much stuff on hand as we could, in case of a hard winter. But I put up so much we never could use it all, and ever year we would wind up a little farther ahead of ourselves. Half of it had probably spoiled. I was the only one left, and I knew I couldn't ever eat half of the good stuff, much less the bad. What looked bad I threw away, and what looked good I stacked in the smokehouse, so I could get Johnny to haul it into Thalia and give it to some poor folks there.

After I got the stuff sorted I set what was left of the jars off on the floor, so I could wash the shelves. Even as cool as the cellar was, it was a hot, dusty job. About halfway through I climbed out and started to the house to get a drink, and there was Gid, standing in the yard waiting for me. He looked all tense.

"Why, hello," I said. "How long have you been standing out here in the sun?" It was only the second time he had been by since the day we heard about Jimmy.

"Just a few minutes," he said. "You look like you been working."

"Cleaning out the cellar," I said. "Can you stay for dinner?"

"I don't imagine," he said. "I just wanted to talk to you a little while."

But that was just what he thought he wanted, I knew that the minute I seen him. Gid had come to me keyed up like that too many times for me not to know what he was needing. I wisht I hadn't been so hot and dusty.

"Well, come on in," I said. "I'll at least get some ice tea down you while we talk."

But I didn't have no intention of fixing him any. I knew Gid too well. If I made him sit around and talk when he didn't want to talk, he would just get self-conscious, and get ashamed of himself, and that would spoil things for him before he ever touched me. The only way with Gid was to keep him from having to face what was on his mind until he was already in the bed. When I could manage that, he loved it. He loved it as much as Eddie or more; but it was just very seldom that he could let himself go.

When we went into the kitchen he was walking right behind me, and I turned real quick so that he ran right up against me. He kissed me without thinking, and I knew I had him for once, so I could forget it too. I wisht I could have gone to the bathroom and washed off a little of the dust, but it didn't really matter. Gid was loose, and that was the main thing; unless he was, neither of us could be.

I slept awhile—I didn't usually—and when I woke up Gid was sitting by me on the bed, washing my face and neck with a washrag.

"You had dust on your eyelids," he said. "I didn't mean to wake you up."

"I'm sweaty," I said. "Let me get some ice tea, I already got some made."

I went and got two glasses and brought them back to the bedroom. He was still sitting on the edge of the bed holding the washrag, but he had put his pants on.

And he had the saddest look on his face. I didn't know why; I felt so happy. I handed him his tea and crawled back on the bed.

"What's the matter, hon?" I said.

He pitched the washrag on the bedside table and didn't say anything for a minute. He squeezed one of my feet.

"I was just thinking about you," he said. "I guess I'm still crazy in love with you, after all these years. What I come out here for today was to tell you I wasn't going to do this any more. I guess I'm sad because it was our last time."

"Oh now," I said. I smiled, but it hurt my stomach, and I wanted to grab him and hold him. Gid had never said anything like that before, and I knew the instant he said it that he meant it, and that he would stick by it. And I knew I oughtn't to say a word: the more I said, the more we would lose. But I loved him, so I fought anyway.

"Well, it just about kills me when I think of it," he said. "But it has just got to be that way, Molly."

I waited a minute. "Gid," I said, "it ain't one bit of my business, but I've always wanted to ask you, and I might just as well. Do you and Mabel ever do this?"

He kinda twisted his mouth. "Oh yes, of course," he said. "Three or four times a year, I guess. But Mabel don't have nothing to do with what I just said."

"Well, Gid," I said. "That ain't very much. If she don't care to give it and I do, what's the harm in letting me? Why make it hard on both of us? Don't you know I need to be able to give somebody a little something?"

He didn't say anything; he still had one hand on my foot.

"Are you ashamed of me, too?" I said.

"Ashamed of you 'too'?" he said. "Who's good enough to be ashamed of you?"

"Jimmy was ashamed of me," I said. I didn't feel happy at all, any more.

"Who I'm ashamed of is us," he said. "The both of us. And Jimmy's part of the reason I made up my mind like I have."

"Why is it you're ashamed and I'm not?" I said. "Am I just sorry? I always thought really caring about a person made a difference in what was right and wrong."

"I don't know," he said. "I was raised to believe that what we done is wrong. The Bible says it's wrong. The churches say it's wrong. The law says it's wrong. And I've always believed it was wrong—except when we did it. But any no-count bastard can get around something that way. Lots of people think stealing's wrong, except when it's them stealing. But if this here's wrong, it's wrong when we do it too, now ain't it?"

My leg was trembling. I knew I had come to the wall, and I don't know why I even argued, but I had to.

"Gid, I'm just me," I said. "I ain't the law, and I ain't the church. All I say is, if it's wrong, then let's go ahead and have the guts to be wrong. We can't but go to hell for it, and that would be better than doing without you."

"We could do a lot worse than that," he said, and he put his head in his hands. "We could have another Jimmy. You ain't too old. And I've got a little girl now that's got to be thought of too. We ruined one child's life and we could ruin another. That's worse than any going to hell."

There wasn't one word I could say to that.

"Molly, you could marry Johnny," he said. "He's always loved you too."

"Johnny don't want to marry," I said. "And I don't either. You know you've always been my mainstay."

"Then why did you marry that sorry bastard you married?" he said. He'd been wanting to say it twenty years. "Why didn't you marry me? It's just about ruined my life, Molly!"

It *had* just about ruined his life, and I was to blame. And Jimmy's too, and I was to blame for that. And Gid was going to quit me. That was the way.

"I wish I knew what all was involved in this loving somebody," he said. "Mostly a lot of damn heartbreak, I know that."

"I know we've done at least a little something that was good," I said. "Please don't quit me, Gid."

"Oh, I'll be by," he said, "whenever I can risk it."

That was what finally made me cry. "Well, good-by then, damn you," I said, "because you can't ever risk it, not even if I am forty-three. I've liked it, even if you haven't, and I ain't ashamed of it, even if you are."

"What about Jimmy?" he said.

"Jimmy's dead. You quitting me won't make nothing up to him."

"Molly, it ain't quitting," he said. "We got to do it. Don't you know this is killing me? I never quit nothing in my life."

"If you can think of a prettier word for it, fine," I said. "You're the one that has clothes on."

Things were just a blur, but I reached out for him and he got up and put his shirt on. "I don't have much pride where you're concerned," I said, but he left, and I laid on the bed and cried for a long time.

nine

Gid kept his word. I knew he would. He never loosened the reins on himself agin. It was over ten years before he ever touched me, and then it was just a pat on the shoulder.

Right after he quit me I couldn't stand to think he would actually make it stick. I was determined I'd bring him back the next time I saw him, whatever it cost me, or him. I knew I could make him come back; I had ways I had never had to use.

But I didn't lay eyes on him for two months, and when he finally did come I knew in five minutes that I wouldn't do what I had planned to do. It was October when he came; I was in the kitchen; and he knocked and came in with a coyote puppy. He had brought me one or two to raise before that.

"Well, I killed his momma, Molly," he said. "You want to raise him?"

"Of course," I said. "I'll get him a box."

And when we had the puppy fixed I walked to the gate with him. Only I stopped inside the fence and didn't go to the car, the way I usually did.

It would have been easy to have touched Gid, that day; he was just starving for somebody to. But it wouldn't have been loving him much to have tricked him into doing something he had suffered so much to quit doing. And the two months had really told on Gid, I guess worse than they had on me. If he really wanted to quit that bad, I thought I would do better to help him keep his word. If he broke it, it would just be that much more agony for him. But I don't know; never will know. The way he looked before he drove off, I think he was wanting me to help him break his word. Those things are awful complicated. Or more likely it was both he wanted: me, on the one hand, and to do what he thought was right on the other. I never will know which one he wanted the most. I don't imagine he knew himself. But when he drove off and I went back in, I thought he had sure been right about the heartbreak.

That last day, when he asked me why I married Eddie instead of him, I didn't have no answer for him. I thought about it a lot after that—too much, I guess—but I never came up with an answer for myself, either. Not one I could be sure was right. There may not have been no one answer, but if there was, I didn't know it. I guess that said something pretty bad about me, that I didn't know why I married who I did. I knew an awful lot of little things about myself, what I liked to eat and smell and do. And I knew some bigger things than that—about giving and taking, and the things Mr. Fry had talked about the one time we talked. But marrying Eddie may have been the most important thing, for all of us, that I ever did. I didn't know why I done it, and I don't know what good it would have done me if I had. Knowing wouldn't have made it any less done.

For a month or so after Gid quit me, I like to have run Johnny ragged. He came over a lot. Sometimes I wouldn't let him in ten feet of me, and other times I went to the other extreme. I wasn't in very good control of myself. Finally one night at the supper table he brought it up.

"Well, I guess I better tell you off, Molly," he said. "You been getting me mixed up with Gid, lately, and it's about to get me down. You know me and him are different fellers. It ain't fair to me for you to pretend I'm him."

I was so ashamed I couldn't say a word. We sat for several minutes.

"You're right," I said finally. "I'm sorry, Johnny. Don't hold that against me, will you?"

"Of course not," he said. "Now that you've quit. I couldn't hold anything against such a good cook."

"Gid's changed his way of thinking about me," I said. "I guess you knew that. It made me pretty miserable."

"Not as miserable as it made him," he said. "I've been thinking he'd probably kill himself. But since he's made it this long, I guess he'll probably survive."

I let him know I appreciated his patience, and his finally speaking up. It made me feel a lot better after he had. I felt calm for the first time since Gid left the bedroom that day.

"Now see," Johnny said. "Me and you may not kill nobody over one another, but we're comfortable. We've always been comfortable, and I want us to keep on being that way."

"I don't know," I said. "I might kill a person or two for you. It would depend on who." That made him feel good. He knew I probably meant it.

But I guess Gid was still heavy on my mind, because I had to talk about it.

"Johnny," I said. "What do you think about this we do? Is it right or is it wrong?"

"Well, it's enjoyable," he said. "I ain't gonna bother to look no farther than that."

But that wasn't answer enough, just then.

"You quit worrying," he said. "That's the kind of thing Gid has to worry about. There's no need in you worrying about it too."

"But you know I've done it with him, too," I said. "Do you think it's wrong for me to do it with both of you all these years?"

"Of course not," he said. "Gid's even more crazy about you than I am, and he deserves a little enjoyment too. Only he's so crazy he reasons himself out of it.

"After all, we raised a son," he said. "And a good one. You and Gid had bad luck with yours, but that's life. The stars were just set wrong for Jim. I never lost a night's sleep in my life from being ashamed, and I don't intend to start."

"You're right about it," I said. "In a way, you are. I never lost much sleep over it, either, not till lately. I just wish Gid agreed with us."

"Oh no," he said. "That wouldn't be Gid. Somebody's got to take an interest in the right and wrong of things."

All the same I would always miss Gid, even if Johnny was right.

About nine o'clock I woke up and he was pulling on his boots.

"You ain't leaving tonight, are you?" I said.

"Oh, of all the stupid things," he said. "I left my damn milk cows in the lot; I just now remembered. If I don't go turn them out, there's no telling what they'll get into. I hate to leave."

"Oh, it's all right if that's all it is," I said. I got up and put on my nightgown and got a flashlight and walked out to his pickup with him.

"I guess you'll be barefooted the day you die," he said.

He had just half-thrown his clothes on; one of his sleeves was flopping, and I made him wait till I buttoned it at the wrist.

"You come back when you can," I said. "Now that I'm straightened out on who you are."

"Don't you worry," he said. "You won't hardly know I ain't living here."

It was a beautiful warm night and I walked around to the porch and sat on the glider awhile, in just my nightgown. I didn't feel very sleepy; I heard a coyote, back off toward the Ridge. The moon was just rising; it was full, and I sat and watched it, a big old gold harvest moon, barely up above the pastures. My hair was down, but I didn't have no comb, and I didn't feel like going in the house. While I sat there my menfolk begin rising with the moon, moving over the pastures, over the porch, over the yard. Dad and Eddie, they was drunk, had whiskey on their breath. Jimmy was looking away from me, thinking of school. Joe, he was laughing, and Johnny was lazing along, grinning about something. But Gid was looking at my face, and wishing he could put his hands on my hair.

But, Lord Christ! whan that it remembreth me
Upon my yowthe, and on me jolitee,
It tickleth me aboute myn herte roote.
Unto this day it dooth myn herte boote
That I have had my world as in my tyme.
But age, allas! that al wole envenyme
Hath me biraft my beautee and my pith.
Lat go, farewel! the devel go therewith!
The flour is goon, ther is namoore to telle;
The bren, as I best kan, now moste I selle. . . .

The Wife of Bath

Oh lay my spurs upon my breast, my rope and old saddle tree,
And while the boys are lowering me to rest, go turn my horses free.

TEDDY BLUE, from *We Pointed Them North*

GO TURN MY HORSES FREE ✸ III

I had just dropped a post in a hole and was tamping the dirt around it with my shovel handle when I looked up and seen Gid hot-footin' it for the lots. He never said a word to me—he just struck out. Well sir, I thought, we'll both go. I knew he had some cold beer on ice in the water can, and I thought I'd help him siphon off a little. When I got there he was plopped down in the shade of his new GMC pickup, swigging on the first can. I opened me one and sat down and rested my back against the rear wheel and settled in to listen. Gid had pitched his hat on the running board and set his beer can down between his legs, so he'd have both hands free to wave. I seen the sun had blistered his old bald noggin agin, right through the straw hat. He had the hailstorm on his mind. Molly had come out that morning and argued with us a little about the fence line, and for some reason arguments with Molly always made Gid think of that hail.

"I'd been over at Antelope, getting the mail," he said. "Old Dirtdobber thought the cloud was just threatening, but I knew better. You can't fool me when it comes to hail."

"Hell no," I said. "Nothing simple as weather could fool you."

"The Montgomery Ward catalogue had come that day," he said. "I yanked it out of my saddle pouch, and then I took down my lariat rope. 'Run, you old bastard,' I said, and I keewawed him between the ears with that rope. It broke him into a lope he was so surprised."

"Watch out, Gid," I said. "You're going to knock that can of beer over if you don't."

But he didn't give a shit for beer when he got to talking. Gid never started talking till he was sixty years old, and then he never stopped. That hailstorm hit Thalia in the spring of 1924, and Gid hadn't forgotten it yet. None of the old-timers had—in the long run it done more damage to the people than it done to the windowlights or the wheat crops. I guess the worst was Old Man Hurshel Monroe getting his skull cracked outside the door of the bank. They say Beulah Monroe found the hailstone that conked him and kept it home in the icebox for nearly ten years, till one of her grandkids ate it for an all-day sucker. I've heard that so many times I probably even believe it myself.

"We made it to a little mesquite tree," he said. "Old Dirt was slowing down."

"I guess so," I said. "What a man gets for riding a twenty-two-year-old horse."

"So I got down and yanked the saddle off. Uuuups . . . !"

"I knew you'd spill it sooner or later," I said. "Half a can of good beer nobody gets to drink."

"You wasn't gonna get to drink it nohow," he said. "What difference does it make to you?"

"Your beer all right," I admitted. "Why open it if you ain't gonna drink it?"

"Why buy it if I ain't gonna open it?" he said, reaching in the water can for another one.

"Here," I said. "Let me pour this one out for you so it won't interrupt your story."

"Just shut up," he said. "I've emptied two cans of beer to your one."

"Why sure," I said. "In the first place you're older than me. And in the second place, I've always had to drink my cans. I never been able to afford just to pour them out."

He stopped and swigged beer till there wasn't much left in the new can. "If you worked as smart as you talked, you have something to show for your long life," he said. That was Gid—he thought my working for wages was a disgrace. But I got my pleasure out of doing what I wanted to, not out of owning no damn mesquite and prickly pear. I told him that a hundred times, but he never did understand it.

"I figured old Dirt would stand," he said. "So I crawled under him and scrunched up under the saddle." He kept wiping his face with his shirt sleeve, and I knew the sweat was stinging his old nose, where it had blistered and peeled. "Shore hot," he said.

"Finish your story. It'll be sundown before we get back to work."

"About the time I got under the saddle I heard water falling on it. I thought it must have quit hailing and gone to raining, and then I smelled it, and it didn't smell like no rain water I ever smelled. I peeped out to one side and saw some of it trickling along the ground, and it didn't look like no rain water I ever saw. It was still hailing to beat the dickens, and all I could do was sit there thinking about it. Finally I raised up and jobbed him in the stomach with the saddle horn. 'Damn you,' I said. 'You could have waited a minute.' "

"Haw," I said. "That's pretty good. I'd have paid money to have seen that."

"I wouldn't laugh, if I was you," he said. "It wasn't nothing to be ashamed of."

"No, but it ain't much to brag about, either," I said.

He waved his beercan in my face. "You better not talk," he said. "Where was you when we had that storm? At least I was home where I belonged. I wasn't off in New Mexico living with no Indian woman."

"Neither was I," I said. "I knew you'd drag that in. I can tell what you're going to say before you even say it. For the nine hundredth time, I wasn't off in no New Mexico. I was right near Baileyboro, Texas. And I wasn't where no horse could weewee on me, that's for damn sure."

"Not on me! On the saddle!" Gid was very particular about that point.

"It's too hot to listen to you explain." Actually, when they had that storm, I had done been busted up in my horsewreck and was in the hospital. I wasn't even living with Jelly.

"When I jobbed him, he kicked me," Gid said, and he looked kinda sad, remembering. Contrary as he was, I could feel sorry for Gid sometimes. He was getting old, and he wouldn't admit it. Middle of July, hot as a firecracker, and the old fart wouldn't stretch out and rest for love nor money. Telling them old stories, getting himself in a stir, remembering them. I wish I could have talked some sense into him, sat him down and told him, "Now goddamnit, Gid, you're getting about old enough to slow down. It won't hurt you to take a little rest in the afternoons." But when it come right down to saying it, I just let him go. Making him mad would have done more damage than the advice was worth. Besides, I kinda got a kick out of hearing the stories agin myself.

"Put your hat on, Gid," I said. "You'll go off and forget it and take a sunstroke."

"That was the first time Dirt had kicked in ten years," he said. "It surprised me. And then he run off."

"Did you cuss him?" I said.

"Yeah, but it didn't do no good."

"Why no, that don't surprise me," I said. "It don't do no good when you yell at me, either."

"Yeah, but you ain't a horse," he said.

"That's all right. Neither one of us can understand you when you yell. You don't talk plain."

"Bullshit," he said. "If you'd just get you one of them little invisible hearing aids, you could hear fine. Nobody's going to blame you for getting old."

Gid was the worst about that kind of remark I ever saw. "Who said anything about old?" I said. "You splutter when you yell; maybe it's them false teeth, I don't know. And the next time I wish you'd buy Pearl if you're going to buy beer. You let this get a little warm and it tastes like horsepiss."

He threw his beer can on the pile we were building up by the loading chute. "You know, Johnny, we're going to have to haul them cans off, one of these days," he said. "Cattle will get to where they won't load with all them tin cans shining at them."

I chunked one on the pile myself. It's nice to have a pile to throw a beercan at. A man can see he's been accomplishing something. "Leave them cans where they are," I said. "The pile's just now getting big enough it's easy to hit. Besides, we ain't gonna load no cattle recently."

"That's about the size of it," he said. And that can pile is still right where it was. We never got around to hauling it off, and I'm glad. It's kind of a monument.

"When are we going to get to work?" I said.

He had to strike five matches to get his stogie lit, and then it went right out. He just bought them to chew, anyway.

"Looks like you'd be willing to rest," he said. "I try to ease up on you in the heat of the day and you go to rearing and tearing. You have to sit on an old bugger like you to keep him from killing himself. I guess you just want to prove you can still work."

"Blame it on me," I said. "I'm handy."

"Now if you were able to work in weather like this, it'd be different. I seen you get the weak trembles yesterday, digging that corner posthole."

"It was hot yesterday," I had to admit. "Anybody that works hard can get too hot."

"Sure, sure," he said.

"Don't be sure, suring me," I said. "You had the weaves your-self a dozen times. You just had the crowbar to prop up on or you'd have gone down fifteen times."

"Aw," he said, "that's just your imagination. The sweat drips on my bifocals and I stumble once in a while, that's all."

"Of course," I said. "That must be it. That's why you're going to have that operation next month. Sweat's what does it."

"Making fun of a sick man," he said. "Let me finish my story."

I knew that story like a good preacher knows the Bible, but I listened anyway. I liked to hear what new lies Gid would put in.

"What happened," he said, "was old Dirt squashed my hip when he ran over me."

"No wonder you're so bunged up nowadays," I said. "You ought to have taken better care of yourself when you were young."

"There's a blister bug on your hat," he said. "You better get him before he gets you. What do you mean bunged up? I've got a crick or two, but I ain't feeble."

I caught the brim of my hat and flipped the blister bug half-way across the lot. "Them sonofabitches are going to take this country," I said.

"Yeah, them and the mesquite. And the government. I hope I ain't alive to see it."

"You won't be," I said. "The country ain't that far gone."

"Then it don't like much," he said. "Ten more years like this and it will strain a man to make an honest living in this country." He flipped about four inches of stogie over toward the can pile.

"It strains the ones that make an honest living now," I said, "but that don't affect the majority. What was the matter with that cigar?"

"Nothing. Good cigar. That little piece I threw away wasn't worth lighting."

"Kiss my butt," I said. "I guess if you laid down a dollar and they give you two bits change, you'd let it lay, like it wasn't worth keeping."

"That's right," he said. "It ain't worth keeping. Won't buy nothing."

"Now, Gid," I said. "Think a minute. That's a hamburger you'd be throwing away. That's five Peanut Patties."

"Think yourself," he said. "Who wants a goddamn Peanut Pattie anyway, much less five of them? You'd think a man your age would get over craving candy."

"Nothing wrong with Peanut Patties. They stick to your ribs." Everybody hurrahed me about my sweet tooth. But I've craved candy all my life, and I don't believe in doing without something just because a bunch of idiots thinks it's silly. Delaware Punch is another thing I like.

"And anyway we're letting the cool part of the day go to waste," I said. "I guess it'll be a hundred and ten tomorrow."

"We ain't gonna work tomorrow," he said. "I promised Susie I'd take her to see *Snow White*." Then he went back to his story. "I don't know how I survived," he said. "Finally the hail was piled up around me and the saddle like it was an igloo, I remember that."

I reached in and got my pocketknife and slipped the boot off my right foot. "You're gonna talk till suppertime I might as well trim my corns," I said.

"Poor bastard," he said. "I guess a man's feet give out first."

"Not mine," I said. "I've had sense enough not to use mine much. I just got a few corns."

"Mabel talked me into having Susie a pair of little boots made," he said. "Made outa javelina skin. Shore purty."

"I bet," I said. "And probably didn't cost over five times what they were worth. What'd you want to spend money on that javelina skin for?"

"Soft. Don't hurt a kid's feet so much."

"That's the way the whip pops," I said. "The first pair of shoes I ever bought felt like they was made out of tin."

"Mine did too," he said. "No wonder we're both cripples."

"What'd you do when it quit hailing?"

"Stood up," he said. "When I looked around I seen I wasn't but just across the peach orchard from the Eldenfelders' house. So I got me a limb for a crutch and hopscotched across the orchard."

"A man's taking his life in his hands, going up to a Dutchman's house on one leg," I said. "It's a wonder the dogs didn't rip you up."

"I thought about that," he said. "We was near neighbors, and the dogs knew me a little, else I wouldn't have gone up at all. I picked me up a pocketful of big hails, just in case."

"Just in case what? You couldn't hit a dog with a hailstone in fifteen throws."

"I don't know," he said. "I could always chunk good and straight. Remember the time we played that baseball game in Thalia and I chunked that Methodist preacher they had playing second base. I chunked him good enough."

"Yeah," I said. "By god I do remember. I remember he got you down and beat hell out of you after the ballgame, too. You didn't chunk him hard enough."

"He surprised me," he said. "Got in the first lick. I didn't figure a preacher would hit a man without warning him."

"A preacher's got that much sense," I said. "He may not have much more." And there's a sad end to that story. The preacher waited a year or two and got in a hell of a last lick—he was the one married Gid and Mabel.

"Anyhow I didn't need the hails," he said. "The dogs come charging out all right, thirty or forty of them, but that little bitty old rat terrier they used to have was the only one actually went for my legs. The rest just stood around growling and showing their teeth."

"By god now, that took nerve," I said. "If you'd a fell, there wouldn't have even been a belt buckle left. I might not have ragged you so hard all these years if I had seen that. I admire a man with the kind of backbone you showed."

"Just shut up," he said. "I limped on to the house. That rat terrier give me hell, too. I meant to come over some day when the folks were gone and kick the shit out of that dog, but the coyotes got him first. Finally the old man heard the commotion and came out on the porch. He thought it was funny, me fighting that rat terrier with my peach limb. 'Get up steps,' he said. 'Dead cow's for dinner.' Only I didn't find out what he meant till it was too late."

"Find out whose cow it was, you mean?"

"Naw, how long it had been dead. I thought it tasted all right for Dutchman's cooking. So did old Wolf. 'Good-cow,' he said. 'Dead mit de lightnin' vee days ven we find her.'"

"Poison you?"

"No, it didn't hurt me. Wasn't as spoiled as some of the stuff you buy in grocery stores nowadays."

"Was Bartle home then?" I asked. I remember Bartle Eldenfelder; he was a fighting demon.

Gid had to stop and laugh when I mentioned Bartle. "No, he was gone," he said. "That bastard." He had to wipe the laugh tears off his cheeks. "Frank Scott come by my place one morning and said he was going to whip Bartle for dancing with his wife. I told him I hoped he'd eaten a big breakfast—it just made him madder."

"Who won?" I said. I had underestimated Frank Scott's fighting ability once myself.

"Bartle whipped him right off. Frank came dragging back by

bleeding like a stuck hog. Said Bartle hit him with a hoe handle."

"That was about the time his wife left him, I guess. She told everybody Frank hit her with a hoe handle, but nobody believed her, neither." But if he never, he should have. She was too pretty for her own good, and a whole lot too pretty for Frank's. Once I was taking her out the door at a dance and met Frank coming in. If he hadn't taken time to hit her first, I would have got whipped worse than I did.

"Anyhow, that's the story," he said. "After I ate the rotten cow Annie hitched up the wagon and took me home. I had to wade the creek."

"Okay now," I said. "It's what you and Annie did before you waded the creek that I been waiting all this time to hear. Just tell that."

Gid grinned a little. "I swear you got a filthy mind," he said.

"No, I just like to know the feller I'm working for. If I'm working for a sex maniac, I want to know about it."

"That ain't it," he said. "You just got the damn nostalgia. You wish you was young enough to have a shot at Annie agin yourself."

"You damn right I am," I said. "And kiss my butt. I was better off then than I am now, it don't take no college degree to know that."

"Maybe you were and maybe you weren't," he said. "I know one thing, them times were hard. You couldn't drag me back."

I just snorted. "Okay," I said. "How about if I could show you Molly, looking like she looked in 1924. I don't guess that would tempt you none."

That hit him right on the sore spot; I knew it would. I stood up and brushed the dirt off my pants.

"Well, that might change my mind all right," he said.

I was sorry I said it. I could remember how she looked in 1924 myself.

"You want me to bring the water can?" I said.

"Naw, we ain't gonna work very long. Take a big drink."

We started back down the fence row, with him a little in the lead. I stumbled and like to fell; memories had kept me from seeing the ground.

"She could make my mouth water," I said.

"I'd just as soon not think about it," he said. "I'll be glad when I get that operation. My kidneys shore do ache."

"You don't reckon Molly will really get upset about the way we run this fence, do you?"

"I don't think so," he said. "But then I never could predict Molly very well. Anything that's connected with her dad she's touchy about."

When we got to the working place, Gid began to tamp the posts and I began to dig. The damn ground was so hard it took me half a dozen licks to get through the top crust, and then the sand-rock started. I don't know how long we worked, but after a while I looked up and seen the old red sun sitting right on top of Squaw Mountain, ten miles away. That brought her back too. When we were young it was an awful good picnicking place—there was supposed to be an Indian woman buried there, and me and Molly spent many an afternoon looking for her grave. Squaw Mountain was where the rattlesnake bit her. It wasn't even coiled but it got her right in the fat part of her calf. She shut her eyes when I got ready to cut around the bite; I barely had the nerve to do it. "If you don't I won't be your girl," she said, and I went ahead. While I was working the tourniquet she kissed me. "I'm still your girl," she said. I had the devil of a time getting her home.

"She's going down, Gid," I said. "Let's quit."

He leaned on his tamping bar a minute, looking at the sun. He was so hot he was sweating on the ears. "One more hole," he said. I dug it and he dropped the post in and tamped it while I took my sweaty shirttail out so the evening cool would get to my belly.

"That's a day," he said. He dropped the tamping bar and stood there leaning on the post, panting a little and glaring at me.

"What's the matter?" I said. "Wasn't that hole deep enough?"

He snorted through his nose. "You never have believed how bad that hailstorm was," he said. "Out in New Mexico, living with an Indian woman. Your old man never made a bushel of wheat that year."

"So what," I said. "He knew about hail when he decided to plant the stuff in the first place." But I guess I should have been sorry where it concerned Dad. The hailstorm turned Dad back into a poor man, and that turned him into a drunkard. But I guess if the hail hadn't, something else would have.

Gid picked up the crowbar and I shouldered my diggers, and we started back up the fence row.

"Nearly seven o'clock," I said. "Too many hours for an old-timer like you to work. You ain't no wild coyote any more."

"You're no young stud yourself," he said.

We made it to the lots and pitched our fencing stuff in the back of the pickup. Gid flipped a coin to see which one of us would drive, and he won. He was an expert coin flipper, or else the luckiest man alive. He never had to drive over once a month.

"Don't run over that rock," he said, after we started off.

"You just settle down," I said. "I'm driving this vehicle, now. Tomorrow, is it, you're taking your granddaughter to the picture show?"

"Tomorrow," he said. "*Snow White*. Get you in a good game of dominos."

I drove out of the pastures and onto the highway. "Pretty sundown," Gid said. "Looky how the sky's lit up. Looks like somebody set the world on fire."

"It wasn't neither one of us that done it," I said. But the sky was awful bright, over west of Thalia. The whole west side of the sky was orange and red.

"I wish we had time to go by and see Molly," he said. "Maybe we can day after tomorrow."

two

Three days later, I met Gid on the road. He never showed up in the morning, so after I ate my dinner I decided I'd go in to the domino hall and play a little. I didn't figure he was coming; but I just shouldn't have figured. Before I got halfway to town I seen his car, about two hills up the road, coming like sixty: I knew right then I'd made the trip for nothing.

Usually, when I met him on the road, he'd come flying over some hill and get nearly by me before he even seen the pickup, much less recognized it. I'd get to watch him go skidding by, cussing and talking to himself. I always just stopped my vehicle and waited: there wasn't no sense in both of us trying to back up in a narrow road, no better than either one of us could drive. Gid would grind into reverse and back he'd come, leaning out the window and spitting cigar and backing as fast as a six-cylinder Chevvy would back. Usually he would swerve off in the bar ditch a time or two, and run over a beer bottle or an old railroad tie somebody had thrown out to get rid of. Most of the time the damage wasn't serious. Some times were worse than others.

It had rained that morning, and I met him right at the top of the hill by Jamison Williams' goat pasture. The old claytop hill was a little slippery. Gid went somewhere down the south side of the hill getting stopped. I kept one foot on the clutch and the other on brake and sat there on my side of the hill, waiting. In a minute I heard the gears grind, and then I seen the back end of the Chevvy come over the hill. I saw right off it was coming in sight too fast and too far to the west, so I pushed in on my clutch and rolled on down out of the way. It looked like what happened was Gid's hands were sweaty and slipped off the wheel. Anyhow, the Chevvy went into a slide and came sideslipping down the hill and kinda bounced the bar ditch and went through Jamison's fence and made a little dido and came back through another part of the fence and headed for the road agin. Only by then it was slowed too much to bounce the ditch, and it hit the soft dirt and turned over.

Well, when I seen that I jumped out of the pickup and ran over and yanked open the first door I came to and helped Gid out. The glove compartment had come open and he was practically buried in maps and beer openers and pliers and old envelopes; he kept that glove compartment about as full as Fibber McGee kept his hall closet.

"Are you hurt, Gid?" I said. The only thing I could see was a big skinned place on his nose. It didn't look deep, but the blood was dripping on his new gray shirt. "Is your nose broke?" I said.

"No, goddamnit!" he said. "Get to hell away if you can't do nothing but stand there asking questions."

"You must have bumped the windshield," I said.

"Hell, I bumped the whole damn roof," he said.

"Don't talk," I said. "Sit down here a minute. You was just in a wreck, don't you realize that?"

But he went walking up the hill, bending over so his nose wouldn't drip on his shirt. He acted like he was going on to the ranch, afoot. "Hey," I said. "Don't go walking off that way. Your insides may be hurt."

"I lost my cigar coming down here somewheres," he said. "I

just got it lit and I don't intend to let it go to waste." Now if that wasn't consistent. I sat down on the Chevvy and he went on and found his cigar and came back.

"Get up from there," he said. "Get the pickup and chain and we'll drag this sonofabitch out."

I got up and looked around, and if it wasn't just my luck. When I jumped out of my pickup I plumb forgot about it and the bastard had rolled off in the east bar ditch and stuck itself tight as a wedge. Gid was moderately mad when he seen he had two vehicles not fifty feet apart that wouldn't neither one budge.

"Shit," he said. "Looks like you could have taken time to stop that pickup, Johnny. I guess if I was chasing a herd of cattle and my horse fell, you'd just bail off and let the horses and cattle go."

"I might," I admitted. "There ain't much telling what I'll do." A kid would have known better than to leave that pickup out of gear.

"I thought I heard you yell at me when you went through the fence," I said. "That's what made me in such a big hurry."

"Aw, you got to do something when you're running over a fence," he said. "I just yelled to be yelling. What do you think I'm paying you for?"

"Damned if I know," I said. "I haven't worked for you but thirty-eight years, you ain't had time yet to tell me what you wanted me to do."

"Well, it's not for driving into the domino parlor every day, that's for sure," he said.

"I thought I better come in and get the news," I said. "The country could have gone to war, for all I knowed."

"You got a radio," he said.

"Yes, but when I turn it on I don't get nothing but music or static. And most of the time I'd rather listen to the static."

"Okay," he said. "Don't stand out there in the road arguing with me all day. Let's dig her out."

"Which one?" I said.

"Yours. It wouldn't do no good to dig mine, it would still be wrong side up when we got it dug."

"Dig her out yourself, by god," I said. I thought the car wreck must have driven him out of his mind. "Why, there's a tractor at the Henrys', not two mile away. I can go get it and be back before we could get the shovel sharp."

"Dig her out, by god," he said. "I don't intend to borrow from the Henrys."

But just then a hundred or so of Jamison Williams' goats came out of a post-oak thicket and made for the hole in the fence. When Gid seen them coming it sobered him in a minute.

"Run," he said. "Let's stop up them holes or them bastards will be all over the country and we'll have to round them up."

And by god they would. Goats could hide in weeds and badger holes where it would take you a week to find one, much less a hundred.

"Get your rope," he said. "Maybe we can string it between the posts."

"I've seen eight wire fences that couldn't stop a goat," I said. "What good do you think a lariat rope would do?"

"Okay," he said. "You take the north hole and I'll take the south."

"Take it and do what with it?" I said. "You don't mean patch it, do you?"

"Goddamn, Johnny," he said. "Ain't you got any initiation at all! Have I got to tell you ever move to make?"

"If you mean go-ahead, I don't guess I got any," I said. "You whipped that out of me long ago."

He went trotting over to the south hole, no faster than I could walk. I guess he thought he was running. I walked on to my hole and stood there.

"Wave your hands and yell," he said.

"Gid," I said. "Why don't you try out for the Olympics? You were really picking them up and laying them down. I'd hate to think what would happen if something got after you someplace where there wasn't nothing to climb."

But he was mad enough to bite somebody, and I was the only one handy, so I shut up. We made what noise we could, and it kept the most of them from just walking right on through. But the old Chevvy had cut a pretty wide dido, and there was about thirty yards of fence between me and him. It wasn't exactly hole, but it wasn't no goat fence, either. Gid was yelling like the Choctaw nation, but one old billy went right on through. I thought Gid might call up an ambulance or the volunteer firemen, though. The old billy stood in the road blatting and trying to get the rest to follow him.

"Chunk that sonofabitch," Gid yelled. I couldn't find nothing to throw but a clod, and I missed with it. Gid was farther up the hill, where there was more sandrock, and he begin giving the old goat hell. Only about the fourth throw he led him too much and the sandrock went sailing right on through the rear window of the pickup and rattled around in the cab.

"Goddamn," he said. "Of all the places you could have stopped that pickup."

"Of all the places you could have thrown that rock," I said. "If it broke that bottle of screwworm dope I had sitting in the seat, I'm quitting you for good. I don't intend to ride along smelling that stuff for the rest of my life."

About then the rest of the goats decided to move. They spread out and come for the fence like a covey of quail. We did our best to turn them, but there wasn't no way, short of actually grabbing hold. I wasn't in the mood to wrestle no Jamison Williams goat, so I stood there and tried to get a count on the ones that went through.

Gid gave up the hardest of any man I ever saw. He grabbed a nannie and fought her around and got her turned and then let her go and grabbed an old billy. The minute he did the nannie whipped around like a bobcat and jumped the bar ditch and run down the road a ways and jumped the off bar ditch and went on through the barbed-wire fence into the brush and was gone. Gid and the old billy went to the ground. It looked like Gid was getting the worst of it, only sometimes Gid had more stubbornness to him than a billy goat. A lot more, actually. It ain't no exaggeration to say he was the stubbornest man I ever knew, except his dad. It ain't no miscompliment, either. He was determined that at least one goat was going to stay in Jamison's pasture, and by god one did. We tied him with our belts, and Gid sat on him.

Gid sure did look worn out. He looked so old all of a sudden it worried me. His hat had got mashed in the struggle and was laying off to one side; he leaned over to reach for it and the old goat hunched and over Gid went, on his face. It wasn't particularly funny, and I reached down to help him up, but he wouldn't move.

"I'll just stay down awhile," he said. "I ain't no good when I'm up noways. I can't even stay on a tied-down goat."

I remembered the time, up on the plains, when Gid had ridden eighteen wild horses in one day. Falling off the goat was a real comedown. He sat there on the ground, wiping his skint nose on his shirt sleeve. I handed him his hat.

"And take this handkerchief, too," I said. "You'll get infected wiping that nose on your shirt."

"Don't give a damn if I do," he said.

"Maybe it won't be so bad," I said. "Maybe Jamison's got those goats trained to come to a horn."

"Aw, you couldn't call them up with an elephant horn," he said.

I never knew there was such a thing as an elephant horn, but I didn't say so. I squatted down on my hunkers. The old billy thought he was plumb to the high and lonesome, since he'd got rid of Gid, and he went hunching along the ground on one side.

"If I had the money, I'd just buy them goats," Gid said. "Then we could let them go, and anybody found one would be welcome to it."

"We'll get 'em a few at a time," I said. "Jamison oughtn't to be in no hurry."

Jamison was the slowest white man either of us had ever seen, and pretty near the most worthless. He kept him a little herd of sorry Mississippi cows, that he let run loose on the road in the summertime. Ever evening his old lady and his boys would have to get out and gather them up. I've seen them many a time, moving the herd, Jamison poking along behind in his old blue Dodge, and Judith and the boys driving the cattle down the road afoot.

"Oh hell," Gid said. "He's slow, but he ain't dumb. He'll figure out how much to charge us for this fence. If you had just have stayed home a few more minutes, all this never would have happened."

"No, nor if you had started a few minutes sooner. Same difference. If you could drive worth a shit it wouldn't have happened anyway. Whoever heard of a grown man letting his car get out of control that way?"

"I have," he said. "It happens all the time."

I noticed he kept rubbing his elbow, like something was wrong with it. Finally I asked him about it.

"Why nothing's wrong with it," he said, and then he looked at it and winced. He rolled up his sleeve and it looked like a rattlesnake had struck him; his elbow was the size of a grapefruit. I guess the blood vessels in it had burst; it was about the color of an old inner tube.

"That beats all," I said. "Wrestling with a damn goat and your arm nearly knocked off. Look how black it's getting."

"It's that damn steering wheel knob," he said. "It's as dangerous as a snake. I seen it whipping around at me when I first lost holt of the wheel, but I thought I got out of its way. Reckon my arm's broke."

I figured so. He had done broke that arm three times. One time a whirlwind blew him off the barn roof, and one time a little mean Hereford bull knocked him down. Once I think he even broke it slamming a pickup door on himself.

"I hear a car," I said. "I'll flag them down and they can run you into a hospital. You better get it X-rayed. I'll stay here and dig that pickup out." Actually I meant to go on up to the Henrys' and get that tractor.

But Gid wouldn't even get up and walk out to the road. I never seen a man turn down as much good advice as he done.

"Let them go," he said. "I'll rest a minute, and help you dig."

"No sir," I said. "That arm needs tending to."

I went out to the road. And of all the people to be coming along just then, it had to be Molly. I knowed it was her before I even seen the car; she always went in to sell her eggs on Friday. And sure enough, it was her old Ford, the only car she'd ever had. We were humiliated for sure, one wrecked and one stuck, and I just turned my back to the road. As proud and contrary as Gid was, he wouldn't ride in with her if his jugular vein was cut.

The way she drove, I thought she might go by without seeing us. The driver's seat on her old car was sunk in, and she had to drive with her chin way up in order to see at all. Usually she never looked to the sides of the road. Actually, I don't know that she did see us. She may have smelled us. Anyway, she threw the skids to the Ford, and if the hill had been about one degree slicker there would have been three cars in the ditch instead of two. I wish she had stuck it—it would have evened things up. Her and Gid was ever bit as bad a driver as one another; the only difference was that when Molly got in a tight place she slowed down, and when Gid got in one he speeded up. Anything fancy was out of their category.

But by pure luck she got stopped all right. Gid was still sitting there, feeling of his arm, and the old billy had hunched and floundered about thirty yards away. Molly had on her sunbonnet and her blue milking overalls, and an old pair of men's overshoes that had belonged to me at one time, so she didn't exactly look like Lily Langtry. But she would be a good-looking woman the day she died; she always kept enough of her looks to make me remember how much she had when she had them all. She stood there in the road, taking her own good time looking the situation over. She shoved Gid's car with her foot, to see if it would shake, and then she studied the car tracks on the hill awhile, trying to make out what happened.

Gid couldn't stand the wait. "Come on over here," he said. "We ain't ashamed to admit we had a wreck. We'll tell you all about it."

But she walked off up the hill a little ways, trying to get it settled for herself.

"Look at her," he said. "Hog on ice. She's too independent for her own good. Somebody needs to take Molly down a notch or two."

"I could spit on two fellers who've been trying it for forty years," I said.

"Yes, and I've accomplished it," he said, "and I'll accomplish it agin."

"I never knowed you was such an optimist," I said.

In a minute she came stepping across the bar ditch. She looked perfectly peaceful: it was the way she usually looked. Lots of times I'd go by her place and find her sitting at the kitchen table, looking rich as cream. Life had took different on Molly than it had on me and Gid. She rested her hands on her hips and looked down at him a minute before she said anything. She had tipped her bonnet off, and her hair was blowing around her face. It was getting a sprinkle of gray, but it was still mostly black, and as long and pretty as it had ever been.

"Well, you sure skinned your nose," she said. "You look like you had an accident."

Gid snorted.

"Oh no, it wasn't no accident," I said. "We set out on purpose to see who could make the biggest idiot of himself."

"It's hard to say who won," she said, grinning at me.

"I don't want a word out of you," Gid said. "As many times as I've pulled you out of ditches and off culverts."

"I know it," she said. "I don't claim to be a good driver. But I'm going to town after while, and what are you going to do?"

"Sit here till my nose scabs over," he said. "I don't intend to walk a dripping blood."

"Aw, get your hook and chain," she said. "I can pull the pickup out."

He had just been waiting for her to offer so he wouldn't need to ask.

"If you think your old hoopey can do it, we'll sure be glad to let you try," he said. He reached out a hand for me to pull him up, but when I took it and pulled he bellered like a bull. He had stretched out his sore arm before he thought, and I had to ease him back. Molly squatted down and rolled his sleeve back up and had a look at the elbow. He tried to wave her away with his good hand, but she paid it no mind.

"Quit flapping that hand in my face," she said. "You look snake-bit." His arm was hurting so he couldn't talk, but he held up his good arm and I got him to his feet.

"Let's go," he said. "You get the chain and she can pull you out." He wouldn't look at Molly; he was afraid she was going to take him up to her place and doctor him awhile. And before I had time to move he went across the road to the pickup and began fishing around for the chain himself.

Molly grinned. "He never will learn," she said, "and I'm glad. You better go find that chain if you can. He's liable to drop it on his foot and be down agin."

"I wish he would. If he had an arm and a leg out of commission, we could slow him down enough that he wouldn't really hurt himself."

I went over to the pickup to see what I could do. Gid had about half the stuff under the seat slung out on the road.

"Get out of the way," I said. "A one-armed man ain't got no business trying to handle a chain."

The chain was tricky to get out once you found it. It was between the hydraulic jack and a big pipe wrench that had got wedged in so tight a couple of years before that we couldn't move it. I had to be awful careful about moving that jack: with the slightest excuse it would have wedged itself, and the chain would have been gone for good. Damn the man that invented pickup seats anyway: you can't get nothing under them without skinning your knuckles, and then you can't get it back out if you do get it in. Gid was grumbling because I'd pushed him out of the way.

"That's how it is," he said. "I pay a fortune in wages, and then I'm the one gets ordered around."

I had managed to ease the jack past the seat brace, and I finally captured the chain. Molly came up about that time and Gid shut up like a terrapin shell.

"I wonder where all those goats will go," she said. "They were strung out clear back to the bridge."

"I hope the sonofabitches starve to death," he said. He had given up trying to do anything and was leaning against the fender. "I hope the creek gets up tonight and drowns ever one of them. A man that would own a goat would own a hound dog—they ain't no worse."

"Why, I think goats are okay," she said. "They probably make Jamison good money."

They went on that way, having a nice friendly dispute to settle their nerves, and I drug out the chain. Then I gathered up all the stuff Gid had drug out and stuffed what I could of it back. I was just getting ready to hook on the chain when I seen Jamison Williams coming over the hill riding his old fat blue horse.

"Looky yonder," I said. "Get your checkbook ready."

"Damn you," he said. "If you wasn't so slow, we'd be in town by now."

"He's riding old Blue-ass," I said. "We could outrun him on foot."

Molly got tickled, but she tried not to show it.

"Why Jamison won't hurt you," she said. "I've never seen him mad."

"Oh no," Gid said. "I ain't scared of him hurting me. It's his ideas I'm scared of. He'll have some crazy idea about how much that old rotted-out fence is worth to fix. You watch and see."

"Don't let yourself panic," I said. "Think up a good story to tell him. Say a hit-and-run driver knocked you through that fence."

"Naw," he said, "what's the use? Jamison's too dumb to lie to.

It'll be all he can do to understand the truth."

Actually, Jamison managed that without much strain. He rode straight up to the hole and slid off old Blue-ass and came right over to Gid, sticking out his hand. Jamison was foolish about shaking hands. He tipped his hat to Molly and came and shook hands with me before he ever said a word.

"By god, Gideon," he said. "I see you run through my fence. These roads are slick, would you say?"

"A little slick," Gid said. When he was in a tight corner he got mighty scarce with his conversation.

"Well, Gid," Jamison said, "I wonder how long it will take you and Johnny to bring them goats back in? Judith don't like for them goats to run loose on the road." Which was a lie. Judith Jamison never cared. In fact, she might have been glad.

"Depends," Gid said. "How much are they worth to you, Jamison, by the head?"

"Well, you know, Gid," Jamison said. "You know how I knew them goats was out. By god, if that old one-eyed billy didn't come right up in the yard and butt that littlest boy of mine. He butted that boy good and hard and was after the dogs."

"Goodness," Molly said. "Why, they looked so gentle. You wouldn't think they'd hurt anybody."

"That's what I told my wife," he said. "It's too bad she can't shoot no better. She would shoot that good dog before she hit the goat."

"Probably should have used the shotgun," Gid said. "Rifles are a little hard."

"Well, you know, Gid, it was the ten-gauge she used. I don't know whether her shoulder's broke or not. I guess the doc can X-ray it when we take the boy in. He would butt him through the garden fence."

"These roads are pretty slick, Jamison," Gid said. "If I was you, I'd wait till they dried up a little before I went in. A man can get off in the ditch and wreck his car before he knows what's happening to him."

"I guess forty dollars apiece for them goats," Jamison said. "They got to be drenched if I keep them, and they ain't due to wool till September."

He tipped his hat to Molly agin and went over and began to climb on old Blue-ass. I watched that, because Jamison Williams getting on a horse was a sight not many people got to see. Jamison was a little short fart; he led old Blue over to Gid's car and got up the car so he'd have elevation and got on from there. Gid didn't get much kick out of that performance. He was in a fairly solemn mood.

"Forty *apiece?*" he said. He was trying to let on he thought that was too high.

"Why, you could have them for that, Gid," Jamison said. "There was eighty-six of them. If you don't want to buy them, you and Johnny just feel free to bring them in any time and leave them in the pen. Judith and the boys can take them back to the pasture after they milk." We found out later it was Judith's collarbone that broke. I guess we ought to be glad she didn't shoot one of the children.

"We'll get them back tomorrow," Gid said. "And I'll get a crew out to fix your fence. Shore sorry all this happened. Send me them doctor bills."

"Well, Gid, such is life," Jamison said. "By god, this rain did us good. Just leave the goats in the pen. We don't mind helping our neighbors, me and the wife."

"Okay. You'll all come to see us," Gid said.

"Sure, sure. Go, Blue. By god, I hope that boy's stopped bleeding when I get home."

He turned old Blue-ass toward the barn, and off they went. "Ain't that a sight?" Gid said.

"Get in and back her up, Molly," I said. "This chain ain't very long."

It didn't take long to get the pickup out, once I got her hitched to it. It's just a wonder she didn't pull it in two.

"Now you got about ten feet of slack," I said. "Go slow till the chain gets tight. Then give her hell."

"You reckon she can do it?" Gid said.

"You just stand back so the mud won't splatter on you," she said.

She gunned that old Ford like it was a B-36. I just braced myself; I knew what she was going to do. Directly off she went, and it like to popped my head off when she hit the end of the chain. But we sure came out of the mud. Gid gave a jump for the running board, but he wasn't close enough, so he got left. I went to honking for her to stop: the road was still so slick I was afraid to tap my brakes. I just sat loose in the seat and got ready to jump if it come to that. There wasn't no limit to how reckless Molly could drive. Once I was riding with her when she turned over a trailer with two sows and eleven shoats in it; a Greyhound bus passed us and honked. "He never needed to honk at me," she said. It took me half a day to gather those squealing bastards up.

For a change, I was lucky. We came to a corner, and when we got around it she felt a little jerk on the chain and remembered me. I was out of the pickup and had the chain unhooked before we quit rolling good.

"I'll be," she said. "I guess we left Gid."

"He's coming down the road." I hadn't looked, but I knew Gid that well. I was fixing to back up for him when I heard him holler.

"Just hold on," he said. "If you was to back up you'd run over me." He was red in the face as an old turkey gobbler.

"What's the matter with you?" he said to Molly. "I wish you'd been tied to a tree."

"You didn't need to walk," she said. He didn't bother Molly. "Now git in this car. We won't go to town, we'll just go back to my place. I want to work on this arm a little." She slipped up and got him by his sore arm, so he couldn't pull back, and led him right on over to the Ford without another word said. He knew better than to fool with her when she had the advantage. We stopped at the wreck a minute, so he could fish out a box of cigars. I bet it blistered him a little to have her drive him up the hill he'd just slid down.

Molly was still living on the old Taylor place, where she had lived her whole life. It was on a hill—some say the highest place in the county—and you could see it for miles and miles around. The first time I ever saw Molly was on that place; she was carrying a jug of the old man's whiskey up the cellar steps. It was the first time I had ever been visiting anywhere. All my folks were blonds, and I never will forget how surprised I was to see them black-headed Taylor kids. Pa and the old man sat on the back steps and drank whiskey out of the same jug for half an hour, and then they chased me and Molly down and made us drink a little. We cried and run off down to the pigpen together and made some mud pies out of the pigwallow and ate them, to get the whiskey taste out of our mouths. When we went back the old man thought of some more devilment: he sat a bucket on the fence and said he'd give me a dime if I'd shoot it off with his old twelve-gauge shotgun. I didn't know what a dime was, but I was crazy about guns. Pa steadied it for me, so I don't guess I caught the whole kick, but I caught enough. I missed the bucket, too, so the old man wouldn't give me the dime: I never found out what one was till two years later. Molly took up for me and led me down in the cellar and showed me the still.

And she stayed right there and done all of her living right up on that hill. I guess she just never saw no reason to move around. Her old man and old lady were dead before she married Eddie, and all the other kids had left home. Eddie never had nothing but a pack of turd hounds and a pair of roughnecking boots from the day he was born till the day he fell off the derrick; their getting married was just a matter of finding a justice of the peace who was sober enough to talk. But it's still strange to think of her spending her whole life there on her hill. One night when we were younger and were laying up together, I was awake listening to the wind rattle the windowpanes, and I asked her about it.

"Ain't you curious to see the world at all?" I said.

"No," she said. "I'm doing just as much living right here and now as I could anywhere." And she hugged me and we went back to sleep.

Probably, in the long run, she was right. She done her share up on that hill. She was born there, and went to school what little she went over in the Idiot Ridge schoolhouse. The flu killed the old lady in 1918; the old man drank lye. Her oldest brother Shep, I don't know what became of him. Mary Margaret married a store clerk, and Rich got caught stealing saddles and sent to the pen; Molly said once he was out, but he never came our way. Eddie fell off that oil rig, and then the Germans got Joe and the Japs got Jimmy. All that time Molly stayed there and went on. Sometimes I wonder what will become of the old Taylor place when Molly and the rest of us are gone. I can't imagine that hill without her. But I guess there ain't nothing that don't come to an end sometime.

When we got there she took us in the kitchen and fed us peach cobbler and coffee. Gid was quiet as a mouse. After a while she went out in the smokehouse and brought in some kerosene for him to soak his arm in.

He perked right up. "Oh, is that all?" he said. He couldn't get his sleeve up fast enough. I guess he thought she went after the dehorning saw.

"Yell if she gets too rough," I said. "I got to go outside. Smelling that kerosene ain't good for a healthy man."

I went out back and sat on the steps. You could see way off west, across Molly's land and a lot of Gid's. Her back bedroom was a nice place to wake up. The clouds to the west were peeling away like layers of gauze, and it wasn't long before the sun was shining on the wet mesquite. I could hear her and Gid talking through the screen door. It was childish, but it made me feel left out. I knew all about it. Old as they was, Gid was still halfway talking about leaving Mabel and coming to live with Molly, and she was halfway encouraging it. And it would have been a good thing for Gid and her both, I guess; it just made me feel a little left out. We had both hung around her so long. Course Gid ought to left Mabel. Living with her thirty years was no judgment, in my book. But she had a grandkid to hold over him. I got up and walked around to the garden, to see how the tomatoes and the roasting ears were holding out. I seen I was going to have to make it around for supper a little more often, if I was going to beat the blister bugs to what there was. Molly kind of expected me for supper anyway, a lot of times.

When I came out of the garden the sun was so bright that I went around to the front of the house, where the shade was. In a little while Gid come out on the porch; he had about half a bedsheet wrapped around his arm, and he was grinning like a possum.

"I'm as good as new," he said.

Molly came out with three big glasses of buttermilk and a plate of cold cornbread. Nobody had much to say, so we sat quiet for a change, eating cornbread and buttermilk. Once in a while the conversation would kinda settle; I guess we were all thinking about old times. Finally I looked around and Molly and Gid were staring off across the pastures, not seeing anything.

"What time is it?" I said. They both jumped.

Gid fished out his pocket watch, but it was stopped.

"Shadows are pretty long," Molly said.

"Time we got on," he said.

"Aw, you'all stay for supper. I've got some fresh black-eyed peas shelled. We'll dress a fryer."

"I guess we can't," Gid said, sounding a little gloomy. He set his empty buttermilk glass down on the tray. His nose still looked raw and stingy.

Molly walked out in the yard and began to pick on the lilac bushes. "I don't see why you'all don't just sit a few more minutes," she said. "Supper won't take no time."

"We'll have to put it off till some other time," Gid said. "We're much obliged."

"I don't want your much obliged," she said, kinda snappy. "I want you to eat with me."

Then we walked around the house and stood by the cellar a minute, the cellar Old Man Taylor had built. The sun was down and it was clouding up agin over in the northwest.

Gid said let's go and Molly tried one more time to get us to stay. She walked out to the pickup with us, looking down in the dumps. Gid bragged on her bandage a little, to try and perk her up.

"You'all come by and see me," she said.

"I'll be by," I said. "I might even get back tonight."

"I wish you would, if it ain't out of your way. I'll keep something on the stove."

"No, don't go to no trouble," I said. "No sense in you waiting up special. I might not get by till eleven o'clock, I don't know."

"Okay," she said. "Do as you please."

We told her good-by and I drove on out through the cattle guard, into the lane. Molly was still standing by her windmill, watching the world, or maybe just watching us.

"She's getting lonesome in her old age," he said.

"Tell me where to go," I said. "I don't want to get blamed for taking you someplace wrong." He never had found out I wasn't no mind reader. Once when we was younger and got drunk I took him to a rodeo in Newcastle and it turned out he had paid his entry fee in one in Waurika, Oklahoma, a hundred and fifty miles the other way.

"Just take me home," he said. He was blue; he always got blue in the late evenings—had been for years. If I had to face Mabel, I wouldn't have had no fondness for sundown, either.

"Molly's been lonesome a good while," I said. "Her independent talk don't fool me."

"We're the only ones that ever go and see her," he said. "Wonder why she don't like womenfolk."

"Same reason I don't. They're silly as hens, all of them except her."

He turned it over in his mind for a while. It wasn't quite dark good, but all the lights were on in Thalia. Ever time we topped a hill I seen them flashing. The shower had cooled things off and the country smelled nice and green. Being in wrecks made Gid thoughtful.

"Molly's had a lot," he said.

"Yes," I said. "But I wouldn't call it no whopping success of a life."

"She's made mistakes," he said. "So have I and so have you."

"At least I ain't made the same ones over and over agin," I said.

"Why not? You might as well make them you're used to as to make new ones all the time. It don't do no more damage."

"Anyhow," he said, "I wish she wasn't lonesome."

We drove through Thalia. Two or three cars were parked in front of the picture show, and a couple more outside the domino hall.

"Television's got the picture show business," he said.

"No wonder. They quit making good shows. The last one I seen that was any count was *Red River*."

"Good night," he said, "that was years ago."

"So were a lot of good things," I said. Six or eight kids were scuffling and fighting on the courthouse lawn, under the mulberry trees.

"You don't keep up," he said. "*Shane* was made since then. So was *The Searchers*."

"Them was so-so," I said. "All the good movie stars are getting too old."

"I wish I had the energy them kids have," he said.

"You'd waste it," I said. "Just like they're doing."

We passed the drive-in eating place, and it looked like 90 percent of the cars in town were there. "Them things are what makes the money," I said.

"I know it," he said. "I hate a drive-in. Them jukeboxes are awful."

"Susie'll be right there in a few years," I said. "Right in the middle of it."

"I guess so," he said. "I reckon so."

I pulled up in his driveway and stopped. Gid opened the door, but he kept sitting there.

"How'll we get those goddamn goats?" he said.

"I favor a thirty-thirty," I said. "The ammunition's cheap."

"But the goats ain't. We'll just get out there about daybreak and get them ourselves."

"I knew you'd decide on the hardest way."

"If you stop at the domino hall," he said, "tell Charlie Starton to get his wrecker and go get that car. You might show him where it is." What he meant was, be damn sure I didn't let that car sit out there all night.

"Okay," I said. "See you when it gets light. Any special horse? You got one that's good on goats?"

"Bring me any one you can catch," he said.

He was out, still holding to the car door. I began to back up. The only way to get loose from him was to drive loose. When I swung into the street my headlights shone on him, standing outside his door cleaning his boots.

Charlie Starton was standing on the sidewalk in front of the domino hall, smoking a cigar.

"What's the matter with Gid?" he said. "Can't he drive?"

I never cared to stand around having no conversation with Charlie Starton.

"His reflexes don't work too fast," I said. "Are you coming or ain't you?"

When there was money involved Charlie's reflexes worked awful fast. He followed me right out and winched up the car. I turned in at Molly's, but it was past ten, and she had gone to bed; I hated that. I hated to see Molly lonesome, and I had been counting on some cold supper besides. But it wasn't no go. I went home and fed the chickens and ate me a bowl of Post Toasties and went to bed.

three

About two weeks later we met Molly at the feed store one morning. It was August then, and the country was drying up, so Gid wanted to feed his old cows a little. I was in town early and we thought we'd be the first customers, but Molly's old Ford was sitting by the loading platform.

"She's getting her chicken feed," I said.

Gid looked a little nervous. Him and her might have been having arguments, I didn't know.

Her and the feed-store hands were sitting in the back of the store on the sacks of dogfood, drinking coffee. Samuel Houston was petting his old mangy dog and telling a big windy. He didn't own the feed store, he just foremanned it: His boy T.I. and a crew of Mexicans did what little work got done.

Molly looked up and said hello to us, but Samuel H. never broke his stride.

"He caught me about two miles this side of the stop sign," he said. "Come walking up to the car with a big gun on his hip and a badge on his chest. 'I'd like to see your driver's license,' he said, like it was a friendly conversation. 'I'd like to see your funeral notice, you sonofabitch,' I said. 'Now, mister, don't use that foul language,' he said. 'What are you going to tell the judge when you have to show him this ticket?' 'I guess, by god, I'll tell him I run a goddamn stop sign,' I said. 'Now give it here, I got to get this feed unloaded this morning.'"

"Why, I'd have stomped that mother into the pavement," T.I. said. "Where he needed to be stomped." He might have, too. Once at a medicine show T.I. won what they said was a genuine white

Mormon wife, only it turned out to be a genuine White Rock Hen. He stomped a little that night. His real name was Texas Independence.

"Why, hello, Gid," Samuel Houston said, "have you seen my dog? This here's the smartest dog I ever raised, and I call him Billie Sol. He can suck the eggs right out from under the hens without them even noticing."

Gid just looked impatient. "I hate to bother you fellers," he said. "But if it ain't too much trouble, I'd like about a dozen sacks of cottonseed cake."

The three Mexicans got the biggest laugh out of that. They led such easy lives sitting around that percolator, I guess they could get a big laugh out of anything.

"Oh, it's no trouble," Samuel H. said. "No trouble atall. That's what we're in business for. Sit down and help yourself to some coffee."

"No thank you," Gid said. "I believe we'll get the cake and get on. The longer we wait the hotter it will get."

"Then, by god, why go? A man can get too hot out working, if he ain't careful. It'll be cool agin this afternoon."

"Oh, sit down a minute," Molly said. "I got a favor to ask you."

But Gid was having a stubborn fit; he kept standing up fidgeting. Finally I got tired of standing and sat down.

"We'd sure like to get on," Gid said. "Maybe me and Johnny could just load the feed ourselves, if you'd show us where it is."

"Why sure, Gid," Samuel Houston said. "It's right over there in the corner. Just feel right at home. Show him where that cottonseed cake is, T.I."

T.I. yawned like he had just got up. "Sure," he said. "Why don't you let these boys help you pitch it in the truck? They don't mind."

I knew it would eventually come down to me helping load it. Gid would have soon handled a rattlesnake as a sack of cattle feed. He never lifted one except in emergencies. But as soon as I stood up and moved, the Mexicans grabbed the sacks and had the feed loaded in a minute and a half. And as soon as Gid saw that, he was perfectly happy to stay awhile; he felt like things were getting done.

Only he said the exact wrong thing, and Molly thought he said it to her.

"That's the stuff," he said. "We can get going in a minute now and get some work done. I wasn't raised lazy, like most people."

I don't know what possessed him to say it; maybe it was being nervous. And I don't know what possessed Molly to take it wrong; he never meant to aim it at her. But she sat her cup down and gave him the strangest hurt look.

The elevator boss drove up then, and Samuel and T.I. and the Mexicans jumped to get to work. Just us three stayed there, and it was real quiet. I tried my hardest to think of some conversation to kinda pass it all over, and I know Gid did too, but we couldn't come up with much. It was plain silly, but it was awkward as hell; five minutes of it would have made me sick.

But it never lasted over two. Molly broke down crying; I knew she would. "That wasn't a very nice thing to say to me, Gid," she said. She bent over with her head between her knees and we could only see her hair, and her head shaking. Then all of a sudden she straightened up and looked right at me. "Well, aren't you going to take up for me?" she said, and went to crying agin.

I didn't know what to say. None of it made sense. I guess she took it as something against her dad—she always tried to fool herself about him. Gid never could appreciate how hard some people worked to fool themselves.

She cried hard when she cried, but it didn't last too long. Gid was just flabbergasted. In a minute her back got still, and she looked up. The tears were dripping everywhere, but she was kinda calm agin, and nobody would have believed she had been so upset. I went over and filled her coffee cup and handed it to her. "Thank you," she said. She rested her elbows on her knees and bent over, sipping coffee, with the tears running off the corner of her mouth and dripping right in the cup. Gid couldn't stand it—he got up and fished out his handkerchief.

"Here, don't ruin that good coffee," he said.

She took it and kinda grinned at him. "What am I going to do with myself?" she said.

"Why, I'm terribly sorry, Molly," he said. "I never meant a thing by that remark."

"Oh, I know you didn't," she said. "It's silly. I don't know why some things upset me so. You ain't to blame."

But he was, really. At least he sure thought he was. We sat for about five minutes, all of us a little bit worried, drinking our coffee.

"I thought of something while I was crying," Molly said. "I hadn't thought of it in years. It was when all of us kids were at home, when we still used blackstrap molasses for all our sweetening. Daddy went in to Thalia and bought the winter groceries one day." She stopped and looked out the feedstore door, at the hot, dusty street and the houses of Thalia on the other side of it, with television aerials sticking up on their roofs like I don't know what. She looked like she was looking through a telescope at something as far away as the moon. And I guess they was about that far away, them days. It takes a long memory to sit on a bunch of dogfeed sacks and call up Old Man Cletus Taylor riding off to Thalia in a wagon. I bet he had a whiskey jug on the seat beside him, too.

"When he come back, just before sundown," she said, "he had a big barrel of sorghum molasses sitting in the front of the wagon. Him and Shep went to unloading the flour and stuff, and the rest of us kids stood there looking at that syrup barrel. I couldn't hardly imagine that much syrup. It was the sweets for the whole winter. Pretty soon Dad and Shep came back and walked the barrel to the back of the wagon, so they could lift it down." Her talking quavered a little. "I never did know how it happened," she said, "but anyway, when they were lifting it out of the wagon, one of them lost his grip and it fell and busted open on the ground. The molasses stood by itself, just a second, and then it all spread out and began to run down the hill toward the chickenhouse. We all just stood there; we couldn't move for a minute. The first was when Richard stuck his toe in it. It ran real slow, and ants and doodlebugs got caught in it. There wasn't no way to scoop it up. Then we all begin to cry. Mary Margaret took it the worst. She held her breath and ran all the way around the house before anybody could catch her to pound her on the back; then she went over and began to bang her head on the cellar door. She was the worst to hold her breath and bang her head I ever saw. Even Shep was crying. Richard was the only one that showed good sense. He squatted down and stuck his finger in it and kept licking it up that way till after dark. I couldn't believe it. Nothing had hurt me that bad before. After a while Richard put a horned toad in it, and it got stuck. I went in the house and got in one of the woodboxes and wouldn't come out till after supper. Shep and Daddy argued over whose fault it was till Shep just finally left home, and Daddy stayed down in the cellar drinking whiskey nearly that whole winter."

"My god," Gid said. "That was a tragedy."

"Nothing will ever make me forget watching that sorghum run downhill," she said.

"What was that favor you wanted to ask?" Gid said.

"Oh, Old Roanie got out in the big pasture the other day," she said. "I can't get her back." Roanie was her milk cow. She was a wild old bitch.

"We'll come right on and get her," he said, standing up. Molly put up her coffee cup and got in her car, and we got in the pickup. "You drive," he said.

"Don't worry," I said. "This pickup is the only means of transportation I have. I ain't anxious to let you under the wheel."

"I wish we didn't have to get that cow in," he said. "We just barely will have time to do the feeding."

"I'm glad to do it today," I said. "Another day or two and you'll be gone to have your operation, and I'd have to do it by myself."

"Molly needs to be married," he said. "She ain't able to run that place by herself. I never meant to get her so upset this morning."

"She's too touchy sometimes," I said.

"I had heard that molasses story before," he said. "That was awful. I can imagine just how them kids felt."

When we got to Molly's house she was just going in the back door. Had her mind on dinner. I went on down to the barn. Gid was out before I got stopped.

"Let's pen the old hussy and eat dinner and go," he said. "Which one you want, Chester or Matt?" Molly named her horses after *Gunsmoke*.

"Chester, I guess," I said.

"Goddamn," he said, trying to saddle up. "This old bastard's so big around it's like trying to saddle a whiskey keg."

He didn't get no sympathy from me. I had reared back to throw my saddle on and heaved and Chester had got one of his big front feet on the girt. It like to broke my back. I dropped the saddle, too.

"Well, I've shot my wad," I said, "I never will get up strength for another throw."

Gid got a big laugh out of it.

And at that the horses was easier than the cow. She was standing right in plain sight, down by the salt lick. The sight cheered Gid up.

"Well, looky there," he said. "This won't take no time. I was afraid the old bitch would be off in the mesquite somewhere."

"She may be yet," I said. "I can remember cattle closer to the gate than she is that ended up getting away. How about Mick and Big Shitty?" They were two old outlaw steers Gid had owned for about ten years. We chased them up and down Onion Creek all one summer and finally tricked them into the lot with some hay. We kept Mick, too. But Gid got careless and Big Shitty ran over him and a water trough and tore up three fences and got plumb away.

"Aw, she's just an old milk cow," he said. "You sickle around behind her thataway."

I did. Old Chester loped about as graceful as a roadgrader. At first old Roanie came along fine; actually, I just don't think she had noticed us. I think she just thought it was Chester and Matt by themselves. Molly just sooked her afoot; she might not have never seen men on horses before.

But when she figured things out, the race was on. She had her head down and her bag swinging from side to side, and she was covering country. I was closest and I whipped up: I knew if I let her get in the brush, it would be my fault from the conception to the resurrection. Chester had no idea what it was all about, but he done his best. We barely got her turned before she hit the brush; then she struck out south, just as fast, and Gid and Matt struck out to head her agin. It was the funniest sight I ever seen. Old Matt didn't no more care about that cow than if she was the moon, and when it come time to stop and turn her he just went right on into the brush. The brush went to popping and the cuss words come a-flying back. But I took in after Roanie; I didn't have no time to worry about Gid. Actually, she turned out to have about twice as much speed as Chester, and I was just hoping she'd stop for the south fence when I seen Gid and Matt come flying out of the brush ahead of me, hot on her trail. Them thorny thickets hadn't helped Gid's disposition, I knew that; he didn't have his hat any more, or all his shirt. But he had his rope down. Nobody in their right mind would try to rope off a plowhorse, but Gid would rope an elephant off a Shetland if he took a notion. He was whopping old Matt with the rope about every two steps, and Matt was going to the races. Gid came roaring over a little knoll, swinging his rope and yelling, and pretty soon he let fly and caught him a cow. It was where his troubles began. Any horse with a grain of brains would have stopped when Gid threw the rope: Matt wasn't in that category. Gid reared back on the reins—he seen his fix immediately—but Matt went right on. I guess he seen the old cow when he run by her, but he sure never dreamed him and her were connected. She was just landscape to him. Roanie got a big surprise. One minute she was headed for the high and lonesome, and the next minute Matt had got to the end of the rope and she was tearing up the land like a plow. Gid, he was just a spectator, but his sympathies were all with the cow. Finally Matt figured out he was dragging an anchor. When I rode up all three of them were panting.

"She's caught now," I said. One of her horns was broke, and her front leg stuck out sideways, about as useful as a dishrag.

"Why can't nothing go right?" he said. Not "Why can't I do nothing right?" And if I had done it, it would have been "What in the goddamn hell did you mean pulling a stunt like that?"

"One consolation," I said. "We won't never have to get her up agin."

But Gid was too blue to rag.

"Nobody's fault," I said.

"No, but I'll get blamed," he said. "And I'll furnish the new cow."

"Oh no," I said. "Molly wouldn't want you to do that. We were just being neighbors. Accidents happen sometimes."

"Mostly to me," he said. "Let's go. She'll stay till we get back."

"She won't be hard to track if she don't," I said. "Where did you lose your hat?"

His hand flew up to his head, and he turned a shade bluer. He hadn't missed it till then. Me and Chester sat on the hill and waited while he went and found it.

Of course Molly was as nice as she could be about it. If it fazed her at all, it didn't show. She had meat and beans and gravy on the table when we got there, and some roasting ears steaming in a big bowl. Sweat was dripping off the ice-tea glasses.

"I hate to lose her," she said. "But she was wild as a wolf anyway. I had to hobble her all the time." She wouldn't hear of Gid furnishing her another cow, and she wouldn't even let us go down and kill the old hussy for her. Gid was out of the talking mood, so we ate and loaded our saddles and left. Molly was standing on her back porch tying her sunbonnet strings when we left.

"I shore hate that," Gid said.

I knew he would have to get over it in his own time, so I never said nothing. Nobody could talk Gid out of feeling bad. When something happened to get his mind off things a minute he was all right, and along came one of Jamison Williams' kids to do it. He was running right down the road.

"My god, ain't he running," Gid said. "Take to the ditch, he don't see us. Get out of his way and let him go."

But when he got even with us the boy stopped right quick and went to crying. He stood there in the road crying, picking one foot and then the other out of the hot sand and cooling it against his trousers leg.

"Nelson drowned in the horse trough," he said. "Just now."

We grabbed him and went. Judith was sitting in the porch rocker, rocking and crying and hugging the boy so tight he couldn't have breathed if he had been in perfect health. "Oh St. Peter," she said, "he's drowned and gone." Gid jerked the kid away from her and turned him upside down, and I ran to the back yard and kicked the rain barrel over and got it around there. Me and Gid squeezed the boy over it till about half the horse trough ran out of his mouth, and finally he came to. Gid carried him back and gave him to Judith; she was still hysterical. I don't think she ever knew it was us that drained him; she might have thought it was St. Peter. Anyhow, we went on.

"What a day," he said.

When we got to the ranch it was done too late to feed. I unloaded the twelve sacks of feed while Gid was trying to make up his mind what to do.

"I don't never get nothing done any more," he said. "These old pens need rebuilding. And that damn fencing ain't finished. Why does a man even try?"

"I've often wondered," I said.

"Well, you damn sure don't ever accomplish nothing if you don't try," he said. "Let's sit down in the shade here a minute."

"Some people get rich without trying," I said. "Look at Pearl Twass. She used to go in the bushes with just about anybody, and now she drives around in a big Chrysler and sends her kids off to fancy schools."

"Yeah, but that's just rich," he said. "That's just diamonds on a dog's ass."

"Maybe so. But Pearl don't go in the bushes so cheap any more."

"Now I got to organize," he said. "Before I go to the hospital. Wisht I never had agreed to this damn operation. No telling how long it will tie me up."

"I thought it was just a standard operation for kidney trouble," I said. "Like grinding your valves."

"Oh it is," he said. "But you never know. I'm pessimistic, I guess."

"Well, don't worry about the ranch," I said. "I've taken care of it for thirty-eight years. I won't lay down on the job now."

"That's what worries me," he said. "How well you've taken care of things. That's why nothing on this whole outfit works like it ought to."

"No, it's because you're too tight to buy good equipment," I said.

"Anyhow," he said, "and be that as it may, I'm going to draw you up enough orders to last you till I get back."

"Glad to have them," I said. "Then I'll at least know what not to do."

He wet his pencil and went to figuring, and I whittled some. The big white thunderheads were bouncing along on the south wind like tumbleweeds and the lot was a little dusty.

"I guess this will hold you for a while," he said, handing me four or five pages out of the little book. "I wrote them down so you wouldn't forget any. Don't lose them."

I gave them the once-over. "The first thing I need to do is lose these here," I said. "I ain't got no crew of Mexicans working for me."

"Just a few little chores," he said.

"I want to straighten one thing out," I said. "When Mabel took you off on that boat trip, I had a little trouble with your brother-in-law Willy. Now if he shows up this time trying to tell me what to do, he's liable to get his feelings hurt." Willy was the state representative from our district, and a fat-ass politician if there ever was one. Every year he'd show up at the town baseball games, passing out little old scrawny peaches. Once he offered me one. "You ain't too old to vote," he said. "I will be before I vote for you," I said. He shut up like I'd poured him full of alum.

"I never told you about him coming out," I said. "I didn't see no sense in embarrassing you."

"Well, by god, I like that," he said. "Willy trying to give you orders?"

"Just trying to get me to quit," I said. "Him and Mabel still think I'm a bad influence on you."

"That fat bastard," he said. "It's no wonder to me he'd try something like that."

"It ain't to me neither," I said. "I just wanted to tell you, so you wouldn't be surprised if he shows up at the hospital to tell you how nasty I was to him."

"I wouldn't care if you drowned him," he said. "Damn I wish Mabel wouldn't scheme around like that—she's behind it. Seems like the older I get, the less I know for sure."

"Well, don't lose no sleep over Willy," I said. "I just wanted to mention it."

"Just don't let him make you mad enough to quit," he said. He was so gloomy all of a sudden; he was practically planning his own funeral.

"I like that," I said. "We been friends sixty-five years. You don't think a fat-ass like Willy could run me off, do you?"

"Course not," he said. "I'm sorry."

We didn't say anything for a while.

"Molly takes her age pretty well," he said then, out of the blue. "I'm half a notion to quit Mabel and go live with her yet. I might have a few years' peace. If I live over this operation, I might just do it. You don't need to tell nobody though."

"Oh, I won't," I said, and he looked at me pretty close.

"Would that bother you much?" he said. "If I was to move in with Molly? I hadn't really thought about it from your angle."

"Why, it wouldn't bother me a bit," I said. "I think it would be good for both of you. Besides serving Mabel and Willy right." The part about it not bothering me was a plain lie, and he knew it; I kept whittling on my stick and didn't look at him.

"I guess it would though," he said, kinda sad. "We've kinda split her, haven't we? Anyhow it's just one of my crazy ideas. I doubt she'd want to do it anyway."

We sat there an hour, watching it get dark, and didn't say another word. He sure was lonesome for Molly. I was too. And neither one of us had the other fooled.

four

I was sure right about Willy coming. About a week after Gid went to the hospital I was out one morning doctoring some puny calves, and I seen Gid's big Oldsmobile driving up to the lot. Willy got out and came toward me like I was the President. He was peeling off the glove on his handshaking hand.

"Put her there, Johnny," he said. "By god, it's been some time."

"I got screwworm dope on my hands," I said. "What can I do for you, Willy?"

"Oh, not a thing, not a thing," he said. "I was just in town staying with Mabel while Gid's in such a bad way. I thought I'd run out and see if I could be any help. To tell the truth, I could use the exercise."

"Aw, I've seen worse overweight men than you," I said. "One or two."

Actually he was just a fat tub of lard.

"Well, whatever you need doing, just show me. I wasn't raised on a dry-land farm for nothing."

"You wasn't?" I said. "I thought it was being raised on nothing on a dry-land farm was what caused you to go into politics. Or was it because you couldn't *raise* nothing?" I just came right out and got insulting when I talked to Willy. I didn't have no time to fool around.

"It's just like Mabel says," he said. "You don't try to get along with people. I came all the way out here at my own expense to see if I could be of some help, and you insult my ancestry."

"Get off the goddamn soapbox," I said. "There ain't no voters around. You know damn well whose expense you come out on—Gid's. It's just a pity he didn't throw away his car keys and cancel his charge accounts before he went in."

"Now you listen, McCloud," he said. "My sister and I have had about enough of you."

"Listen yourself," I said. "I've had a damn sight too much of you and your sister. Now you see this jar of screwworm dope? It's the blackest, shittiest-smelling stuff they ever put in a bottle. Unless you want about half a bottle on the front of that white shirt of yours, you better get in that car and skedaddle." I started around the feed trough, holding my bottle ready to throw. I would have thrown, too, if he'd opened his mouth, but he never. That's one quick way to get rid of a politician.

Only the next day I ran into him agin, and he had me at a disadvantage. I had just stepped out of the domino hall.

"Well, I see you been working hard today," he said, "looking after my sister's interests."

"No, I been playing dominos all afternoon," I said. "If it's any of your business."

"Mabel's business is my business," he said. "And you're working partly for her. So I guess we ought to talk."

"My checks are signed Gideon Fry," I said. "He's the one I work for."

"That's why we need to talk," he said. "Of course you haven't seen Gideon since the operation. If you had interest enough to go see him, you'd know he won't be in any shape to give orders for a long time."

"Hell, he don't have to be in very good shape to give orders," I said. "Besides, I'm going to see him day after tomorrow."

"Well he's a very sick man," he said. "The doctors have told him he'll have to quit work completely. Now what do you think of that?"

"It don't surprise me," I said. "They're always telling him something like that. But he ain't quit yet, and even if he had I wouldn't take no orders from you or Mabel. You can take your orders and put them where the monkey put the peanut."

And that ended conversation number two.

That one worried me just a little, though. On my way home that afternoon I stopped by Molly's. She met me at the back gate.

"I was hoping you'd come by today," she said. "I've been wanting to talk to you."

"You know, I talk a lot better when I'm full," I said.

She grinned. We had black-eyed peas and turnip greens and beef for supper. And I had about half of a custard pie and the better part of a pot of coffee.

"I've got to get the weeds mowed around my barn," she said. "I nearly stepped on a snake yesterday."

"One nearly stepped on me today," I said. "He was a political snake."

"Willy Peters," she said. "I was down to see Gid yesterday."

"I was hoping you'd been," I said. "How was he?"

She looked a little worried, too. "He was still a little dopey," she said. "I never got to stay but about ten minutes."

"Willy said they told him to quit work," I said.

"Oh, they told him that ten years ago," she said. "They just tell him that on general principles. One of the nurses told me they found some kind of little old tumor, but she didn't know if it was malignant or not. I think Mabel was in the building somewhere, what made them run me off so quick. I hated to leave."

"Well, I'll be down and see him tomorrow," I said. "Maybe we'll get to talk awhile. Let's go out on the porch."

The chairs were done out there; we went out and sat down. It was dark and we sat quiet awhile, enjoying the south breeze. The white clouds were rolling over, and the moon was done up. I wished old Gid could have been there with us—he would have enjoyed the cool. I could just barely see Molly, rocking in the dark. I reached out and patted her hand.

"What ever become of that old glider?" I said. "Tonight would be a nice night to swing a little."

"Good lord," she said. "I gave it to some high-school kids who come out hunting scrap iron. I wish I had it back."

"Want to ask you something," I said. "Just out of curiosity. Gid mentioned to me once that he was kinda thinking about leaving Mabel and moving out here with you. You'all ever decide about it?"

Molly sighed and didn't say anything for a while.

"Oh, we've talked about it a lot, Johnny," she said. "But we haven't decided. Gid hates to lose little Susie. Besides, I don't know, they may take him off to the Mayo Clinic now."

"I'd make a bet they don't do that," I said.

"Well, I just wish he'd come on out here where he'd have a little peace," she said. "He's done without it all his life. I believe I could take better care of him than he's been getting."

"Well, I just wondered how you felt about it," I said.

"I guess it will come down to whether he likes me better than he does Susie," Molly said. "He's got such a conscience, you know. You got to convince him something's right or he won't touch it. Or else you got to trick him someway."

"Why hell, tricking him's twice the easiest," I said. "I can trick him nine times an hour, but I never have been able to convince him of nothing."

We sat there watching the night till almost ten o'clock. The whippoorwills were calling all over the ridge.

"Bedtime for me," I said.

She walked to the pickup with me and told me to tell Gid hello for her. "Glad you came by," she said. "Come a little oftener."

She was standing by the running board, and I reached out and patted her shoulder. When I drove off I remembered a lot of the times when we was younger and I'd stayed the night. It wasn't that I wasn't welcome no more, either. We were just different. Use to we could chase around and have fun doing nearly anything. Now we both just got yawny. It seemed plain sad.

five

I had wonderful luck at the hospital—Mabel and Willy had already left for the day, and Gid hadn't had no sedative. He had his bed cranked up so he could see out the window and watch the traffic. I knew the minute I seen him he wasn't in no danger.

"Country getting dry?" he asked. He was white as a bleached sheet, but he didn't seem weak. At least his voice wasn't.

"Some," I said.

"What do you mean, some?" he said. I could see he was primed for a long conversation.

"Just some," I said. "A rain wouldn't do no harm, but then I've seen it a damn sight dryer. We had a good shower down on the River country the day you went in."

"Just an inch, Molly said," he said. "That's already burned up."

"Now just back up," I said. "You've been lying here half-unconscious in an air-conditioned room for ten days, and you're trying to tell me how hot and dry it is?"

"I got eyes," he said. "I can see that lawn out there. They water it ever day and it's still dry.

"How's the cattle?" he said.

"They all died of blackleg and a whirlwind blew the windmill over," I said. "How's that for calamity? When you coming home?"

"Be out in two days," he said. "Don't tell nobody though. They think they're gonna keep me two more weeks." Gid was a great one for walking out of hospitals; he'd done it four or five times in his life.

"Glad to hear it," I said.

"Willy's been driving me crazy," he said. "Been bothering you?"

"Not much. I chased him off with some #62 screwworm dope. That the right tactic?"

"It'll do till I get out," he said.

"Molly said they want you to ease up," I said.

"Hell, don't they always?" he said. "If doctors had their way, the whole world would be sitting on its butt. But I'll tell you a secret. This is the last hospital I ever intend to go in. If I get to hurting too bad to live, by god I'll shoot myself, like Dad done. He had the right slant on this business, that's for sure."

"I better give you my present," I said. I had picked him up a good smooth cedar whittling stick, and I handed it to him. I didn't figure he'd hurt nobody with it. Once I give him a stockwhip, and the doctors and nurses like to ate me up. They figured he had weapons enough as it was.

But the stick tickled him to death. "Many thanks," he said. "Looks like a dandy."

About that time the door opened and a little red-headed doctor popped in.

"Well, how's the patient?" he said. We didn't say anything, and he went over and checked the charts. I knew he had come to run me out.

"Now you're coming along fine," he said. "How would it be if this gentleman left, so you could take a little nap?" He said it just a little timidly; I guess he had already had a run-in with Gid.

"It wouldn't be worth a damn," Gid said, popping the stick on the sheet.

"Well, you know a sick man needs lots of rest," the doctor said. He wasn't Gid's regular man. "I'm sure this gentleman wouldn't mind leaving."

"What do you know about me?" I said. "I might not leave for love nor money."

"Get out of here," Gid said. "I've got some business to talk with this man. I'll sleep when I get sleepy, like I've done all my life."

"Hospital rules," the doctor said. "If he won't leave, we'll have to show him out."

"That'll be fine," I said. "Just bring a few pretty nurses to help you."

"You old cowboys seem to think the world revolves around you," he said. "We'll see about this." And he left; he was plenty mad.

Gid was popping his stick against the sheet.

"That makes me just mad enough to leave," he said. "Two days or no two days."

I didn't say a word. He looked out the window for a while.

"Bring the pickup around the side," he said. "I've had my craw full."

And twenty minutes later me and him was on the road to Thalia, and everbody but the FBI was after us. The doctors and nurses acted like it was Judgment Day. But Gid didn't pay them any mind. That Wichita hospital was nothing to the one he walked out of in Galveston one time. That time he chartered a private airplane and had himself flown home. I guess having money is right convenient sometimes.

"Now I guess you'll die," I said. "Only I'll get the blame for killing you, instead of the doctors."

"Oh, I'm all right," he said. "I'll have to be careful of my side for a while."

"Take you home?"

"Yeah, I reckon."

We drove about fifteen miles and he was feeling a little sore.

"No, by god, take me to Molly's," he said. "If I go home, they'll just knock me out and haul me back to the hospital. Take me out there. The doctor can come and see me, and you and her can help me fight off the ambulance drivers."

"Okay," I said. "Once you get strong enough to take care of yourself, I can cart you in to town."

"You know, I may never get that strong," he said. "Won't this surprise Molly?"

Myself, I figured that question was settled, if he didn't die before I got him out there. I figured he'd stay right there the rest of his life. Where that left me, I couldn't tell.

six

Getting Gid out tickled us all. I came up the hill to Molly's honking, so I guess she thought the war was on agin. Coming over those country roads had bounced Gid up enough that I think for a while he was kinda wishing he had stayed where he was; but Molly ran out and we helped him in the house and got him installed in the big south bedroom, where he caught every breeze there was, and he picked up pretty quick. Molly asked him what she could get him, and he said fresh tomatoes, so she sliced him up a bunch fresh from the garden and brought them in to him. He ate tomatoes and drank coffee till he got his spirits back. Late that afternoon his regular doctor showed up and tried to get him to go back, but Gid wouldn't do it. The doctor had to come out and see about him every day for a while.

Just getting away from the hospital done Gid a world of good. There was a day or two when he didn't feel too spry, but in the long run he got better a lot quicker. Molly fed him good and watched after him and made him sleep a lot, and he didn't have Mabel or Willy always worrying him.

Of course I had a big run-in with Willy. I had been at the

filling station, drinking a Delaware Punch. All the boys got a big laugh out of hearing about Gid. Then I ran into Willy on the sidewalk, and he motioned with his hand for me to stop.

"Willy, don't be waving me down," I said. "I ain't no motorcar."

"I guess you realize what a serious thing you done," he said. "Taking Gid out of everybody's reach."

"Whose reach?" I said. "The doctor was just out this morning and said he was improving fast."

"Well, out of the reach of the people who love him," he said. "Anyhow, when's he coming back?"

"When he gets ready, I guess," I said. "He told me yesterday he was going to start fencing agin next week. Does that ease your mind?"

"Not a bit," he said. "You know he ain't to work."

"Oh sure," I said. "I know it. But I ain't agile enough to stop him, are you?"

"Well, I just wanted to warn you," he said. "Just don't you get crosswise with the law. I got some friends who are judges."

"You'll probably need them," I said, and he left.

Molly and Gid enjoyed hearing about it. Gid was propped up in bed eating ice cream.

"I wish there was some way to run him out of the country," I said. "That's the damn trouble with democracy. You got to wait around and vote, and then the people are so stupid they put the scroungy sonsofbitches back in office."

"I don't like to hear that kind of talk," Molly said. She was democracy-crazy.

Gid handed Molly his ice-cream dish. "Uum," he said. "This is mighty nice. Only I got to get up from here and start getting a few things accomplished."

Molly frowned, but he never noticed; he was already planning. I knew right then he wouldn't be in bed much longer.

Molly done wonders, though. She fought him and argued with him and dominoed him and ice-creamed him and kept him down another week. She was working so hard keeping Gid down she was about to get down herself.

I didn't know what they had decided about him staying and living there. Molly wanted him to, that was plain as day, and I guess they must have talked about it. But never while I was there, which wasn't too often. Running the ranch kept me busy all day, and usually I got over about suppertime to see how the invalid was doing. The nights weren't too hot, and we all sat around on the porch and talked.

Then one morning it come to a head. I was over helping Molly set up an owl trap in her chickenyard. We worked on it about an hour and looked up and seen Gid coming out the back door, all dressed and carrying his suitcase. Molly was just crushed; I guess she thought he was going to stay for good.

"Now where's he fixing to go?" she said. "He don't have to go nowhere."

I was kinda wishing I wasn't nowhere around.

But she grabbed my wrist before he got to us. "Listen," she said. "Now if I can't talk him out of going, you be sure and see he takes it easy on his work. Will you do that for me?"

"Of course I will," I said.

Gid had put his gear in the pickup, and he came over, looking proud of himself.

"Owl trouble," he said. "Can I help?"

Molly was all over him. "You sure can," she said, "you can go in out of this hot sun and get back in bed and stay there. That would help me a whole lot."

But Gid put up his bluff.

"Can't," he said. "I've got to get to working."

And we stood there. I kept on working on the trap. Molly was trembling and about to cry, I could tell. But Gid was determined.

"Don't think I ain't much obliged to you," he said. "But I've got to go to work, Molly."

She looked at me kinda funny. It was really tearing her. I was surprised to see she still had those terrible strong feelings, at her age. I never had felt things that hard, at any age.

"All right, go to work," she said. "But, honey, you don't have to leave, you can go to work and come back."

She had never called him honey in public, in all the years I'd known her, either. I was trembling a little too, from just watching, and I don't know what held Gid up.

"Yes I have, Molly," he said. "For right now, anyway. Just running off from a hospital like that ain't the right way to settle anything."

She was crying then, but neither one of us quite dared touch her.

"There never will be a way right enough for you," she said.

He said maybe there would. "And much obliged agin, for taking care of me."

I guess she thought Gid was sort of leaving her for the last time. "You're mighty welcome, Gid," she said. "God bless you." And she turned and went to the house, crying and snuffling.

"We better go if we're going," I said.

It upset Gid a good bit too. We were pretty quiet, driving to town.

"I wish I could have thought of a nicer way to leave," he said.

"I hate to upset Molly."

"Well, Gid," I said. "My god, you ought to stay out there with her, if you want to. It's about time you pleased yourself a little, if you're ever going to. Or it looks that way to me."

"Well, I want to," he said. "And I may do it. In fact, I guess I intend to do it. But you can't just go off and do something like that on the spur of the moment, without making no arrangements. There's a right way and a wrong."

"And you're the only man alive that can tell them apart," I said. "Or maybe just the only one that bothers to try."

When I let him out at his house he told me to buy a keg of steeples. He said he'd be out Monday and we'd start steepling the fence. I never stopped by Molly's, going home. I couldn't think what I would say to her.

seven

It was a good thing I got the steeples, because Monday morning he was there before I got the milk strained. I stayed about that far behind the rest of the day.

"Are you ready?" he said.

"I'm bound to be readier than you are," I said. "I'm well, anyway."

"Shut up and let's go," he said. I sat the milk in the icebox and got my steepling hatchet. I had soaked it in water all night so the head wouldn't fly off and kill Gid.

The wires were done stretched; I had done that; so all we had to do was steeple. We didn't waste no time. I got off from him a hundred yards or so, and we started in. I guess I steepled forty or fifty posts before I thought to look around, and Gid wasn't nowhere in sight. It scared the sense out of me: I thought he'd passed out. I started running back up the fence row, but I wasn't used to running and I thought I was gonna collapse. If he hadn't of hollered, I'd have passed him right by. He wasn't over fifty yards from where he started steepling. There was a little shady shrub oak tree there and he was sitting under it fanning himself with his hat. I never saw a man so wet with sweat in my whole life.

"I didn't know you could run so fast," he said. "Where's the fire?"

"By god," I said, trying to get my breath. "It looks like it's underneath you." I had to sit down and get my breath.

"I just came out here to rest," he said. "I was getting too hot."

"My god, Gid," I said. "If you're sweating like that already, what you better do is sickle in to town and rest on some nice cool bed. It ain't good for a man in your shape to get that hot."

"Oh, I'm all right," he said. "You're more give out than me, just from that run."

"I may be out of breath," I said. "But I ain't sweated down from steepling no ten or fifteen posts."

"It was more like a hundred and fifty, the way my arm feels," he said. "But it's just sweat. Must have been them drugs they gave me. I never sweated this much before."

"Hell of a note," I said. "Why don't you let me hire a Mexican or two, to finish this fence? They work a lot cheaper than doctors."

"I never asked for no advice," he said. "I guess I know when I'm able to work and when I'm not."

"I doubt very seriously that you do," I said. "But I can't do much about it."

"You can get to steepling," he said.

And that was the way it went, the rest of the week. Gid couldn't work but thirty minutes at a time without having to rest, but he wouldn't quit. The whole week he was just up and down. I finally just let him alone about it. I guess he just had so much sweat to get out of his system. After we finished the fencing we spent a week spraying the cattle and getting them shaped up. He finally got where he could work an hour or two at a stretch, but he wasn't the hand he used to be.

I asked him once if he'd been by to see Molly, and he said he had. Mabel was off on a vacation in Colorado and had Sarah and Susie with her, so Gid was batching. I imagine he seen Molly a lot. I never asked him what they decided about living together, and he never said. I knew he wouldn't do nothing till Mabel got back; that would make him feel too sneaky. He didn't much want to talk about it, and I couldn't blame him particularly, so very little was ever said.

One morning he came out looking kinda blue—he had got it into his head to fix the windmill that day. It was the mill on the old Fry place, where I was living. I had used it for years and years, without no particular trouble except a worn-out sucker rod now and then. But he had done ordered a new set of pipes and a new running barrel, and everything: a man was going to bring them out from town that morning. It looked like a hell of a hard day's work, and I tried to head him off.

"Just think a minute, Gid," I said. "It's the first of September. In another month it'll be cool, and that mill won't be half as hard to fix."

"I know it'll be a little hot," he said. "But we'll just fix it anyway, while we got the time. We might be doing something else in another month. Let's go get the sucker rod out."

The sucker rod in itself wasn't much of a job, and we had it out in no time. The job was going to be lifting that old pipe out and lowering the new pipe in. I never had been much of a pipe hand, and the old stuff was corroded at the joints. It had been in long enough to be petrified.

While we were waiting for the man with the pipe to come, we sat in the shade of the waterhouse and told some old windmilling stories we saved up for days like that. I had had an uncle get killed on a windmill, and I was scared of them as I was of a rattlesnake. I told Gid about it.

"It was a steel mill," I said. "Lightning struck it while he was up working on it. Electrocuted him."

"They're dangerous," he said. "If it's a wooden mill, the dam frames are apt to break and let you fall. Remember Clarence Fierson? He got his neck broke falling off one."

"Yeah, I remember," I said. "Went around with his neck in a brace for years. Lucky at that."

Pretty soon the pipe man came and the hard work began. It was all we could do to carry the new pipe over to the windmill where we needed it. Gid got as hot as a pistol, and I wasn't cool, myself.

"I don't believe we better fool with this stuff," I said. "You'll strain your operation, lifting this shit. I can barely hold out myself."

"You want to work on the mill or on the ground?" he said.

"I'm trying to think what will be the best for you. If you get up there you'll get dizzy and fall, and if you stay down here you'll get all the heavy lifting."

"Shut up about me," he said. "I ain't collapsed yet, and I been windmilling all my life. You stay down here."

He began to unscrew this and unscrew that, and in a little while it was too late to back out, we done had the thing torn into. We spent the rest of the morning unscrewing the old rotten pipe and lifting it out.

When dinner time came we were both give out. I went in the

house and fried us a little steak and made some tea, and for dinner we had steak and bread and about a gallon of iced tea apiece. We were too tired to tell any windmill stories, too. Gid flopped down on the living room couch, and I got me a pillow and stretched out on the floor. We couldn't get ourselves moving agin till two o'clock.

"Godamighty," I said, when I finally sat up. "I sure hate to go back out there."

"Yeah, them pipes will be hot," he said. "Hot and heavy."

"I can't figure you out," I said. "As much money as you got, and you're still fighting a goddamn windmill. Why do you do it, Gid?"

"Sometimes I wonder myself," he said.

We got up and went back to work. The sun was just a blur in the sky it was so hot, and the new pipes would fry an egg. It was all we could do to keep ahold of them, gloves or no gloves, and we had to cut threads in three or four joints. That took half the afternoon. Then Gid got back up in the mill and we raised the pipe and let it down in the well, a foot at a time. Once Gid lost his grip and I thought the whole shebang would go to the bottom, but I managed to slow it with my pipe wrench till he could get another hold. Finally we got the pipe run and he came down to rest. We were both wringing wet.

"Well, we're nearly done," I said. "It'll be cool in another hour. I'm kinda glad we done her, now."

"Me too," he said, mopping his face. "One thing about it, when we get this bastard fixed this time, me and you oughtn't to have to ever lay a hand on it agin. It ought to last at least twenty-five years."

"So ought we," I said. "We might get to fix it agin. We're better windmillers than I thought we were."

"A man has to be experienced like us before he has enough know-how to fix one of these things."

"Watch out now," I said. "I fixed a lot of them while I was getting the experience, and you did too. Besides, it wasn't the know-how I was worried about, it was the do-how. Two weeks ago you were flat of your back eating soup."

"Laying around in bed's what like to ruined me," he said.

We put the sucker rod in, but it liked about a foot coming up to where it was supposed to connect. So we had to go down to the barn and get another piece and replace it. The barn was beginning to make a shadow and the big heat was over for the day. Gid went up and made the connection and came back.

"Turn her on," he said. "I want to see the water run."

I turned the mill loose and a little south breeze caught the wheel. Pretty soon the old rusty water began to pour out of the hydrant, and we stood there waiting for the stream to get clear. It was still an hour to sundown, but we were two tired cowboys, I don't mind to admit. Gid was squatted down watching the water run, and I was propped up against a standard with my shirttail out, letting my belly cool. Pretty soon the rusty water washed out and the water came out of the faucet good and cold and clear. Gid stuck his mouth to the faucet and drank awhile, and then caught his breath and drank some more.

"Be careful you don't founder," I said, "drinking so much cold water."

"Sure good water," he said, leaning back on his heels. "I remember when me and Dad had that well dug. It sure has been a good well."

Then we heard water splashing behind us. We looked up and seen it was the overhead pipe, the one that went to the storage tank. We had forgot to connect it.

"I'll get it," I said. "Just take a second."

"No, go on and get you a drink," he said. "I left my pliers up there anyway."

"You're the derrick hand," I said, and went to drinking. I took about three good cool swallows and heard him yell: he had just hit the ground. I guess he lost his grip, or else his foot slipped, but he couldn't have been over three or four feet up the ladder when it happened. It didn't look like he hit very hard, either, and I seen him start to get right up, he even got his hand on a rung. Then he hesitated, and I thought one of his legs might be broke.

"Wait, Gid," I said.

I got to him and eased him down on one elbow and he never acted the least bit hurt or wild, but I don't believe he recognized me at all.

"Well, boys, he threw me agin," he said. "I'll ride him yet."

It made the hair stand up on the back of my neck for a minute. But I wasn't really worried. I thought he was just out of his senses for a minute. He had gone out of his head that way several times. He tried to get up but I held him.

"Let me up, boys," he said. "I ain't hurt."

"Okay, now, Gid," I said. "Just lay a minute and get your breath."

He minded me. "That bastard threw me, Johnny," he said. He had quit fighting to get up and lay there, looking real weak. I think that scared me the most.

"Here," I said. "Where do you think you are? You just fell off the ladder a couple of feet. That you're talking about was a long time ago."

I knew just exactly what he was thinking. When we was young there was a horse called Old Missouri, that everybody tried to ride. Dad owned him, God knows why. One day he threw Gid six times. He never threw me but once, because I never tried to ride him but one time. But there never was a horse that Gid couldn't wear down eventually, and he finally got so he could stay on Old Missouri.

"I've been throwed harder," he said.

He went on like that for a while, and I didn't try to stop him. I figured he'd come out of it in a few minutes. But he looked weak as a fish, and I finally decided to take him on it—getting him in the car was a real job. I stretched him out on the back seat and went back and turned off the faucet at the windmill. Gid's doctor was in Wichita, but I struck for Thalia, it was closer. I started out slow, trying to miss the bumps, but I finally let that go and concentrated on speed.

When I come to the highway I stopped a minute and Gid opened his eyes and looked at me. He seemed perfectly sensible.

"What you reckon Molly's doing?" he said. "I must be slipping." Then he went off agin. "Sounds like I hear a train," he said. "Let's me and you go to the Panhandle. I'm tired of this country."

It made me sad to hear him talk that way, when it was forty years too late and him out of his mind. I begin to let the hammer down on his old Chevvy.

And then, by god, he come completely out of it. "That goddamn old windmill," he said. "Did you turn it off?"

"Last thing I did," I said.

"Well, it won't take long to make that connection," he said. "My damn side hurts. I wish I'd woke up a little sooner, I'd had you take me over to Molly's, I ain't sick enough to go to town. Maybe this time I'd have sense enough to stay there where I belong. Why don't you just take me back? I'd kinda like to see her."

"Aw, we better let a doc look at you first," I said. "I can run you out there tonight or in the morning."

Then he looked out the window, I guess: he said what he always said when he looked at the country in that part of the summertime: "The country's too dry, I sure do wish it would rain. My grass is just about gone."

I didn't say nothing to that, but I was relieved he was back in his senses. I was trying to pass a Dutchman; he was pulling a load of hay.

"Oh me, Johnny," Gid said. "Ain't this been a hell of a time?"

"It sure has, Gid," I said. The sun was near enough down to be right in my eyes, and I needed all my concentration just to drive. I thought Gid said something else, to me, to Molly, to somebody, and then he didn't say no more and I was hoping he had dozed off to sleep. But when I caught the red light by the courthouse in Thalia, and had to stop, I looked back at him and knew right then that Gideon Fry was dead.

eight

At the clinic they said he couldn't have been dead over ten minutes, or maybe fifteen. But I guess to Gid ten minutes was just as final as ten years. A bloodclot done it, they said. Some people blamed me for bumping him over them old roads. But I don't think it would have made any difference. I couldn't have gone off and left him there on the grass by the windmill, while I drove twenty-five miles in and the doctor drove twenty-five miles back. The doctor at the clinic said the fall had started internal bleeding.

The meanest, hardest part of it all, for me, was going off that night and leaving Gid at the hospital. They wheeled him away somewhere on a stretcher, and when I asked the doctor what I could do, he said, "Nothing." I called Buck, Gid's son-in-law, and he told me which funeral home to have Gid sent to; I asked him if he knew where Mabel was, and he give me her hotel number in Colorado Springs. When I got her I said, "Well, Mabel, I've got some pretty bad news for you." "What's happened to him?" she said. "He fell off a windmill," I said. "The fall never hurt him but it caused a bloodclot and the bloodclot killed him, Mabel. He died about an hour ago." "The Lord help us," she said. "Are you sure? What am I going to do?" They said she got hysterical after she hung up.

After that, things was kind of out of my hands; there wasn't no reason for me to stay. But I couldn't hardly go. It didn't seem right to just go off and leave him there. I kept wondering which jobs around the ranch he wanted me to get done in the next day or two. But I finally seen there wasn't nothing I could do but go. None of the hospital people paid any attention to me, and I hated the smell of the place.

I drove out to Molly's then, and broke it to her. She came out in the yard to meet me, it was done way after dark, and I told her about it and she cried, there by the yard gate. She was awful broke up. After a while we went over to the ranch and she drove Gid's car back to town for me and I followed in the pickup. We left it at Buck's. When we got back to Molly's she had quit crying for a little while.

"Well, come on in, let's make some coffee," she said. "You'll stay here with me tonight, won't you?"

"Of course," I said.

It was a sure sad night for us, but we didn't say fifteen words. We drank a good bit of coffee.

"You know, the night we got the word about Jimmy, me and Gid played dominos," she said.

"You want to play some tonight?" I said.

"Oh lord no," she said. "I'd rather not."

It was the first time I'd spent a whole night with Molly in three or four years, maybe longer than that. She went in the bathroom and put on her white nightgown and I got in bed. I held her hand and we both lay there awake for an hour and a half, on our backs. Once in a while Molly sniffled, but she wasn't crying much.

"Well, he was some feller," I said. "I don't expect to ever see another like him. You know that saddle he gave me? That's the most expensive saddle ever made in the Thalia saddle shop. Me and him had a big fight the day he give it to me. Over you, I guess."

I guess it was worse for Molly. Him and her had associated so much there, in the house, right there in that same bedroom we was in, there was no telling what all she was remembering. I guess he was all over the room, for her.

"Gid was my favorite," she said. I finally went to sleep, I don't know whether she did or not.

In the morning, when I woke up, an unusual thing happened. I had turned over during the night and I had my arm across Molly's middle and my face was in her hair. When I got my eyes open she was looking right square at me. There were dark circles under her eyes, but she had just the trace of a grin on her face. For a minute I didn't know why, and then I noticed myself. As old as I was, too, and on a morning like that. And Molly had done noticed, that's why she was watching me. At first I was plumb embarrassed.

"Well, I swear," I said. I didn't know what else to say.

But she grinned, and squeezed my hand. "That's the first time I've ever seen you embarrassed," she said. "I've had to wait sixty-two years."

"Well, it ain't because of that," I said. "You've caused that many a time. You've stayed too pretty. It's because of Gid I'm embarrassed."

"I don't want you to be," she said. "That's nature, she ain't no respecter. I don't want you to be embarrassed even if we're a hundred years old." Then she grinned a sad grin; for a minute she reminded me of herself when she was twenty years old. "And you better not waste it, either," she said.

"You're an unusual woman," I said, rubbing her side. "Only it ain't much to waste. If old Gid can't, then by god I won't neither, how's that?"

"About as foolish as something he'd say," she said. "Only thank god you won't stick to it like he did." And she rolled over and hugged me and cried for an hour, at least. I had to get up and hunt a box of Kleenex.

nine

A week after the funeral I stopped by Molly's house; she never heard the car come up. She was out in the garden, and I walked around the house and stood by the gate a minute, watching her. The garden was just about gone. When I walked out she was down on her knees, pulling onions and putting them in her apron.

"You're getting a little deaf," I said. "A person could sneak up on you."

She grinned, happy and jolly as could be. "Hold these onions for me," she said.

"Let's go sit in the kitchen, where it's cool and there's something to eat," I said.

But she took me to the porch, instead. "You can eat here, what there is," she said. "Cold potato pie is all there is, and you don't like it. I didn't figure you'd come tonight."

"I just like two kinds of pie," I said. "Hot and cold. Go get me some."

We ate a little pie and rocked awhile and she brought out some coffee.

"Well, I'm all packed," I said. "I guess I'll move tomorrow." They had fired me, of course—I was going back to the old McCloud place, three mile off. It wasn't a very long move.

"They didn't allow you much time," she said.

"Aw yeah," I said. "They said no hurry. But it don't take much time to move what little I got."

We talked a little while, about Gid and the will and one thing and another. Gid had left me the old pickup and a thousand acres of land—he couldn't stand for me not to increase my holdings by at least that much. So I was set pretty for my old age—I done had two sections I inherited from Dad. That thousand acres sure burned Mabel and Willy; they thought the pickup would have been enough. He just left Molly his dad's old pocket watch. I guess he knew Mabel would have gone to court if he had left her anything more. Molly was plenty satisfied.

After a while the new moon came up, about the size of a basketball, and the conversation petered out. I could see Molly's face, and she looked tired. I was too. I gave her my pieplate to take in the house, and when she came back we walked around to the pickup together. The moon was so bright we could see the chickens roosting on the chickenhouse.

I had something big on my mind and I didn't know how to get it up. It just seemed like I better ask Molly to marry me, for the sake of all our old times, but I didn't know whether she'd much want to, and I didn't even know if I much wanted to, we got along so well like we were. Finally I came out with it; I was standing with my arm around her.

"Well, Molly, what would you think about us marrying?" I said.

"I'd think we ain't the kind, honey," she said, "but thank you a whole lot for asking."

It was kind of a sad relief. "It's a damn strange time for me to do it," I said. "I could have asked you forty years ago."

"We lived them pretty good," she said. "It ain't as important a question as a lot of people think."

"Don't you miss Gid?" I said. "I never thought I'd miss such a contrary so-and-so so much."

"Oh yes," she said.

"Molly, just for curiosity," I said. "Do you think you and him would have taken up together for good, if he had lived?"

She put one of her hands in my hip pocket and pulled out my handkerchief to see if it was clean. She had to smell it. This one wasn't, and she kept it so she could wash it.

"We'd decided to," she said. "I guess we decided about thirty times. And I think in about another year I would have got his conscience quiet enough and his nerve worked up so he could have come out and stayed."

We thought about it a minute.

"You know I think he worried about you as much as he did Mabel," she said. "He kept saying it wouldn't be fair to you if he moved out here." She gave me a long look. "I got sick of him wanting to be so fair to you," she said, "and I even got sick of you being around for him to worry about. You may have noticed."

"No," I said. "But I imagine it's true."

"Johnny, when it came to him, I just never cared to be fair," she said.

"I don't blame you none."

When I got in the pickup she leaned in and kissed me on the cheek. "I'll take you in to a ballgame one of these cool nights," I said.

"I wish you would," she said. "I ain't been to a half a dozen games since Joe quit playing."

I started to drive off, but she had ahold of my arm. "I'll have a better supper tomorrow night," she said. "Just because we ain't marrying don't mean you're free to miss a night. You're welcome here every night, all night, when you feel like putting up with me."

"I'll be here in time to carve the beef," I said, and drove off. I felt pretty blue driving down the hill, and kinda wished I had stayed that night. But sometimes you can't get around being lonesome for a while.

I took my time driving home on those old bumpy roads. When I got back to the house I put the pickup in the garage and shut the doors. I had me some Delaware Punches in the icebox and I got one and went out on the screened-in porch. Over at Molly's I had been a little sleepy, but the drive had woke me up.

The porch was cool, and the night was real quiet. I set my Punch bottle down and stepped out in the yard to take a leak. I could hear an oil rig working way over in the Dale, but except for that and a few crickets the night was perfectly still. When I got through I didn't much want to go in, so I walked around the old Fry place for a while, watching that white moon circling out over Gid's pastures. It was strange how I never knowed till Gid died just how used to him I was.

"You old so-and-so," I said. "You wouldn't listen. I offered to go up and fix that thing, but no sir, you had to do it yourself."

"Aw, you couldn't have fixed it if you'd a gone," he said. "You never was no hand with pipe."

"Hell no, a cowboy ain't supposed to be," I said.

"That's all right. Who made the fortune, and who worked for wages all his life?"

"You might have made the fortune," I said. "But I'd just like to know what good it did you. Working like a Turk. Which one of us was satisfied?"

"Hell, that's easy," he said. "Neither one. We neither one married her, did we?"

Talking to myself. Gid was off in the Great Perhaps. I looked around at the house and down toward the barn. One man's whoop is another man's holler, anyhow. At least Gid was stubborn about it. I remembered one election day, when I gave him hell. Me and Molly had the first shift. The bloom was really on the peach, as far as she was concerned. She wore a blue dress with white dots on it and never wore nothing on her hair. About two weeks before that I had got to spend my first whole night with her. We was there an hour by ourselves, and kissed and walked around and had the best time: I pumped my hat full of water so she could get a drink. Then Gid come and talked her into staying with him after I was supposed to leave. Only he had old Ikey for a partner and had to scheme around someway to get rid of him, I don't remember how he finally done it. It tickled me. He thought he'd have Molly to himself for two hours or so. I left about the time Ikey did and circled around and intercepted him; he was riding that old crippled mule. "Ikey, you ought to be ashamed of yourself," I said. "Living in a free country where they let you vote. And the first time the government gives you a little job you let somebody send you off on some damn errand. If you know what's good for you, you'll turn that mule around and get back up there where you belong." I broke me off a good-sized mesquite limb and handed it to him. "See if you can get that mule in locomotion," I said. I guess he thought I intended to use it on him. "Yes suh, Mistuh Johnny," he said. "I sure get back. I didn't inten' to leave in de fust place." So poor Gid got about twenty minutes. I guess it was kinda mean, really—nobody gets enough chances at the wild and sweet. But he would have done the same thing. There's just two things about it that I really regret. One was not being there to see the look on Gid's face when he heard that crippled mule clomping up, and the other is forgetting to bring a Kodak that morning, so I could have got a picture of Molly while she was sitting in her blue and white dress on the schoolhouse steps.

THREE GRAVESTONES

GIDEON FRY—1896–1962

MOLLY TAYLOR WHITE—1900–1976

JOHNNY MC CLOUD—1898–1985